God's Frozen Chosen

by

Larry G. Johnson

Vabella Publishing
P.O. Box 1052
Carrollton, Georgia 30112
www.vabella.com

Cover art by Dr. Julie Chibbaro

Manufactured in the United States of America

ISBN 978-1-942766-59-9

Library of Congress Control Number 2019904075

10 9 8 7 6 5 4 3 2 1

This book is dedicated to Dan Pak. Providence had a hand in this kindred spirit coming into my life. His remarkable story has been a source of endless inspiration. Thank you, Dan, for being who you are and for the very special friendship we share.

This novel was written in memory of Jesse Richard Merrell (1961-83) for whom the frozen chosen one was named.

Moving Parts

Part I: Frozen in Time

The parcel
Pushing the envelope
Are you kidding me?
Forever and ever
Numbness
MPD
IVF
Polly
Close enough
Providence
Strike one
Phone dates
"It"
Sleepless in Seattle
Butterflies
Knickers
Muddling
Fresh out of words
Picking up the pieces
No fooling
The wildcard
A tailspin

Part II: The Gift

He's a boy
Hello . . . Jesse
Leverage
Well, Dad . . .
We're home
Have a nice day
Fleeting glimpses
Little Brother
Christmas presence
Postcard from the edge
Y2K

Surprises
Two remarkable women
Envy
What's stopping you?
Sissy
Forget-me-not
Hyperbole
Urges and nudges
Plain Jane
Forgive me, Lord
TDH
No kidding
You're not going to believe this
Christmas spirit
How's all that working out for you?
Ice
Adamsonville
Sunday clothes
Merry Kiss-mas
How cool is that?
Hogwash and brainwashed
Different places-different spaces
The Chosen Frozen
Amazing Grace
Mama
Plum tuckered
Ep-i-sus

Part III: A Preexisting Condition

Look at you!
Filling in the blanks
Sorting stuff out
Like a kid at Christmas
Tomfoolery
You'd better take a look at this
Damn, woman
Keep me posted
A card-carrying member of the digital age
What are the odds?
Yes-sie promise

Plans change
Taking bullying by the horns
A pee in the creek
A peck on the cheek
Brooding
Like daughter, like father
Mama Bear—Papa Bear—Baby Bears
Sourdough Spice
How did I do?
Tonya!
Welcome to Alaska
W'us eat
P. S.
What about Hannah?
Aunt Polly
Sounds like a plan
Bloody hell . . . Othell
The safe-haven
Vanity
Little pitchers
Who is Darleen?
Jesse's girls
Who is Hannah?
That damn shovel
Oh, well . . . Othell
The elf on the shelf
Kicking the can
This is so exciting
Morning breath
Ta-licious
What to do with his eyes?
Teamwork
Game on
The earth moved
A good plucking
On the road again
A woman's touch
Always on my mind
Plans change, again
Get a grip, girlfriend
Striking out
The balls
Unintended consequences

A cool kid
Radar
A mentor
Think snow
He's the one
Auf wiedersehen
A proud day
AVALANCHE!!!!!
Baby Robin

Part I: Frozen in Time

The parcel

"Othell . . . Miss Bizzy Belle is *so* swell."

Walter Othell Williamson's best friend had always been his inner child, and he addressed this alter ego by his middle name. Throughout the ironic twists and erratic turns of Walt's improbable life, he was prone to say with resignation, "Oh, well . . . Othell." On occasion, a rhyming expletive came in handy.

Swell was the word of the day. Sitting in the seat next to him on the plane, was his twenty-nine-year-old daughter, Tonya. Her daycare worker had aptly applied the Miss Bizzy Belle label.

Walt's daughter was raised by a mother who refused to tell her who her father was. Only after her mom's tragic death in a fiery car crash, did she connect the dots.

Numerous times in and around Ephesus, North Carolina, Walt had crossed paths with the child he never knew. When Tonya finally found him, they discovered another remarkable connection. Both were current residents of towns on the Kenai Peninsula in Alaska. They were going home—looking forward—together.

After boarding a flight in Asheville, Walt and Tonya held hands as the airliner raced down the runway. He always had his own way of putting things. "Touch up," he whispered as the plane lifted off the ground.

Walt Williamson was of the generation just older than the baby boomers. This "war baby" was born under mysterious circumstances during World War II, and a big family secret always overshadowed him. Before starting to school, he taught himself to read. The first time the precocious lad ventured into unknown territory, he deciphered the children's classic "The Ugly Duckling."

Something about that tale resonated. After struggling with contentious parents, Walt figured out eventually, that he, too, hatched in the wrong nest. Coming to Alaska was the culmination of a quest to see his championed swans in the wild.

While some had said his life resembled a soap opera, Walt's graduate school buddy, Eli Pierce, deemed it more like a Greek tragedy. That did not exactly fit Walt, because tragedies don't have good endings. Just look at his daughter.

"Othell . . . My *spell* is *bound*. My *awe* is *struck*."

Walt was not fond of the expression "reinvent yourself." Rather, he preferred framing it "redirect yourself." He had already done just that more than once, and unbeknownst, he was on a collision course with yet another redirection. This time, it might well be more like an actual reinvention.

Tonya booked her flight to the city of Kenai for a stopover at her dad's home. He would then drive her to Homer, where she lived. Walt could hardly wait to share his corner of Alaska with his daughter, and she was equally excited about showing off her newly found father to her friends.

After they touched down for the fourth time, the duo hailed a cab. The driver deposited them at the house where Walt lived with the love of his life, Ginny, before he lost her eleven years earlier in a plane crash. He made no explanation when he unlocked the front door, stepped inside, and bellowed, "Hi, Honey . . . I'm home." Neither did he utter a sound when he promptly lit a candle.

Following a brief tour of the house, Tonya busied herself unpacking. The plane had landed, but Walt's being had not yet found grounding. His daughter had filled so many empty spaces in his mountain home in North Carolina. She was now inside the walls of his other abode at the top of the world.

Walt brought Ginny's old Ford F-150 to life the next morning. He headed to the post office to stop the forwarding of his first-class mail and to pick up the accumulation of everything else. As he shuffled through the pieces of junk, one card caught his eye. The checked box indicated a registered letter addressed to his deceased spouse, and it had to be signed for.

The official-looking parcel piqued his curiosity, but not wanting to shred the envelope, it could wait until he got home. He did notice that the return address was from Ginny's hometown of Seattle, Washington.

The smell of coffee brewing greeted Walt when he went in the door. Tonya was yawning her way into waking up. She was up at three for an hour and then tried to get some more sleep. It would take a few days for both to upright themselves from the four-hour time differential. He deposited the circulars on the counter and called on caffeine for an assist.

Tonya left Alaska to bury her mother, fearing that her mom had taken with her to the grave any clues regarding the identity of her father. She returned with her long-lost daddy by her side.

Walt was gone for a couple of years, spending time with the mother who gave him up at birth, but who reclaimed him before she died. He was sitting across the table from the child he was led to believe was aborted.

"What's next?"

This they said in unison. The father and daughter were still getting used to both starting and finishing each other's sentences.

"You first."

"No—you first."

Walt weighed in with a bit of philosophical wisdom gleaned from the wealth of his experiences.

"What a relief it is not to have to know everything all at once. Think of three words starting with the same letter. Being open to *whatever*, to *whenever*, and to *wherever* is the first step in embracing the possibilities— as their moments in time announce themselves."

"That's easy for you to say. You didn't think you had a kid and lie awake endless nights wondering where she was. I knew I had a father. I was certainly open to all three, but I grew increasingly impatient, and then resentful, that their moment in time might never come."

"But it did. If I had obsessed over why my mother gave me away, had harbored feelings of abandonment, and anguished over everything we missed during our separation, I would be in the nut house by now. I determined to let it all go and to grasp what time we had left."

Reflection took up residence on his brow.

"It was much more difficult for Mother. I'm not sure she ever forgave herself."

"Will I ever be able to forgive my mom?"

"I don't like what Michelle did, and you certainly don't, but we have to give her the benefit of some doubt. She started out thinking that she was doing what was best for all of us. Maybe the redhead got stubborn along the way. Yet, one thing is undeniable. Both of our mothers had to live with the consequences of what they had done. There's no way for either of us to measure the weight of their burdens."

"I confess that I did not make it easy for her."

Tonya rose from her chair and took a deep breath. She stood behind her daddy and put her arms around his neck.

"Now that I've found you, I don't ever want to lose you."

"Baby girl—that's the least of your worries."

As she returned to her chair, Walt slumped forward, let out a deep breath, and mused.

"I've had enough excitement for a while—perhaps even for a lifetime. I'm looking forward to some good old laid-back Alaska therapy. Now that I have a daughter, I cannot think of anything yet unfulfilled in my life—except maybe being a grandpa someday."

Tonya rolled her eyes in precisely the same way he had seen his mother do when he amused her. He retired for the night, still unaccustomed to being a father, but relishing every moment of it.

3

"Othell . . . How can a child be radically different from the parent who raised her, and yet she so mirrors the one she never knew for the first three decades of her life?"

Fatigue overtook him. He still had not opened his mail.

Pushing the envelope

"If we're going to eat, we need to make a grocery store run. Old Mother Hubbard's cupboard is bare. Except I guess it's Old Mother Sullivan's cupboard—although Ginny was never a mother—God rest her soul."

"I'd love to hang out with you for a few more days, but I really need to get back to Homer. I do have a job you know. Do you think you could take me today?"

Tonya did not say as much, but she had a hunch that they both needed some alone time. Walt offered no resistance.

"Of course, dear, if that's what you want. We can drive into town, find some breakfast, and then head on down the road."

As they left the restaurant, Walt mentioned that he needed to gas up Nellie, his other mode of transportation.

"There's a special place I want to do that—where I met Ginny."

The convenience store had changed little. As Walt aimed the vehicle toward the pump, Tonya sat up in her seat.

"I've been here before. I filled up my old blue Volvo, Agnes, here one time."

"Did it still have Washington plates on it?"

"It most certainly did."

"I was here at the same time. I remember thinking that the beautiful, dark-haired young woman was likely another cheechako about to fall in love with this great place."

Tonya rolled her eyes again. This time the corners were leaking.

The silence was broken only briefly as the aging pickup plodded along on the rough highway. Nellie was the vehicle that first heralded Walt to Alaska laden with a camper. He asked his daughter to tell him about her job and said he looked forward to visiting the gallery where she worked as an artist in residence.

The volcanic snow-covered mountains across the Cook Inlet were the beginning of the vast Aleutian Chain. Overcast skies enshrouded them as though they were not even there. The passengers were likewise engulfed in the cloak of so many unknowns and uncertainties.

It had only been two weeks since Tonya had dialed Walt's number back in Ephesus. After the fairy-tale-like union of the daughter with her father, they had not been separated. Neither could envision what was about to evolve next.

Walt helped Tonya take her belongings up the stairs to her apartment.

"Othell . . . This must be what it's like taking a daughter off to college."

Nothing had prepared him for Tonya's paintings hanging all around the walls. Their eyes kept meeting, but soul words made no sounds. He stood for several moments looking out over the majestic mountains across Kachemak Bay. Promising to get together again soon, they both stumbled awkwardly over goodbyes.

When Walt turned right on the Sterling Highway, the shored-up levies were inadequate to contain his memory bank, and it overflowed. Homer was the "end of the road" on his first voyage to Alaska. Now—his own daughter lived there. WOW!

After almost five thousand miles, his dream was fulfilled seeing swans in the wild in the Moose River near Sterling. Afterward, he meandered down to the "Cosmic Hamlet by the Sea." Sleeping in his camper, he struggled with a letdown. There was only one way to go—back the way he had come.

Had he reached life's pinnacle? Was everything all downhill from there? The very next day, Walt met an Alaska woman. He had already fallen in love with America's Last Frontier. His heart then took a totally unanticipated plunge.

The driver tried to disengage his mind, but it was not cooperating. A half hour up the highway, he got a glimpse of a pair of swans on a lake. Nellie took to the shoulder as the motorist grabbed his binoculars. This was the sign he was looking for. Walt was at peace.

History has a strange way of repeating itself. Walter Othell Williamson had no way of knowing that this Homer turnaround heralded yet another new chapter about to open in this ugly duckling's implausible life. Furthermore, this startling episode, soon to unfold, did not pertain to his recently discovered daughter. It was rather inextricably entwined with his late wife, Virginia Arlene Sullivan, the Alaska woman he met the first time he lumbered back up that road.

When Walt went inside, the first thing he noticed was the stack of junk mail. It could wait a while longer. First, he must light a candle. Missing

Ginny, and the emptiness of the place without Tonya, took turns ruling his seesaw emotions.

It was only mid-afternoon, but the melancholy man decided it was not too early for Happy Hour. As he retrieved a bottle of "Sin Infidel," memories of Tonya's mother's malapropism brought a smile to his face. The Zinfandel was smooth, and soon, tranquility transpired all around him.

Walt closed his eyes. His thoughts revisited the day he said goodbye to Ginny on her last mission as a travel nurse. Blinding snow almost aborted the flight from Kenai headed toward an island in the Aleutians. Unknown to the crew and passengers, a vast winter storm was in the path of the twin-engine plane.

He tried to imagine his beloved's last moments, but nothing in his repository came even close to what actually went through her mind. As the plane was spiraling out of control, the entirety of Ginny's life energy was fixated resolutely on the one tangible thread still connecting her with Walt, and whether or not it would wither on the vine.

After a welcomed good night's sleep, he was jarred awake by the pleasant sounds of Ms. Robin's distinctive song, resonating through the open window. Before he woke up Mr. Coffee, he went outside, and she greeted him on the clothesline.

"Well . . . Hello!"

He had done it again. To this seasonal resident that nested in a backyard tree, Walt had uttered his and Ginny's hallowed word. He had enunciated "Hello" so reverently the night their bodies had merged, their spirits melded. They had repeated it with every greeting after being apart.

Following her death, he had vowed never to say the sacrosanct word again as a salutation. For some strange reason, it did not feel like a betrayal when he used it to address the robin.

The mother bird took a particular delight in the little reunion. Memorial Day was just around the corner, and the beautiful orange-breasted creature celebrated it each year nestled atop the next generation in waiting.

"Okay . . . If you insist."

Walt went for the step stool, and the soon-to-be parent sat by approvingly as he looked into the nest. Three blue eggs were awaiting their mother's warmth and nurture. Ms. Robin burst into song. Walt gazed into her eyes, and she grew still.

He walked away wondering about the lifespan of birds. Was this the same robin that first connected with him after Ginny's death, or was it a second or even a third generation? For certain, there was no loss of continuity.

After putting the stool back beside the refrigerator, he reached for the mail. Shuttling through the unsolicited advertising material, he had no expectation of anything requiring action. Then, he took the registered letter and held it up. It was from a clinic in Seattle. Walt reasoned that it was likely nothing important, possibly just something related to Ginny's nursing school days. He was right about the second part.

Where was the letter opener? He did not want to mutilate the return address. Perhaps, he needed to inform the clinic of his wife's death so they could update their files. Retrieving it from the office desk drawer, he sliced open the envelope and took a seat in his easy chair.

Where were his reading glasses? When did typewriters start using such small print? He retraced his steps and settled again. Walt read the cover letter and replaced it carefully. He got up, went back outside, and Ms. Robin had taken her place over the eggs.

The F-150 fired up again. Not long after the fatal plane crash, Walt started calling the old truck "Radar." Radar was Ginny's Husky.

Are you kidding me?

Bekka looked up with surprise when Tonya sauntered into the art gallery on the Homer Spit. Her assistant had left abruptly when she learned of the sudden death of her mother, and the owner had opened it for the summer season while she was away. No customers were in the shop, and Bekka was dabbling with the outlines of a new painting.

"You don't look any the worse for wear. How did everything go?"

"Shall I start at the beginning or go to the end and work backward?"

"I don't know. The latter sounds more intriguing."

"Okay—but put down your brush. No need to ruin a masterpiece."

"Hmm."

"Fasten your seatbelt. I did not fly from Anchorage to Homer. Rather, I had a layover in Kenai. My daddy drove me down this morning."

"Your what?"

"That's right. As unimaginable as it might seem, Mother inadvertently left a clue that led me straight to him."

"Are you kidding me?"

"Not a chance. And guess what? Our paths have crossed many times. He owns a house in North Carolina—and another one just eighty miles right up the road. Do you remember the plane crash several years ago when a Kenai nurse was among the casualties? She was his wife."

"I had just come to Alaska when that happened. As I recall, her husband was a well-known author. Is that your father?"

"The one and only. Poor man—he's emotionally depleted. I wanted to stay with him for another couple of days, but I knew he needed his space. I suspect he's going into the wilderness, at least figuratively if not literally, for some time trying to wrap his mind around everything."

The bell over the door signaled that some tourists had wandered in. Tonya mumbled as she turned to assist them.

"Later."

"Oh, yes—I want to hear everything."

Forever and ever

Walt had no plan. The truck, now considered an antique, was still his winter mode of transportation. Ginny was driving it the day they met. He was making a pit stop when she came out of the convenience store. Concerned that his camper had her blocked, he gave hand signals, waving her through.

Pulling alongside him, she rolled down the window. Apparently miffed by his condescension, she responded rather demonstratively.

"I'll have you know—I'm an Alaska woman."

Not to be outdone, Walt shot back.

"And I'll have you know—I'm a southern gentleman."

The pickup lunged forward slinging gravel. Before entering the highway, the driver hit the brakes and backed up. Walt had no notion of what was coming next. The Alaska woman surprised him, the first of many, many times.

"I could get used to that. Park your rig and get in."

He did just that—clueless about what he was getting himself into. She drove to a beach, and they walked on the rocks and glacial sand for more than an hour, bantering and jousting—a pursuit that would prove to be ongoing.

Walt steered the old truck to the same spot. The breeze from the inlet was brisk, but he did not notice it. Processing the contents of the registered letter would not be completed by the time he returned to Radar. Neither would he get much sleep that night.

He wished for the opportunity to talk it through with Father Nicholas, the Russian Orthodox priest who performed his and Ginny's storybook progressive wedding. However, the cleric had been transferred to a church north of Anchorage.

The introverted man headed to the grocery store the next morning, but his mind was not on food. He rather made his way to the church with the beautiful blue domes where the extended wedding ceremony began. After assuring the attendant that he needed no guided tour, he went and knelt at the altar.

Trance-like, he spent the rest of the day retracing the route to each nuptial site. It was back to the beach where Father Nicholas had given an inspiring discourse on the nature of love. Clouds of the day before had lifted, and the mountains across the Cook Inlet were out in all their glory. The veil shrouding the widower still hung heavy all about him.

Over the next forty miles, Walt grimaced each time he saw wildflowers gracing the roadside. He took the spur to an overlook of the emerald-green Kenai Lake—nestled among the mountains still sporting pockets of snow. Standing on the edge of the precipice, with a solitary tear stuck between his nose and cheek, he revisited the vows they made to each other on that wondrous day. He reached for his bride's hand, but it was not there.

Unable to eat, he decided to forgo stopping at the summit for lunch, as the wedding party had done fourteen years earlier. Instead, he ambled along to Beluga Point on the Turnagain Arm.

On Walt's first voyage, it was at this venue that he felt a strong kinship to Alaska. It was also where the couple later exchanged wedding rings. He stood facing the brisk wind sweeping down from the Chugach Mountains and had to brace himself to prevent being blown over.

The drive to the last wedding setting took two hours. He was in no hurry. The priest had pronounced Walt and Ginny husband and wife—with the massive Exit Glacier as a magnificent backdrop.

Afterward, his beloved placed the bouquet of wildflowers that he had picked for her along the way on a shelf carved by the glacier. Walt returned to the spot after the plane crash and found remnants of the faded blue ribbon that he tied them with. He looped it through her wedding band, recovered from her body, and framed them in a shadow box.

Over time, alders and willows had reclaimed the area, and that ledge was no longer distinguishable. Yet, the words Ginny spoke to him were still fresh in his mind.

"My darling . . . I love you so much for picking this bouquet for me. They were meant just for this wonderful day. The wildflowers are already beginning to wilt, but my precious Walt, my love for you will never wither or fade. It is forever and ever."

Forever and ever. What did that mean?

Walt made his way back to the bench that the wedding party had used as an altar. He pulled the neatly folded letter from his pocket and read it again.

Before Ginny met Walt, she went to Seattle to attend a nursing school reunion. During the proceedings, the director of the program updated the alumnae about the progress being made with infertile couples. Experiments were underway fertilizing eggs in Petri dishes—with the prospects of eventually implanting embryos in wombs in a procedure called "in vitro." An appendage fertility clinic to the hospital was looking for donors to provide eggs for research.

Ginny was among those who volunteered. These young women were assured that they had far more eggs than they would ever need, and that harvesting some would not hamper their own reproductive abilities.

The letter to Ginny was to inform her that the clinic had recently discovered three of her unused eggs—still frozen. The director was inquiring of her wishes for what to do with them.

Walt had not eaten all day. He considered going into nearby Seward for the night when a sign at a rustic old roadhouse advertising fresh halibut caught his eye.

The sustenance revived him. The past prime time Radar was cumbersome during the two and a half hours back to Kenai in the twilight.

The spectacular drive from Tern Junction to Seward was one of Walt's favorites in all of Alaska. He never tired of it, but on the way down, his focus was elsewhere. Going back the other way, with the evening sun bathing the snow-cover peaks, he worshiped in awe and wonder.

The news from Seattle refused to take a back seat in his mind. Parts of his beloved were still alive. Her DNA did not perish when her body was cremated. How could he know what her wishes would be for the eggs?

Walt recalled what he had said to Tonya after they got back to Alaska about embracing *whatever*, *whenever*, and *wherever* as their moments in time announced themselves.

A cosmic moment—frozen in time—had just declared itself.

Numbness

Bekka shooed Tonya an hour before closing time and told her she could come in late the next morning. Miss Bizzy Belle's cupboard was also bare, but first, she had to dispose of perishables gone bad while she was away. Only a month before its summer solstice, the sun was nowhere near ready to retire for the night.

Sipping soup, picked up at a deli on the way back to her apartment, Tonya realized how spent she was. Over the past few weeks, her wits had run the gamut, and her being was screaming, "Enough already." Her body clock told her she was still on Eastern Time. Trying to occupy her mind a little longer so not to wake up early the next morning, the artist grabbed her pad.

Methodically, she began sketching a caricature of her father sitting in the front porch swing of his mountain home. Her thoughts went to what he had said about wishing one day to have a grandchild, and how she teased him about putting all his eggs in one basket. She smiled as she recalled baiting him.

"Who else might come knocking on your door?"

Nonetheless, Tonya knew the weight was on her shoulders. She celebrated her twenty-ninth-birthday on the day after finding her father. Being a single mom was not in her plans. If she could not raise a kid with someone she loved—and with a man who loved her and their baby—she would remain childless. The prospects of finding a mate who embraced life as she did were dim.

Tonya could only dream of the father Walt would have been. Any child would be so fortunate to have him as a grandpa. Nodding, she got up and put herself to bed.

"Gus . . . What now?"

Walt smiled as he recalled his annoyance when the phone interrupted him as he was almost out the door to catch a flight back to Kenai. Years earlier, he started calling his phone Gus after the elusive trout that his Granddaddy Williamson rightly said would make you cuss. The phone in his mountain bungalow was dubbed Gus I, and the Alaskan, Gus II.

Walt was hoping the same person would be on the other end of the line as was on that fateful day almost three weeks earlier. It was.

"Yes."

This was the way he answered sidestepping "Hello," his and Ginny's sanctified word. If the call was an intrusive telemarketer, the positive rejoinder was followed with a resounding, "No."

"Hi, Dad. What sort of troubles have you gotten yourself into since you've been back?"

"Why, Tonya. Why would you even think such a thing?"

"Are you coming this way again anytime soon? This place is abuzz about wanting to meet the famous author, and I'm sort of looking forward to showing off my father."

"I'm flattered. There's also something I want to discuss with you. How about I drive down tomorrow?"

"Perfect—it's Memorial Day weekend, and the Spit will be bustling. You can crash for as long as you wish. I'll even give you the bed and sleep on the sofa. I will have to work, though. Evenings are free. Anyway, I have something special to show you."

A few wildflowers were on the shoulder of the road, but it was too early for most including the vibrant fireweed. Walt wondered what Tonya's take would be on the information in the letter.

The father and daughter still knew so little about each other. With every rendezvous, they filled in more blanks. Walt beamed with pride as Tonya introduced him around. He had heard little of how she got to Alaska, and they set aside that topic for Saturday night's entertainment.

The art gallery opened when the owner unlocked the door, somewhere around ten-ish. Tonya demonstrated her cooking skills—if fixing breakfast with eggs, reindeer sausage, and Alaska style hash browns required any particular talent. Walt registered an immediate complaint.

"But I wanted grits."

"Next time, you'll have to bring your own. You're not likely to find them on any grocery store shelf in this town."

Walt pushed back from the table, and Tonya immediately protested.

"You don't have to wash the dishes."

"Busted. That's not what I was about to do. Hold that thought, and we'll discuss it later. I have something I want to show you."

Walt handed the letter to Tonya without explanation. She removed it from the envelope and made no comment as she perused it. When she finished, she put it back, handed it back, and took a moment before she spoke.

"How did you feel—or perhaps what did you feel—when you first read it?"

"Numbness . . . I'm still not sure what I think."

"What are you going to do about it?"

"I keep drawing a blank. I've not been able to pick the phone up and call the number. I tried to draft a response to put in the mail, but I came up empty. The inquiry has to do with what Ginny would want to be done with the eggs. Thus far, I have been unable to channel her in any sort of way."

"Maybe you should go to Seattle and talk with them directly."

"Wanna go with me? I would love for you to meet her family."

"I know I would enjoy it, but I've already missed so much work, and the tourist season is just getting underway. How do you think they'll react when they find out you have an illegitimate child?"

"They already know their daughter married a bastard, so I think they can handle it."

"Go on to Seattle. I feel strongly about that."

"You go get ready for work. I'll do the dishes."

"Yes, sir!"

Before she was out the door, Tonya reminded her father of a surprise still awaiting him.

"Follow me in Nellie."

Before getting to the shops on the spit, she veered her own vehicle left onto a dock access road. A quarter mile later, she came to a stop. On an abandoned rusty old pylon rising out of the seawater, a bald eagle was nestled in a crude abode made of twigs, awaiting the stork. Her mate was atop a light pole guarding his family.

MPD

Fertility rites hovered all around the man trying to figure out what to do about his own. Using his initials, Walt had kept a journal for years that he called, WOWs, and another volume was full. He sat and looked at the blank page in a new notebook several moments before picking up a pen.

> *My Precious Darling . . . I miss you*
> *so much at this moment.*

His eyes welled up, and he put down the pen.

When Walt informed the Sullivans that he was coming to Seattle on a little business trip, they did precisely what he anticipated. Ginny's old bedroom was his when he wanted to borrow it. He gave them no sign regarding the nature of his business, nor any hint about their late daughter's stepdaughter.

Ginny's parents fretted over getting everything just right for their son-in-law's visit. Mr. Sullivan met him at the Seattle-Tacoma Airport while his wife pored over sweet onion pie, twenty-four-hour salad, and a cobbler made from fresh cherries.

Walt minced no words in his praise for their genuine hospitality and for the superb cuisine. He was reticent, however, when it came to telling them about Tonya. Once he got it all out, he was perturbed with himself for being tentative. They made him promise that his daughter would accompany him the first possible opportunity. Mr. Sullivan could be direct.

"Walt . . . We have a great appreciation for your southern culture. I always looked forward to trips to Atlanta and Charlotte and never tired of waitresses calling me sweet little pet names. But this is the Pacific Northwest. Please dispense with the formalities. It's about time you started calling us Dave and Alice."

David Sullivan retired from Boeing after a distinguished career as an electrical engineer. Alice never got a profession off the ground. After their son was born in the second year of marriage, followed by two daughters spaced out a bit, she found being a stay at home mom much to her liking. The eldest moved east, the middle child went north, and the baby of the family stayed close to home.

Walt supposed that his in-laws were comfortable financially, but no flair of pretentiousness was about them. The couple still lived in the stately two-story house they raised their brood in. It reminded him of the one on "Father Knows Best."

IVF

Walt woke up in fits and jerks all during the night. His appointment at the clinic was at ten the next morning, and Dave offered him the use of a vehicle. After signing in, he was soon called to the director's office.

Dr. Hamby expressed condolences for Walt's loss, and he apologized for the insensitivity of him receiving the letter. Their files had not been updated, and they sent the document to Ginny's last known address. He said he never met her personally because he had only recently come to the clinic.

Recognizing that Walt did not know what questions to ask, the director explained the legal tangle. As Ginny's heir, he presumed the eggs would be transferred to him, but he would need to consult the hospital attorney to make sure.

"Supposing that's the case, Mr. Williamson, what do you want us to do?"

"What are my options?"

"For one thing, you could direct us to destroy them. Or, you could have them reassigned to infertile couples."

Walt had a question nagging him since he first opened the letter.

"Were any of my wife's eggs used for that purpose?"

Dr. Hamby did not have to check with anyone before answering.

"In a word, no. The contract she signed only authorized their use in laboratory research. She would have been required to sign a further release before they could have been used in vitro."

Walt breathed a sigh of relief, but he was about to catch his breath.

"Mr. Williamson . . ."

"Please call me Walt."

"Well, then, Walt. Unless someone tells me differently, there's still one other possibility. You might want to consider finding a surrogate mother and use your own sperm to fertilize an egg. IVF has come a long way in a short time, and we're having some amazing results. The chances are good that with three shots at it, you might hit the bull's eye."

What was this physician saying? Walt mind had refused to go there.

"There's no particular hurry. The frozen eggs are safe, but I would encourage you to move right along—if this is the option you choose. You're not getting any younger. Why don't you give it some thought and come back in a couple of days?"

Not getting any younger, indeed. If something that improbable might actually happen, he would turn fifty-four before the birth of his and Ginny's child.

When Walt took his seat behind the steering wheel, his wheels were spinning faster than the SUV's. Approaching an intersection, he was oblivious to a cop directing traffic because of a malfunctioning light. When he breezed past with her finger darting back and forth, he called out the open window.

"We're going to have a baby."

He laughed that the policewoman must have presumed that they were right then on the way to the hospital.

"Othell . . . What did I just say? We're going to have a baby? Is that what Ginny would want?"

Polly

"Walt . . . It will be leftovers. When Polly found out you were here, and what we had for dinner last evening, she put her foot down that both of hers would be under the dining room table tonight."

Polly was the baby of the family. Walt's late wife got her tall angular features from her father. Her sister was shapelier and a couple of inches shorter like their mother. The career high school English teacher divorced when her son, Frank, was two, and she had remained single.

"Wonderful—I look forward to seeing her. Do I have time for a little nap before she arrives?"

"Sure . . . Sweet dreams."

Walt's eyes refused to stay shut. Sweet dreams?

"Othell . . . Am I sleepwalking? Is this all a dream?"

Hardly able to keep a secret from her surviving daughter, Alice had naturally already told Polly about Tonya. It was not just her mother's cooking that was bringing her to the table. Inquiring minds wanted to know more. Polly was a sport, and she tried to put Walt on the defensive.

"Let me see if I've got this straight. You knocked up a woman and then vanished. The lieutenant was missing in action when diapers needed changing, you were not around when she was an insufferable brat, and you were AWOL as she became a surly teenager. You sat out paying for her college, and now you take full credit for how wonderful your daughter turned out. I'm impressed."

"Polly . . . I'm glad somebody appreciates me. I do have some regrets, but the biggest of all is that Ginny is not here for me to share my Tonya with. They would have loved each other almost as much as I love both of them."

Walt formed his own favorable impressions the first time he was around the Sullivans. Unlike with his upbringing, everybody always seemed to work together. They had welcomed him unconditionally into the family, and that had never wavered.

He was glad Polly was present. Bracing himself to share the other big news he had brought along with him in his pocket, her blitheness was a welcomed addition to the mix.

After savoring the last bite of the cherry pie, he handed the letter to Alice without explanation. The others looked on curiously and expressions intensified as the one on Ginny's mother's face morphed. Polly grew impatient.

"Well?"

"I'm speechless. I really don't know what to say."

Ginny's sister reached for the document, and her mother offered no resistance. Polly was uncharacteristically mute when she laid it down. Dave was accustomed to being in the dark.

"Will somebody please tell me what's going on?"

In his own words, Walt restated the contents of the correspondence.

"Unless the attorney sees a problem, I'm the lawful owner of Ginny's three frozen eggs. The clinic wants them disposed of one way or the other. I can just walk away as though I never knew anything about them, and they will be destroyed.

"I could also designate the clinic to use in any way they choose, including offering them to an infertile couple. Dr. Hamby indicated that if the parents consented, Ginny's family could be a part of her genetic child's life."

Walt paused. He was not sure if he wanted to go any further. Polly knew there was more.

"Or?"

"Dr. Hamby mentioned one other possibility—finding a surrogate mother—using my own sperm—and having Ginny's baby. My mind cannot fathom what would be involved in finding such a person, or how it might all play out."

Polly came out of her chair, literally. For a nanosecond, Walt thought she might have found that possibility repugnant. But no.

"If that's what Walt wants, **I'll do it.** I'll stand in for my big sister. Look no further. My incubator oven has a proven track record, and it's still in good working order."

"Are you sure about this?"

Those words were said in sync by the others around the table. Alice took it from there—expressing concerns and reservations.

"Polly . . . You're in your forties. Don't put your own life at risk. I can't bear the thought of anything happening to you, too."

"Oh, Mother, chill. I've never felt so right about anything in all my life. When Walt said, 'a surrogate mother,' joy ran up my toes, right through my heart, and it lit up my brain."

"This will not be your child. Are you sure you can let Walt take the baby you carried and birthed back to Alaska, maybe even to North Carolina, and raise it as his own?"

"It will be Walt and Ginny's baby, not mine. Of course, I can."

"What will Frank think?"

"My son is off in college and my nest is empty. This will take nothing away from him, and he will not interfere. Good thing he's not a girl. That would be a different story. I think he will find this amusing."

Very much aware of the gravity of the situation, Mr. Sullivan remained silent no longer.

"Walt . . . Have you thought this through? There is so much to consider."

"Uppermost on my mind is what Ginny would want. I cannot rule out anything at this moment. I have a follow-up appointment at the clinic in two days. If Polly is serious, perhaps she can accompany me, and we can learn more about what is involved. Dr. Hamby specified some stringent requirements, so they might veto it."

"Perfect—my last day of post planning is tomorrow."

The men got up and cleared the table. After the dishwasher was loaded and started and the food safely in the refrigerator, they retired to the parlor and watched CNN.

When Walt went to bed, the mother and daughter were still sitting around the table talking. Each time he walked past, the conversation paused, and they looked up and smiled. He had the distinct feeling that Alice was trying to dissuade Polly from making good on her proposal. Maybe, she was right.

Again, sleep did not come easily. Mind-boggling seemed too lame a word to label what was going on inside him. No matter which wild tangent his thoughts went off on, they always circled back to what Ginny would want. Caution flags were waving everywhere, but he could not discern a stop sign. If the clinic precluded it, or Polly did not meet their requirements, the point was moot, anyway.

That night, he wrote in WOWs.

My precious Ginny . . . Please send me a sign. What "must" I do?

Wide awake and looking at the ceiling, Walt smiled. He had methodically put "must" in quotes. Unable to time travel to the future, his mind reverted back into the past.

He reminisced about when he and Ginny were out for a night on the town in Anchorage and the tickle box kept getting turned over. Back in their hotel room, he was annoyed when she took so long before coming to bed. When she finally emerged from the bathroom, he was smitten and muttered mischievously.

"You look good enough to eat."

Whimsically, she threw her head back.

"If you must . . ."

Close enough

Walt arrived a few minutes early to alert Dr. Hamby about Polly's participation in the session. This gave them a chance to go over some of the procedures. Surprisingly, the physician expressed optimism about the possibility of the sister of the egg donor becoming a surrogate.

When escorted into the office, Polly was cheery. Dr. Hamby was a no-nonsense professional, and he got down to business.

"If we go forward with IVF, you will be a gestational surrogate in that another's egg will be used instead of your own. Our first attempt will involve attaching the egg and then inserting the semen with a syringe. Should this fail, we'll try again using the same procedure. As a last resort, we will take the third egg, try to inseminate it first, and then affix the resulting embryo.

"But we're getting ahead of ourselves. There are some standard guidelines that we must follow. Polly . . . Nod in the affirmative as I go over them if they apply to you. You must have already had a successful pregnancy with a normal birth. We need to see your OB/GYN records. So good so far?"

"Yes."

"You must be a nonsmoker and not have any smokers living under your roof. You must have no mental health issues and live a healthy lifestyle."

Walt stopped him at this point.

"Polly might be a little touched in the head to even consider something like this."

After obligatory nods and smiles, the physician continued.

"You must have no criminal record and be financially stable. Whatever monetary arrangements the two of you make are up to you. Have you discussed that?"

Polly spoke with no hesitation.

"I'm doing this for my sister, and I'll take full responsibility for what my insurance does not cover. This will cost my brother-in-law nothing until I hand off the brat to him. Then, he's on his own."

"Polly, I cannot let you do that."

"I don't see you having any other choice."

Dr. Hamby was taking both written and mental notes.

"There are a couple more items we need to check off. Our clinic thinks it's too risky if the surrogate mom is older than forty-two."

For the first time, Polly did not nod.

"Close enough—what is the time frame we're working with? I'm out of school for the summer. Can this be expedited so I don't have to miss much class time?"

"Let's not get in too big a hurry. This is still new to both of you. Step back and give your emotions a chance to catch up with the novelty.

"Polly . . . We can go ahead and schedule you for the required complete physical. And Walt . . . We can make sure you're not shooting blanks. You will both also have to spend some time with our counseling staff. They will ask questions that you have not thought about and press hard about your understanding of the long-term ramifications."

Dr. Hamby paused a moment.

"If we continue, we will be doing something most irregular. In vitro fertilization is designed for couples. We've never brought a baby into a single mother's home, much less one for a widower father. Walt . . . If our staff approves this, we will require absolute assurances that you will have all the resources necessary to take care of a newborn."

Polly interrupted.

"Let me put your mind at ease. My mother and I will both be there for Walt and this baby. You can rest assured that this child will not be neglected."

Turning to Walt, the physician continued.

"I did learn from your application that you have a grown daughter so parenthood is not a new experience for you."

Walt winked at Polly when they made eye contact. He nodded to the physician, but she understood, "Close enough" was left unsaid.

The doctor asked if Walt's Alaska residency would create any complications during the interval. Polly assured the physician that he had two places to stay in Seattle. If he wore out his welcome in one, he could move to the other for a few days.

"Then again, all we'll need from you is to make your donation. After that, your whereabouts are irrelevant until the baby gets here."

If he intended that as a joke, it fell flat. Signaling the meeting was over, the clinic director arose from his chair.

Walt was fortunate to get the last window seat on the right side of the plane. The coastal panhandle was in and out of the clouds—somewhat parallel to what he was going through. A part of him was walking on air—the rest flying through a haze.

Being on the other side of the counseling desk, was a new experience. Apparently, he passed the muster. Four days earlier, he had not signed his name so many times since his last book tour. With a brief explanation of what he was agreeing to, the assistant kept putting one document after another in front of him.

The donor asked the physician how they would know for sure it was Ginny's egg and not Polly's that got impregnated. Dr. Hamby tried out his deadpan again and said they might never know.

"There's really nothing to worry about since the baby would come from the same gene pool either way."

Walt was not amused.

"Seriously—we have ways of working around that."

Apparently, *how* was more information than his patient needed to know.

Walt was kept mostly in the dark until the day he was called upon to make his contribution. His modesty was brushed aside by the technician who approached the deed as just all in a day's work.

Polly was exuberant. She passed her physical with flying colors, and Dr. Hamby said nothing more about her age. Mr. Sullivan kept his thoughts to himself, but it concerned him that the clinic might be seeking publicity. Alice turned into a chatterbox. Walt assumed that this was a normal reaction to her apprehensions.

The prospective father was not on the guest list for the conceptual party. Both the implantation and the injection took place in sequence, and only time would tell if the egg attached itself successfully to the womb, and a spermatozoon had made love to it.

Providence

Walt had no need to hang around. He was promised updates on all developments. As they applied to him, he was just not sure what was considered a development.

Tonya had no phone in her apartment, and from a pay phone at the airport, he had tried to reach her at work. Bekka said she had left the gallery to pick up a take-out order. They were so busy that an actual lunch hour was impossible. He left a message about his travel plans and said he would fill her in when he could.

The ticket price for the commuter flights between Anchorage and Kenai had risen steadily. Walt was glad he had driven into the city and left Nellie at the airport. Once his feet were on the ground after the four-hour flight, the three-hour drive was just what the doctor ordered.

The pullover at Beluga Point gave him a chance to stretch both his legs and his lungs. Ah—that Alaska seaside air. The Dall Sheep were visible halfway up the mountainside. Not clear was how to prepare himself for what was ahead. Walt imagined Ginny's child beside him, holding his hand, watching the Beluga Whales cavorting. He could not make out whether the kid was a boy or a girl.

"Hi, Honey . . . I'm home."

Walt went directly to the drawer, reached for the matchbox, and lit the candle beside Ginny's photograph. Next, he went out the back door to check on Ms. Robin. The eggs had hatched while he was gone. Both dutiful parents welcomed him with exuberance.

Chup . . . Chup . . . Cheer up, Cheerio!
Chee . . . Chee . . . Chee . . . Tut . . . Tut . . . Tut.

> *Dearest Ginny . . . If everything goes well, we're having a baby. This is truly unbelievable. Your sister is making this happen, but I promise you, my darling, this child will always know who his real mother is. Providence had a hand in your decision to donate those eggs. In a few months, I might well be holding our baby in my hands. I love you so much.*

The first thing Walt noticed when he entered Tonya's apartment was the pencil sketch of him sitting in the swing. He had gone to the gallery and picked up the key that she had made for him. After getting over his amusement, he mused.

"Othell . . . I look like an old man. If this baby thing happens, will I be more like a father or a grandfather?"

Having surrendered to the sleeping arrangement, he put his bag in the bedroom. In some things he had rank—in others he had none. He did not see a closing hour posted at the gallery and was unsure when Tonya would be home. She came in the door full of questions.

"Had you even thought about the possibility of using the eggs?"

"You mean Ginny's sister just up and volunteered?"

"Does she have a husband?"

"Any children?"

"How do the parents feel about this?"

"Will you move to Seattle? Did you know I've been there?"

"Now, tell me the truth. Do you want a boy or a girl?"

"Can I be its nanny?"

Walt had a question of his own.

"How do you feel about all this?"

If he had been paying closer attention, there would have been no reason to ask.

Walt had heard tales of expectant fathers treated like useless appendages, and he was getting an early taste. No word came from the lower forty-eight for the next few weeks.

When Sockeye salmon were in the river, he went to a local fish market and purchased enough to fill his smoker. Tonya must have gotten a whiff and drove unexpectedly into the yard just as he was taking them out. She followed her nose and came out the backdoor sporting a bottle of Sin Infidel.

Around the table, the two reminisced about the first time they shared this dual delicacy just weeks earlier the day after they discovered each other. The real reason for her visit was to check on her father. His own introspection hardly took a timeout.

"Othell . . . Help me out here. The newness of me and my grown daughter still getting to know each other has nowhere near worn off. Simultaneously, I am stumbling along in the shadows of the unknown, sorting the ins and outs of having my own kid to raise. What happened to the solitary man tucked safely away in his sanctuary?"

Meanwhile, he missed his mother. She left this world, not knowing that she was a grandmother, and now might be again. In the short time they shared, Maggie became his sounding board. How he wished that he could talk this over with her.

Tonya was still basking in the glow of finally finding the father denied her. Being an only child, she had felt deprived. A hole was in her heart from the untimely death of her mother, and much between them was left resolved.

In still another bizarre twist in the astonishing tale of her own life, the realization of a sibling was impending. She wondered if she would feel more like a big sister or an aunt.

"Dad . . . Are you okay?"

"At this moment, I have no concept of what *okay* even resembles."

Strike one

The day after Tonya went back to Homer, Walt finally got a call from the clinic. Strike one.

> *My love . . . I do not know whether I am disappointed or relieved. Maybe this was just not meant to be, but we still have two more chances. Please send me something to go on. Always, Walt.*

Dr. Hamby required a fresh batch of semen for round two. The next call was to Alaska Airlines, and the donor booked a flight for August 12.

Walt Williamson's body had never been on a roller coaster at an amusement park. Nevertheless, his emotions were on a wild up and down ride. During the flight south, he entered into a grieving process. All over again, he was on the verge of losing the last vestige of Ginny.

He rebounded rapidly from that low point when Polly met him at SEA-TAC. She greeted him with a hug that would have made a mama bear proud. Unexpectedly, she put her arm around his waist as they headed for baggage claim. Waiting for the carousel to begin making its deliveries, the potential proxy mother said her intuitions were pointing to success this next time.

Polly turned and faced him squarely. Taking both of his hands, her moist eyes penetrated Walt's armor.

"Trust them. Trust me."

The sperm donor went to the clinic the next morning to take care of business and was hoping for a chat with the director, but Dr. Hamby was nowhere to be seen. Later that afternoon, Alice accompanied Polly to the clinic while the men went to the fish market to snag the catch of the day for dinner.

Going forward, the rules of decorum had not been written for this sort of thing. Walt was unsure if it was proper to ask Polly to keep him posted, or if it were permissible for him to check in with her from time to time. Should Alice be his contact person? Not much was kept from her. For certain, the clinic would not divulge much information. He returned to Alaska with no established lifelines.

The body contact at baggage claim had rattled Walt. It was reminiscent of Ginny's touch and like looking right into her eyes. He was relieved when Dave drove him to the airport. As a counselor, he had worked with clients dragging along their baggage. On the long flight, he grappled with his own.

Three weeks went by with no word. Did the folks in Seattle think that he was disinterested, or did they even think about him at all? Polly was already back in the classroom and had assured Walt that the school understood her condition. She had accrued numerous sick and personal leave days and could take them as needed. What he needed, was to hear from her.

When the gallery closed for the season, Tonya looked forward to devoting more time to her own painting. Once again, Walt had an unannounced visitor. When she unloaded an easel and announced her intention to stay a few days, he rubbed his chin.

"Do I have any say in this?"

"No—that's why I didn't call ahead."

Walt fired up the grill on Labor Day, and the two feasted on pork ribs, barbecued southern style. Tonya made potato salad. After a week of frivolous and frolicsome fun, his spirits were more upbeat. Her big accomplishment was a painting of the house, with the F-150 in the drive. Its namesake, Radar, was superimposed on the front porch.

Tonya encouraged her father to give Polly a call. Not yet a month, he waited a while longer. The next Sunday afternoon, he got her answering machine. He was unsure if his message was intelligible, but apparently, it was. Two hours later, Gus II put him on notice.

Polly was talkative. So far—so good. She was convinced that she had felt twinges of morning sickness. Sensing his anxiety, she tried to make it easier for him.

"Walt . . . You can call me anytime you wish."

He deflected.

"When do you think you'll know for sure?"
"I have an appointment on Friday afternoon."
"I'll give you a call Friday evening."

My precious darling . . . Our baby is on the way. So much in need of your loving presence. Hold me in your heart.

Phone dates

Sunday evenings became phone date nights. Polly clarified specifics and answered Walt's questions without him stammering to find the right words. With the embryo attached successfully, the biggest risk going forward was that it would abort spontaneously. She reassured him that this possibility existed in any pregnancy.

The chats were not just about her or her condition. Polly wanted to know all that he had been doing, and she shared amusing anecdotes from school. Initially, Walt approached each call with a measure of dread, fearing the worst, and she picked up on his anxiety. She pledged to call him immediately if anything went wrong. The expectant father became more comfortable in the conversations and began looking forward to them.

After the fall equinox, darkness started overtaking daylight by a few minutes every solar cycle. By the first of November, a few snowflakes had moseyed through the elements. When Gus II announced an incoming call one Sunday afternoon, Walt assumed that Polly was calling early. Instead, it was her mother. Alice extended an invitation for both Walt and Tonya to spend Thanksgiving with them.

Leaving on Tuesday, the father and daughter took their second flight together. Walt had wondered but not pried about Tonya's finances. On the way to Seattle, she told him about Mrs. Thornhill—and the inheritance she had received from her mentor and second mom.

"She gave me my first car—the blue Volvo you saw. When I was a toddler in her daycare, I could not say her name and called her 'Cornfield.' Now you know why I gave that name to my little Subaru Legacy."

Walt thoughts turned to Polly. She was about a third of the way to the finish line. Her sprint might soon be over, but his marathon was only beginning. He tried to imagine how much she would be showing but would have to wait for two days to see for himself. Mr. and Mrs. Sullivan both met them at the gate.

After Walt received a warm welcome, the attention shifted to his daughter. As they walked through the terminal, Alice took this newest member of the family by the arm.

Tonya made herself right at home in the kitchen helping with the cooking. She had flashbacks of the many delightful childhood hours shared with her Granny Addie around the stove.

Polly and her son, Frank, arrived just in time to help with the finishing touches. She was given a food preparation pass but promised to take charge of the cleanup. Walt had not seen Ginny's nephew since the memorial service following her death.

Mr. Sullivan handed the carving knife to his son-in-law, but he passed it along to Frank. The only grandson considered it a rite of passage and went right to work. Polly's brother Robbie was spending the holiday with his wife's family.

The conversation around the dinner table was spirited. Dave proposed a toast to Tonya. This was followed by one to the family member still on the way. Polly lifted her tea glass. She said new research indicated that an expectant mother should refrain from alcohol. Walt saw further evidence that the stand-in mother of his child was taking good care of herself.

As the others retired to the parlor, Walt and Polly cleared the table. She pulled him over to the side and gave him a big hug. He could feel the bulge between them. Releasing her grip and placing her hands on his shoulders, their eyes locked.

"Thank you so much for letting me do this."

Walt felt more needed saying, but his words stumbled getting out of the gate. Polly then reached for his right hand. Not breaking their gaze, she placed it on her tummy.

"Walt . . . This is your baby, *too*. Don't be shy. It's okay for you to feel it."

My dearest Ginny . . . Are you hoping for a boy or a girl? I already have one daughter but another would be fine. Since I will be raising this kid without you, a son might be less complicated.

"It"

On the flight back to Alaska, Walt was unable to secure adjoining seats. He surrendered the window to Tonya and took one on the aisle a few rows back. It was just as well. Many things were on his mind.

When Polly invited them for Sunday brunch, Dave announced that he was taking Tonya to a Seahawks' game. Her eyes lit up, but Walt winced at the notion of going alone. He had not been to Polly's and presumed Frank would provide some cover. Alice hinted for an invitation, but it went ignored.

Walt did not want to go empty-handed, but he could not take the customary bottle of wine. Neither would it be a Champagne brunch. He had never been sure of himself around women, and Ginny had picked up on that. She made it mostly easy, but she was fully capable of messing with him. Polly was something else.

The woman carrying his baby lived in a modest suburban home. He noticed the moss hanging from the gutters, common in an area with so many rainy days. On the way to her house, he also observed vehicles with the green stuff growing on side panels.

"Othell . . . That must take some getting used to."

Walt was uncertain what to expect when he rang the doorbell. His edginess exhaled when she only extended a hand. When she said Frank had already left for Washington State, his uneasiness inhaled.

After a little tour of the house, Polly invited him into the kitchen. Her guest noticed the nautical theme and commented on it. She said she was a Pisces, and that in another life must have been a sailor. He suspected that she could cuss like one if the circumstances warranted it.

The Sunday brunch entailed bagels and lox with a cream cheese topping and a pastry that Walt was not sure of. The tête-à-tête was also light and fluffy.

When they moved to the den, he wondered how long they could keep sidestepping the inevitable. Polly poured more coffee and preempted further circumventing.

"Walt . . . What is our end game here? This is awkward, but there are things we need to discuss. When the baby comes, are you moving in here to help me take care of *it*? Dr. Hamby says that ideally, I should breastfeed *it*. Might you be more comfortable at Mother's? I certainly hope you're not just going to whisk *it* away back to Alaska."

Walt heard every syllable, but one hit a nerve each time she uttered it.

"Can we stop calling Ginny's baby an '*it*'?"

In the words of that great twentieth-century philosophical guru, Yogi Berra, Walt had just made the wrong mistake. Visibly shaken, Polly bolted from the room. When she returned half an eternity later, she was still drying her eyes.

"I'm so sorry. This really is my sister's baby, not mine, as I fear I was allowing myself to believe. And you are right. 'It' is a little human being whose gender we do not yet know. Dr. Hamby asked about ultrasound, but I was not sure what you wanted."

The sperm donor and the surrogate mother patched things up, but he left with none of her questions answered. Another circumstance was beginning to trouble Walt. What kinds of feelings might Polly be developing for him? He closed his eyes and tried in vain to take a nap on the plane.

"Othell . . . I just can't dwell on that right now."

Sleepless in Seattle

Tonya was glad for the solitude. Going back to Seattle had conjured up some ghosts from her past. When they were circling to land, she could see the Space Needle below and broke into a smile recalling the day Ranger Rick was with her there. Having just been to the Pike Place Market where he had "caught" a flying fish and placed it in the cooler for later, he was self-conscious about how he smelled. As they orbited the observation deck, he did slip his arm around her.

They had come to the city to see the movie, "When Harry met Sally," oblivious to the impact it might have on them. Afterward, they contemplated getting a room and crossing a line that they had tiptoed around for months. Tonya wondered how things might have turned out if they had.

When she took Mrs. Thornhill on their last voyage together, the one to Alaska they had planned for years, Tonya was only planning to be gone for two weeks. She had supposed the separation might be healthy for the relationship with Rick. Instead, she put her mentor on the plane back to D.C., meandered down the Kenai Peninsula to Homer, and never went back to her old job.

When returning from Mrs. T's funeral, Tonya took a side trip to Bashville, Washington where she had worked as a newspaper reporter. She checked on Rick, and the Park Ranger had been reassigned.

Was that her one and only chance for love? She would be thirty on her next birthday, and the prospects around Homer were scant. Several guys were more than willing to play rough and tumble, but she wanted romance.

Tonya found some hope in how her father met Ginny. At the same time, the fulfillment of his dreams was cut so short. Would intimacy ever be elusive? During the Thanksgiving weekend, she had discovered firsthand the meaning of "Sleepless in Seattle."

Furthermore, she was worried about her father. She offered to change seats with him about halfway to Anchorage, but he pointed to the clouds outside and teased her about an empty gesture. He had not mentioned how things went at Polly's, but from his demeanor, he seemed unsettled. Much was up in the air.

The phone dates picked back up where they left off. Walt had never been one to spend much time on the telephone, and the long-distance rates from Alaska to Washington were steep. Not an independently wealthy man, he had to keep an eye on his finances.

He owned homes in Kenai, Alaska, and Ephesus, North Carolina, both bequeathed to him. His modest book royalties and the proceeds from Ginny's life insurance were invested wisely, and he lived off the dividends. Raising a child, was one thing Walt Williamson had not budgeted for.

Polly inquired about his Christmas plans. He deferred until he could discuss it with his daughter. Travel during the holidays was not cheap. Tonya encouraged him to go, but she preferred to sit it out. Walt wished to spend his first Christmas ever with his not so baby girl.

Butterflies

Norman Rockwell would have struggled to find anything from that holiday scene worthy of something to paint. Nothing was traditional about the way Walt and Tonya celebrated. She had no Christmas decorations, and Homer had not yet had any measurable snow that hung around.

Walt drove down on the winter solstice. Leaving soon after lunch, he arrived barely before the sun started setting, but no gloominess hung in the bayside air.

The following day, a walk beckoned. A city moose was also out for a stroll, munching on alder shoots in a vacant lot. After the amblers deposited their boots and shed their jackets, Tonya made hot chocolate, and they both made conversation.

With every visit, Walt spent more time admiring the paintings hanging on the wall. He was not sure from whence his daughter's amazing talent had sprung. One pencil drawing captivated him.

"Tell me about this sketch."

Tonya handed him a mug and lifted it from its perch. It remained on her lap as they slurped their beverages noisily, each trying to outdo the other. Since neither had anything resembling a typical childhood, juvenile playfulness came naturally.

"I'm not surprised at all that you were drawn to this."

Slowly and reverently, she told her father about the little church in the wildwood that she visited on her cross-country journey. The preacher's theme centered on following your still-small-inner-voice. She described Mrs. Hattie who came in and sat beside her and then invited the church visitor to go home with her. Tonya recounted helping the saintly woman make biscuits and fry chicken.

She paused after unfolding each development. Walt's senses went on high alert. Before saying goodbye, her hostess instructed her to follow her own "inner voice." Handing the framed draft to him, she described sitting in the swing and penciling the sketch before leaving it on the kitchen table.

"Daddy . . . I've never talked to anyone else about this except one other person. She believed me. I remember thinking then how I longed to share that experience with my father because I knew somehow he would understand."

All four eyes were moist. Tonya went on to portray how something compelled her to return to Mrs. Hattie's later that evening only to find a dilapidated house not lived in for years.

"From the musty and dusty ruins, I retrieved what you hold in your hands. The likeness is the spitting image of my Granny Addie."

The solidifying bond between a father and his daughter just grew stronger.

My dear loving late wife . . . How I
wish that you could have lived to

know my Tonya. Then again, the two of you would gang up on me for sure, and I wouldn't have a chance. I don't know what I would do without her. She wants to be our baby's nanny.

Sitting around the little kitchen table the next day, sipping soup and smacking on sandwiches, Walt delved into the depths of Tonya's Mrs. Hattie/Granny Addie visitation.

"You know—there is so much more to life than what we perceive only with our natural senses. In fact, that's where we usually go wrong. If we cannot see it, hear it, feel it, smell it, measure it, and put a label on it, we presume it does not exist."

"I know one thing. What happened to me, changed me forever. I'm aware of my limitations, but I do get that the universe is alive with all kinds of energies. I had never thought much about the migrations of animals until I moved to Alaska. The birds and waterfowl travel the same routes, thousands of miles, each year. They must be tuned into a guidance system that mere humans don't receive."

Walt jumped in.

"Just think about the salmon. If they were not tapped into something directing them, how could they possibly find their ways back to the very beds where they were spawned?"

After a moment for reflection, he continued.

"When I was undergoing my own metamorphosis before my first trip to this great place, two concepts started making sense to me—*synchronicity* and *spontaneity*. People are endowed with all kinds of inexplicable intuitions. If we follow them, we align ourselves with those energies of which you speak.

"As we are open to unknowns—when we surrender our fears of them—we can embrace a connectedness. How else do you explain inspiration? We are most alive when aligned with the dynamism of the Creator and His creation."

Tonya paused as the significance of what her father had said settled in. Then, she backtracked.

"Funny, you should use the word metamorphosis. You already know that I have always had a fascination with butterflies. I once wrote in my journal. 'Why do some people get stuck as caterpillars, never able to emerge from their cocoons and become butterflies'?"

In addition to his phone date, Walt had called his in-laws before he left Kenai to wish them a Merry Christmas. The day after Santa bypassed at least one apartment in Homer, he knew it was time to get back up the road. Christmas fell on a Friday in 1998, and he wanted to be home for his next chat with Polly.

"Tonya . . . Someday you will have to get a phone."

"Why don't you just give me Gus II? Most folks would rather talk with me."

"Any other time, I would do so gladly. I need Gus, for now, to keep me updated about my baby on the way."

Knickers

Snow was falling when Walt loaded his gear. Perhaps, he should have driven Radar. Other vehicles had blazed a trail, and he only went through a couple of treacherous patches. Accumulations were piling up as he pulled into the drive.

When he trudged to the mailbox, an envelope with David Sullivan's return address was the only thing inside.

"Othell, what the . . . Ugh, Hades is this all about?"

He went looking for his reading glasses and took a seat in his chair.

>
> Dear Walt,
>
> I trust you and Tonya had a delightful Christmas. Naturally, we were disappointed that you could not be with us but understand fully your decision to spend it with your daughter. I kept imagining next year celebrating our new grandchild's first Christmas, pulled up to the table in a high chair, and the center of attention.
>
> The reason for this letter is that I had planned to have a private talk with you if you had been able

to come our way. I will instead use this means to convey what I would have said.

Our family understands that many decisions are yet to be made about your plans. We wish you to know that we are nothing but supportive and will play whatever role in our grandchild's life that you make possible.

Ginny is not here to help you raise this child. When Polly hands the baby off to you, her obligations will be fulfilled. Walt, I have made a decision regarding a way my family can assist you. It is my hope and desire that what I am suggesting will be received in the spirit of helping to fill the void Ginny left.

Now, let me cut to the chase. I have an annuity that just keeps rolling over. My broker tells me that I must start making withdrawals. If you concur with what I am proposing, please send me a voided blank check. I will make arrangements for monthly deposits to be credited to your account. This is money that we are not using and will not miss.

I remember so well how you took some of Ginny's insurance settlement and established a scholarship in her name. I cannot begin to tell you the joy that brought to her family. It is now payback time for your thoughtfulness and generosity. And one more thing. Let's keep this just between the two of us.

Sincerely yours,
David Sullivan

   Walt's male ego had a power surge. By the time he raised the mailbox flag on Monday morning, he had reset his emotional circuit breaker.

He could laugh at himself by then, but it was not funny at the time. Walt Williamson was no ward of the state—no charity case. He scrutinized the letter looking for what might be crouched between the lines. Was his father-in-law staking out his claim to assure access to his grandbaby? Did he think Walt's integrity was for sale or see his son-in-law as incapable of providing for his own flesh and blood?

As he settled back down, he remembered what his Grandpa King used to say.

"Son . . . Don't get your knickers in a knot."

Walt had never observed anything but genuineness in Mr. Sullivan and had no cause to suspect his motives. The family patriarch just wanted the best for everybody. No mention was made of the amount of the monthly deposit. Likely, it was nothing worth fretting over.

> *Darling . . . You have a most wonderful family. Your sister is making such a sacrifice for us, and your parents are being so supportive. I promise that our child will always be a part of their lives.*

On New Year's Eve, the light began fading by mid-afternoon. As a brilliant sunset illuminated the southwestern sky, Walt lit candles throughout the house. Around ten, he raised a toast to himself and turned in for the night. He tossed and turned—pondering how remote the year 2000 had seemed when in his youth. Now, it was only a year away. When he aroused at six the next morning, the calendar had turned over for the last time in the twentieth century.

The reclusive man thought about his Grandpa and Grandma King and how much the world changed during their lifetimes. This "war baby" had come a long way himself. In a few months, he would have a child, part of "Generation Z," or a "Millennial," he was not sure. The fifty-four-year-old expectant father simply did not have the tools to imagine what was in store for either his firstborn or his yet born.

In no hurry to kick-start the new year, Walt replayed in his mind the conversation he had with Tonya about connectedness. Maintaining his own equilibrium was problematic. The vastness of the Yukon and British Columbia hampered the bond building between him and the living being that would be handed off to him within the next few months. The weekly phone conversations were helpful but left him wanting so much more.

Muddling

Sorting out his feelings for Polly was an ongoing effort for Walt. He stood in awe of her for taking on this responsibility. His vocabulary simply did not contain the words to convey gratitude that his beloved Ginny would live on because of her sister.

Neither was he certain of Polly's feelings for him, but he kept the guard up. She was more comfortable talking on the phone than he was. He got detailed reports with reassurances of no signs of complications. It seemed easy for her to discuss intimate things about her body.

With Ginny, Walt's amorous hankerings had finally found a worthy recipient and were unleashed. As Valentine's Day approached, the incurable romantic wondered if he should send her sister a card. When he discussed it with Tonya, she proposed something else.

"Why not flowers?"

The red-letter day was Sunday. Should he request delivery to the school on Friday or at home on Saturday? It got too complicated, and in the end, he decided it was not a good idea. The gesture might send mixed messages and muddle things.

During the long-distance prearranged Sunday conversation, Walt listened intently to the news of the past week. As the call was coming to its conclusion, he just blurted it out.

"Happy Valentine's Day."

The typically gregarious Polly went mute, and his well-wishes were met with a pregnant pause. How Walt wished he could reach through the telephone line and pull those words back.

Polly found her voice eventually, but it was wobbly.

"That is so sweet."

Walt had muddied the waters anyway.

MPD . . . Please help me with this Polly thing. It has become more than a simple arrangement to get our baby here. I fear she is becoming attached to the child in a way other than through the umbilical cord. I'm afraid she sees me as more than just the donor. Should I stop talking to her every week, or would that only make matters worse?

When Walt's January bank statement came in the mail, nothing out of the ordinary was deposited into his account. He had no reason to doubt his father-in-law's credibility. The wheels of business and banking often grind slowly.

The February statement was a different story. What his eyes beheld, threw him back on his heels. Two deposits had been made, one near the beginning of the month and another toward the end. Both were for the sum of $988.34. Instead of a round number, Walt presumed that was the tally of each monthly dividend.

"Whoa, Nellie!"

Within an hour, he made the call—to Alaska Airlines. That initial deposit was going toward the purchase of a round trip ticket to Seattle.

Alice assured him that someone would be waiting at SEA-TAC when he touched down. He was relieved when it was her husband. While waiting for the chute to disgorge his well-worn luggage, Walt thanked his father-in-law for his generosity. Dave gave him an update.

"I have already spoken with my accountant, and after the baby is born, I will add his name as the beneficiary of the principal amount of the annuity. I would just go ahead and sign it over to you for his education, but there are tax ramifications that we must work around."

"Mr. Sullivan . . . You don't have to . . ."

"Did I just say, 'his name?' What are you hoping for, Walt, a boy or a girl?"

"If the baby just gets here all in one piece kicking and raring to go, I'll be happy either way. If she's a girl, she will be spoiled so rotten that, with your experience around females, I might have to turn her over to you to straighten out."

Walt paused and his furrowed brow dissolved.

"A son would also be nice. Is Polly doing okay? From our phone conversations, things seem to be going well. There's always the nagging doubt that she might not be telling me everything."

"Relax, my boy. I don't think it could go any better."

Alice met them at the door with open arms. Walt was unsure when he would see his baby's surrogate mother, but he did not have to wait long.

"Go get unpacked. By then, Polly should be here."

He had not seen her since Thanksgiving, and she was entering her third trimester. Walt had never been around expectant mothers and assumed that she might be wearied and haggard. He was startled when Polly waddled in with a glow about her.

Fresh out of words

The first words out of Polly's mouth caught him by surprise. No, "Hello." No, "How are you?" No, "Did you have a good flight?" Not even, "It's so good to see you."

"I'm a little pissed off with you. I thought you would be staying with me."

Alice chimed in.

"Now Polly . . . You're still teaching, and there's no need for Walt to twiddle his thumbs while you're off helping to cure the world of ignorance. Anyway—you can have him this weekend."

The houseguest stood by sheepishly, unaccustomed to others charting his comings and goings. Walt Williamson's newest expedition in the world of unfamiliar turf was rummaging for traction.

As Polly escorted Walt to the guest bedroom, he glanced through the open door of hers. A baby bed was tucked away in a corner. She measured his reaction and was waiting after he unburdened his arms.

"My—how things have changed since I had my first child. Baby furniture is so much more functional. Can you believe this one will fold up in seconds and fit in the back of an SUV?"

His head turned slowly, but its mouthpiece was mute.

"Walt . . . We have so much to talk about. My family does not know what your intentions are after this baby is born. But will you do something for me? Can we bring it, ugh *he* or *she* here when we leave the hospital?"

She did not miss the little glint that announced itself.

"I want so much for this child to spend some time in the house where *he* or *she* grew inside me. We can load up and move to Mother's if or when you wish."

Walt did not have a plan.

"That sounds reasonable to me."

"Something else—are you sure that you don't want to know if he's a boy or she's a girl? Ultrasound is used widely now. I think my insurance will pay for it."

"I thought ultrasound was only for emergencies and if there might be complications."

"Oh, Walt . . . You are so 1980s."

As though protesting the putdown of *his/her* daddy, Polly got a swift kick in the ribs—and then another.

"Ouch! Come feel this."

That was one of those moments Walt had dreaded. Before he could offer any resistance, Polly took his hand and moved it slowly and methodically from her face, pausing as it went down her body, and then to the bulge.

Right on a cue, Walt felt the movement. He was not much of a dancer, but his soul's feet were waltzing with the stars. Polly brought him back down to earth.

"I don't know about this kid *we're* creating. He or she is certainly a spirited one and going to be a handful."

Polly failed to mention that she already knew the gender of the baby. The one question she wanted so much to ask would have to wait.

The atypical couple talked long into Saturday night. Polly knew little about Ginny's life in Alaska. She kept prodding him for juicy details about their love life, but he had years of experience as a professional and knew just how and where to draw the line.

The conversation turned to Tonya. He had no reason to hold back in his enthusiasm regarding his daughter. Speaking openly was cathartic. Walt appreciated Polly's interest and was glad to have someone to talk to. When she announced bedtime, little had been said about his other child on the way.

Walt had visited her house before, but this was his first time to stay overnight. Polly disappeared to prepare for the night, and he wondered if he would see her again before morning. With just his shoes off, he stretched out on the bed. Nothing about the room felt familiar.

"Othell . . . Will I always feel like an intrusive stranger?"

Polly poked her head in to say goodnight. Walt went to her and kissed her on the forehead, but he was fresh out of words.

Picking up the pieces

Walt offered to fix breakfast, and Polly had no objections. She took a seat on a bar stool and pointed him in the right directions.

"You do that so well—I could get used to this—I might just keep you around."

She saw that he was pleased with a bit of praise. The foot was in the door, and Polly was not about to let Walt slam it shut. Between bites, her sentiments started spilling out. She wanted Walt to know that she still had not regretted, even for a single moment, her decision to have the baby. The woman carrying his child then confessed that the most difficult part was being by herself.

"You can only imagine how much I look forward to our weekly chats. Even so, I walk away from them feeling so alone and isolated. I have longed for you to be here with me so we could go through this together."

The woman was trying hard to keep the tears under wraps, and the dam holding them back was paltry. So also, was the weir restraining her from asking the one question he feared most. The dike ruptured from the stress and escaped her lips.

"Walt . . . How do you feel about me?"

My darling wife . . . If this were a fairy tale, I suppose, I could fall in love with your sister. We could then all be one big happy family. I am so grateful to Polly for what's she's doing, but my heart just can't go there. You do understand, don't you?

As Walt fastened his seatbelt, he was ready for the airliner to taxi across the tarmac and take to the skies. It had been a taxing few days. At least, they now had a game plan. Unless the baby took matters into *his/her* own hands and made good on an early escape, the expectant father would fly down in plenty of time for the delivery. He agreed to stay with Polly so he could take her to the hospital.

He also pledged to bring the baby to her place when discharged. They would figure out as they went along if the party would move to the grandparents' house.

Everybody understood that when he was ready to take his child to Alaska, Tonya would come down and assist him during the flight. She would become the child's nanny and stay with them as long as necessary.

Not everyone was pleased with this arrangement. The Sullivans braced themselves for the inevitable. When Dave came to his daughter's house and whisked his son-in-law to be on his way, Polly went to pieces.

No fooling

"Dad . . . You know what? This baby will be born on my birthday."

"Is this just wishful thinking, or are you tapped into something I'm not?"

"You'll see."

"How do you feel about that? Are you willing to share it?"

"Seems to me—I don't have much choice. No—seriously—I would be thrilled."

Tonya had driven up from Homer so they could get serious about making sure everything was ready to bring a baby home. Mrs. Sullivan had asked both Walt and Tonya to bring an extra suitcase along to transport all the clothes and other supplies she had already purchased for her new grandchild.

"The big item we need to find is a baby bed."

"And a dressing table. You don't want to use the dining room table to change diapers."

"Let's hit some yard sales today. We might come upon a moving sale or even an estate sale and find just what we need."

Single-focused Walt did a quick perusal at each stop and was soon ready to move on. Tonya engaged the folks in small talk and left knowing their life stories. By lunchtime, the only prize in Nellie's cargo area was a well-used old wheelbarrow with a flat tire that Walt planned to salvage. She had picked up a few items for her kitchen.

After burgers and fries, the treasure hunters decided to check out a new furniture store still celebrating its grand opening. This time, they hit pay dirt but the payout was greater than for something used. Walt strapped the boxes down with bungee cords.

The two spent the rest of the afternoon putting the baby furniture together. Tonya's adeptness amazed Walt. Un-manly-like, she read the instructions instead of plummeting ahead. Before she left the next day, they went shopping for sheets.

"Daddy . . . I can just see you in the grocery store, with a baby in your arms, and a diaper bag draped around your shoulder."

"Walt . . . You'd better get here as soon as you can. Dr. Hamby says I've started dilating."

"Ugh . . . Are you sure? How long does he think it will be? Do you think I have time to get there? I don't even know what the flight schedules are."

Polly paused while Walt gulped for air.

"April Fool!"

Walt did not have to punch a clock, so he did not always pay close attention to a calendar.

"Congratulations! You got me. You really got me good."

"Actually, I've just come from the doctor's office. Everything seems to be right on schedule. He thinks the baby might just up and make a grand entrance around Mother's Day. Wouldn't that be a hoot?"

Walt's mind took a little vacation. Tonya was born on Mother's Day. When he realized that Polly was in mid-sentence, and he had no clue what was at the beginning of it, he feigned a poor connection and asked her to hit the restart button.

"What I said was, 'Why don't you plan to come down around the first of May?' Of course, that's always subject to change if junior has other designs. Did you hear me this time?"

"Loud and clear."

Walt awoke each morning in a holding pattern. His phone did not ring often, but he jumped with every Gus II interruption. The edgy expectant father turned the ringer up to full throttle so it would wake him at night. By the middle of the month, things were still progressing predictably. Phone dates multiplied by two.

Tonya took a break from helping to get the art gallery readied for the busy summer season and spent a weekend with her dad. She was concerned that Bekka might be displeased with her assistant going on maternity leave when it was not even her own baby, but her boss reminded her that this is Alaska. The enormity of what lay ahead made Walt understandably jumpy.

"Tonya . . . Can we do this? Look at me. I'm fifty-four-years-old, and I've never been around babies. You're about to turn thirty, and you have no mothering experience. What makes us think we can raise a kid?"

"Talk to me, Daddy. Didn't you basically raise yourself? I certainly did not receive much in the way of positive parenting. Just so long as we don't let this little fellow starve to death, I doubt that it will make much difference what we do one way or the other. This kid has both your genes and Ginny's. He'll be who he is—regardless. You can count on that."

"Did you just say, 'he'?"

"Oh, Dad . . . This baby is a boy. I thought you were Mr. Synchronicity. You mean you still have not figured that out?"

"Every time I think I have something figured out, somebody upsets the old applecart, and the props get knocked right out from under me."

"Trust me. You'd better start thinking about boy names. And this one will not be a junior. Why don't you pack up and go on to Washington? You can walk the floor down there just as well as you can here. Polly might really need you these last few weeks."

"I've not told you everything. Polly is not as emotionally detached as when you saw her Thanksgiving. I'm worried about her. I want to make this as easy as possible, and I feel strongly that we need to avoid complicating things."

"Are you telling me that she might have problems handing over the baby, or that she has developed feelings for you?"

"Both."

"Oh, dear."

Gus II broke his silence, but it was a local call. Walt's broker said they needed to talk, and he set up an appointment.

"Walt . . . As you know, our firm prides itself in making as much money as possible for our clients while minimizing the risks. We got you into technology stocks gradually, but when things started heating up, and per your agreement, we kept adding to your portfolio. On paper, you're worth about three times more than you were just a few years back. It is that *on paper* part that concerns me right now. Our best consultants do not see how this bull run can continue indefinitely. I'd hate to see you get burned."

"Are you suggesting that I start selling?"

"I think you should give it some serious consideration. I know capital gains would take a bite, but this is no time to get greedy. The profits you would be taking far and away exceed anything you could have imagined. Let me make this perfectly clear. We do not have a crystal ball. If you stay put, this time next year you might well have a 400% gain."

It did not take Walt long to process this information. The broker was unaware of one important factor in the investment equation. His client was about to have a child to raise. It was time to put some hay in the barn while the sun was still shining.

The next call was from Polly. She suggested that he come down around the first of the month. Walt packed all his lightweight clothes, not in North Carolina. He was not always so compliant, but his ticket said May 1. May Day.

Tonya was on her way to take him to the airport, and to lend moral support. Her dad offered some advice in return.

"I have not discussed your investment strategy with you, but my broker thinks it's time to get out of overpriced technology stocks. I just liquidated a wad and reinvested in interest-bearing bonds. Think about it."

While taking a stroll around the yard to keep his legs loose before the long flight, Walt heard a familiar sound. He wondered how long she had been calling before finally gaining his attention. Someone else had arrived just in time to see him off.

"Well, hello, Ms. Robin. Where is Mr. Robin?"

The male bird was reticent, but Walt spotted him on the ground at the edge of the forest. He turned his attention to the ladybird.

"By the time I get back, you might well be a mother again, and I'll be bringing home my own little tyke."

Ms. Robin flew to the clothesline and grew still. He looked into her eyes, and goose bumps ran up his spine. Abruptly, the bird burst forth in song. Walt was transported back to the first springtime after Ginny's death when he was also about to leave and felt the same inexplicable presence.

About that time, something wrapped itself around his heartstrings and rattled him to the core of his being. Once more, he had let his guard down and uttered, "Hello." Again, the consecrated word had escaped his lips.

Ginny . . . I just keep letting it slip. I vowed never to use our sacred greeting again. Yet, it seems so natural when I say, "Hello" to Ms. Robin. Please do not think that I'm disrespectful of you. The bird gets all animated when she hears that word. Try to understand.

The wildcard

Walt's seatmate seemed determined to tell him all about her troubles. He indulged her for a while and then suggested that he needed a nap. His mind was stuck in sorting things out mode. That his eyes were closed did not mean he was dozing.

Polly had always been the wildcard. Although the feelings she had developed for him might have been predictable, they caught him by surprise. Briefly, he entertained the notion that they might raise the child together, but nothing about that felt right.

The plane hemmed and hawed as it descended. That did not sit well with the butterflies in his stomach. After a rough landing, Walt breathed an audible sigh when the plane finally came to a jarring halt toward the end of the runway. Waiting for the seatbelt sign to go off, he tried to imagine the next time he would buckle up in the seat of an airliner.

Dave waved to Walt when he came into sight. The handshake dissolved when his father-in-law uncharacteristically pulled him into a hug. There was no semblance of insincerity when Dave told him how proud he was to see him.

Waiting for the baggage carousel to jumpstart, Mr. Sullivan shifted from one foot to another, trying to circumnavigate a gaffe. Eventually, he found his voice.

"Walt . . . All of this still seems a tad strange. Well, more than a tad. Alice and I want you to know that you're always welcome in our home. I'll take you there now if that's what you wish. Polly is expecting you to stay with her, but we want you to be at ease. We dare not get ahead of ourselves, but our doors are open for as long as you want to stay with us after this child's safe arrival. If you want to make this area your home, I will be happy to help you find a place of your own."

It was Walt's time to squirm. The intrusive noise of the upstart luggage roundabout provided cover. He spotted his bag coming down the chute and lunged for it. Walking to the parking lot, he decided it best not to say too much, even with the one family member he trusted most.

"I have promised Polly that I would stay with her and take her to the hospital should the stork come knocking on the door in the middle of the night. This is all new to me, too. I'm not sure what will happen after that. I guess we'll just have to do what seems best as we go along."

"We're naturally concerned about our baby daughter. Her mother was dead set against her going through with this. In time, she accepted it, but she's troubled about how Polly will handle everything once her job is finished. I know you'll be gentle with her fragile emotions. Walt . . . Women have issues that we know nothing about."

The counselor did know something about transference. He wondered if Polly's parents were aware of how she had gotten her feelings all tangled up with the man whose baby she was carrying.

"There's no way I can ever compensate Polly for what she's doing. I'm still dumbfounded that she so eagerly took this on. I doubt seriously that I would have even looked for a surrogate mother if she had not stepped forward. I do want to make it as uncomplicated for her as possible—if we can just know what that is as we come to it."

Dave was not totally sure what he was seeking to elicit from Walt, but what he got was not precisely the sum of it. He wanted to be more direct but knew that might push his son-in-law further away from divulging his plans.

Walt redirected.

"And I will never be able to repay you for the financial contribution you are making. With my little nest egg and the proceeds from the annuity, *I'll* not have to put the kid in daycare."

Walt had just answered one question that was not asked. If he had looked at Dave, he would have seen dismay written all over the man's face.

A tailspin

Polly was larger than Walt had imagined. Despite her center of gravity so far out in front, she was rather steady on her feet. The pregnant woman kissed her father on the cheek and turned toward Walt. He extended his right hand, but that was not what she wanted.

Dave unloaded Walt's gear and put it in the guest room. Unsure what else to say or do, he excused himself.

"It's about time you showed up. I was beginning to think you might miss the grand opening. Dr. Hamby thinks I'll go full-term, but this kid seems to have a mind of his own. I wonder where that came from."

"From your sister, no doubt. That couldn't possibly have anything to do with me."

"You fathers are all alike—always just innocent bystanders."

Like an aircraft gaining altitude too steeply, the conversation suddenly stalled out. Walt did not know whether to hit eject or try to pull it out of the lull. He was where he needed to be, where he had to be, but far from where he wanted to be. The teardrop making its way down Polly's cheek did not help. The pilot reached for the emergency compassion control switch and stretched out his arms.

"Walt . . . Will you go lay on the bed with me and just hold me?"

The aeronaut went into a tailspin.

Of all the possible things Walt might have anticipated, he never saw that coming. He later apologized profusely for bolting from the room. Polly had no way of knowing that those were the exact words Ginny had said to him on the night when they first made love.

"You really loved her, didn't you?"

"There are no words to describe just how and how much."

"My sister was so fortunate. Do you think you can ever love again?"
"Oh, yes. I will bestow all my love upon Ginny's child."

Walt conjectured that the word had not yet been coined to describe the awkwardness that encased them. There was no definitive division of labor. Accustomed to taking care of himself, he had no illusions of being waited on hand and foot. Still, he was not familiar with another woman's kitchen and was uncertain of her expectations of him in general. To make matters worse, his feeble attempts at humor fell woefully flat.

Nevertheless, the anomalous couple muddled their way through the next few days. Polly talked often with her mother, and the Sullivans came over once. Walt took walks through the neighborhood but was anxious about being gone for long.

He escorted Polly to the doctor's office on the following Friday. The physician thought the patient was perhaps beginning to dilate. He told her to go home, and if nothing happened during the weekend, to check into the hospital on Monday. Walt was not sure how Polly was resting, but he hardly got any sleep.

The clock moved agonizingly slowly, as did Polly's progress. Sunday was Mother's Day. Polly received both a card and a phone call from Frank, but they made no mention of it.

On Monday morning, she informed Walt that labor had begun. He jumped to attention, but she seemed in no hurry. After she gave the house the once over, he carried her bag to the car.

On the way, in his own ineffable way, he tried again to thank her again for the sacrifices she had made. Polly once more expressed no misgivings, and in her own attempt at levity, said she had not done this for him but for her sister. They both smiled.

"You know Walt . . . I only want what's best for this child."

She left the rest unsaid, but he knew what she was thinking.

When they rolled into the ER parking area, Polly insisted on walking to admissions. With every shift change, the staff learned that the two were not a couple. When labor got serious, the father declined to go with Polly to the delivery room. Instead, he went looking for a pay phone. He had barely enough pocket change to get a call through to Tonya at work, now in her own holding pattern.

"See . . . I told you my baby brother would be born on my birthday. That's tomorrow, and I'm betting he won't get here until after midnight."

Alice jumped at the chance to be with her daughter. Walt sat alone in the waiting room during the overnight vigil. Except for the brief time he was with Ginny, he had been alone the better part of his life. Soon, opportunities for solitude would be few and far between.

Part II: The Gift

He's a boy

Just before sunrise on May 11, 1999, Walt's son took his first breath—thirty years to the day after his then unbeknownst daughter took hers. When the new father was finally granted passage to see his baby for the first time, a big banner streamed across the room.

"He's a boy."

Regretfully, Polly did not see the sly smile that pried itself free. An LPN already had her on her feet, and she was in the bathroom.

The baby's grandmother cradled the infant in her arms under wraps, and she did not offer to remove the little blanket. She did, however, unearth an observation.

"He looks just like his mother."

Walt was in no position to suggest otherwise. He had never seen baby pictures of either parent.

Dr. Hamby and Polly converged from opposite directions at the same time, and the father received assurances that everything went well. While Walt waited outside, the physician did a cursory check to make sure everything still was. The doctor then took the new daddy by the arm and directed him to a consultation room.

"Walt . . . We knew from the onset that this was most out of the mainstream—the first time a surrogate mother has been a member of the family. As I'm sure you're aware, Polly is not handling this too well. She finally relented, and we are giving her shots to dry up the milk. I understand that her mother will stay with her for a few days. What are your plans on down the road?"

"They are what they've always been. When this baby is able to travel, my daughter is coming down to go with us, and we're taking this little boy home. How long do you think that will be? Tonya is moving in with me to help out."

"These little fellows are tougher than we give them credit. I would say in about a month. Do you have a pediatrician in Alaska?"

"There's one in Kenai. My daughter has already spoken with her."

"Good—I do hope things go well with the family here. These are really fine people."

When Walt returned to the room, his son was nestled beside the woman who carried him. She began removing the flimsy blanket and the father got his first good look. Walter Othell Williamson stood once again on sacred terrain. Tears trickled at glacial speed. Neither spoke. The infant slept right through their first moments together.

Baby Williamson was soon returned to the nursery. As Walt stood peering through the glass, conflicting emotions mimicked alternating current. The joy in his soul was immeasurable. Yet, the sorrow of missing Ginny was just shy of unbearable. His attention was averted by a tap on the shoulder.

"Fine boy you have there, son."

"And a fine grandson you have, too, Dave."

The guys continued their man to man talk although neither said anything else that reached the other's ears.

Only two visitors were allowed and Walt yielded so his father-in-law could join his wife in their daughter's room. Meanwhile, the newborn started making his displeasure known. The cries were barely discernible from within the enclosure, but his body language was unmistakable.

A nursery nurse gathered him up and gestured toward Walt. The proud papa nodded. She smiled and brought him to the window.

"Good lungs."

Walt concurred again. She whisked the infant away to attend to his needs.

When Dave came out, Alice was with him, and Walt returned to Polly's room. That was where he needed to be but unavoidably where he did not want to be. They had hardly spoken since she was swept away to the delivery room. Walt broke the ice.

"*He's* a boy. Nice touch. Thank you."

Polly's eyes were brimming with questions that Walt did not want to address. Her voice kicked in with one he could.

"Walt . . . What are *we* going to name him?"

"His name is Jesse Sullivan Williamson. Jesse comes from the Bible, and it means 'A Gift.' This kid is certainly that. I also want him named for his mother, but I'm not sure she would be happy with a boy named Virginia Arlene. So—his middle name is *her* family name."

Congratulations, my darling, you're a mother. Your family says little Jesse looks just like you. How I wish you were here to nurse him and to cherish him as much as I already do. Keep sending me your strength. I feel so inadequate to raise him without you. We'll just have to take it day by day, but one thing is not in doubt. Jesse will always know who his mother is.

Hello . . . Jesse

Dr. Hamby said Polly came through the birthing ordeal about as well as any woman her age might well have. Attention shifted back and forth between her and the baby, with the father endlessly in the backdrop. Before Polly and Jesse were discharged, Walt stayed with the Sullivans. Dave shuttled his wife and son-in-law back and forth to the maternity ward during visiting hours. The new daddy got to hold his infant son for the first time on day two.

> Hello . . . Jesse. I'm your daddy. You might not be able to hear me, but I know you're in there somewhere. I so much wish your mother could be here with us. You'll learn to love her in time. Promise me something, son, that you'll always make her proud. I cannot imagine what it will be like when it's just the two of us. I can promise you one thing, though. We will have so much fun.

"Othell . . . My *awe* is so much more than just *some.*"

The birth mother and the biological father reached a nominal truce with Walt ever steering the conversation away from daunting conjectures. He learned the neighborhood around the hospital well. Hints of adversarial snippets slipped out, but Walt sidestepped the shards. He had given no one any reason to suspect that he might settle in Seattle, and he began bracing himself for the month ahead.

The charge nurse brought the baby into the room with an unmistakable look of delight about her. After handing him off, her smile brightened.

"I just learned something that makes me woozy. I would have never been able to attend nursing school except for a scholarship. I found out that it was endowed by the family of Little Jesse in honor of his biological mother. I cannot begin to tell you how much this means to me, and what I feel when I hold that precious infant."

Polly gestured toward Walt.

"This is the man who made it happen. Well—actually—the scholarship and the baby."

The nurse grabbed Walt's hand and yanked him from the chair. After a hug that might have violated hospital policy, she thanked him with words.

Dr. Hamby thought Polly might be ready to go home on Thursday, but he kept her for another day. The Sullivans provided the chariot for little Jesse's first ride. Walt was directed to sit up front, and Alice held the baby directly behind him.

Still tapering off the pain medications, Polly apologized for her vocalized grimaces. The driver and front seat passenger made small talk about traffic and the weather while "uh" and "ah" sounds filled the empty spaces.

The inevitable comparisons of the newest family member to the previous offspring amused Walt. Alice was certain that Baby Jesse had the same temperament as Ginny. Polly was convinced that the infant was much like her own son. The father's role seemed immaterial.

The new daddy stood back the first day or so before asserting himself more in the baby's care. If the birth mother and the grandmother had any grasp that he would soon be raising the kid on his own, they gave no indication of it. About every other feeding, he had already gathered the baby from its bed when the bottle was warm.

There was no discussion within his earshot of how much longer Alice would continue sleeping in the room with Polly and the baby. Neither was there any mention of what might happen when she moved back home.

On the third day, Alice went with Dave to fetch some clean clothes, and she returned in her own vehicle. Thereafter, she left for several hours but came back in time to prepare supper. Polly was on her feet more each day.

Walt stood in absolute awe of his little boy. As was his lot in life, he kept his feelings mostly to himself. Overcoming initial clumsiness when holding Jesse, and especially when changing diapers, his confidence gained momentum. He had not yet been granted the privilege of bathing the baby, but he was about to usurp that authority, too.

Oh, sweetie . . . Jesse is so fragile.
Please do not let me break him.

Polly had a doctor's appointment before Jesse had his first. Alice did not know whether to accompany her daughter or stay with the baby. Walt assured them that he was fully capable of taking care of his son while they were gone. Dave was sent over to babysit the babysitter.

When they returned, Alice had a grim look on her face when she told the men that Polly had "the baby blues." As a professional, Walt had counseled clients with postpartum depression. He also understood that Polly's despondency was not just hormonal and wondered if Alice intended for the doctor's report to make him feel guilty.

The stand-in mom, grandmother, and father all accompanied Jesse for his first checkup. The pediatrician found everything in working order, but the baby boy was a little annoyed when jostled so much.

When Jesse finished a bottle after they were back home, Walt placed him on his shoulder. The tot burped and passed gas simultaneously. The daddy broke into a laugh but noticed that no one else joined him. Rather, Alice retorted.

"You men are so disgusting."

Laughter—that was the first time Walt could remember snickering since he flew south. His sense of humor had always been such a vital part of his survival nature. In the short time that he and Tonya had been together, they had spent much of it laughing.

As Walt placed the infant back in his bed, he leaned over and whispered to him. Jesse's eyes were trying to focus on the face right in front of him.

> **They might not have seen anything funny in what you did, but your old pappy certainly did. Let that be a lesson. Learn to laugh at yourself. Life is so much more fun when you don't take yourself so seriously.**

Leverage

When Dave came over to join the others for dinner, he invited his son-in-law to take a walk with him afterward. Walt was right to suspect that the outing was not just about getting some exercise.

"Walt . . . I want to give you an update on the annuity. My broker was able to leverage the tax liability against a loss from another investment. What

I am saying is this. The annuity has now been signed over to you, with Jesse as the beneficiary. The paperwork is on its way."

"I do appreciate what you have done. Just as soon as I get back to Alaska, I'll open a savings account for my son and let the proceeds start accumulating. I think we can get by without having to tap into it. It will be his education fund."

"Now that this little fellow has come into our family, we have all fallen in love with him. We know it's your call, but is there any possibility that you might stay around here and let us help you raise this boy?"

"I do so much understand that you have your grandson's best interests at heart, but just, please . . ."

"Now, hear me out. I'd hate to see you have to put a mortgage on the house you inherited from my daughter. I'll be happy to lend you some money for a deposit or even a down payment."

"That's mighty nice of you, but . . ."

"We've already lost one daughter, and now we're concerned about the other. Alice and I stood back and let the two of you make the decision to go through with this risky procedure, although my wife certainly expressed her misgivings. Polly knew full well what she signed on for, but she obviously had no concept of how difficult this part of the bargain would be. We're worried about her. We don't know what might happen if the baby is taken from her."

"I do share your concerns, and I know Polly is struggling. Perhaps, once her body gets regulated again and school starts, she can move on. I will forever be in her debt. Let me remind you that I never suggested in any way whatsoever that relocating was in my plans. For one thing, that would be so unfair to my daughter—denied her daddy for almost thirty years. She would now also be separated from her little brother."

Walt hesitated a moment to let that sink in before he went on.

"Even more important—I want Jesse to grow up in the house where his mother lived. It will be hard enough for me to explain to him how he came to be. Feeling her presence and connecting with her spirit will make it easier."

"I see . . ."

When Alice no longer stayed the nights, the buffer between Walt and Polly was removed. He was certain that her father had told her about the walk and talk, but she made no mention of it. They shared cooking duties, but she would not let him help with other household chores.

Walt did not seek her approval as he sprang into action when Jesse announced the need for some attention. The doctor had said the baby would be able to travel when he was about a month old, and he was halfway there.

The new father grew increasingly more uncomfortable with Jesse sleeping in Polly's bedroom. He wanted to move the baby bed into his but agreed to a compromise. They relocated it to the living room. She rested several hours during the daytime, and he had his son all to himself.

Walt was delighted when Polly went on her first outing alone. She returned with several bags of groceries, which he unloaded and helped put away.

He was torn. Polly needed to talk with a professional, but probably not him. She was also due for another examination. Alice came and stayed with the baby, and he went with her to the doctor's office. When she was called, he requested a private conference with Dr. Hamby. The nurse ushered him back while the patient was getting dressed.

Making no mention of the consultation with Walt, the physician broached the subject of counseling when she came to his office to pick up her prescriptions. With her consent, he scheduled an appointment with the psychologist on the clinic's staff.

Walt called in reinforcements to help engineer Jesse's next move. The agreement was to let the baby spend his first nights with the surrogate mother, but the plan all along was then to move him to the Sullivans. They had stayed longer than he had anticipated. When the grandparents came for a visit, he broached the subject. Polly got up, went into her bedroom, and closed the door. Her mother joined her.

When Alice emerged about fifteen minutes later, she said everything was arranged. She and Dave would return the following day. After they left, Walt did not see Polly again for the next couple of hours. Nothing was said about the impending move.

The relocation went about as smoothly as it could have under the circumstances. When her parents arrived, Polly disappeared. The men folded the bed and put it in the cargo area. Alice started carrying things to the car. Holding his son secured in his infant seat, Walt squirmed in the back among the stacks of baby stuff. Little Jesse slept right through the move.

The next few days passed without incident. Alice was helpful but understood that the primary responsibilities for the baby's care fell on the shoulders of his father. He anguished for his hosts. Celebrating the birth of a grandchild should be a happy occasion, but smiles were short lived.

Polly came for Sunday lunch. She was restrained, and Walt suspected that she was under medication. He made sure that Jesse was not the center of attention, and she left without having any physical contact with either.

"Hello," mother of our child. I will soon be taking Jess home—to our house. The first thing I'll do after we go through the door, is to show him your picture. I simply cannot put into words what I experience when I hold him and look into his eyes. I feel your arms around both of us. Always!

Well, Dad . . .

Tonya and Walt booked their flights—hers a round trip and his one way. She had waited long enough to get her hands on her little brother, and the father was so ready to take his son home.

Walt called Polly and invited her to come and see them off. She said she would think about it, but in the end, was a no-show. After the obligatory assurances that Walt and Jesse were always welcome at their house, they headed to the airport.

The nanny was waiting for them at the gate. Politeness trumped terseness as they said their goodbyes. After preferential boarding, Walt buckled up and simultaneously took a deep breath. Tonya framed it.

"Well, Dad . . . Here we are. You finally have the child you always wanted, and I've got the little brother I never had."

After the door closed, the atypical family moved to a row with an empty seat, and Tonya took charge of the infant. Walt was pleased with how his daughter was already bonding with her baby brother. Jesse opened his eyes, appeared to smile, and she was sure he squirmed with delight as she talked to him.

As the plane taxied on the runway, Walt gathered his son in his arms and held him cheek to cheek.

> **Jesse . . . We are about to fly on the wings of a big bird. It might get a little bumpy, but don't be afraid. Sit back and enjoy the ride.**

> I am right here. When it lands, we will be almost home.

Little Jess was a tad fussy as the plane started gaining altitude but settled down as his father's loving hands soothed away his discomfort. The flight attendants made a fuss over him throughout the flight. The one who gave him his wings said he was the youngest she had ever presented them to. The tiny passenger slept right through the improvised ceremony.

Tonya remembered well the time she got hers. The flight seemed endless, but Walt got in a catnap. An attendant warmed a bottle, and big sister gave her baby brother her first. She also insisted on changing him.

After wiping his tiny bottom and sliding another disposable diaper underneath, another urge overcame the tot. A surge of pee hit Tonya smack dab in the face.

"So—that's how you feel about me, huh?"

After a layover in Anchorage, the homecoming continued. Thirty minutes later, Cornfield was waiting and ready.

We're home

Home at last. A party of two formed an unofficial welcoming committee. Ms. Robin called from the power line and began chattering. Her mute mate was perched in a nearby tree. The pair had faithfully performed their paternal duties while he was away and faced an empty nest. For the man who lived in the big house, parenting was just beginning.

As Tonya began unloading the luggage, Walt took the baby inside.

"Hi, Honey . . . *We're* home!"

He took Jesse straightway to a picture of Ginny.

> Son . . . This is your mother. She lived here with me before she took a flight on another big bird, and it fell to earth when it could not find a place to land. But Jesse, our precious son, her spirit still lives here. I feel it every day, and one day you will, too. I don't have the words to explain how much I loved your mom. And there's no way I can tell you how much she would have loved you. What she

would want for you more than anything else in the world is for you to grow up and be who you are. Now, Jesse Sullivan Williamson, you just make yourself right at home.

Tonya had spent the two previous days getting things ready. The baby bed was fluffed, diapers stacked on the changing table, a case of formula ready, and enough groceries purchased to get them by for a few days, with some food already cooked.

After being gone for almost two months, Walt was not sure Nellie would start. The Alaska winter grade battery did not even struggle. When he picked up the accumulated mail, the annuity documents were with the other stuff. Walt wondered if Dave might have regretted making that decision when it did not have any "leverage" on his son-in-law's plans.

After being pitched from pillar to post, Jesse thrived with his new routines. He still slept more than half of any twenty-four-hour span, with more concentrated at night. Night was a relative term since he took up residence in his new home on June 23—just two days past the summer solstice. His caregivers opened and closed curtains to simulate a normal cycle.

Walt thought the crib would be in the master bedroom, but Tonya pulled rank. She insisted that her father get some much-needed rest. Little Jess did not seem to notice that the two people caring for him had no prior parenting experience.

Jesse's hands were his first big discovery. A serious look came over his face as he pondered them. Then, he broke into a smile when he started sucking on some fingers. Walt noticed that the infant was holding his head up longer each day.

Ginny, how can I simultaneously feel so exhausted and energized? The stresses of the past few months have drained my batteries, but they get a quick recharge each time I behold our son. He is indeed our precious gift.

Have a nice day

In the annals of non-traditional families, this was one for the books. However, nothing seemed out of the ordinary about a middle-aged man and a woman in her early thirties, out and about, with a little tot in tow. Nevertheless, the customer behind them in the grocery store checkout line got more than she bargained for. Walt was holding his little boy while Tonya placed the items on the counter.

"What a cute baby. Is it your grandchild?"

Walt looked her in the eye.

"First of all, this child is not an *it*. And no—*He* is not my grandchild— *He's* my son."

Gesturing, he added.

"This is my daughter."

The woman was wearing a Dallas Cowboy sweatshirt. Walt supposed the oil industry likely brought the family to Alaska from the Southwest. Something did not add up, and she was compelled to dig deeper.

"I've seen you in here before, but I've never met your wife."

"I'm raising Jesse alone."

Her curiosity was now really piqued.

"Are you a widower?"

Befuddlement only intensified with Walt's response.

"Yes—my wife died twelve years ago in a plane crash."

She was not about to let it go at that. The tenor in her voice ratcheted up a notch or two.

"Did you adopt this baby?"

"No—he's mine."

Tonya was observing the exchange. As they turned to leave, she smiled at the bewildered woman.

"Have a nice day."

Even in Alaska, where off the chart is often commonplace, this was some eyebrow-raising stuff. Not much of a socialite, Walt had kept a low profile. Folks in the Kenai area had come and gone since Ginny's tragic death, and he did not sit among the town fathers.

Somebody leaked enough of the story to the local paper that they sent a correspondent out to investigate. Walt knew of only one person who might be the culprit. During the interview, Tonya did not mention her newspaper experience. She did, nonetheless, understand just how to help the rookie reporter fill in the blanks.

After the piece was published, replete with photos, they did attract some attention. It mattered little what other people thought, but Walt sensed that his neighbors were unsure whether to feel sorry for him or to give him high-fives.

"Hello," mother of our son. Our little boy is now a celebrity. Can you believe that? Pictures in the paper and a story about us. The last time our names were news was when you crossed over. This edition was a proclamation that you live on through this miracle child.

Fleeting glimpses

Little Jesse grew less contented playing in the background. He became assertive when letting his needs be known and more expressive when showing delight. Walt could not imagine a healthier or happier baby, but he yielded to Tonya's pressure to set up an appointment with the pediatrician. The physician concurred with the father's assessment.

"Dad . . . You need to take more pictures."

"I know. I'm just so busy making memories that I forget all about my camera."

"Don't forget Jesse's grandparents."

"When I do take a roll, I always get double prints and send the extras to Seattle."

"Have you heard anything from Polly?"

"Not a word."

Tonya needed to go check on things in Homer and to pick up some stuff. She asked her father if he could manage for a day or so. Beset with a dose of cabin fever, Walt suggested rather that he and Jess tag along. She was insistent that first, they purchase a child's seat belt restraint.

"You'll need this when you take him out by yourself. They're designed for the rear, but since neither of your trucks has an airbag, you can use it in the front."

Then, she added.

"And it's the law, even in Alaska."

Tonya had to do some calling before she found a store that carried them. Merchandise and services were not as clear-cut as elsewhere. Businesses often wore many hats. One storefront advertised handmade knives, taxidermy, small engine repair, a bookkeeping service, and prom dresses.

With no selection to choose from, Walt picked up the only model available and started for the register. Tonya called him back.

"Here's something else that we could really use. I've seen tourists hauling their little ones around in these shoulder harnesses, and I think it's a neat idea."

As she plunked one down on the counter, she commented.

"I'm surprised you had these."

"Just put them out. Folks kept asking for them, and it took me some time to find a distributor that would ship them here. One of these days, Alaska will catch up with the rest of the country. I hope when it does, things are not so expensive."

Walt was learning that he could no longer just up, get in a vehicle, and go wherever he wanted, whenever he pleased. Taking a child along was an ordeal. One part of the preparation became routine—talking things over with his son.

> Jesse . . . We are about to go on a long ride in Tonya's car. You'll get to try out your brand-new car seat. You see . . . Your sister is only here with us for a while. We will stay with her a day or so. As you get older, I know you'll spend lots of time with her. She loves you very much.

Tonya drove and Walt insisted on sitting in the back with his baby. Jesse slept almost the entirety of the trip. Once they got things situated, his daddy was ready for a power nap.

Walt awoke to an empty apartment. A note on the counter informed him that Tonya had taken her little brother to show him off at the art gallery. After passing him around, Bekka inquired about the plans of her employee on leave. Tonya said it was doubtful that she would return before the end of the season.

"When I see who you're holding in your arms, I understand perfectly. We're managing."

On the way back, Tonya picked up a Coho at the fish market. The silvers were running, and it was reeled in that very morning.

"I don't have a grill, but my oven works fine. Let's bake it."

My dear Ginny . . . Little Jesse did not come with a how-to manual. I have always more or less assessed things as I went along. I suppose, raising this child will be no different. What I want more than anything is to let the cute little fellow just be himself. Isn't that what you want, too?

This implausible dad saw no need for guidelines to obsess over, apprising him of what his son should be doing at different stages of his development. Food was no exception. The three-month-old was already being introduced to a sampling of table food. No place would ever be set at his table for a picky eater. Jesse got his first taste of salmon, and Tonya captured the moment with her camera.

The shoulder harness got its initial workout. Tonya modeled it before adjusting the straps for Walt. The three then took a stroll into downtown Homer. The walk was punctuated with pauses along the way.

Look. Jesse . . . There's an eagle coming right up over us.

You see that big noisy bird up there? That's not a bird at all. It's an airplane like the one we flew in.

Jesse . . . The greenish water down there is part of the ocean. Mountains are beyond it with snow on their tops. This winter, we will play in the snow. Can you see the blue ice between those mountains? It's a glacier. When you're older, I will take you right up

to a glacier where your mother became my
wife.

Not wanting anyone to see her face, big sister strolled on ahead. She had just gotten a fleeting glimpse of Baby Tonya suspended in that sling.

Cornfield's cargo area was almost full on the way back to Kenai. In addition to the baby's stuff, it was packed with two easels and a slew of art supplies. Tonya was trying to decide if her next painting would be a mini portrait just of Jesse or one of him with his daddy. The image in her mind of her father holding her brother and pointing to the eagle floating right overhead prevailed.

By the time they got home, Jesse was ready for his bedtime bottle, and Tonya took charge. Walt hovered over them for a few seconds and then abruptly turned and went into the bathroom. In a moment, in the twinkling of an eye, he envisioned Ginny rocking her baby to sleep.

Little Brother

Jesse went right to work on his first bottle of the day. Tonya snuggled him tight and looked into his eyes.

"Little brother . . . I don't know how you will turn out. I never knew your mother, but from what I've heard, she was a wonderful woman. You sure picked yourself out a good daddy, though. If you are ever disrespectful of that fine man, I can promise you one thing. I'll take it out of your sorry hide."

After the boy's morning nap, Walt was restless.

"Let's go walk on the beach."

Tonya detected a note of passion in her father's voice. It was a ten-minute drive, and she insisted on strapping Jesse into his car seat.

The parking area was only a short distance from the beach access trail. Walt gently gathered his son into his arms. After they had walked across the glacial gray sand to the edge of the Cook Inlet waters, he paused.

Jesse . . . Your mother and I walked on this
rocky beach the day we met. Actually, we
got off to a rather rocky start. You see . . .
She was driving her truck, and I tried to
assist her, and she informed me that she

63

> was an Alaska woman. I smarted off back to
> her and told her that I was a southern
> gentleman, which I suppose, was not much
> of a gentlemanly thing to do. It's a thousand
> wonders she did not just drive on off and
> leave me standing there.

Tonya did not want to intrude, but neither did she want to miss a word. Over the next several moments, only lapping waves and seagulls fussing over a fish stranded by the fast retreating tide filled the airwaves. Walt stopped abruptly.

He was holding the infant cradled in his left arm, and Tonya was walking on their right side. She could see Jesse's eyes looking right into his daddy's.

> Anyway—she told me to hop in. Your mom
> had a big dog named Radar. He sat between
> us so she had no fear of any unwanted
> advances, southern gentleman or not. She
> drove us to this spot where we talked as we
> walked. I wish that Alaska woman was here
> walking with us now.

Walt stopped in his tracks yet again. This time, he handed Jesse off to his big sister and ambled on alone. An eagle ended the squabble up ahead as it swooped down and snatched the disputed prize from the disenchanted gulls. No one remembered to bring a camera.

On the way back to the house, Tonya asked her father if he had any inkling of how much Jesse watches him and listens to him. Walt shrugged, and then she went in another direction.

"Do you think you can manage for a few days? Bekka starts packing things up at the gallery around Labor Day. Her summer help is gone now, and I know she could use a hand."

"Tonya . . . You'll never know how much I appreciate you being here with us this summer. I could not have managed without you, but I know you have your own life. Jesse is my responsibility. We'll be fine."

"I'll come back in a couple of weeks for a visit if that's okay. And if you think I was doing this all for you and Jesse, get over it."

Tonya was giving her baby brother a tight hug after loading her things into Cornfield.

"Don't squeeze the life out of him."

"Now Jess . . . You take good care of your daddy while I'm gone."

> **Well, Son . . . It's just you and me babe. Why don't we celebrate by lighting a candle and lifting a toast of Sin Infidel to your mother? I think we'll both then be ready for a nap.**

Walt was in awe watching his own flesh and blood turning into a little person. Jesse had outgrown the middle of the night feeding. Mealtime was a favorite part of the day for both. With the moving sale high chair pulled up to the table, the two guys took turns taking a bite. If the daddy pretended to ignore the boy and keep eating, Jesse protested.

Not much seemed to faze the little fellow. It amazed Walt how little it took to entertain the toddler who spent hours amusing himself. He was irritable as a gum swelled but learned to mimic his father's finger by rubbing the tooth trying to push through.

Christmas presence

As they were finishing breakfast one morning, Ms. Robin's repertoire had a plea in it—as the melody wafted through the kitchen window.

Chup . . . Chup . . . Chup . . . Tut . . . Tut . . . Tut.

"Come on Jesse . . . Let's go see what that's about."

"Bird? Do you see the bird?"

Walt then turned his attention to the balladeer.

"So—today's the day. Ms. Robin . . . I do hope you have a good flight, and we look forward to seeing you again next spring. I wish I knew where you spend the winter. Send us a postcard when you get a chance."

The days were getting progressively shorter, and Jesse was outfitted with winter clothes when they went out. The fall foliage paled in comparison to the colors Walt had grown up with. He talked to his son about taking him to North Carolina to their other house when he was older.

By Thanksgiving, new territory was added to the tot's expanding sphere. No longer confined to a bed, infant seat, high chair, and his daddy's lap, the pallet on the floor gave him room to roam. He could turn himself over and exercise his limbs.

My, how our son is growing and changing right before my eyes. I'm trying hard not to spoil him. I already detect an independent streak in Jess. Wonder where that came from?

Tonya came for visits at least once a month. She articulated the advancements in Jesse's development from one trip to another and asked her dad if he was recording things in a baby book. Walt acknowledged that he had not thought about such a thing and added that he would just let the kid make his own marks.

She put in her request for the day of gratitude cuisine well in advance. Neither she nor Walt had feasted on a turkey in years. He purchased a frozen breast from the limited supply, and she baked it in the oven. Walt attempted to make cornbread dressing with giblet gravy but was glad his Grandma King was not around to express her opinion. Jesse was not too sure about the taste but could not get enough of the sweet potatoes.

"Othell . . . My *over* is *abundant*. My *grate* is *full*."

After Jesse was down for his afternoon nap, the subject of Christmas came up. As they were going over the options, the phone rang. The Sullivans were on the other end, one on each extension. After wishing the Williamsons a Happy Thanksgiving, Dave broached the upcoming holiday.

"Walt . . . We've talked it over. Rather than ship Christmas presents to our grandson, we would rather give them to him in person. As our gift to you, we want to cover the cost of your flight to Seattle. What do you think?"

"Funny you should mention this. Tonya and I were going over the possibilities when the phone rang."

"Oh, she is certainly invited, too. If you're agreeable, go ahead and book your flights."

After the conversation was over, Walt started thinking aloud about reciprocal gifting. Tonya had her own thoughts.

"I don't think the Sullivans expect any presents other than the presence of their grandbaby. Let me take care of anything else. I'll start tomorrow on a painting of Jesse just for them from all of us."

Postcard from the edge

A check came in the mail the following week sufficient to cover both tickets. Jesse was still young enough to get a free pass.

The dispatch was not the only mail from Seattle that day. A postcard also arrived from the pediatrician's office where Jesse had his first checkup. It was a notification that the baby was overdue for another office visit.

Walt wondered if some mindless assistant had not even noticed his Alaska address. Before discarding it, he turned it over. The medical staff had chosen a colorful bird series upon which to send out their reminders. He held in his hand an artistic rendering of a beautiful American robin. Wow!

Word origins fascinated Walt. He was captivated by complex terms with separate concepts welded together, and he loved playing around with their unintended connotations. The wordsmith was also enamored with expressions that seemed to act out their meanings. Gruesome jargon automatically brings about grimaces, while pleasant utterances produce smiles.

Jesse had started babbling, and his daddy repeated the sounds. Since the little boy could not see himself in a mirror, Walt also mimicked facial expressions much to the tyke's delight.

Before retiring for the night, Walt reached for WOWs.

> *Dearest Ginny . . . Jesse is jabbering. He is developing his own language. Soon, he will begin converting this primitive speech into perceptible communication. I so look forward to the time he looks into your eyes on the photo and says, "Mama."*

Showing Jesse, the picture of his mother, was a regular part of the day. He was now able to grasp the frame and unsteadily shake it. While Walt yearned to hear his son say, "Da-Da," he hoped the little tot's first words would be, "Ma-Ma." He was wrong on both counts. When offered a bite of squash a few weeks later, Jesse pushed it away and said, "No."

As they strapped in for the short flight to Anchorage on the way to Seattle, Walt reached for Jesse, and Tonya surrendered him reluctantly. The proud papa held the boy out and gently shuffled him back and forth. His elated son responded with smiles and giggles. Then, he stilled the boy and looked into his eyes.

> **Jesse . . . It's about to get noisy. Then, it might be a bit bumpy, but everything will be fine. Daddy will hold you tight. It's okay if you don't like it and want to cry.**

The boy's sister swiveled her head toward the aisle so their father could not see the teardrops trickling down her own cheeks. Big girls cry sometimes, too.

After liftoff in the much bigger bird, Jesse settled into Tonya's lap and decided he needed some shuteye. Never able to get much sleep on planes, Walt was glad his son could. He tried to find a movie but nothing appealed to him.

His thoughts turned to possible scenarios for the days ahead. Someone was wandering around in the shadows of his imagination, and she decided to step into the center stage limelight. Walt closed his eyes and banished Polly back into the wings, knowing full well that he was not the director of this unfolding drama. Tonya interrupted his thoughts.

"I gave myself a Christmas present last week. After you mentioned the volatile stock market, I decided to keep pressing my luck. Last week, I figured I had put what Mrs. Thornhill left me at risk long enough.

"I dumped about half of what was vulnerable, and the rest will sell after the first of the year to divide the capital gains. The bulk of my savings will be in government ensured short-term CDs. I can always get back in the market later. Thanks for the tip. I don't know what the future holds for me, but I did not want to squander potential opportunities by being too greedy."

"Tonya . . . It is humbling to think how fortunate we both are."

Y2K

With only a couple of surprises, the Christmas celebration was not that different from what Walt had envisioned. Predictably, the grandparents fawned over their grandson. The soon to be a toddler would need no new clothes until some time after his first birthday. Walt was grateful that the Sullivans exercised some restraint in giving Jesse toys. Even so, suitcases would be crammed for the return flights.

When the portrait of Jesse was unveiled, Alice and Dave were genuinely moved. The day after Christmas, she and Tonya went to a frame shop and ordered one custom-made. While they were gone, Walt asked his father-in-law a question.

"Do you have any robins around here?"

"Oh, yes—they're here year-round. The population swells as birds from as far away as the Arctic Circle winter here. Why do you ask?"

"Just curious. I've always wondered where the robins went that nest at our house."

Attention shifted to the TV news. Commentators were obsessing over possible computer malfunctions with the turn of the century. It had something to do with Y2K, but Walt did not understand what that meant. Dave added his own byline.

"I guess you'll be glad to get home before New Year's Eve, supposing everything crashes, figuratively speaking, of course. We were using computers extensively at work before I retired, and they are the wave of the future. Every now and then, I get a hankering to play around with one here at the house. You do know that Seattle is where much of the revolution is taking place?"

"Yes, I did know that, but it's about the extent of my expertise on the subject."

"I wonder what kind of world that boy of yours will grow up in."

"Me, too. I'll do my best to teach him to be true to himself, and he'll have to take it from there."

"After all, he wouldn't be here apart from cutting edge technology. Alice and I want you to know that we're so honored to have you as our son-in-law. Jesse is such a happy child. You're obviously doing lots of things right. Tonya tells us that you're already reminding the boy who his real mother is."

"I do that just about every day. When he's old enough to catch on, Jesse will learn that you are Ginny's parents, too."

Strangely, Polly was not mentioned before or after Santa came. That circumstance did not get past the ever-observant Tonya.

"This is eerie. Do you think I should say something to Alice?"

"No . . . As my Granddaddy Williamson would say. 'Let sleeping dogs lie'."

On the morning of the afternoon flight back to Anchorage, Walt decided to stretch his legs. The mist was almost heavy enough to be light rain, but his hooded windbreaker was sufficient. As he turned back into the drive, he did not notice it at first. Then, it grabbed his full attention.

Chee . . . Chee . . . Chee . . . Tut . . . Tut . . . Tut.

"Ms. Robin? Is that you?"

Cheer . . . Cheer . . . Cheer . . . Cheerio . . . Cheer . . . Cheer . . . Cheer . . . Cheerio!

My precious darling . . . Thanks for the postcard.

As the entourage headed to SEA-TAC, the grandmother insisted on holding her grandson. Walt was relieved that things had gone so well. At the gate, Alice reached in her purse and handed him a neatly wrapped small gift.

"This is from Polly. She sends her regrets for not being here to celebrate with us. She and *her* son decided they needed some quality time together, and they went on a holiday cruise."

Sensing Walt's hesitancy, Tonya reached for it. With everyone looking on curiously, she meticulously removed the colorful paper. From inside a little box, she retrieved an ornament and held it up by the string.

"Baby's First Christmas" was inscribed on one side. Smiles signaled a sense of both relief and appreciation. When Tonya turned it around, the air was sucked out of the room. The likeness of an Eskimo was on the other side. "God's Frozen Chosen" was spelled out underneath.

"Dad . . . Have you ever thought about getting a computer?"

"What on earth would I do with a computer?"

"For one thing, they have word processors in them. I hope you'll do some more writing. Maybe you should consider something like a memoir—using your journal as the springboard."

"Do you really think anyone would be interested in my humdrum life?"

"Ah, come on, Dad. Your story is so out of the ordinary that you might have another bestseller on your hands."

"Even if I did write another book, I'm not sure how much use I could get out of a computer. My thinking flows through the thumb and index finger of my right hand."

"I'll bet you could retrain yourself to compile on a keyboard. I keep hearing about something called the Internet. People are actually sending electronic messages."

"I don't know. Let me think about it."

"For sure, you want to raise Jesse with traditional values. Just keep in mind that this kid will find another big world out there waiting to be discovered. A computer might be a wonderful teaching tool."

"How expensive are they?"

"Let me do some checking around."

"It might be a moot point if they all crash—as the news is hyping. Are you staying up to see the new century in?"

"Of course, I am. What about you?"

"When I was a youngster, the notion of a calendar starting with a two was so far-fetched that my mind could not imagine it. Now that it's about to happen, I think I'll join my son and sleep right through it. I told you my life is mundane."

"Fine then. I think I'll go into town and watch the fireworks."

Walt switched the lamp on and slid off the bed. Jesse had entertained himself long enough and was hungry. Tonya would not rouse until closer to the mid-morning sunup. While the bottle warmed, the baby got a change. Cradled in his daddy's arms, the boy slurped louder than usual. After two good burps, the father sat his son on his knee.

> Jesse . . . Today is the beginning of a new century. I know you have no idea what that means, and in many ways, neither do I. Your old Pa is feeling like a relic, but I promise you that I will not hold you back. Things have changed so much since I was a kid. From what I'm hearing, much more is to come. I want you to have all the tools necessary to make your way when you go out there to take it on.

Tickling his tummy, Walt added. "Most of all, I just want Jesse Sullivan Williamson to be himself."

His son smiled and squirmed. It was playtime, and he was ready to get started.

71

Surprises

A few days after returning to her apartment, loneliness shrouded Tonya like the darkness of the long winter nights. Many were overcast, and artificial lighting was not very enticing when she tried to paint. Furthermore, nothing on canvas was calling her.

She fought the urge to fold her tent, so to speak, and go spend time with her father and brother. The welcome mat was always out. Yet, she did not want to intrude further during this special time of bonding.

Tonya was too young for a mid-life crisis, but it certainly felt like one. One morning in the lamplight, she stood before the sketch of Granny Addie. Her cognizance revisited the happenstance with Ms. Hattie. The saintly old woman told her to find her inner light and follow it. That candle was flickering.

When growing up, nothing in the furthest stretches of her imagination would have put her in Alaska. Any notion that she might share life in America's Last Frontier with the father she feared she would never find seemed outside the realm of possibilities. The likelihood, that she might one day have a sibling, was even more inconceivable. Presently, the eighty miles separating them seemed more like attempting to cross the choppy waters of the Cook Inlet in a rowboat.

Tonya was in the year of her thirty-first birthday. She had been in only one serious relationship, and it just died a slow death. Apart from the bequest of Mrs. Thornhill, she would not be able to support herself in pricey Homer. That her artwork hung on walls in several states gave her some satisfaction.

Turning away from the drawing, something hit her right between the running lights. As a child, she had pined and pined for the opportunity to talk things over with her father. The other side of that gulf was suddenly not so inaccessible.

Putting her few perishables in a cooler, and packing enough clothes to stay several days, Tonya was soon behind the wheel of Cornfield. Already, she was feeling a lift in her spirits.

Any qualms about encroaching were dispelled when her dad was genuinely glad to see her. Tonya took off her boots at the door and went directly to her little brother. Walt put on his and unloaded her stuff, making note that this was more than an overnight stay.

The next member of the welcoming committee was on the job. The big smile signaled that the tot recognized her, and the reunion was rousing. After putting Jesse back on his pallet, daddy and daughter both started to speak at the same time.

Tonya yielded.

"Age before beauty."

"What I was about to say was how really proud I am to see you. If you had a phone, I would have called. These long winter nights and short days start closing in on you."

"You got that right. It seemed such a shame that we could not commiserate."

"Now—what was it that you were about to say?"

"Just that I didn't want to intrude and be a bother, but I would like to stay a couple of weeks."

Walt sensed that *bother* was the operative word. Something was troubling his daughter, but he would let her approach it, in her own way.

"I have a surprise for you. When Jess and I were out the other day, we stopped at an estate sale. I brought home a futon and put it in the corner of the office. You can sleep there and not disrupt your brother's schedule. Come as often as you want and stay as long as you wish. I promise that I will not treat you like hired help."

"I promise I won't just be another mouth to feed. And I have a surprise for you, too."

After dinner and Jesse down for the night, she turned to him.

"Dad . . . I'm afraid this turn of the century thing has put my biological clock on steroids."

"I suspect that's true for lots of folks. From what little news I get, there seems to be some widespread anxiety and much uncertainty about the future. But this is not about other people. What's going on?"

During the next hour, Walt probed and prodded, and Tonya poured her heart out. Sensing that the session had gone on long enough, he suggested that they continue the next morning around the breakfast table.

After Jesse had navigated through his morning rituals, and the dishes washed and put away, Walt refilled the coffee mugs.

"Didn't you say something about having a surprise for me?"

"We got so engrossed in my misery that I forgot to mention it last evening. I went by to tell Bekka that I would be gone for a couple of weeks, and she was unpacking a new computer. She said a tourist called and purchased a large painting that she had coveted when visiting back in the summer. It was just enough to cover the cost of a new Windows 98. Bekka got a desktop with a monitor and separate keyboard."

Mischief was in Tonya's eyes. He had seen that look before.

"Now for the best part. She gave me her old Windows 95 notebook. I think some people call them laptops. I can't wait to start learning my way around on it."

The day was filled with grocery buying, lively conversation, and Jesse time. After dinner and the guys were off somewhere in La La Land, Tonya's juices were flowing. She booted up the computer and went exploring. Bekka had assured her that she could not break it, and she showed her how to undo any unwanted changes.

Walt was unsure whether it was his bladder or Jesse's whimpering that roused him. Apparently, both needed attention at the same time. He saw the office light switch off as he came out of his bedroom. With Tonya sleeping in, daylight eventually made its way over the horizon.

Jessie . . . Come and look. The world turned white while you were asleep. Let's bundle up and go outside. It's still snowing.

Sheer delight was in the little boy's eyes as they followed the falling flakes. He extended his hands and flexed his fingers trying to catch them.

Two remarkable women

When Tonya finally crawled out, her brother was already taking a nap. The boy was mostly down to one a day, but some mornings he got fussy and needed to sleep it off. She fired up the coffee maker again and went looking for her father. He was shoveling snow, the first accumulation of the season.

"Looks like you got here just in time. Are you ready for some breakfast? I waited for you."

"Too lazy to cook your own? Here we go—treating me like your personal servant."

"If you insist, but I'll clean up your mess."

While Walt was standing at the sink doing just that, Tonya brought her new toy to the table.

"Dad . . . I do hope this contraption does not intimidate you."

"Intimidate me? I thought it was yours."

"I'll share. Maybe we can learn how to use it together."

"You already have a head start. I know what time you flipped off your light."

"So . . . You're intimidated already."

"If I were, I wouldn't admit it."

"It's been so long since I did any typing that I was not sure if my fingers would remember the keys. I guess it's like riding a bicycle. It's strange, though, not hearing the clacking."

"I took a year of typing in high school and did peck out some of my college papers, but Hannah typed my master's thesis."

"I've heard you mention Hannah a time or two, but I know very little about her."

"She was my first love. The night we met, our eyes locked, and something clicked inside both of us. I had never had that feeling before and really haven't since. I loved Hannah with my mind. Out intellects meshed as one. In contrast, I loved Ginny with my heart and soul."

"Why didn't things work out for you and Hannah?"

"Simple—she was already married, and her husband was in Vietnam."

"Did you ever meet him?"

"Twice. He was a patient briefly at Walter Reed where I was stationed when I met your mother. I also saw him in the auto parts store he managed."

"Oh! Was he injured?"

"Yes, he was paralyzed from the waist down."

"Ouch! Do you and Hannah keep in touch?"

"We kept bumping into each other now and then, figuratively speaking, of course, but I have not heard from her for some time. Ginny got to meet her at a book signing. They hit it right off. If we had not been living in Alaska, I think they might have become best friends."

"That would be weird."

"Not if you knew them both—two such remarkable women."

"How did we get off on all that? Now—back to this thinking machine. I've already mentioned that you might want to do some more writing. I think you'll find the word processor user-friendly."

"I could certainly use some help with spelling."

"Maybe you should consider writing an autobiography of some kind."

"You know—Hannah suggested the same thing one time. She said I already have a title."

"What would that be?"

"*The War Baby*. Hannah only knew bits and pieces about my childhood, and so much has come to light since those days. I never saw her after my mother found me, and I learned about the big family secret. She certainly knows nothing about, first you, and now Jesse."

"Dad . . . You do have a remarkable story. Please think about it."

"What about you? How will you use the computer?"

"The first thing I plan to do is type my diary entries into it."

Walt and Tonya found it most interesting that they both dubbed their journals, WOWs. His designation came from his initials. She derived hers from Willa-O-Wisps, a play on her middle name.

"Should I ever want to do anything with them, my musings will already be recorded electronically."

"You already have a title, too. Mrs. Thornhill gave it to you—*Miss Bizzy Belle.*"

"Bekka told me to be sure and back everything up. She gave me a box of floppy discs and showed me how to use them."

"Floppy what? Is this like learning a foreign language?"

"Come and look over my shoulder. Let me give you a brief tour of what I've learned, thus far."

The computer lesson was cut short. Jesse stirred and Tonya was on her feet. After a quick change, she started bundling him up.

"Let's go build a snowman."

From his infant seat, the bright-eyed tot watched with fascination as his daddy and sister labored. Unlike the heavy wet snow, they grew up with, the dry, powdery stuff was not cooperating. After some serious pounding, an unsteady form took shape.

Walt remembered his camera when he went inside to get a scarf, a hat, and a carrot for a nose. After taking a couple of shots with Jesse in the picture, the wobbly snowman toppled. Babbling and laughter commingled.

Jesse has your laugh. That twinkle in his eyes also looks so familiar. I'm beginning to wonder if he got anything from me.

Envy

After Tonya gave Jesse his night bottle, she rejoined her father. He still knew so little about his daughter's childhood and had a question.

"Who was your best friend when you were growing up?"

"Samantha Ringer—she's a doctor's daughter. Her dad's name is Ebenezer and her mother's, Florien. To everybody in the town, they were Mr. Ebb and Mrs. Flo—and they were a hoot."

"Ebb and Flo—how cute."

"Oh, how I was jealous of Sammie having a family that cared about her and so involved in her life. Her parents took such pride in their children. Mrs. Ringer dressed her daughter in the nicest clothes that always looked so good on her. Mother reminded me at least once a week that she did not make enough money to compete with the Ringers."

Tonya took a deep breath.

"When we went our separate ways after high school, we drifted apart. Well, actually, I was the one who dropped out of her life. While I was home settling Mother's estate, I went by their house unannounced, as I had done so many times before. Mrs. Flo looked at me as though I had come back from the dead. She ushered me in, and to my surprise, called out to Sammie."

Two deep breaths this time.

"Sammie ambled sheepishly into the living room. She looked bedraggled, and that's putting it nicely. Her first words stunned me. 'I'm so ashamed for you to see me like this.' The very personification of pride—ashamed?"

Walt nodded for her to go on.

"To make a long story short, Sammie never got her college degree. She married herself a law student who wanted to go into politics. Two children later, he traded her in for a newer model. With his legal connections, he was avoiding hefty child support. Unable to take care of herself and the children, she moved back home. Now, Mr. Ebb and Mrs. Flo are having to raise their grandchildren. From what I saw, the holy terrors really need a steadying influence."

Tonya sat back and took three deep breaths.

"It was what she said as I was leaving that really got to me. 'Tonya . . . I am so envious of you.' Sammie Ringer? Envious of me?"

All Walt could verbalize was a prolonged, "Hmm."

"Let's clear the table, and then there's something I want to ask you."

Rattling the dishes seemed therapeutic for Tonya, so he went to check on Jesse. The contented little guy was sleeping peacefully. Walt propped his feet up and waited for Tonya to proceed when she was ready. He did not have to wait long.

"I know you discussed this in your book, but I still don't get it."

Tonya went to the bookcase and retrieved a copy of *I. D. - The Identity Dilemma*. She fumbled through several pages and then read a couple of paragraphs.

"In essence, here's what I need you to explain for me. How is it that one child, who is the apple of his parents' eyes, takes that validation and turns it into believing in himself, while another kid transforms that same kind of support into a continuous need for approval? Don't answer. I'm not through.

"Why do some children, repeatedly told how worthless they are, grow up with boundless self-assurance and self-confidence, but other kids, endlessly praised and promoted by their parents, wind up with no self-respect or self-esteem?"

"Tonya . . . I've been a student of human behavior for a long time. It never ceases to amaze me how some offspring grow up and simply replicate their raising. Many just pass down family dysfunctions from one generation to the next."

"I can see that."

"Then again, there are the exceptions to the rule. Some kids come of age with the determination to be everything that their parents were not. They see their folks' failings and resolve that their own families will not be subjected to the harangue they endured."

"Why is that?"

"Tonya . . . If you ever figure that out, you can write your own book."

"I think I'll stick to painting and leave that to you."

Walt went to bed feeling admiration for his daughter's courage to escape the past and carve out a whole new life. She reached for her journal.

"I wonder if Sammie would still be envious of me if she knew how trapped I am in my freedom and independence?"

What's stopping you?

Over the next couple of days, Walt learned of such things as Save, Save As, Copy, Paste, and Delete. He was still not sure if a computer would ever be of much use. Tonya, on the other hand, could not get enough of it. After Jesse was down for the night and the laptop put to sleep, she bounced something off her dad.

"I'm wondering if maybe I should go back to college."

"What's stopping you?"

"I might pick up a few classes at the campus in Homer and round out my basics, but I'd have to go elsewhere to finish my degree."

"Any idea what you would major in?"

"I'm thinking about art education. I can't live on my savings, part-time summer work, and selling an occasional painting forever. Surely, I could get a job somewhere teaching art. I could certainly use some benefits."

"You do know those are the kinds of programs that get cut first during a budget crunch."

"I might be able to give private lessons, but that would not help me with health insurance."

Just like that, her father made a proposal that sent her head spinning.

"You could always live in my other house and go to Ephesus State. Of course, Jess and I would want visitation rights."

When Walt left his bungalow in North Carolina, he had no concept of how long he would be gone. Customarily, he came and went every year or so. Still basking in the glow of his daughter finding him, and now with a son, not yet a toddler, a return trip was some ways down the road. Having someone in the house during the interval would ease his mind.

Tonya was reenergized. She packed up and headed back down the road, soon to embark on the next phase of her life's journey. She requested a transcript and filled out the paperwork to jumpstart her formal education. With an open-door policy for nontraditional students, her application was expedited so she could begin classes during the winter semester.

Sissy

Jesse's first birthday and Tonya's thirty-first was on a Thursday. The college student took her last final exam the day before, and Cornfield was already packed and ready to roll. A late cold front was moving through, and the Subaru drove through snow flurries. She bounded through the door ready to get the party started.

"We've got so much to celebrate. Where do we begin?"

"Let's see—birthdays, all A's, and one big surprise."

Jesse was standing alone using a chair for support.

"Reach out your arms, and tell him to come and give his sister a hug."

The toddler broke into a big smile and ambled unsteadily in Tonya's direction. She reached out and grabbed him before he lost his balance. They snuggled big time, and she tossed him into the air.

"You just couldn't wait, could you, Little Bro? I thought we had agreed that you would take your first steps to me."

"He has something else to show you, too."

Walt gathered the boy in his arms and went to the photo of his mother. "Who is this?"

Jesse decided to make a game out of it.

"Da-da."

"No—I'm Da-da. Who is this?"

Making sure Tonya was watching—he got it right on the third try.

"Ma-ma."

Walking back toward Tonya, Walt put his hand on her shoulder and asked his son what his sister's name was.

The little tyke went mute. No amount of prompting could get him to say anything resembling Tonya. As his daddy put him back on the floor, he looked back up at her.

"Sissy."

No self-respecting Alaskans would ever celebrate a birthday without ice cream. Tonya said she saw a sweatshirt with the inscription, "Life is short. Eat dessert first." They did.

The birthday girl got to choose the main dish, and she had put in her request ahead of time. Her father had smoked a ham, and it was ready and waiting.

Jesse was determined to see how much Jell-O he could get on his face and how little in his mouth. Around the table, Tonya announced that she had some surprising news.

"I've been accepted at Ephesus State University. There's not much more I can take here, and I want to move forward."

"Oh, Tonya . . . That's wonderful."

"Can I take Jesse with me?"

"No—but I'll make sure he doesn't forget you. Remember—you'll be living in my house, and we'll have to come and check on things now and then."

"Not everything will fit in Cornfield. I'll have to ship some stuff. Do you think I can drive that far by myself?"

"I have an idea. Why don't you fly? Leave your wagon here and drive Brusky when you get there. We can just swap Subarus for the time being. I need more reliable transportation here with the trucks getting old. What do you think?"

"I think I have the best daddy in the world. You, too, little bro."

Little bro no longer stayed where he was put. His crawling skills allowed him to go exploring to slake his escalating curiosities. Learning to get around upright, meant new challenges for his father. Walt was getting his first good taste of setting boundaries.

On Sunday, he made a simple entry in WOWs.

Happy Mother's Day!

Tonya threw herself into her work at the studio. When she pitched her tent in Homer, she had no concept of the future. Ten years later, she was about to move on, but one lesson she had not yet learned. Just when you think you have plotted a way going forward, inevitably, something pops up in your path.

Bekka came bounding through the door the morning after Independence Day an hour after Tonya had unlocked it. From the shopkeeper's demeanor, something was up.

"Would you like to take over the studio? Kelvin proposed to me last night. He has taken a job in Montana, and I'm going with him."

Tonya was aware that her boss was seeing a man, but she had not met him.

"That must have been some fireworks last night. When are you leaving?"

"At the end of the month."

Take over the studio was well put. Since the building was leased, the only things that Bekka owned were the name and her personal effects. Little of a capital outlay would be required of Tonya.

"This is so sudden. Let me think about it."

Think about it she did. The words of Mrs. Hattie echoed throughout her being. What was her inner voice trying to tell her? Was this proposal intended to protect her from making a colossal mistake or geared to give her the confirmation she needed to pursue her education? With no time off in view to go to him, her dad got a call.

"Can you guys come and spend a couple of days with me? I need to discuss something with you."

Walt stopped all along the way and pointed things out to Jesse. The various colors of the wildflowers particularly fascinated him. When Tonya explained her dilemma, her dad quoted his Grandpa King.

"If you think God doesn't have a sense of humor, then just tell Him your plans."

A "For Lease" sign was hanging on the studio door the next day.

Forget-me-not

Most of Tonya's apartment furnishings had come via moving sales. The last weekend in July, they were recycled. Her art supplies, along with clothes and other personal effects were boxed up with an Ephesus, North Carolina address. Walt found room for other things she did not want to part with.

He insisted on driving his daughter to Anchorage. For months, he had thought about dusting out the camper and attaching it to Nellie. So much of Alaska was just waiting for him to share with his son, and they could take their sleeping quarters along with them.

Tonya gave most of her attention to the tot while Walt seemed lost in his thoughts. He was thrilled that Tonya was taking this big step. At the same time, the separation was already taking a toll. The father found satisfaction in being able to provide for his daughter—something denied him most of her life.

The itinerants picnicked at a park on the Portage spur to Whittier. A babbling brook provided background music for Jesse's jabbering. Snow-covered mountains and ice-blue glaciers seemed so close that you wanted to reach out and touch them.

"I'm really going to miss this place, but I'll be back. When do you think you'll head my way?"

"I can't say right now, but you never know."

The early August sun was nowhere near ready to retire, but the day of the fifteen-month-old was about over. Tonya crawled in back with him and put him to bed. Jesse was weaned except for his bedtime bottle.

"You cute little fellow—I'll miss you, too. Don't you forget me. I put a picture of the two of us on the dresser beside the one of your mother. Underneath, is a dried blossom of a forget-me-not, which just happens to be the state flower of Alaska."

"Sissy."

Around ten, Nellie pulled into a level spot in the airport parking lot. As his daughter wheeled her luggage away, Walt locked the cab and went to join his son in the camper. This was as good of a place as any to hitch Nellie for the night. Tonya looked back, just as he disappeared inside. Waiting for her flight, she dug in her tote bag for her WOWs.

"It must not be easy being the father of a grown woman still figuring out who she is—and a toddler just beginning to."

Hyperbole

"Okay, pod'ner . . . Which way you wanna to go? North, you say. Me, too. Let's find a little breakfast, grab some grub to take along with us, top off the tank, and head out."

Jesse protested when his daddy buckled him into his car seat. Walt was negligent when they had been out for short distances.

"Okay—but if we get a ticket, it's coming out of your allowance— whenever you're old enough to have one."

As the little boy stood up in the seat and took his place beside his father, he noticed something for the first time.

"Sissy . . . Sissy."

"Sissy got on a big airplane last night while you were sleeping. We won't see her again for a while. But son—you can rest assured of one thing. Your big sister won't forget about you."

When Nellie headed out from Kenai, Walt had no inclination about which way she would go from Anchorage. A plan was now taking shape in his mind.

"Jesse . . . Let's go for a long ride. I want to show you where your mother and I went on our honeymoon."

"Ma Ma."

Walt was unsure how much the child restraint law was enforced. With the camper blocking light from going through the rear window, it was doubtful that an oncoming trooper could even see much of anything in the cab. The driver was certain of one thing, though. He was in no danger of getting a speeding ticket.

Mother of our son . . . I wish you could hear him say, "Ma Ma." We are off on an adventure. I promise that I will not neglect Jesse, but so many of my thoughts will be taking a stroll down memory lane. You made me so proud to be your husband. I now feel that same pride in being the father of my bride's child.

After a grueling overnight flight with layovers in Salt Lake City and Atlanta, Tonya finally landed in Asheville. Her dad's friend, Eli, was waiting with Brusky, fresh with a new battery. The vehicle was several years older than Cornfield, and it took some getting used to. With little sleep and jet lag overtaking her, the hour drive to Ephesus tested her senses.

The weary traveler nearly fell asleep during a delay as she was entering the town. Traffic was stopped for a funeral procession. Still early afternoon,

Tonya knew she did not need to go in and collapse on the bed. Steeling herself, she stopped at a café for a pick-me-up before picking up a few groceries.

Once her order was placed, she picked up a local paper and saw the headline about the death of a paraplegic Vietnam veteran businessman. She wondered if it was his body on the way for burial. The obituary stated that the man was survived by a devoted wife but no children. Something sounded familiar about the names, but she was too drained to sort it out.

The bungalow had been locked up for more than two years and was musty. She opened windows and turned on a fan. Fatigue was a blessing in that it insulated her from a passel of unknowns. Instinctively, she went to the phone and dialed her dad's number. When no one answered, she surmised that her guys were off rambling somewhere.

Jesse had two speeds and one was sound asleep. As his guardian sat under the wheel, the toddler had the run of the rest of the cab. He arranged his toys systematically, only to send them flying. Periodically, he ran across the bench seat, wrapped his arms around the driver, and kissed him on the cheek. One hug was interrupted.

"Moose! Moose!"

Walt slowed the camper as a cow and twins were grazing along the roadside. Jesse had seen one moose when it wandered through the yard. Pointing, he mimicked his daddy.

"Moose! Moose!"

After several hours of lumbering along up the Parks Highway, the RV hung a right toward the historic little village of Talkeetna. The father and son wandered through town and decided to spend the night.

Walt rustled up some vittles, and while he was washing the dishes, the other passenger had experienced enough excitement for the past two days. He was mostly potty trained but still needed a diaper for overnight. Not long after the tot was out for the count, Walt realized something. Jesse did not ask for his bedtime bottle.

Spotting a pay phone as they were heading on up the road the next morning, Walt turned aside and placed a collect call to his house in North Carolina. When no one answered, he figured Tonya was busy tying up loose ends to resume her schooling.

As Tonya strolled through the beautiful, well-manicured grounds of Ephesus State University, dichotomous emotions flip-flopped. Her maternal grandparents and both parents had earned degrees at that institution. Still, nothing felt like she was carrying on any kind of tradition.

She relished the memories of the summers spent with Granny Addie and Papa Doc when her mother was getting her master's. As a child in her own world, the campus might well have been on Mars.

In her early thirties, Tonya was continuing her education in a town half an hour from where she grew up. The spatial map was in extreme hyperbole. She felt much closer to the Kenai Peninsula in Alaska some four-thousand-miles away.

> *Jesse went to sleep tonight snuggled atop my bare chest on our honeymoon bed. MPD, I could feel your heartbeat.*

Matriculation was a breeze compared to her first college experience. Computers took much of the hassle out of it. Tonya was so grateful for her own little notebook. Before putting her foot in a classroom, she purchased an inexpensive printer.

> **Jesse . . . We are on the Denali Highway. Yesterday, I pointed out to you the highest mountain in North America. Can you say Denali?**

Walt chuckled when the little boy tried to say the word. What came out was probably close to the way Native Americans pronounced it.

> **Son . . . This might be called a highway, and it does go through some high passes. It is unpaved for almost a hundred miles. We are in a wilderness. That means wild animals live here. I have been here before with your mother.**

"Ma Ma."

Jesse did not understand how the camera worked, but he enjoyed seeing the pictures after they were developed. He also took charge of the binoculars, which he dubbed the "noculars."

After settling up with the business office, Tonya was already feeling in a financial pinch. When she purchased her textbooks, the anxiety proliferated. Before walking away from the counter, she inquired about part-time employment. The clerk told her she would have to discuss that with the manager and pointed her to his office.

The balding, rotund, middle-aged man with look-over specs, a comb-over, and ring around the collar put on his noncommittal face until Tonya mentioned her bookstore experience. Mr. O'Quinn's countenance changed, and so did the rest of his body language. When he spoke, the second-generation Irishman had lost much of his brogue.

"My biggest problem is finding students who see their job as more than just a paycheck. Most have difficulty following instructions, and just about the time I think I have them trained, they depart for greener pastures."

"Did you know my father wrote a bestseller published by the university press? He did his first book signing right here."

"No kidding. Let me see your schedule. What hours can you work?"

> Jesse . . . This world is so beautiful. Out here in the wilderness, everything has a purpose. So, do we. This is such an amazing place when we are in sync and attuned to the natural world. We must take care of the earth so it can sustain us . . .

When Walt realized that he was not getting any reaction, he looked down at the toddler in his arms. Jesse had dozed off during the over the top soliloquy. The driver laid the lad gently on the seat, fired up Nellie, and continued on in his own thoughts.

Tonya's academic advisor helped devise a plan where she could graduate in two years—if she took no time off. Ouch! Summering in Alaska was not going to happen.

When classes started, she was surprised to see a few other older students. The course work did not seem insurmountable, and with few distractions, she delved right in. Tonya did become a tad concerned when the phone in Kenai went unanswered.

Work was a welcomed diversion. Out of curiosity, she looked over reading lists and found that her father's book was still on the Psychology Department's. She had presumed that it was out of print but found a copy on the shelf. No one was around to see her smile.

Living in the house where she and her dad first got to know each other seemed eerie. She could feel his presence and that was reassuring. Since the college student was stuck in North Carolina, she yearned for the time her men could come for a visit.

"Jesse . . . Can you say mosquito?"

The picnic was cut short by the pests desperate for their own feast. A couple followed them inside the camper.

The toddler's vocabulary was increasing faster than Walt could keep up. He was not sure how much his son was grasping that he still could not put into words. Inching along the Denali Highway, they saw swans swimming in marshes, black bears foraging on berries, and a big bull moose that had descended from the higher elevations in search of a mate.

Back at the edge of civilization, Walt spotted a pay phone at a convenience store. It was midday, and Tonya was likely in class. Both the driver and passenger were getting weary from disrupted routines. In two nights, they would be back in their own beds.

My dear Ginny . . . Our son is so much like you. He already has your spirit of adventure. I wish you could have seen his bright eyes with every new experience. When we got back home, he walked straight to your picture and said, "Ma Ma."

Tonya did not get home from work until after eight, and two appetites competed for her attention. Food could wait. The hunger to hear the voices of her dad and brother compelled her to dial the number yet again. This time, she finally got an answer.

"Where in blue blazes have you guys been? I was beginning to think your phone was out of order."

Walt filled her in.

"We had such an amazing time. Wanna talk to your little brother? He's trying to take the phone away from me."

The tot's inquisitive eyes shifted into gleefulness when he heard Tonya's voice.

"Sissy . . . Sissy."

On the morning of the fall equinox, Ms. Robin announced that she was closing shop for the season. She hopped along on the ground ahead of Walt, chattering with every pause.

Chup . . . Chup . . . Chup . . . Cheer up, Cheerio! Cheer up, Cheerio!

"Maybe we'll see you in Seattle during the holidays. If not, we'll be waiting for you next spring."

Chee . . . Chee . . . Chee . . . Tut . . . Tut . . . Tut.

Urges and nudges

Walt felt an urge to take his son to a community-wide Thanksgiving service. A teenage girl was behind them sitting with some friends. The eighteen-month-old flirted with her until she reached over the bench and took him. Jesse could not yet speak in sentences, but his facial expression communicated a full paragraph when his daddy looked back.

Freed of the squirming boy, Walt tried to concentrate on the service. He had not exactly rebelled against his conservative religious upbringing but did not find fulfillment within the institutional church.

One thing was not in doubt. Gratitude filled his heart. No preacher had to explain providence to Walter Othell Williamson.

After the final "Amen," the girl handed her handful back to his father.

"He's so cute. What's his name?"

"Jesse."

The boy perked up when he heard his name.

"Is he your grandson?"

"No . . . Jess is my son. I'm raising him alone."

The perplexity of the situation was beyond the sphere of the young woman's attentiveness, but something else was not.

"Do you ever need a babysitter?"

"Hmm . . . I've never thought about that."

"My name is Jane. Let me give you my phone number should you ever need me."

Being sequestered on holidays was nothing new for Tonya, but that changed after she found her father—followed so soon afterward by the birth of her brother. Aloneness had a way of asserting itself back into her soul as fall transitioned into winter. Limited finances and her work schedule would not allow for going back to Alaska during her Christmas break. First, she had to get through Thanksgiving.

The disciplined student kept pace with her assignments. The time off would be put to good use writing papers due at the end of the semester. Tonya's computer had become an extension of her fingertips.

She had not been in a church since the bizarre day she met Mrs. Hattie. Finding her still-small-inner-voice expounded by the country preacher had taken her on a pilgrimage apart from organized religion. A poster in the student center announcing a citywide Thanksgiving service grabbed her attention.

Tonya almost talked herself out of going to the Wednesday evening gathering, but a little indefinable nudge kept niggling from somewhere inside. Recalling with a smile her strategy when entering the little country church years earlier, she thought to herself that she could always get a seat at the end of a row and slip out.

The sanctuary of the First Baptist Church was overflowing when she arrived, and ushers were putting chairs in the aisles. A deacon gestured for her to take a seat in one of them. With not enough hymn books for everyone, they were passed around and shared.

After the preliminary announcements and everyone welcomed, the music director asked the congregation to stand and sing "Great is Thy Faithfulness." Tonya was transported to a portal where her Pa Bell was whistling that tune. The vision was interrupted when a man stepped across the narrowed passageway and held a songbook between them. She looked over at him and smiled.

As the second stanza began, Tonya reached a hand to help support the book. Unintentionally, two thumbs were touching. Neither made any attempt to separate them.

> Summer and winter, and springtime and harvest,
> Sun, moon and stars in their courses above,
> Join with all nature in manifold witness
> To Thy great faithfulness, mercy and love.

The Refrain reached a crescendo, their eyes met.

> "Great is Thy faithfulness!" "Great is Thy faithfulness!"
> Morning by morning new mercies I see;
> All I have needed Thy hand hath provided—
> "Great is Thy faithfulness," Lord, unto me!

Tonya's path was unblocked, but she would not be cutting out early.

Plain Jane

Walt mulled over the babysitter's offer. Perhaps, his son was too sheltered. Jesse had never shown any fear of strangers, but this father understood that socialization goes through stages. Just maybe—this dad could use an occasional break from round the clock care of the boy.

He called the number the teenager gave him, and she answered the phone. Walt suggested that she come by for a visit. Jane asked if her mother could accompany her.

"She would never admit it, but she's overprotective."

"I understand her position. She's just doing her job as a parent. Of course, she can come with you to make sure I'm not the big bad wolf."

When Walt met them at the door, the woman looked familiar. She recognized him immediately.

"You're the man I met in the grocery store when your daughter was with the two of you. You must have known how mystified I was when you said the baby was not your grandchild, nor your adopted son, and that his mother had been dead for several years. The article in the paper cleared it all up for me."

After a tour of the place with Jesse the self-appointed silly-maker, they settled in the living room. Walt turned his attention to the girl.

"Tell me about yourself."

"First of all, my parents named me well. I'm just Plain Jane McCain. What you see is what you get."

With nods of approval from her mother, Jane filled Walt in on some details about her family. She did not remember her father, killed in an explosion on an oil platform when she was two. Her mom decided not to return to Texas and had remarried. Jane had a little brother, Nate, a few months older than Jess. After teaching for several years, Mrs. McCain was a stay at home mom.

Forgive me, Lord

"Tonya Willa Bell . . . What were you thinking? More specifically, why were you not thinking? You mean—from the thousands and thousands of words in your vocabulary—the only thing you could come up with after that tall, dark, and handsome stranger walked beside you to the front door of the church was the lame, 'Happy Thanksgiving?' Then again, he didn't do any better, did he?"

She was grumpy all the next day. Because of the four-hour time difference, she had to wait until almost noon to call her dad and brother to wish them a Happy Thanksgiving. Tonya considered telling her father about the encounter, but it was apparently a non-starter.

Walt did mention the babysitter hookup. When he told her who the teenager's mother was, she smiled for the first time all day.

The bookstore was closed until Monday. Tonya concentrated on her assignments, but something was playing persistently in the background, and a Miss Bizzy Belle little scheme began taking shape. The chances of the man who almost held her hand attending the church where it happened were only about one in five since that many congregations had come together for the service. She decided to take those odds.

On Sunday morning, she gave a little more attention to her personal appearance than usual and retraced her steps to First Baptist. This time, she slipped out unnoticed during the Offertory.

"Please forgive me, Lord. I went to church for all the wrong reasons."

As her activity level shifted back into overdrive, Tonya was unable to get the man off her mind.

"You know, God . . . I might have to visit every church in this town before I find the right one for me."

Plain Jane arrived ten minutes early. She had told Walt that he might have to pick her up and take her back home, but her mother relented and let her use a car even though she was only fifteen.

"I think she wanted me to have a means of escape if you turn out to be an ax murderer."

Walt felt lost when he fired up Cornfield. The things he had thought about for his night out now had no attraction. He doubted that he could sit through a movie. December darkness prevented much of anything outdoors. His mind simply could not release images of this being a date night with Ginny.

The clear December sky was dark except for the twinkling stars, but he drove to the beach anyway. The floundering man retrieved a flashlight from the glove compartment. Once he reached the area smoothed by the tides, he turned it off and started walking aimlessly. Something in his peripheral vision turned his head, but nothing was there. It happened again.

Then, magically, the northern lights began putting on a spectacular light show. Inadvertently, Walter Othell Williamson had stumbled once again onto hallowed terrain.

My Precious Darling . . . Tonight, I was one with the Aurora Borealis. My spirit merged with the energies of the universe. You were right there with me. Hello—again—MPD.

TDH

"Stop acting like a teenager. If Mr. TDH had any interest in you, he would have shown it when he had the chance."

Tonya was not as creative as her father in naming things. TDH stood for tall, dark, and handsome. She wrote in her journal.

"God might forgive me for going to church for something other than worship one time. Maybe I should mend my ways before getting into some serious trouble with the Almighty. Then again, my Pa Bell used to say, 'God helps those who help themselves'."

Many changes had taken place in higher education since she first enrolled as a freshman. One thing had not. Few faculty members and not many students had their minds on academics during the days leading up to the Christmas holidays. She was coming down with a good old case of the holiday blues.

Mr. O'Quinn was already out of town and left Tonya to lock up. The hours dragged with hardly a customer after lunch. Then, time stood still. Be still my heart.

Mr. TDH had come through the door. He was browsing near the front and seemed not to notice her. The customer looked up as the clerk approached him. Tonya thought he did a double take. Did he recognize her?

"How may I help you?"

"I might give you a good answer if I only knew what I was searching for."

"Is it a textbook or something from a reading list?"

"I'm not sure I'll find it in a book."

Tonya was stymied. How would her dad handle this?

"Maybe I could recommend something."

Mr. TDH realized that he was putting the employee in an uncomfortable position, and that was not his intention. He extended his hand and redirected.

"My name is Tom. I remember you from the Thanksgiving Service. Do you recognize me?"

Did I recognize him? Is he kidding me? Blood went rushing to her face.

"Yes—you kindly shared a hymnal with me."

"I'm looking for a particular book. The store on the square said it's out of print, and the two copies in the library are checked out. I know it's a long shot that you might have it, but I really would like to read it over the holidays."

"What is the title? I'll see if by chance we have a copy."

"The book was recommended by a friend. She said it changed her life. The author is an alumnus of ESU. If I remember right, the title is, *I. D. – The Identity Dilemma*."

Tonya tried not to imagine her face going from flushing red to pale white. Her first attempt at speech ended licking her lips. On the second try, words tumbled out.

"As a matter of fact, we do have a copy. Let me get it for you."

Tonya was grateful for the opportunity to turn her back to the man and buy some time shuffling through the stock as though searching for it. Approaching him, she held the book near her waist with the cover facing forward to draw his eyes away from hers.

"I guess you might say I'm pathetic. I'm thirty-five-years-old. I have a Ph.D. in American History, have a cushy teaching job, and make rather good money. Yet, I'm still trying to figure out what my life is all about. Do you know anything about this book?"

"I'm familiar with it. I actually quoted from it in my high school graduation speech."

"I know you're about to lock up and go home. Let me pay for this and be on my way. For tax purposes, I would like to write a check. Here's my business card if you need any identification."

"I do hope you enjoy the book. And oh, by the way, it was written by my father."

Mr. TDH's blood pressure spiked. He walked away without looking back.

Tonya locked the door and was taking the receipts from the register when she heard someone knocking. The last customer of the day had circled back. Miss Bizzy Belle had regained a measure of her composure and did not make it easy.

"Sorry . . . We're closed until next year."

Tom feigned dejection and turned as though walking away. He did an abrupt about-face when he heard the click of the cylinder lock.

"I hate to bother you again, but may I call you?"

"Why? What would we talk about?"

"I don't know. I might ask if you would consider having dinner with me sometime."

"You mean—like tonight?"

No kidding

They had almost finished eating before Tonya got Tom to loosen up. The man who routinely lectured a hall full of students struggled with the one on one. The Sin Infidel story finally broke the ice.

When he asked for the check, she had no sense of what might happen next. Since they had met at the restaurant, if left to him, he would likely shake her hand, and they would go their merry ways. She was not about to make the same mistake and simply wish him a Merry Christmas.

"Can we go somewhere and talk? The night is still young, and this is the official beginning of my holidays—no work or school for a week."

Tonya felt certain he would not suggest going to his place. Something might be out of place.

"I have a bottle of Sin Infidel in the fridge. Follow me."

Tom liked it when she took charge. The first thing he noticed when he went through the back door into the kitchen was the old movie poster.

"Guess you didn't know that you're dating a famous movie star?"

She had a fix on him when he heard "dating," and his reaction would have been about a 3.8 on the Richter Scale.

"No kidding. I had a bit part in that film, some of which was shot in nearby Knoxo Springs, where I grew up."

Tonya then made a calculated move. Her out of the ordinary story need not be an open book. It might spook the cautious man.

"I'm guessing that since you teach at the university, you're not from around here."

"No, I'm not. I'm originally from Georgia. I grew up in a small town in the northwestern part of the state named Adamsonville."

"No kidding. My father went to college at Adamson State. I have a great-uncle and aunt who live there, but I've never met them."

Oops. That might raise a red flag. Best to move on before he finds that odd.

"You likely know them. Earl and Mary Beth King are retired now, but he was both a tractor and an automobile dealer. I believe he was also once mayor of the town. Mary Beth was a teacher and then a principal."

Tom could hardly wait until she finished.

"I bought my first car from Mr. King, and Mrs. King was my fourth grade teacher. Shall we say it together? 'Small world'."

Tonya's guest might be reticent, but he was a historian.

"How is it that you never met your uncle and aunt?"

"That's a long story. Let's put it on ice for later."

Did she just say later? Would there be a later after that night?

Banter became Tonya's strategy of choice for the rest of the evening. She was careful not to upstage him, but that did not come easy. Tom knew when it was time to say goodnight, and he also understood that the next move was his when she stood in the door.

"I've had so much fun tonight. Can we do this again?"

"Thought you'd never ask."

As Tonya was preparing for bed, she found Tom's business card in her pocket. Her eyes then did an undeniable double take as she saw his full name—Thomas D. Howard. His initials were TDH.

You're not going to believe this

Around the time Walt set out on his adventure to Alaska, he encapsulated a basic part of his lore and recorded it in WOWs.

"I cannot always tell you where I'm going to be, but there are two places you need not look, for I will be in neither. One is where I'm not wanted, and the other is where I do not want to be."

He was certain that he and Jess were wanted in Seattle during Christmas, but he was struggling with the other part of that equation. The boy's grandparents had not seen him in a year. Thoughts of feasting on someone else's cooking, tipped the scales.

Tonya suggested that he give the Sullivans a couple of gift cards. Walt was not too keen about that proposal, but he had nothing better to offer. That was not the purpose of her call.

"You're not going to believe this—well, maybe you will. One of the professors here is from Adamsonville. Okay, that was easy. The unbelievable part is that he came into the store looking for your book."

"Did you have one?"

"Yes—he purchased our last copy. I guess it's now officially out of print. He knows Earl and Mary Beth."

"Interesting . . . Jess and I are going to Seattle. What are your plans for the holidays?"

"I guess I'll just hang around here. Don't have any money to do anything else. If the weather holds, I might do some hiking. Say hello to Dave and Alice for me."

As they were coming into town, Walt saw the twin-engine commuter plane headed toward the airport. He knew it would not be on the ground for long before taking off again. They arrived just in time for a lesson.

Son . . . See the airplane? Next week, we will fly in two different airplanes, and they will take us to see your grandparents. You have met them before, but you don't remember it. They are your mother's parents, and they love you very much. We'll eat lots of good food, and I'm sure they will give you a bunch of Christmas presents. We will have so much fun. Can you say airplane?

"Ah-pane."

"Gus . . . Don't you think you've been silent long enough? Your ring tone is my favorite sound in all the world."

Favorite or not, Tonya jumped when the phone rang. Dr. TDH called and suggested a movie. She just loved it when she put him back on his heels.

"One of us gets to pick the flick and the other the bistro. Which do you choose?"

"I don't remember saying anything about dinner."

"Tom . . . Are you forgetful? Am I about to go out on a date with an absent-minded professor?"

During the dinner part of the date, Tonya had trouble keeping him misdirected. She feared too much information about her past might push him away. Tom sensed unusualness about a woman going back to college at her age and kept probing. Little by little, she filled him in with some of the timeline, including her Alaska connection. The real-life clock kept ticking.

"Tonya . . . You have just convinced me of something I guess I've known all along. I've lived such a monotonous life."

With that, he glanced down at his watch.

"The movie is starting right now. Will you take a rain check?"

Since he had picked her up this time, Tom had to drive Tonya home. He offered no resistance when she invited him in. After a couple of glasses of Sin, what came stumbling out of his mouth surprised even himself.

"I'm leaving on Friday to go home for Christmas. Why don't you go with me? It's not like I'm taking you home to meet the parents or anything. Do you think the Kings might like to finally meet you?"

"Dad . . . You're not going to believe this. Wait—I've already used that line. Tom's going home for Christmas, and he's invited me to hitch a ride. Do you think Earl and Mary Beth might put me up?"

The pause on the other end of the line was not helping. Walt was busy processing what his daughter had just said and how to make it happen.

"They would love to meet you. I've only spoken with them once since . . . Let me give them a call and I'll get back with you."

"Gus . . . You're giving me that old silent treatment again."

When she went to bed, Tonya had heard nothing further from her father. Because of the time difference, it would be at least midday before the next opportunity.

"Talk to me, Gus. Don't make me cuss."

He was defiant until almost suppertime. Walt apologized, but Earl had just returned his call. The childless couple had been to Atlanta to celebrate their 55th Wedding Anniversary.

"Earl is still a sport, and Mary Beth is forever the love of his life. They said they would welcome you with open arms. You'll get to sleep in my old bedroom. Can you believe that?"

Christmas spirit

> MPD . . . My mind keeps retracing the Christmases we spent together. I remember so fondly the time you dressed up as Mrs. Santa and whispered in my ear, "Sometimes, naughty is nice." I do not want to disappoint you, but I've been a good little boy this year. Jesse, on the other hand, has been a bit naughty at times. You would be so proud of him.

Walt could only imagine what was going on in Jesse's mind. The little lad listened intently as his daddy described the kinds of things about to happen. Undoubtedly, the boy understood far more words than he could articulate.

This was their first flight without Tonya. Walt did not buy a ticket for Jess and was hoping for an empty seat somewhere on the plane, but it was packed with holiday travelers. During takeoff, the toddler's ears perked up as he heard other kids crying.

Before reaching a cruising altitude, Jesse was already squirming from the aisle seat. Walt pointed to the seatbelt sign and assured his son that he would put him down when it went off.

"See the light?"

"Dight."

Not wanting his own child to become an annoyance to other passengers, Walt tried to keep a tight rein. As the boy ventured farther up and down the aisle, the widower father soon learned that he was among an improvised extended family. In the spirit of Christmas, smiling faces and friendly voices greeted his son. With a nod of approval from the daddy, one woman became a substitute granny, took the tyke in her arms, and entertained him for several minutes.

> Son . . . The airplane will be landing soon, and your grandparents will be waiting for us. I mentioned earlier that you've already met them, but you do not remember it. Dave and Alice are your mother's parents. They took care of her when she was a little girl, and they love you just like they did her. We'll be staying at their house for a few days. Your grandmother is a great cook so you'll get a break from your old pa's cooking. You will also get to open some Christmas presents. We are going to have so much fun.

Walt offered to tote Jesse off the plane, but the boy resisted. He did consent to holding his daddy's hand. Dave and Alice were both waiting at the gate when the two came walking out the passageway. As folks approached that he did not recognize, the toddler relented when his father picked him up.

The grandmother restrained herself until her grandson signaled that he was ready for her to take him. Walt smiled reassuringly amidst hugging and kissing mingled with some giggling. Jesse looked over the woman's shoulder back toward his daddy as they went through the corridor. Both were grinning big time.

They did not go directly home. With Jesse sitting in her lap, Alice apologized for not having dinner ready. She had ordered take-out Chinese, and they went by and picked it up.

"I've already done some baking, but the serious cooking has not begun. Polly is coming over tomorrow to get her hands in it. I suspect she will also put in her two cents' worth."

"I cannot remember the last time I had Chinese. Jesse . . . Can you say Chinese?"

How's all that working out for you?

Dr. TDH picked Tonya up right on time. He was a morning person and wished to get an early start. Punctuality was also one of his passions. Having him as a captive audience for the three-hour drive, Tonya fully intended to find out what else made Tom tick.

"Have you had a chance to look at the book?"

The driver looked straight ahead but reacted with a mild grimace and a shallow breath.

"I read the first few pages, but I'm still pondering something your father said in the prologue. Here I am a history professor, and I had never thought about how humans are the only species that struggle with their destiny. Every generation has to go through the procedure all over again. He mentioned that a dog does not fret over what it means to be a dog. A dog just goes about living a dog's life."

"That's right. Neither does a deer wake up one morning all bent out of shape. Oh, dear . . . I'm a deer. Dear me. What must I do today to prove that I'm worthy of being a deer?"

"Why is that? How come it's not in our genes? Why can't this just be passed down from generation to generation?"

"I don't know why. I believe the author said that it's just part of the human predicament."

"Tonya . . . You seem so sure of yourself. From what little I know about you, your mother was not exactly a role model, and you did not have a father in your life when you were growing up. Here I am the product of what I presumed was perfect parents, and my life is Exhibit A of what Walt

100

Williamson described as a person with identity voids. I'm a textbook case of someone who thought that if I just filled all those spaces, I would find happiness and fulfillment."

"How's all that working out for you?"

"Not so well, I'm afraid. I keep measuring myself by the yardsticks of others. My parents could not be any prouder of me. I seem to have the respect of fellow faculty members. I'm on track for tenure and a full professorship, and my students typically give me good reviews. But . . ."

As his voice trailed off into space, Tonya realized that not much she could say at this point would make any difference. She had to trust her father to spell some things out for Tom.

"Keep reading the book. You're asking the right questions, and you just might find some answers in its pages. Did you bring it with you?"

"Yes . . ."

Ice

"What do you want Jesse to call you? I've already explained that you're his mother's parents. He's big into naming things. If you have preferences, maybe we can steer him in that direction."

"I'm no granny, and I doubt that Dave wants to be called a grandpa."

"What does your other grandson call you?"

"Just by our given names."

While he was taking everything in, the seventeen-month-old just took most stuff for granted. If his daddy was okay with what was going on, that was good enough for him. As they were sitting around the dining room table after a scrumptious feast, Walt put his hand on Mrs. Sullivan's shoulder.

"Jesse . . . Who is this?"

The little boy's version of a shrug was to ignore the question. His daddy persisted.

"This is your grandmother. Can you say, grandmother?"

Same response.

"Her name is Alice. She is your mother's mother. Can you say, Alice?"

A smile lit up the boy's face.

"Ice . . ."

Just like that, it was settled. Jesse could not say her full name, but he connected with the last syllable.

How he would refer to his grandfather took more time. His tongue did not seem able to shape anything resembling Dave, much less David. No amount of cajoling got him to produce any sound.

Adamsonville

The house where Tom grew up was six miles out on the road coming into Adamsonville. The first thing Tonya noticed as they turned into the drive was an American Flag on a tall pole in the front yard. At least, no Confederate one was hanging with it.

"The parents" were understandably curious. Had their oldest child and only son finally met someone? Tonya was certain he had not told them much, and this only whetted their appetites.

Cliff Howard was a construction foreman. The contractor he worked for built mostly institutional structures, such as schools, banks, and office buildings. Some projects were far enough away that he was gone for weeks at the time. Marsha was both the CEO and CFO at home.

Nothing was elaborate or pretentious about the residence. Slate-gray vinyl siding was added a few years back with a metal roof to match. The word drabness came to Tonya's mind.

As Mrs. Howard's son unloaded his luggage, she explained that she was taking a break from cooking before the headlong rush. They were going into town for soup and sandwiches at Cliff's favorite diner.

"Tommy tells us your father went to school here, but this is your first time to visit our town. We'll take the scenic route and point out some landmarks."

In the South, that meant downtown churches and the historic old courthouse.

From the passenger seat, Marsha informed their guest that they did not go to any of the big city churches. She was also delighted that Tommy had her met in church. The years of Tonya keeping a straight face when dealing with her mother were still paying dividends.

"You came right by ours. We'd love to have you go with us on Sunday. Tommy . . . Did you point it out when you went by?"

He made no audible sound but meekly shook his head.

From the driver's seat, Cliff picked up the conversation.

"We're conservatives. Liberals are ruining our country. I don't know how Tom deals with it."

It was Marsha's turn.

"Our college is out on the edge of town. It's now a university. Praise the Lord for Adamson State—at least for what it was back then. We could not afford to send our children away for their schooling. Tommy graduated, but the girls dropped out. It was a different place when they were students. We hear it's now a cesspool."

Back to Cliff.

"Our preacher told us someone actually heard a professor say that the school's primary responsibility is to teach students to think for themselves. How dumb is that? Their job is to teach students **what** to think."

Tonya surmised that riding through the campus was not on the itinerary. They might all get contaminated even with the windows rolled up. She reached for Tom's hand, and they shared a moment. Then, she released it.

Tom called to get directions, but Earl insisted that they come out to get Tonya. Her first impression of her great-uncle was that he might have been a very successful public servant, perhaps even an ambassador. After putting her stuff in the trunk, she was directed to sit up front.

"Why don't we take a spin through town and show you around? Let's start with a little tour of the campus where your father went to college. You know . . . That place has never been the same without Walt."

Any qualms on Tonya's part about putting these folks out were quickly squashed. She had a hard time getting a word in edgewise as the couple took turns making her feel welcome. The tour continued when she was ushered into their beckoning home. After seeing all the rooms on the main floor, they went to the basement.

"So—this was my daddy's apartment. I'm beginning to think I enrolled in the wrong school."

"You can transfer any time you wish."

"What do you want me to call you?"

"Boy, does that bring back memories. We went through the same routine with Walt. It seemed to go against the grain of his raising, but we insisted that he call us by our given names."

"Then, Earl and Mary Beth it is. Thank you. And by the way—a belated Happy Anniversary!"

Sunday clothes

"Walt . . . Sunday is Christmas Eve. We want to go to church and sit together as a family. If you were not here, we'd likely go anyway, but I guess I'd better fess up. It would be really nice to show off our grandson."

"Go to church? Sir, I didn't bring any Sunday-go-to-meeting-clothes."

"I'm ahead of you, my boy. You and I have basically the same build, only you're slimmer. I have some suits hanging in the closet that I've not had on in years. My feet are bigger than yours, but nobody will be looking at your shoes. I think I can also fit you in a shirt and tie that no one would think anything about. There's a Christmas tie back there in the closet that Polly gave me several years ago. I've never worn it, and she probably doesn't remember it."

It was understandable that Polly's name kept coming up in conversation because she really was family. Each time, it made Walt feel ill at ease. He reluctantly consented and wondered if she would sit with them.

The Seahawks were playing the Falcons on Saturday. Walt had never been to a professional game in any sport so this invitation he gladly accepted.

"I grew up in North Georgia and you might not know it, but I was in college just an hour from Atlanta when the Falcons joined the league as an expansion team. We'll be pulling for different teams."

"Do you want to make a friendly little wager?"

"Not a chance. I would never bet on the Falcons."

After watching his team get thrashed, Walt was ready when Dave suggested they get ahead of the traffic. Polly's car was in the drive as they approached. He wondered if this might have been part of a plan to get him out of the house so she could spend some time with Jesse.

Not surprisingly, his son was holding court. Somewhere in the future, Walt would have to explain the role the surrogate mother played in birthing him, but for the time being, she would just be Aunt Polly.

Walt was pleased when the usher at the Covenant Presbyterian Church took his sister-in-law by the arm. Alice fell in line behind her. Dave yielded so his wife could be seated beside her grandson and son-in-law.

Jesse was not about to sit on anyone's lap for the duration. He stood and turned to the folks in the row behind them. Pointing to Walt, he said, "Daddy." Then his finger did a one-eighty. "Ice."

It occurred to Walt during the Christmas sermon that Jesus did have some rank, born of a virgin and such, but Jesse's story ran a close second. At the end of the service, the southern gentleman stood in the aisle for the ladies to exit. Polly winked at him.

"Nice tie."

"Tonya . . . I do hope you're planning to go to church with us, but you won't have to sit through a sermon. The choir will be presenting a cantata."

"I didn't bring any Sunday clothes."

"Not to worry. I want to do something very special. When your father was a kid and came to stay with us for a few days, I always took him shopping. This soon became a tradition. His parents never bought him anything that fit, so Earl and I helped fill that void."

When Mary Beth looked to Tonya for a response, she was surprised to see her eyes red and moist.

"I would have never had any pretty clothes, either, except for Mrs. Thornhill. I was in her daycare center, but she was more like a mother to me than my own."

Come Sunday, Tonya sat between Earl and Mary Beth at the First United Methodist Church wearing an elegant blue suit. The choir sang about angels.

Merry Kiss-mas

Sometime during the night, Santa came for Jesse. He brought some toys and several new outfits. Other gifts were still under the tree. As the family assembled for the ritual, Walt called his son to come to him.

"Christmas Tree—can you say Christmas Tree?"

"Kiss-mas Twee."

"Jesse and I have something very special that we would like to add to the beautiful decorations."

Walt was glad he remembered to bring the "Baby's First Christmas" ornament Polly gave them the year before. The lad did not instantly get the hang of it, but with his dad's help, they found a place.

Quietly, Polly moved toward them. She reached under the tree and handed Jesse a small present wrapped in colorful paper.

"Go ahead. Open it."

With Walt's help, out came something else to go on the tree. "A Little Boy's Second Christmas" was inscribed on one side. Etched on the other, was the image of a robin looking over into a nest with three blue eggs. Walt's eyes met Polly's, but she had no way of knowing what he was thinking.

"Before everybody digs in, I want to take a Christmas Dinner picture for Tonya."

Polly reached for the camera.

"Walt . . . You need to be in it."

Alice leaned over next to Jesse. He patted her on the shoulder and said, "Ice." The boy was not too sure about the flash, but it did not distract him for long. Once his food was mashed and cut up, he went right to work. So, did everyone else.

Walt imagined the mother of his son sitting in that very spot when she was a little girl. He tried to remember what she was wearing when he first sat at that table with her. Some memories of Ginny were vividly clear. Others were fading in time.

He never failed to mention the Christmas china. Alice said it was a shame that she only got to use it once a year. It was so old that it was not dishwasher safe.

"Son . . . As your Great-Grand Pa King would say, 'I'm tight as a tick.' Are you going to help me wash dishes?"

"Get along. You boys go watch a football game or something. Polly and I will put the leftovers away and stack the dishes in the sink for later."

With his son already sleeping off the excitement of the day, Walt reached for WOWs before he switched off the lamp. This entry would not take long.

Merry Kiss-mas, my darling, from both of us. And from Ms. Robin, too.

Earl suggested they go out for Christmas lunch, but his wife reminded him that they would not find anything open between Adamsonville and Atlanta. He then did the next best thing. Walt's uncle first learned to cook when he was in the military. He made no claim of being up to his mother's standards, but he never forgot his way around the kitchen. The girls talked shop.

"Come and get it. The possum and taters are ready."

It had been a while since Tonya had sat down to good old southern cooking, served, of course, with sweet iced tea. Taters were on the table, but a pork roast stood in for the possum. As they were about to be seated, Tonya went for her camera.

"I want to take a picture of the table for my daddy."

"Here—you should be in it, too. Your camera has a timer on it. Let me set it and put it on the counter. I guess what turns out will be potluck."

The talk moved as slowly as the dishes were passed back and forth. No one was in a hurry to leave the table. Tonya had some questions, and she eventually ventured beyond her hesitation.

"May I ask you something? If you don't want to answer, or if it's none of my business, just say so."

Mary Beth was puzzled, but Earl was rather sure where this was going. He nodded.

"Daddy's birth mother told him that so far as she knew, only herself, the doctor who delivered him, their friend Millie, your sister Maude who took him to raise, and her aunt were the only people who knew anything about who his biological parents were. Is that true?"

"No—it's not. I'm surprised Walt never asked me that same question. It always amazed me how he took what was dished out to him and then tried to find the good in it. We were there. A lesser person would have been destroyed by the way his custodial father treated him.

"Mary Beth and I tried to help take up the slack, as best we could. I'm not sure if any of that mattered. Walt had a determination to be his own man, and he would not allow anything or anybody to stand in his way."

"Thank you for all you did for him. Who else knew?"

"Daddy figured it out before Walt was even born. He didn't fall for the fake pregnancy gig, but he did not let on to his daughter. He never told my mother, either, but he did bring Walt's other granddaddy on board."

"And you? When did you find out?"

"Daddy took us into his confidence when Walt was about two."

Tonya remained quiet and still.

"Now—you have taken me into yours. If my dad has not already discussed this with you, I doubt that he ever will. He already knows you were there for him, and that's good enough. I've never known anyone who loved his grandfathers as much as he did. And to think—they knew all along that he was not even their own flesh and blood."

"Two such fine men. I hope when my time's up, I'm judged at least half as good as either of them was."

"It's hard for us to imagine Walt now with a son of his own. Earl and I are so looking forward to meeting the little chap."

"Maybe next summer."

How cool is that?

Jesse had mastered what he called his grandmother, but he continued to balk when it came to addressing his grandfather. Alice had the boy in her arms and approached Dave sitting in his favorite chair.

"I'm Alice. Who is this man?"

Something clicked. The little boy's facial expression betrayed him. The question was whether he would share it, but this was too good to keep just for himself.

Jesse pointed to the woman holding him.

"Ice."

He then redirected his finger.

"Ice Man."

"Othell . . . The frozen chosen one has Ice and the Ice Man for grandparents. How cool is that?"

Asked when they might be back, Walt reminded his in-laws that flights go both ways. Dave explained that they went to Alaska once after Ginny moved there, but it was while she still lived in Anchorage. They had never been to the house in Kenai. Walt assured them they were welcome anytime.

Polly came by to see them off, but she was certain the invitation did not apply to her. The tautness had toned-down, and Walt was more relaxed when she was around his son. Only time would tell the nature of the relationship Jesse would have with her once he found out the role she played in his birth.

"Jesse . . . Tell them goodbye."

The boy waved but said nothing.

"Say goodbye to your grandmother."

He let his fingers do the talking for the goodbye part and added something with his lips.

"Ice."

"And what about me?"

Jesse switched from his right hand to his left.

"Ice Man."

Hogwash and brainwashed

The original plan was for Tom and Tonya to go back on Friday. He called and wanted to bump it up a day. She left Adamsonville on more than just a sugar high from the holiday sweets. Walt's daughter had established an important link to his past.

Tonya learned of her daddy getting dumped by his puppy love, and of how he made spending money working at his uncle's John Deere dealership. Laughter filled the air when Earl and Mary Beth told her about her father's college escapades, especially his sparring with the dean. Earl described Walt's first car, an old Chevy that he called "The Rev."

"It was a trade-in from a preacher who had just about run it in the ground. Walt managed to keep it going for several years. I think he was still driving it when he met your mother."

To the extent that Tonya was upbeat, Tom was correspondingly browbeat. As they were going up the road, he told her how he spent the entire time stifling himself. He had nothing in common with the sisters he had tolerated as a youth. Both were alarmingly obese, and their children were rowdy and undisciplined.

He said he struggled most with his parents. Tom described how their minds were so narrow that nothing from the outside was given any credence. Tonya was inquisitive and asked him to explain further.

"It's a simple matter of faith versus facts. Their religion allows them to accept anything, no matter how implausible, on faith. Reality checks are deflected away. As an example, they do not believe in climate change. To them, it is just a bunch of liberal hogwash."

Tom looked straight ahead, and Tonya gave him space until he was ready to continue.

"They not only disregard science, but they also rewrite history to suit their purposes. When I first tried to reason with them, they accused me of being brainwashed by liberal professors. What they believe, is all that matters. As a historian, this is awkward."

"Speaking of awkward, what will they think when they find out that my father and I were both born out of wedlock?"

"I'm not sure they need to know that."

Tonya wanted Tom to know she was hearing him.

"I know this makes it very difficult for you. You don't want to disrespect them, but at the same time, you have to be true to yourself."

"That's the problem. First of all, I'm still not sure who my true self is. I just go along so as not to rock the boat. I allow them to think I see things just like they do."

"Did you find any time to read?"

"Yes—under the guise of doing some course work, I slipped away a few times. I wish I could give you a better report. Your father's book keeps getting in my face. In some ways, I'm just as big a hypocrite as my parents are but in a different sort of way."

"How so?"

"I seem unable to switch on my internal gauges. I've always tried to become what others wanted me to be. As the oldest, and as a son, I felt compelled to carry on the family name and traditions, but I've not even been able to find a wife that my parents would approve of."

Tom paused and took a few breaths. Tonya felt honored that he was opening up to her, but at the same time, she was certain they would never approve of her.

"In my own educational experiences, I tried to please my instructors to get good grades. It worked. Throughout my career, I've jumped through whatever hoops necessary to gain the admiration of those who controlled my status. As a teacher, I seem addicted to the feedback from my students."

"Oh, Tom . . ."

"Walt Williamson nailed it. What I am going through is indeed an identity dilemma."

"Perhaps, I can get the author to sign the book for you sometime."

Jesse had no choice but to keep memories fresh in his mind through photos and voices on the phone. When they got back home, he went immediately to the pictures of his mother and sister.

"Ma-ma . . . Sissy."

After Walt got the holiday film developed, he showed the prints to his son. The boy's right index finger shifted into action.

"Da-die . . . Yes-sie . . . Ice . . . Ice Man."

Aunt Polly was not in any of the pictures.

My precious . . . Jess is changing so much right before my eyes. You would have been so proud of him at your parents'. He conducted himself as a little man. He certainly knows how to put his mark on things, as he perceives them. I'm not sure he will remember it, but he called your mother "Ice" and your father the "Ice Man." Do you think he has them pegged?

When Tonya dialed her dad's phone number, she got a busy signal. Five minutes later, the same thing happened.

"That man hates talking on the phone. I wonder if it's out of order."

The phone was working properly. Simultaneously, he was trying to reach her. Gus II finally got his attention after Tonya kept trying.

"Say hello to your little brother. He's crawling all over me wanting the phone."

"Hey, Jesse . . . This is Tonya."

"Sissy."

Walt could not hear what thoughts she was putting in his ear, but the boy listened intently. Abruptly, he handed the receiver back to his daddy.

"Are you ever in trouble. Earl and Mary Beth told me all your secrets. Your first sweetheart who dumped you was singing in the choir. Too bad. She's a very beautiful woman. I think she's single."

"I knew you guys would get along. I doubt that girl would even remember the kid whose tender little heart she broke."

"The best part is that I now have a family connection I never had."

"Yes—Earl called soon after we got back from Seattle. They really enjoyed your visit and are looking forward to you coming back again. They also like to go to the mountains. Don't be surprised if they show up on your doorsteps. Now, tell me more about this Tom person."

"He's a nice man. He came out of a conservative Christian home much like my mother did. I'm not sure if your book is helping him. Your insights are certainly rocking his boat. Tom wants to crawl out from under his rock, but he's terrified of standing on his own two feet out in the light of day."

"I suspect you'll have a greater influence on him than my book ever will."

"I'm not so sure about that. I don't know how much longer he can tolerate me rattling his cage."

During brutally cold days, Walt and Jesse mostly stayed inside. The boy's pent-up energy and blossoming curiosity made him a handful out in public. It was Plain Jane to the rescue. She came over every Tuesday for a couple of hours after school while Walt bought groceries and took care of other chores.

Gus II interrupted playtime one Sunday afternoon. Jesse figured out the call was from Seattle and served notice that he was not to be excluded from the conversation. When he put the receiver to his ear, his eyes got big.

"Ice."

Walt watched as his son's expressions changed, but he was doing all the listening. Eventually, he spoke again.

"Ice Man."

Winter started losing its grip and the fellows spent more time outdoors. Jesse could repeat the names of objects when Walt pointed them out, and he also remembered more and more of them. If the boy's index fingers were weapons, many things would have been slain.

All looked forward to Tuesdays. Jesse called his babysitter, "Miss-Yane." She insisted that he drop the Miss part, but he balked. The two syllables rolled off his tongue better. As the days got longer, Walt extended her hours.

Sunday was Tonya's only free day. Without formally setting it up, phone calls to Kenai became part of her routine. Gus I could be expected to reach out and touch Gus II right after she finished lunch, which was about the same time the ones on the other end of the line had cleaned up after breakfast.

Different places-different spaces

Tonya and Tom usually found some time to spend together each week. Nevertheless, they were at different places in their pilgrimages, and she grew weary dragging of him along. On one phone conversation, she had a question for her father.

"Do people, who have always gotten their sense of self-esteem from others, ever flip the switch?"

"Tonya . . . It has always been a mystery to me how some folks just come into this world finding self-worth from within, while others see themselves primarily through the eyes of those from whom they need approval.

"As you know, I don't like to hang labels on people. Nonetheless, from my experiences, everybody seems to lean heavily toward one side of this spectrum or the other. It's self-evident that the ones who find worthiness from within like to be appreciated, but they do not let the opinions of others define who they are—one way or the other."

"You certainly didn't."

"To answer your question, I have observed a few persons who experienced something akin to a dramatic conversion after which they took ownership of their lives. But that's rare."

Walt did not address the never-ending frustrations when two people on different sides of the self-worth divide try to overlap their lives. He decided that was something she would have to come to terms with on her own.

To stay on course for graduation, Tonya was stuck in Ephesus during the upcoming summer. Walt began thinking about the possibility of going to see her. The thought of driving was tempting, but the concerned father feared the boy was not ready for a dozen or more days on the road, sleeping in a different place each night.

After Jesse's second birthday, he started speaking in sentences. Walt decided to buy a little more time for the boy to mature. He eventually booked a flight for mid-August, with plans to stay for about a month.

When school was out, Miss-Yane begged for more hours. She said Walt could drop Jesse off at her house anytime he wanted to for free, and she sweetened the pot.

"He always enjoys playtime with my little brother, Nate."

Walt realized that his son needed interaction with other kids and agreed to the arrangement with one exception. The babysitter would get combat pay if the boys did not get along. He also understood that Jane was not just looking out for the little guys. She made no attempt to hide her growing fondness for his son. Likewise, Jesse lit up when she came into his presence.

The Chosen Frozen

After giving him considerable grief, Tonya was eventually invited to Dr. TDH's house. As she anticipated, "A place for everything, and everything in its place" suited Tom to a T. She picked up a church bulletin atop a neat stack of papers on the counter.

"Is this where you go to church?"

"Yes—I visited First Baptist and liked it but knew my folks would be horrified if I went to a big liberal city church—although there's nothing liberal about it. This one's in a little village not far from here. I've found the minister open-minded and the congregation welcoming. Would you like to go with me sometime?"

Tonya was tempted to tell him about going back to First Baptist after the Thanksgiving service hoping to see him there, but she decided that was more information than he needed to know. She was not exactly excited about going to church with him. Yet, inviting her was a big step.

"Sure . . ."

"What about Sunday? Shall I pick you up around 10:30?"

"Okay."

Tonya dressed in her finest, which just happened to be the stylish outfit Mary Beth had given her. Tom looked professor-like in a navy blazer, khakis with sharp creases, and a pale blue shirt with a maroon tie. He opened the car door for her and was surprised when he held her hand going to the church. She surmised that they looked good together.

After they were seated, she glanced at the order of service. "The Chosen Frozen" seemed like an interesting sermon title. The music was not that different from what she grew up singing, and she felt at ease. Tom seemed especially wooden, and she wondered if he might be second-guessing himself.

The minister began his sermon with a recounting of the Exodus when the Children of Israel, "God's Chosen People," escaped Egyptian captivity and began the journey back to their homeland. The preacher framed the setting so simply that any child could get the picture.

Most folks in the congregation were familiar with the Biblical story, but they were not prepared for the sermon's climax. The adroit minister had their attention.

"What happened next, is such a parable of human nature. The *Chosen* became *Frozen*. The sons and daughters of Abraham looked over into the Promised Land, and they blinked. They turned and went back into the familiar wilderness."

Tonya looked over at Tom. The intensity on his face indicated that he was taking it in as the clergyman continued.

"On our own individual journeys, we start out with such promise but often start settling instead of continuously reaching for our ideals. After a string of besetting compromises, we long for a chance to reclaim our visions and dreams. Then lo and behold, just like with the Israelites, we get a glimpse of another chance. Redemption is right before us for the taking. Ladies and gentlemen, that's what God's grace is all about."

The minister paused. When he continued, he spoke softly.

"Do we ever come to our moments of truth and seize up? Do we freeze? Might we turn our backs on what we want so badly, on everything we've been clamoring for, on all that's best for us? Could it be that we turn and go back into old comfort zones and perish in our own personal wildernesses?"

Again, he hesitated. A smile graced his face. Gentleness was in his voice.

"Not all do. Joshua and Caleb defied the odds. They broke with the ranks. They bucked the tide. These two brave men went forward to claim the land flowing with milk and honey. And so, can we."

Tonya was certain the minister had hit one nerve and suspected he hit close to home with several others. Her spirit sensed something resembling a communal groan silently searing its way through the congregation. She held her own hand going back to the car.

> MPD . . . Jesse is talking up a blue streak. He is now stringing words together and has started referring to himself in the third person. It is so amusing when he says, "Yes-sie, no," and "Yes-sie, night-night." Today, he reached out his arms and walked to me. "Yes-sie need a hug." Our son is recognizing that he is his own little person.

Since Miss-Yane was looking after her brother on Saturdays when their mother did most of her shopping, the teenager insisted that Walt bring Jesse. The boys played well together, and this gave the full-time father more alone time. His neglected hiking boots got in some good workouts. So, did his mind and imagination.

"Othell . . . I wouldn't trade places with anyone else on the face of this earth."

Amazing Grace

Tonya asked for some time off from work during the spring break. A visit to her mother's hometown of Bellville, Alabama was long overdue. She had informed her grandmother about her move to Ephesus by phone but had not had an opportunity to go back to her own mother's grave.

"Grandmother Connie . . . You are a remarkable woman. Regardless of the trying circumstances that you were forced to endure, you never allowed them to shape you into somebody you were not."

"Tonya . . . That means more to me coming from you than anyone. The two people who inspired me the most were your Granny Addie, and my father-in-law, your Pa Bell. After you came into my life, you became the third part of that trinity. I'm so proud of you for what you're making of yourself. I know how difficult my daughter made things for you."

"That means more to me hearing it from you than anyone else, too."

"Speaking of Pa Bell, his health is breaking, but his mind is still sharp. He told me he was staying alive to see you one more time. If you like, we'll go out this afternoon. That remarkable man is in his nineties and still managing alone."

"Peanut . . . Come and sit on my lap."

"Only if you will join me in a whistling duet."

The bit off-key melody of "Amazing Grace" floated toward the heavens.

Soon after the old man put himself to bed that night, his spirit joined those wafting notes. Tonya had planned to visit her mother's grave. She had not counted on burying her great-grandfather at the same time.

Mama

With the August trip looming, Walt started both "To Do" and "To Take" lists. Traveling was much different with a toddler, and preparing his son was an ongoing process. Tonya did her part via the phone, reminding her brother on each call that he was soon coming to see her. After one conversation, he hung up and looked up at his daddy.

"Yes-sie go see Sissy."

> Jesse . . . Do you remember when we rode on an airplane and went to see Ice and the Ice Man? This time, we're about to take a much longer trip and go

see Sissy. We will have to get off the plane a couple
of times and then back on another one. We'll be
leaving at night so you can sleep some. Be thinking
about what you want to take with us.

Packing for himself was not that difficult for Walt. Just about anything
he might need was already at his other home. Knowing what to take for Jesse,
was another matter. He let the boy pick out a few toys and some favorite
books. The tyke had become attached to his hat, so it had to go along.

The second piece of checked luggage was a new "Extreme" cooler
guaranteed to keep food frozen for 24-36 hours. It was about to be tested.

Just as Walt was zipping the suitcase, Jesse came up from behind with
one more item. He handed it to his daddy and uttered a lone word.

"Mama."

"Here—let's put it in the middle so the picture frame will not get
broken."

Walt had calculated the itinerary to arrive on Sunday so Tonya could
meet them. The scheduled departure for the return flight was on a Tuesday
morning when she had no classes.

The first short leg of the long journey included a stopover in Anchorage.
Walt held his son's hand as they strolled through the terminal. Jesse stopped.

"Moose!"

He pointed to a gigantic stuffed bull on display. Farther down the
corridor, he paused again.

"White bear!"

"Son . . . That's a polar bear. Don't you remember it from your book
about Alaska's three bears?"

"Polar Bear . . . Brown bear . . . Black bear."

"Which is the largest?"

"Polar bear."

"Which is the smallest?"

"Black bear."

Walt was proud of his son. He was making such giant strides in his
speech.

A bit of strategic planning had gone into the trip. The next stop was in
Seattle, with a three-hour layover. Jesse's grandparents met them at SEA-
TAC, and they shared an early morning breakfast. No one had any way
knowing it, but that would be the last time they would ever be waiting at the
gate.

After only a moment of shyness, Jesse consented to hugs all around.
Alice came prepared to help her grandson with his diction. No matter how
many times she pronounced her name slowly, saying each syllable distinctly,

the boy shook his head. Working with him on his grandfather's name was a waste of time. It was settled law. Jesse's grandparents were Ice and the Ice Man.

Plum tuckered

Tonya was neat but not freakish about it. She wanted to make sure everything was tidy when her family arrived. Adjusting to the separation, was much easier while living in her dad's other house, able to sense his presence. Walt insisted that he and Jesse stay in the downstairs area where he once lived when a graduate student, and she opened the windows for ventilation.

The full-time student with a part-time job was already plotting in her mind how her dad could drop her off and pick her up so he could have access to the old Subaru. Not clear was whether Walt would meet Tom.

When Tonya aroused on the day of their arrival, her dad and brother were already in the air. The next stop after Seattle was the world's busiest airport. With so few flights from Atlanta to Asheville, she agreed to meet them at Hartsfield-Jackson. Facing a long layover, flight time, and the drive from Asheville to Ephesus, she could have them home sooner and before dark.

Traffic was light during the three-hour drive, and it gave Tonya time to think. She tried to imagine where she would be in a year. After May graduation, a whole new phase would open. The chances of Tom being in that picture were fading.

The closer Tonya got to Atlanta, the more her excitement began to build. She was glad not to have to choose which person she would be the happiest to see. The visualized reunion, nevertheless, was nothing as she imagined. When the weary father and son finally emerged from the ramp-tunnel, she just blurted it out.

"You two look plum tuckered."

"We're glad to see you, too. You look beautiful, by the way."

Jesse was suddenly rejuvenated.

"Sissy!"

Walt offered to drive, but no way was he was sitting behind the wheel after just getting his feet on the ground.

"I did not purchase a child restraint, so why don't you get in the back with Jesse. If I see a cop, you can sit on him."

It was not yet four when Brusky had the big city in her mirrors. Walt had gotten little sleep, and his body was confused. He wondered what his son was feeling. When he dozed off, Jesse crawled in the front.

Tonya was in no position to reason with him, so she pulled over and fastened his seatbelt. Minutes later, he squirmed free. She allowed her little brother to get in some kisses, and that seemed to satisfy him. Shortly afterward, he rejoined his daddy and joined him in a nap.

About half-past seven, the reliable old vehicle deposited her passengers, and Walt took Jesse on a little tour of the place. Much of it was as he had left it, but his daughter had put her stamp on things. Tonya took care of the cooler while they began unpacking the suitcase. Back and forth, they went.

"Daddy's drawer."

"Yes-sie's drawer."

When they came to the most precious cargo, they looked at each other.

"Where do we want to put this?"

"Yes-sie's mama. On dresser."

With body clocks still on Alaska time, the guys had a hard time going to sleep. Naps had taken the edge off. Jesse surrendered first, and Walt reached for WOWs.

My dear Ginny . . . Jesse is quite the gadabout. He has already logged more frequent flier miles than many folks do in a lifetime. I fear that I don't get him out enough, but when he is thrust into new circumstances, he just rolls with the punches. MPD, our son is becoming more like you each day. I was never prouder of him than when he insisted on bringing you along for the ride. I love you so much. Jesse does not yet understand everything that means, but he loves you, too.

Ep-i-sus

Tonya was long gone when they got up the next morning. Jesse was full of questions, and after breakfast, they went for a walk into town.

"Yes-sie hot."

"Yes, son—this is August heat and humidity in the South. Now you can see why I love Alaska so much. When they got back home, it was time for a geography lesson."

> Jesse . . . We are now in North Carolina. Let me show you on my old globe. Alaska is way up yonder. North Carolina is all the way down here. Over there, is Seattle where Ice and the Ice Man live. Follow my finger. We got on a plane in Alaska, stopped in Seattle, and then flew to Georgia. Atlanta is right there. Then, Sissy drove us to Ephesus. It is not on the map, but it is about where my finger is. Can you say Ephesus?

"Ep-i-sus."

Tonya had to work until the bookstore closed at six. The weary travelers had thrown together something resembling a meal. Walt felt drugged, and Jesse was cranky. They dived to the basement so Tonya could work on some assignments. She did not want to get behind so they could have more time to play.

Part III: A Preexisting Condition

Look at you!

The grocery store was not crowded. Jesse sat facing the buggy driver with his little legs dangling. He had to personally inspect each item before it was placed in the cart.

A man with a European-style beret waved at Tonya. She explained that he was one of her art teachers, and they met in the next aisle.

"Dr. Perry . . . Let me introduce you to my father, Walt. And this is my little brother, Jesse."

Something about that did not compute, but the professor did not ask for clarification. He just mumbled that he did not realize she had family in the area and moved on. Not so with the next familiar face.

"Walt Williamson . . . I thought I had seen a ghost."

"Hannah Parker . . . Look at you! And that long blond hair is as beautiful as ever."

"When did you start turning gray? I love the mustache, by the way."

Jesse didn't know what to make of his daddy hugging this strange woman.

"Isn't this a school day? What are you doing in a grocery store?"

"I've come through a rough patch, and I'm taking a year off."

"How is Phillip?"

"I can't go into that right now, but who are these people?"

Before Walt could complete the introductions, Hannah turned to Tonya.

"I recognize you. We've met before. Let me think. Yes—in the mall in Asheville."

"I remember you. You were there with your husband in a wheelchair, and you gave me your card. I think it's still somewhere here in my wallet."

Walt's mind was all over the place, but it took anchorage in thinking how some things never change. Tonya had carried his phone number around on a scrap of paper for years before she knew it was his. About that time, she came out with another purse stowaway.

"Hannah Parker, LPC . . . See?"

Hannah was a licensed professional school counselor. Unconnected dots were all over the map, and Tonya realized that she was the one who must instigate the task of linking them.

"Hannah . . . You seem to know this man, but what you don't know is this. Walt is my father."

"What? Walt?"

"Most likely, you've already presumed that this little guy is my child. This is Jesse, my little brother."

121

"Now, wait a minute . . . I'm really confused."

Walt weighed in.

"Hannah . . . You and I have some serious catching up to do, and this grocery store aisle is not the place. Tonya has put in her order for dinner—salmon—flown in from Alaska and ready for the grill. Can you join us? Oh, I'm so sorry. How rude of me. What about Phillip?"

Hannah steeled herself. Walt braced himself.

"Not a problem . . ."

With their eyes locked, Walt spoke in a muted tone.

"Tonya does not get home until after six. Would you like to come over earlier and help me get things ready?"

"I'll see you around five."

"Do you remember the way?"

"Walt . . . I've driven past your house so many times hoping to get a glimpse of you."

Filling in the blanks

While putting the groceries away, Tonya began filling in some blanks. She had shared many things with her father about the pivotal time in her life when she left college. She had told him all about her roommate, Brandi, a paraplegic from an automobile accident. He had learned of the despondent girl's suicide, and of how her parents erroneously blamed Tonya for their daughter's drug dependency.

She had disclosed going to her Pa Bell and of how special it was to sit in his lap as he whistled "Amazing Grace." Of course, Tonya had told her dad about the showdown with her mother who refused to tell her who her father was. She shared the ethereal Mrs. Hattie experience, about living in a tent, of settling in Washington and working for a newspaper, but she had made no mention of the meeting at the mall with the Parkers.

Tonya recalled how unnerving it was when the couple took a table next to her. She had gone there to call Mrs. Thornhill and decided to eat lunch at the food court. Someone in a wheelchair, exactly like Brandi's, made her most uncomfortable.

Sensing her uneasiness, the woman invited her to join them, and she reluctantly relented. Tonya recounted how comforting and reassuring Hannah's words were, and of how afterward, she withdrew money from her checking account and set out on her journey of self-discovery that eventually landed her in Alaska.

"Dad . . . Do you ever feel like you're just a bit player in a much larger scheme being orchestrated by forces beyond you?"

"There's so much more to life than what we perceive in the material world. Remember what I've said about synchronicity and spontaneity? The more we align ourselves with those energies, and the more open we are to Mrs. Hattie's advice about following our inner voices, the better able we are to experience the inter-connectedness and inner-connectedness she also discussed with you."

"Is that what happened when you first learned to read, and you were drawn to 'The Ugly Duckling'?"

"I could have never come up with that on my own. Some people call that providence. I'm always humbled when on the receiving end of things that I am incapable of devising by myself."

"Yes—I know."

Sorting stuff out

For the first time since boarding the short flight to Anchorage, Jesse was not the center of attention. While the grown folks were sorting out some stuff, his physical senses were busy absorbing new sights and sounds. If he needed a little attention, he was not above injecting himself into whatever was going on.

After Tonya left to go to the university, Walt kept watching the clock and almost forgot to get salmon from the freezer. He had an eerie feeling about Hannah's husband. The restless father took his son on a walk up the trail that went off right behind the house. Several birds were stationed all along anticipating some recognition. Jesse giggled in glee when they returned his daddy's chatter.

Hannah did not have to knock. Walt was waiting at the door, with Jesse tugging on his daddy's britches leg. Once inside, she kneeled down to his level.

"What's your name, little man?"

"Yes-sie."

"And who is this big boy?"

"Walt."

That was the first time Jesse had ever referred to his father by his first name, and he was obviously pleased with himself. So also, was Hannah. She had taken the important first step in charming the youngest member of the family.

"Let's go sit in the swing on the front porch. Jesse . . . Take Hannah by the hand and lead the way."

Clouds of uncertainties hung heavy. Neither Hannah nor Walt knew where to go next. He took the lead.

"Tell me about Phillip."

"Give me a minute."

Walt put his hand on her shoulder.

"He is no longer with me."

"I am truly sorry."

"That Vietnam War ruined so many lives. Phillip was such a good person. He fought bravely as a soldier, but his battles were just beginning when he was injured. That man struggled with his career. My husband was never without pain, and the doctors repeatedly ramped up his medications. I cannot say for sure what was the cause and what was the effect, but he grew more and more depressed. God, I hope we learned our lesson and stay out of war."

She paused for several deep breaths.

"I did everything I could for him, but it was not enough. I came home from school one day and found a note on the door. It instructed me not to come inside, but rather to go next door and call the police. I knew what they would find."

Hannah wept. Walt's tear ducts commiserated.

"Phillip left me another note on the dining room table. He said that he did not want me to find his body and the empty pill bottles. See—he was looking out for me to the end."

Walt felt certain more was in that note, but it was not his place to pry. Audible utterances were not always necessary. As these two had experienced decades earlier, an intangible connection joined them across which there was a free flow.

"Walt . . . Yes-sie potty."

"You know where the bathroom is."

"Okay."

Of course, he knew where the bathroom was. He just wanted to impress everyone with his new language tool.

"Which one will you tell me about first, your son or your daughter?"

"I guess I need to take things in order."

Walt described to Hannah how Tonya had found him after years of searching.

"So—her mother was the little redheaded nurse."

He then told Hannah about the time Michelle called him distraught, leading him to believe she had an abortion, and of how something never felt right about that.

"What a surprise that must have been. She looks so much like you. If she will allow, I look forward to getting to know her."

Walt then shared the circumstances of Jesse's birth.

"Walt Williamson . . . What an incredible life you have had. Or I should say, are having."

He looked at his watch as Tonya bounded out the front door.

"I thought you guys would have everything ready."

"We got a little distracted."

Hannah said it was the best salmon she ever tasted. The two old sourdoughs told her it would have been even better straight from the river. Tonya took delight in telling the Sin Infidel tale. Hannah simultaneously rolled her eyes and shook her head as she looked at Walt. When she left, he had no notion of when he would see her again. The adults in the room went to bed that night with more to digest than just the food.

Tom came by the bookstore just before closing time and wondered if she had Labor Day plans. He reminded Tonya of her pledge to get his copy of Walt's book signed. She had not been able to see that far out, but a little Bizzy Belle plan began to form in her mind.

She almost broke things off earlier. Instead, she held things together to get her dad's take. Indicators were pointing toward the Chosen Frozen sermon as a defining moment in Tom's life. Immediately thereafter, he seemed excited about resolving his nagging self-doubts, but he soon began to regress into his same old self-defeating patterns. Tonya was weary of being his sounding board, only to see him give little heed to her supportive gestures.

Walt and Hannah had to back off and cool their jets. On Wednesday of the following week, he received a note from her in the mail. She was reassuringly proud of him and wished him well raising his son. His longtime friend also thanked him for his love and support. The L word knocked him a bit off-center.

Like a kid at Christmas

"Dad . . . There's something else I want to talk to you about while you're here. Actually, two things and they're connected. First, I was awarded an academic scholarship for my senior year. It isn't huge, but it will cover my tuition."

"That's wonderful. Congratulations!"

"The second is about my computer situation. I'm enjoying the one Bekka gave me, but the word processor has limited editing capabilities. Do you know anything about the Internet? It boggles my mind how much information is out there in cyberspace. They say what's available now is but a drop in the proverbial bucket compared to where it's headed. I could really use this tool when doing research."

Walt was not sure where this was going but certain that Tonya did.

"Then, there's something called email. That's short for electronic mail. I need to buy a new computer to take advantage of this amazing technology. We can go shopping while you're here. I want you to listen in as the geeks describe what it can do."

Walt shrugged.

"I've saved the best part for last. I want you to take my little laptop home with you and start using it."

Walt tagged along to the computer store, but he suspected Jesse was absorbing more than he was. Tonya was like a kid at Christmas unpacking and setting up her new electronic toy. She transferred her files to it and handed over the old notebook.

"I appreciate you paying the utilities, but I want to put you on notice. Look for a bump in the phone bill. I'll have to place an order for a dial-up Internet connection."

"I think I can afford that."

"This old laptop can handle the Internet, too, but it will be slow. You can watch me set mine up and get online when you get back. Our computers can then communicate with each other."

"If you say so."

Tomfoolery

The first Monday in September came early in 2001. Labor Day was on the third. Tonya invited the gang, including Hannah and Tom, for a picnic at the base of a waterfall not too far from where she grew up. The weather was still warm enough for short sleeves, but she lugged along a tattered old sweatshirt. Still perceptible on the front, was the image of that very waterfall.

Walt sat amused as his grown girl shared with the others about the time she confiscated her daddy's shirt when but a toddler, not knowing it was his. He smiled with pride when she told them about dragging it along since.

"Watt was always my best friend, and I could talk to him about anything. I never knew why I called the shirt what I did until I finally got around to asking my mother. She said when she pointed to the picture on the front and said, 'waterfall,' I then said, 'Watt.' I told my dad that he should write a book about security blankets, and use his own daughter as the poster child."

The youngest member of the party was paying attention. Jesse walked over to Tonya, took the shirt from her hands, and wrapped his arms around it.

"My Watt."

"Little Bro . . . I would give you the shirt off my back, but you can't have Watt. I'm servicing notice right here and now that he's to be buried with me."

Jesse surrendered it back to his big sister and puckered up his little lips.

Hannah brought most of the food for the picnic—in the same basket she and Walt had used on their yesteryear outings. Both were stumbling along in their separate reminiscences.

Tom felt out of place. His only connection to the group was with Tonya, and it was coming unraveled. Walt tried to draw him into the conversation but with little success.

Tonya had ridden with Tom. Not long after lunch, he pulled her off to the side and asked if she was ready to go. She shot him a bewildered look before answering.

"We haven't cut the watermelon, yet. But if you need to skedaddle, I can squeeze in with the others."

"Wa-wa-ma-yon" was a first for Jesse. When he put his spoon down, he was wearing about as much red juice on the outside of his tummy, as he had managed to get down the hatch.

On the way back, Tonya called out to the two passengers in the front.

"Okay, you professional counselors . . . What's your verdict on Tom?"

Hannah yielded to the father.

"I didn't see anything different from what you had already told me."

"What about you, Hannah? What was your first impression?"

"Actually, my last impression is the one that matters most. I was listening to you but watching Tom when you were talking about Watt. Your self-deprecating humor made him uncomfortable. That says a lot about a person. When he cut out early, I think he conveyed everything you need to know."

"You mean you think it's over?"

"You can stick a fork in it—unless you're a glutton for punishment."

Walt pointed out something else.

"Tonya . . . Sometimes, just being who you are is a threat to other people. Let me guess. That was not the first time you laughed at yourself. More specifically, you also tried to get Tom to lighten up and not to take himself so seriously. People, who need the endorsement of others, cannot let their foibles show for fear of disapproval."

"You are so right. I cannot imagine living in such an emotional straitjacket that I can't make sport when I do something stupid. This became a sore spot in our relationship. You know me. The harder he whitewashed his idiosyncrasies, the more I needled him."

Those in the front seat thought the conversation was over, but the adult in the back was not finished.

"Lordy mercy. If I'd listened to my mother, I would go around today hanging my head in shame. She never let me forget that I ruined her life. I have no doubt that if she had found out she was pregnant early enough, she would have gone through with the abortion."

"Did you know Hannah was adopted?"

"No—you never mentioned that."

"Only, her adoption was not a big family secret. They told her when she was quite young."

"Hmm . . . My head is spinning. What impact did that have? Did you feel abandoned by your birth mother?"

"My adoptive parents were wonderful. As I grew older and started asking questions, they never discouraged me from trying to find my natural mother, but I had no real desire to do so. I gave her the benefit of all doubts and presumed that she gave me up so I could have a better life than what she could have provided. I grew to see it as an act of love. Whether true or not, I also believed that my biological father knew nothing about me."

Jesse filled the empty spaces when she paused. After Tonya tickled both his tummy and his fantasy, he picked up one of his books, and Hannah continued.

"I had a friend in school who was also adopted, but it did not work out so well. His mother never let him forget that his birth mom did not want him. She, on the other hand, was the glowing goddess who rescued him from the garbage heap."

"How did he handle it?"

"I still see them occasionally. I suppose, she will always be the dog, and he will never stop being the tail that she wags."

"Did you call her a bit __?"

"Are you certain your daddy didn't raise you?"

Walt's daughter wrapped her arms around the old sweatshirt and burst into a big smile.

"He was there all right. I just knew him by another name."

Tom did not get his book autographed by the author.

> *Baby—we went on a picnic today to a beautiful waterfall. I wish you could have seen little Jess working his way through some wa-wa-ma-yon. When we went wading in the creek, he announced with some conviction. "Yes-sie feet cold." He and I also went through an important rite of passage. You would have laughed at father and son peeing in the creek.*
>
> *Hannah was there, too, and spoke of the day she met you with such respect and warmth. She is a widow now. Her Phillip carried his burden for as long as he could, and he had to lay it down. I think Tonya and Tom broke up. I was just thinking about something. I'm so glad I didn't get cold feet when you asked me to marry you.*

You'd better take a look at this

Walt and Hannah had only scratched the surface, and he wanted to know more about her plans for the future. She came over the following Saturday for another meeting of the minds, so to speak, just a couple of days before he and Jesse were leaving to go back to Alaska.

"Walt . . . I honestly don't know what's ahead. Taking this year off is about far more than just a time to heal after Phillip's death. I'm in professional burnout. When we were in graduate school, the thought of helping to guide and steer young minds was a basic part of my idealism. I'm now a full-fledged realist."

Walt sat tight not wishing to interrupt the flow.

"When I moved up from being an elementary school counselor to junior high, I thought for certain I had found my niche. Students have changed. Parents have changed. Do you know what the number one guideline is now that I have to follow?"

Walt was detached from the environment she worked in and shook his head.

"I have to fashion everything I do or say around not offending parents. The school lives in perpetual dread of bad publicity and even lawsuits. With no fear of consequences, kids have free rein to do what they please. They grow up with little concept of respect for authority and do not know how to set their own personal boundaries. I doubt that many of them even know what self-respect is."

"Wow! That's incredible."

"I'm not sure I can go back. I so much admire how you laid it all down and walked away, but I don't know how else I can support myself. Fortunately, I have no debt to speak of, and I do have a small nest egg that we managed to scrape together. If I could find a way to pay for what I eat and cover my taxes and utility bills, I would never again sit across the desk from a sullen student or a surly parent."

Walt was a man. Men want to fix things. In this, though, he knew Hannah just needed a listening ear. He also believed that she had, within herself, the wherewithal to go forward in the next stage of her life—although she might need a little nudge.

"Thank you for sharing this with me. I am your friend. You'll never have reason to doubt that. Let's please stay in touch. Ma Bell's reach extends all the way across the continent. Maybe you can come up and visit us sometime."

"At this moment, that sounds like heaven."

Spending time with Tonya and unexpectedly reconnecting with Hannah, had made the trip worth all the effort. Jesse was a trooper. Walt was thrilled with how he had navigated through all the challenges with nary a whimper.

Because of her Tuesday afternoon schedule, Tonya was unable to take her father and brother back to Atlanta. She would rather deposit them at the Asheville Airport for another never-ending day.

On Monday night, they celebrated with a halibut casserole made with Walt's secret recipe. Tonya could enjoy the leftovers for several days. The cooler would fly back to Alaska without any frozen contents, but she had several more awaiting meals from the Alaska fish it brought her way. It would cradle some smaller paintings that Jess had helped with.

Tonya wondered aloud if they should check with the airline to make sure everything was on schedule. Walt said that in his many travels, he had never missed a flight and had experienced few delays. What could possibly go wrong?

When he came back inside from loading the last piece of luggage, Tonya approached him with a look on her face that he had never seen.

"You'd better come and take a look at this."

The television was playing in the background when a news bulletin had grabbed Tonya's attention. Reports were just coming in, but indications were that a plane had struck one of the World Trade Center Towers in New York. Before he had a chance to comment, Tonya said she did not have a good feeling about the situation.

With some extra time built in, they stayed glued to the TV. A second airliner hit the other tower, and cameras were streaming the fires raging on the upper floors of both. Walt dialed the airline's toll-free number and got a busy signal.

"Daddy . . . I don't think you're going anywhere today."

When the phone rang, they both jumped.

"Gus . . . Don't do that."

Hannah was on the other end inquiring if they had already left.

"Walt . . . I'm frightened. May I come over? I don't want to be alone."

She arrived just before the first tower collapsed. A few minutes later, both lay in rubble. Unsure what to do, and still unable to get a call through, the scene on the screen shifted to a reporter announcing that the Pentagon had also been hit. It was hard to keep up with the fast-paced coverage when a commentator reached for a news bulletin.

"I've just been handed this. Until further notice, all commercial flights are grounded."

Tonya was right on all counts. She was not going anywhere, either. Classes were canceled, and the campus was in lock down.

It was hard to sit still, but even more difficult to walk away. The concerned father was not sure what Jesse was hearing and absorbing. The boy certainly understood the airplane terminology, and he knew their schedule had changed. He did not want his son traumatized and took him on another walk into the woods.

The animals of the forest were carrying on as though nothing was unusual about their day. The trees stood stately and whispered gentle choruses as the breezes tickled their branches. A squirrel scampered up a tree. When Jesse tried to say the word, it sounded more like "whirl."

Birds were in trees all along the trail both seeking recognition and eager to show off their musical talents. Jesse focused more on their colors than their songs.

> Son . . . The world has changed today. You will always remember where you were this morning. As history is written, this day will be one of those big ones. Some bad dudes are out there in the world, and they do mean things. When you study in school what happened on September 11, 2001, I want you to think about where we are right now. People might do crazy things that disrupt our lives, but they cannot destroy the peace in our hearts.

"Yes-sie wuv uh, Walt."

When they returned to the house, news coverage was focusing on a crashed aircraft in a Pennsylvania field. Cell phone calls from those aboard indicted the plane was taken down by passengers who overcame the hijacker's, aiming it at another target in D.C., possibly the White House.

Back in New York, estimates of casualties were staggering, with a number of first responders among them. No one was sure who made the observation first, but the reporters were making note of the significance of the numerical representation of September 11. The emergency number 911 was already being indelibly imprinted into the psyches of people all over the world.

Walt, Jesse, Tonya, and Hannah were all processing what was happening in their separate ways. Meanwhile, their bodies kept bumping into each other without always bouncing off.

Hannah asked if she could run home, get a few things, and then come back and spend the night. Her request included the offer to sleep on the sofa in the basement.

She came back with a hot pizza. This was yet another new delicacy for Jesse.

"Dad . . . You guys surely do live a sheltered life."

"And if I ever get my son back to Alaska, it will stay that way."

Jesse learned a new word and how it could be linked to another that he already knew—first responder.

Nobody had to tell Jesse when it was nightie-night-time. Walt had always made it a happy space. When sleep started overcoming him, the little lad put on his pajamas and asked for a bedtime story. Tonya had the honor, and he was asleep before she got to the end.

Walt went downstairs to stay nearby just in case the boy had any sleep difficulties from the day's startling events. Abruptly, something registered with Tonya. Dr. TDH had not called to check on her.

"Hannah . . . You nailed it. As the Brits say, it was done and dusted when he drove away from the waterfall picnic."

Damn, woman

Once Jesse was down, Hannah asked Tonya if she was okay. After a nod in the affirmative, the professional counselor reminded her that she would be on the sofa right underneath if she needed anything. Hannah then said goodnight and made her way down the stairs.

"Walt . . . How long has it been since I was last in this basement with you? I remember so well the time we watched the lunar landing on that old black and white TV."

"I was concerned that we would wake up Mrs. Neumann. That woman was such a dear—taking me in as she did. Leaving this house to me, came as a complete surprise."

"Sometimes our families are chosen for us. At others, we pick our own. Mrs. Neumann had no children, and you were like a son to her. It was only natural that she left everything to you."

"Isn't it amazing how my daughter followed a similar pattern? Mrs. Thornhill became the mother she never had. Miss Bizzy Belle would not be where she is today if not for her Cornfield."

"Now, back to that historic moonwalk—I think it was in 1969. You invited me to spend the night. You'll never know how much I wanted to, but . . ."

"Stop right there. I didn't think I could respect you any more than I already did, but my regard for you skyrocketed when you remained faithful to your husband in Vietnam."

"Just so you know. 'Skyrocketed' didn't go over my head. Now, let me make this perfectly clear. I'll sleep down here tonight, but the outcome will be the same. You're raising another woman's child, and you're still very much in love with her."

"Damn, woman . . . You did it again. Just so *you* know. If you have nightmares, you're on your own."

By the time everyone came crawling out the next morning, the hijackers had been identified from passenger manifests. Few bodies were recoverable, and estimates of casualties were in the thousands. Tensions were ramping up all over the country, and no one knew for sure if other acts of terrorism might follow. Walt would not let the television run continuously.

Around the breakfast table, he asked Hannah if she had a computer. She informed him that she had purchased one to use with her school work and was online to send things back and forth to her office. Walt expressed his ignorance about how it all works, and she offered to give him a lesson or two.

"I appreciate so much you letting me stay here last night, but I must get home today. Would you like to follow me? I'd be happy to show you what little I know."

Tonya had learned that the university was still closed, but the campus bookstore would open at noon. It was a busy time for purchasing textbooks. She offered to keep Jesse until Walt returned.

As his daddy approached him to explain what was happening, his son looked up indifferently.

"Bye . . . Walt."

Walt had only been to Hannah's house once—more than three decades earlier when they were working on a graduate school project together. He had not forgotten how disconcerting it was seeing a wedding picture and a photo of her husband in uniform.

The place was more beckoning this time. As they entered the spare bedroom converted to an office, he took note of a diploma hanging on the wall.

"You didn't tell me you had gotten your doctorate. Congratulations."

"I kept renewing my certification, and when the university added the program, I had already completed a good portion of the work. I guess I also needed a new challenge and something to take my mind off other things. The school system pressured me to go into administration, but I just couldn't see myself as a school principal or office bureaucrat. Now that I have the degree, I'm not sure what I'll ever do with it."

Walt responded in jest.

"I guess you could always become a consultant."

"At the moment, I'm a computer whiz. My humble and unenlightened student, let's get with the program."

Hannah walked Walt through search engines and showed him how email works.

"That's fascinating. You mean I could type you a message and just like zip, it would show up on your computer screen?"

"All kinds of other documents can also be attached. Printers now have scanners. Photos can be converted and emailed. Have you heard of digital cameras? Pictures from them go directly into the computer without being developed. They can also be sent along the information superhighway."

"Wow! That's amazing."

Keep me posted

When Walt returned home, Watt was face up, and Tonya was painting the waterfall. Jesse had on one of Mrs. Neumann's old aprons and was grasping a brush. He showed his daddy that he could paint, too. It mattered not that his sister smoothed out the dabs and blended them in.

"I've got to take a photo of this."

Walt tried again to reach Delta. After a twenty-minute wait, he finally got through to an agent. He told her there was no urgency in rescheduling his flights and to give priority to those in a bind. She reassured him that no additional charge would apply when he rebooked.

"Tonya . . . You're stuck with us for a few more days."

"I think I can handle that, but don't expect me to be your obedient servant."

Hannah had asked him to keep her informed about travel plans and even offered to get them to the airport if the departure conflicted with Tonya's schedule. She said she would also take them to Atlanta, if necessary, and combine it with a shopping trip.

Walt was appreciative of the offer and took her up on it. Tonya was saying her goodbyes as Hannah came into the drive. Jesse took over the back seat, set up shop, and proceeded to entertain himself. Not far down the road, Hannah turned to Walt.

"You said something at my house that I just brushed off at the time as your genius for being clever. Remember when you jokingly said I might become a consultant? I think you might be onto something."

"How so?"

"The people out in the workaday world can't do anything without someone holding their hands and walking them through things. How-to books are bestsellers. You might want to consider getting one of those computer guides for idiots and dummies."

"You certainly have me pegged, and you can hold my hand anytime you want to."

"Oh, hush. You make me blush."

"Glad to know I haven't lost it. Now, tell me more about this consultant thing."

"At the start of every school year, motivational speakers are brought in supposedly to inspire the faculty. They are more entertainers than anything else. I've seen the budget, and these folks make big bucks."

"Hannah . . . With your good looks, charm, and brains, you could blow any audience away."

"I'm not sure that's the way I want to go. I'm thinking more about setting up a consulting business to help schools revitalize their counseling programs. In small towns, and especially in rural areas, many systems are not yet using computers. They're doing things the same old ways and are overwhelmed with all the paperwork now required. I doubt that needful students are getting much help from the staffs."

"Dr. Hannah Parker, Professional Counseling Consultant—That has a nice ring to it. How would you market yourself?"

"I could start by placing ads in educational journals."

"Keep me posted."

Neither spoke, but both were dreading the curbside drop off. After the baggage was unloaded and put on the sidewalk, the youngest passenger had something to say.

"Yes-sie hug Hannah."

"Walt hug Hannah, too."

Everything else was left unsaid.

The first thing Walt noticed when he went inside the terminal was generalized uneasiness, unlike anything he had ever felt before in an airport. He had to deal with his own anxieties about flying after 9-11, but Jesse seemed unaffected.

The newer aircraft they boarded had technologically updated monitors at each seat. He pulled up the screen that followed the plane's flight path and showed it to his son.

"This is like a globe. We can see where we are and how much farther we have to go."

Jesse played with the controls and found a cartoon channel. His daddy rested better with the boy preoccupied. Walt tried to find a movie to occupy his mind, but nothing appealed to him. He was never more relieved than when the big bird finally landed.

A card-carrying member of the digital age

With the daylight hours growing shorter, Mr. and Ms. Robin packed up and left for their winter home. Walt's office sported a new multifunction printer, and he spent hours scanning his voluminous albums of photographs. He got his email set up with only two calls for technical support—one to Tonya and the other to Hannah. The computer went online just in time to receive two electronic greeting cards for his fifty-fifth birthday. Jesse loved the animations.

Tonya exchanged messages with him about once a week. Hannah's came less often. He shared the appropriate parts with his son, taking license to embellish. When the computer was booting up, Jesse came running to help his dad check for email.

Walt was wary of traditions that might generate expectations, but he consented to spend Christmas again in Seattle. Dave showed off his new computer, but Alice indicated she wanted no part of it. That would soon change. On Christmas Eve, Walt's father-in-law suggested they stretch their legs.

"We try not to go overboard with gift-giving. Well, maybe I try a little harder than Alice does. That said, there's a present under the tree, with your name on it, that goes well beyond what we normally spend. Please understand that the present carries with it, a not so subtle hidden agenda. We might actually benefit more from it than you do. You'll see."

After Jesse had opened several gifts, he helped rip the paper off one with his daddy's name on it. The box displayed the picture of a digital camera. Dave winked at the father of his grandson.

Once the batteries and memory card were installed, the first photo snapped was of Jesse sitting between Ice and the Ice Man. When the little man saw the image in the viewfinder, he pushed the camera to his grandfather.

"Yes-sie 'n Walt."

Later that afternoon, with Walt looking over Dave's shoulder, each image streaked across cyberspace to Tonya's computer. Walt Williamson was a camera card-carrying member of the digital age.

Dearest Ginny . . . The world just keeps changing so fast. Jesse and I cannot get on an airplane without going through checkpoints and security gates. People don't stop and chat much anymore. Rumors are flying that we might be in another war soon. I want our son to grow up in a safe place. Speaking of the little guy, he is taking to the computer. Pretty soon, he will be giving me lessons. He is already snapping pictures with the digital camera and runs to the computer to see them on the monitor.

What are the odds?

Tonya did not see the emails with photos attached for the next couple of days. She was spending Christmas again with Earl and Mary Beth. The retired teacher showed interest in the college senior's plans after graduation.

"My advisors insisted that I not just major in art. They reminded me that 'starving artists' is axiomatic. My degree will be in art education with a minor in English. Maybe I could get a job teaching one or the other."

"I've been retired for several years, but I still know people in this town. If you have any interest in locating here, I might be able to get your application on the right desk."

That was not her only job help offer. Tonya and Hannah were becoming close friends, and the former school counselor pledged her full support.

Over dinner one evening, and after two rounds of Sin, they were reflecting on their unusual connection. Tonya framed it.

"What are the odds of a man's first love and his love child being best buds?"

Yes-sie promise

Walt was still familiarizing himself with his computer's word processor and kept discovering things it could do. He liked the thesaurus and found spell check especially helpful.

"Othell . . . My grade point average would have gone up a notch if I had this contraption in college."

Jesse was preoccupied, but when Walt put the computer to sleep, the house was quiet. He called out to him and got no answer.

It had been some time since the boy had ducked into one of the several nooks and crannies throughout the house and made a game of hiding until his daddy found him. Walt became increasingly apprehensive when he did not locate his son in any of the spots he remembered.

After going outside and circling the house, he looked up and down the road. He did not want to go off and leave Jesse if he was inside holed up somewhere. In that event, the boy would not utter a sound until found. If the almost three-year-old had wandered off, he had to find him.

"Jesse! Jesse!"

Frantic was on the verge of becoming panic when the tyke came walking out of the forest behind the house, tapping the ground with the little hiking stick his daddy had made for him. Trying not to show alarm, the father spoke softly to his son.

"Jesse . . . Where have you been?"

"Walt busy . . . Yes-sie go hike."

Emotions from every reach of his daddy's being were vying for recognition. Calmness won out.

Walt had to address his son's action, but the last thing he wanted was to strike fear into the boy's pure little heart. Enough of that was going around since 9-11. The father strived to teach his son to appreciate nature, to respect wildlife, and while at the same time, to recognize danger. The learning curve was ongoing and needed some work.

"What did you see in the forest?"

Jesse answered with a shrug.

"Did you see trees?"

"Yeth."

"Did you see birds?"

He nodded.

The next four questions were answered with a compacted quivering head shake.

"Did you see a bear?"

"Did you see a caribou?"

"Did you see a wolf?"

"Did you see an eagle?"

"What else did you see?"

"Moose."

"A moose! Did you see a moose?"

"Yeth."

"Did the moose run away?"

"No."

"What did you do?"

"Yes-sie say, 'Hello, moose'."

"Then, what did you do?"

"Go home . . . Get camera."

Struggling to control his body language, Walt looked impassively into his son's innocent eyes.

"The moose was also out for a hike. It has moved on now. You can take its picture the next time it comes into the yard."

"Okay."

Right before bedtime, the father-son talk continued.

"Jesse . . . I was worried about you today when I could not find you. Please make Daddy a promise. Always let me know where you are. You cannot walk away from me when we're in a store. And you can't go outside to play without telling me first. Do you understand?"

"Yes-sie promise."

Ginny . . . He's yours. Of that, there is no doubt.

Plans change

Hannah moved forward with setting up a consulting business. Her aim was to have some sessions scheduled during the upcoming school year. Meanwhile, Tonya was hurdling toward college graduation. The ceremony was slated for the same weekend as her birthday, and the best part was that her father and brother were arriving in time.

Plans change. Walt called and informed her that their flight was overbooked. They were bumped and would arrive a day late.

Hannah begged off. She said her graduation dues were all paid up. Furthermore, she was babysitting so a close friend could go. Tonya muffled her disappointment that nobody would be present for this major milestone in her life. Hannah offered one consolation.

"I don't want you to have to celebrate your birthday alone. Come by here after you discard your cap and gown, and I'll take you out to eat. You should be here by five. With all the folks in town, I'll go ahead and make a reservation."

Hannah greeted Tonya with a big smile.

"Congratulations, college graduate . . . And Happy Birthday. Now let's go party."

When Mrs. Parker gave her name at the restaurant desk, the attendant took a second look. The hostess mentioned that they had to open up the banquet room because of the overflow crowd, and she led them to it. The door opened to applause and cheers. Tonya was well-represented when handed her sheepskin after all.

"Hannah . . . How did you pull this off?"

"The flight schedule was the tricky part. There was no overbooking. You've met your father's chaplain friend in Asheville. He's also my old graduate school classmate. Eli met the plane, and Walt and Jesse stayed overnight with him. Your Grandmother Connie is bunking with me.

"I tried to get a room for Earl and Mary Beth, but there were no vacancies because of the university graduation. I finally found a B & B about twenty miles out that could put them up for two nights. And that babysitting I mentioned? That was with your little brother."

Each guest at the roundtable was a distinctive part of a peerless patchwork. One common thread connected them all. After the plates were left with nothing but scraps, that strand rose to his feet.

"Now . . . For the real reason, we're all gathered here . . ."

On that cue, a waiter and a waitress appeared from the kitchen each with a birthday cake in hand. Walt raised one of his own in a toast.

"Here's to my brilliant daughter, Tonya, and to my wonderful son, Jesse."

Mary Beth broke out in song, and others joined in. The little boy took the fingers of his left hand and helped arrange those on his right. When it suited him, he held up three fingers. While no one was watching, Earl picked up the tab.

Walt's uncle had been picking at Jesse since they first met. It continued after they went back to the house. When he was introduced to the boy as Earl King, Jesse skipped right over the first name and dubbed his great-uncle, "King." He also came up a syllable short with his great-aunt and called her, "May Beth."

"Go home with us. When your daddy was a kid, he used to come visit, and I let him drive my tractor."

"Okay."

"Jesse . . . You mean you'd go off and leave your daddy?"

"Little brother . . . You just got here. Would you take off and leave Sissy?"

"Yeth—go home with King. Drive tractor."

"Son . . . I won't be able to come get you when you decide you're ready. Sissy has to go to work, and I can't leave her without a car."

Hannah was no help.

"Tonya can stay with me while you're gone. I'll run a taxi service."

"Are you two ganging up on me?"

"Walt . . . You are so toast."

The father decided it was time to call the boy's bluff.

"Let's go pack your bag."

Jesse bounded down the stairs, opened the dresser drawer, and started throwing clothes on the bed. Abruptly, his enthusiasm took a timeout. With a solemn look on his face, he pointed to his mother's picture.

"Mama stay with Daddy."

Tonya had decided that the cost of a child restraint was likely less than that of a fine. She had already installed it in Brusky, but took it out and fitted it into the King's car. Jesse crawled in the back seat and reached for the seatbelt buckle.

"What? No hug?"

"Bye, Daddy. Bye, Sissy."

MPD . . . Since the day I brought Jesse home from the hospital, this is the first night I am spending without him. I think he knew it was not going to be easy for me. That's why he left your picture here so I would not be alone. And one more thing. For the first time in several months, he called me Daddy.

With degree in hand, Tonya was working more hours at the bookstore. All day Monday, home alone Walt felt like a lost puppy and resisted urges to call and check on his son. On Tuesday evening when he was about to give in, Gus jumped the gun. Tonya answered as she was coming in the door. He heard her say hello to Mary Beth and went for the phone, but she waved him off.

Impatiently, Walt paced. He could tell his aunt was filling Tonya in about what they had been doing. She ended the call and turned to him.

"Mary Beth said they were having so much fun with Jesse and reminiscing about when you were that age, ugh, half a century ago."

"Did Jesse want to talk to me?"

"No . . . He said to tell you hi, and that he got to ride on a tractor."

Taking bullying by the horns

Moments later, Gus intruded again. This time, the phone was handed to Walt, but it was a local call.

"I've been thinking about something, and I want to run it through you. Can you join me for lunch tomorrow? I'll fix a little something here. Although it's been over a year now, I'm just not yet ready to be seen in public with another man. You know how small towns are."

"Sure, Hannah. I'll drive Tonya to work."

"See you around noonish."

Walt was more relaxed going to Hannah's house this time, and she was more like her old self. The widower and the widow woman gravitated back and forth between resuming the playfulness of the past before retreating back into the separate sorrow each was still stuck in. Hannah framed it.

"You know what you are, Walt Williamson? You're a preexisting condition—and I don't have any coverage for that."

After savoring chicken and fruit salads, she was ready to get started. First, an editorial comment.

"Thank you again for that off the cuff remark about me becoming a consultant. That's something about you most people don't appreciate. Your misdirection is often more thought-provoking than straightforward advice. Both in your humor and irony, a seed is often embedded. Even in your insufferable sarcasm, there's usually a kernel of annoying truth. I've always wondered if this was the universe somehow channeling through you, or if you knew what you were doing the entire time."

"Are you talking to me?"

"Somehow, I knew you were going to say that. Moving on. Now, here's what I've been thinking. Perhaps, I should specialize in something from my school counseling experiences. The topic that comes to mind first is bullying. It becomes a greater problem every year. Nobody seems to know how to deal with it."

"I'm listening."

"I'm all into victims' rights and don't blame the victim, but some kids might as well hang a sign around their necks that says, 'Don't look at me. I want to be invisible.' Open season for bullying is not demarcated by a calendar."

"I suspect that's equally true on the other side. The aggressors are exuding, 'Just look at me. I'm special. I'm mean and tough.' Think about that. Do you see the common denominator?"

"I guess not. That's why I invited you over."

"It's summed up in two words—identity voids. The bullies, whether male or female, are unsure of themselves. They feel inadequate and are trying to prove their worthiness in the eyes of the ones they are seeking to impress. Oppressors do this through the intimidation of the weak that generates fear.

"On the other side of the dynamic, the vulnerable ones are void of ego strength. This is not just about lacking the brute force to fight the bully and put the hurt on him. Those with a strong sense of who they are can put an aggressor in his place without lifting a finger."

"That makes so much sense. As always, you go right to the crux of the matter. It's not always that simple, though. Each incident is as individual as the persons involved. How can I incorporate this into workshop presentations? I know I must begin with helping identify the problem."

"Hannah . . . Throughout my experience, that's usually about as far as any plan or program ever gets. The issue is portrayed in glorified fashion, but no substantive measures are advanced to address it. It will not be easy for you, either."

"I know where you're going next. How can teachers do anything about bullying while on the one hand, they are seeking to validate significance through their noble professional standing in the community, and on the other, they need the approval of their students to make them feel good about themselves? Teachers are then bullied by parents not to get their little darlings in trouble. Administrators are bullied by the central office to keep them out of lawsuits and off the evening news."

"And then they all go to their homes at night where there are no pecking orders."

"There's your cynicism again."

"Are you talking to me?"

"Oh, hush. While you were making sport, I think we've hit the old proverbial nail right on the head. In my seminars, I'll build a strong case for pinpointing just how widespread the problem of bullying is. Might even write a book. I'll get an audience all riled up, collect my fee, and then tuck my tail and run."

"I'll look for you on the news when you become rich and famous."

A pee in the creek

Walt resisted the yearning to hear Jesse's voice on Wednesday evening, but it got the best of him Thursday morning. Mary Beth handed the receiver to his son.

"Hi, Jesse. Are you having fun?"

"Daddy . . . May Beth bought me oh'halls. King gave me green cap with deer on it. Today, he take me fishing."

"Are you ready to come home?"

A pause ensued as tiny wheels were spinning.

"No."

The matter was then taken out of the hands of the three-year-old when Earl got on the line.

"Why don't you come down Saturday and go to church with us on Sunday? You cannot even begin to imagine what it means to us having Jesse here. Since Mary Beth and I were not blessed with kids of our own, you were the closest thing to a child we ever had. Your sister never took a liking to us. Tonya has come into our lives and now your darling little son."

"I don't have any church clothes. I wouldn't want to embarrass the Chairman of the Board."

"Walt . . . This is the day of casual. You'll see folks dressed all kinds of ways. Mary Beth could always take you shopping—like she did when you were a tot. Stay with us a few days while you're here."

Walt told Tonya that if she wanted to go with him, they could go down to get Jesse on Sunday morning and come back that afternoon.

"Oh, no you don't. You're just trying to keep me from spending a few days with Hannah. Need I remind you, sir, that we live down here in the same town when you're up there in Alaska?"

Earl had inadvertently put another matter on Walt's not so empty plate. He had not spoken with his sister, Emma Lou, in years, and he wondered if the word had drifted down to her about his real mother finding him, signifying that they were not biological siblings. She would likely know nothing about Tonya, much less anything about Jesse.

Should he go by and see her? It was not that far out of the way.

The excruciating memories of Walt's so-called family exiling him resurfaced. He had no reason to believe the welcome mat would be out and decided just to leave her be—letting her live out her life under the auspices of the fantasy world that her family created for her.

King put a worm on the hook and told Jesse to keep his eye on the bobber. Nothing happened immediately, and the little boy's mind wandered, as did his eyes. Both came to full attention when he heard the words, "Fish on."

After two bluegills were on the stringer, Jesse informed his great-uncle that he needed to go to the bathroom. A big smile came across Earl King's face.

"Come with me."

As they stood on the footbridge crossing the stream that fed the lake, Earl told the young angler that his daddy peed in that very creek when he was a kid. Jesse whipped it out and started taking a whiz. The older man joined him, and they both grinned.

Earl warned him not to stand so close to the edge or lean too far, but the advice went unheeded. Jesse lost his balance, and into the creek, he went. The cold spring water was a shock to the boy's body, and he let out a howl that turned into a scream.

Earl first bundled him up and then told him that he would have to take his clothes off and let them dry in the sun. With not a modest bone in his body, he started peeling them off, and they headed back to the fishing hole.

"King take clothes off, too."

No one else was around, so the eighty-something-year-old man stripped down to his boxers. They had inadvertently turned the recreational area into a nudist colony.

When Walt entered the house, Jesse ran to him.

"I fell in the creek."

"You did? Did you catch any fish?"

"May Beth cooked them for us."

Nobody said anything about fishing apparel or lack thereof, but Walt made note of Jesse's current attire. Earl suggested that the boy tell his daddy what kind of overalls he was wearing.

"OshKosh B'gosh."

"I let my son go off with you for a week, and b'gosh, you've taught him how to cuss."

Jesse took his place between Earl and Mary Beth at church and kept glancing over at his daddy for a reaction. Two could play that game. Walt pretended the boy was not even there. When the sermon began, Jesse switched places and put his head in his daddy's lap. Neither would remember much of anything the preacher said while they were making faces.

It had been several years since Walt had put his feet under his aunt's table, and never with his son. He was not just being polite when he gave his compliments to both chefs.

"When are you guys coming to Alaska? Don't let the statute of limitations run out on the invitation."

"Walt . . . We've been giving that some thought. I would love to go the same way you first did, but I think I'm too old to drive an RV that far. When is a good time to come?"

"I love it all twelve months, but you might want to consider not showing up during the dead of winter."

Jesse chimed in.

"King and May Beth come to Alaska. See moose. See caribou. See eagle. See bears. Eat salmon."

"What we would want to see most is you—you little brat."

Jesse went home with three new prized possessions—a John Deere toy tractor, his King cap, and pair of OshKosh B'gosh overalls. His memory bank had also received some hefty deposits.

> **Jesse . . . Tomorrow we're going back to Alaska. Hannah will take us to the airport. It will be another long flight on the big airplane. We will have one stop where we can get off and stretch our legs. It will be in Seattle. Ice and the Ice Man will meet us there, but we cannot go home with them. We'll have to get back on another plane. Before we get to our house, the weather might be clear enough for us to see the mountains out our window all covered with snow.**

The little boy sat still and attentive. He had only a one-word response. "Okay."

A peck on the cheek

"Okay . . . Let's get this show on the road. Don't want you to miss your flight and be stuck with you again—and we do have a stop to make before we even get out of town."

Jesse was still asleep when Tonya left for work. He seemed to understand that he would not see his Sissy for sometime when she hugged him goodbye at the bookstore.

Walt was conflicted. He was ready to get back to Kenai, but he wanted the drive to Asheville to last as long as possible. Despite their best efforts, the conversation got stuck in the mundane. As Hannah was looking for a temporary parking space, he muttered.

"Curbside drop-offs are so brutal. I really miss family not being able to go to the gate."

The driver took note of the word family. Walt noticed that her hug was longer and tighter than normal. As she broke her embrace, she did something that she had never, ever done. She kissed him on the cheek.

Hannah then leaned down and said her goodbyes to Jesse. She straightened his King cap, drew him tight, pressed her face against his, and whispered in his ear. Walt could not hear what she was saying, but when she finished, the boy nodded.

Hello . . . Ginny. Our son is growing in leaps and bounds. He is certainly going to be tall like both of us. What amazes me most is how his personality is emerging. When I was a kid, except for my grandfathers, I pretty much had to figure things out for myself. Maybe I have been trying too hard to explain things to Jess. He's asserting his independence. More and more, he does not want me to know what's going on in his mind. While this keeps me on my toes, making sure he does not stray into danger, I do want him to think for himself. Wish you were here to help me keep him in check.

Brooding

The phone was no longer Walt's worthy adversary, and Jesse started assuming the role of receptionist. From the little boy's responses, it was not always easy to determine the person on the other end, nor to overcome his reluctance to surrender the receiver.

Tonya called about once a week and the Sullivans maybe twice per month. Walt also used email to stay in touch, especially if he had a photo to share. Plain Jane was not bashful about checking in and volunteering to keep Jesse, and he knew she could use the spending money.

Gus II intruded one evening right after Jesse had put himself down for the night. He bounded from his bed and raced his father to the phone. Walt conceded and had no clue who he was talking to. Eventually, he handed the phone to his daddy.

"Yes."

"Walt . . . I just wanted to hear your voice."

"Hi, Hannah. How are you?"

Winter finally dissolved into spring, and during the summer of 2002, Jesse was experiencing things likely to remain in his remembrance repository throughout his life. Wildlife sightings were times of excitement, and his eyes were almost as keen as his dad's.

Walt taught him to point, and simultaneously say aloud what he was seeing. Caribous from the resident herd and moose scattered throughout might pop up anywhere. Eagles consistently patrolled the mouth of the Kenai River. Jesse learned what a seagull was and that salmon came from the ocean and rivers. He knew his three Alaska bears from his book.

Mr. and Ms. Robin raised another brood. The ladybird especially enjoyed chattering with Jesse who mimicked her sounds. At the end of the season, he learned a new word—migrate. Walt had picked up another globe at a yard sale so he could have one in both houses. The boy's eyes got big when he saw how far the birds flew. The father also introduced his son to a calendar.

> Jesse . . . Each row is a week—seven days. Every page is a month. Today is September 1. The long summer days are getting shorter. Next, will come October, then November, and December when it gets cold and the sun does not shine for very long. Christmas is in December. Then, we will start a new year—January, February, March, and April. Your birthday is in May, and that's the month the robins will come back from their winter home.

"Daddy . . . We go see Ice and Ice Man Christmas?"

"I'm not sure, yet."

"I hope so."

Walt tried to remember the camera when he and Jess were going out. The collection of photographs uploaded to his computer was growing. Tonya taught him how to set up folders and organize them.

Like daughter, like father

The neophyte computer operator was surprised by how easily he could compose things without first writing them in longhand. Directly compiling email messages got him started. He then began chronicling father-son episodes and sharing them with folks in Ephesus and Seattle.

Since WOWs was being devoted to Ginny, Walt began separate journaling in his computer and addressed his entries to Othell, his alter ego. Periodically, he forwarded selected anecdotes. Hannah encouraged him to send more, and this stimulated him to keep writing. After receiving one poignant piece, she gave Gus II a jingle.

"Walt . . . Have you ever thought about submitting something like this to the local newspaper? You might be surprised. Readers love human interest stories, and don't forget, you are a published author."

"I don't know. Let me think about it."

"Tell you what. Send things to me first and let me edit them. Your content is fantastic, but your mechanics leave a lot to be desired. Let me tinker with this one and send it back."

Two mornings later, Walt approached the receptionist at the newspaper office. He handed her a printed copy with a brief resume and contact information. Later that afternoon, the phone rang. The editor requested that he return for a mug shot. She remembered him from the feature article they ran not long after Jesse was born.

"We're not budgeted to pay for guest editorials. If you would like to submit other things, just email them to me in an attachment."

When the paper came out with his article in it, Walt placed a call and shared the news with Tonya.

"Like daughter, like father."

"Oh, Dad . . . That's great."

After two more Hannah edited submissions, Walt received another call from the editor requesting that he drop by. Over coffee and while exchanging pleasantries, she made a proposal.

"As you know, a number of real characters live around here. Regrettably, the old-timers are slipping away, and many of their tales are dying with them. I've been thinking about a series of articles and calling it, 'Peninsula Pioneers' or something like that. Walt . . . You're such a natural storyteller. Would you consider interviewing some of them, and then compiling their profiles? I would want photographs, too. Of course, we would pay you for this."

"I find the possibilities of that intriguing. Would you give me the leads?"

"Yes . . . But I suspect once you get into it, you will follow your own."

Tonya got an email, Hannah received a phone call, and Mrs. McCain was paid a visit. All three were onboard. Jane's mother assured Walt that he could drop Jesse off anytime even if her daughter was not home.

"He and Nate play so well together, and I can sure use some time when my son is not under my feet."

Gin . . . Jesse has learned a new word. Actually, it has been in his vocabulary for some time, but he is just now finding all kinds of ways to use it to his advantage. The word is 'why.' No way will he accept trite or diversionary answers, so I have started answering a question with a question using other W words. 'What' is my favorite. He is thrown on the defensive trying to explain 'what' it is that he is asking 'why' about. I sometimes slip in 'who,' 'when' 'where,' and even 'how.' In most instances, I am then able to point out to him that he has just answered his own question. Not sure how long this strategy will work, but for now, getting glimpses of how his mind operates, is so fascinating. Okay, I know what you

*are about to say. He's figuring out
how mine works, too.*

Tonya was certified to teach English and art but did not actively pursue a position. Instead, she advertised to give private art lessons. One student attended a private academy, and this led to an offer to teach art two mornings a week at that school. With Hannah's encouragement, she also began work on her master's degree.

"You may not have an opportunity like this again with a university in your backyard, and you never know when the degree might come in handy."

Hannah's new business venture was off to a slow start, but by the time the academic year rolled around, three consulting seminars were set. She was also finding it difficult to keep Walt off her mind. The connection they shared years earlier was never severed, and the one obstacle that prevented them from going forward was removed.

Others now stood squarely in its place, and she feared they were insurmountable. They were on different wavelengths far more than he realized, but she was not ready to cut him out of her life without seeing where things might go if given a chance.

Walt had a question for his daughter.

"When you wrote feature stories about people for a newspaper, how did you approach the interviews?"

"Oh, I don't know. I guess I just figured out that when a listening ear shows up at somebody's house, most people like to talk about themselves. They were flattered that someone was interested in their lives. Once I gave them an opening, they usually just took off, and it was sometimes hard to keep up with them. I asked probing questions to the few who were more restrained."

"Like what?"

"The one that seemed to get them going best had to do with the moments in their lives when they could have gone one way or the other. You know— like the times when they were figuring out who they were and where they wanted to go. I sometimes phrased it, 'When did the lights come on?' With the folks you will be interviewing, you'll get some literal answers to that question."

"That's brilliant. Did I ever tell you that you are, too?"

"I can't remember it if you did. And there's one more thing that's so obvious that it's hardly worth mentioning. You just have to let these people be who they are. Tell the tales in their own words. Your biggest problem will be fitting the material into the column space allotted to you."

"Did Hannah mention that she is going to edit them for me?"

"Of course, she did. She probably does not want you to know how excited she is to do this for you. Dad . . . You and I are alike in so many ways, but I guess I did get a few things from my mom. I did learn how to spell."

"For certain, you know how to spell it out."

"I was about to forget something. I always encouraged the people I interviewed to make some kind of record of the character-building moments of their lives to hand down once they were gone.

"Most scoffed at the idea, so I suggested that perhaps they bring a grandchild in on the project and dictate memories that were especially poignant. I actually went shopping with one old codger, helped him pick out a cassette tape recorder, and showed him how to operate it. I wonder what happened to those tapes.

"And oh, by the way, Hannah and I were talking just yesterday about how you need to start working on your own memoirs. Neither of us thinks you have any concept of how out of the ordinary your life is, and how your own story might provide inspiration for others."

"So . . . You and Hannah are ganging up on me again."

"Walt Williamson—just know—two people down here in Ephesus, North Carolina care bunches about you and Jesse."

Mama Bear—Papa Bear—Baby Bears

"Jesse . . . Let's go berry picking."

The fall equinox had come and gone, and the days were getting progressively shorter. A supply of blueberries, raspberries, and salmonberries was already in the freezer. After the first frost, both high bush and low bush cranberries were ready for the picking.

Not far down the hiking trail, the father and son found what they came for. As they worked their way forward, the trail had a kink in it. Just as they rounded the curve, more berry pickers were out ahead. Walt grabbed Jesse, picked him up, and whispered in his ear.

"Bear—see the black bear? Look—she has two cubs."

"Bear—can I pet the bears?"

"No!"

Walt freed one hand and reached into his pocket for the pepper spray, just in case. Mama Bear raised her head and sniffed the air. Then, she turned toward the humans and let out an audible grunt. Instantly, the half-grown coal-black cubs were by her side. The threesome disappeared into the thicket. The twosome returned the way they had come.

When safely inside the Subaru, they had another father-son talk. One did all the talking and the other the listening.

> Jesse . . . Bears are so beautiful, but they are wild animals, and they can be dangerous. An old saying goes something like this. "Never get between a mama bear and her cubs." It doesn't matter whether you intend to harm them or not, she will see the intruder as a threat. It's always best to stop looking at the bear and turn around and walk the other way. You know what? I think that Mama Bear was just about as afraid of us as we were of her. She was not about to come between this old Papa Bear and his cub.

Sourdough Spice

Walt delved right into his newspaper assignment. His profiles began appearing in the Sunday paper in a section called "Sourdough Spice."

The first person he interviewed was a widow who came to Alaska with her husband just for the spirit of adventure. The woman had not only lost her husband in a truck accident but also her three children in a different sort of way. Her offspring moved on when they came of age, and they never looked back. She had no knowledge of where they were, or even if she had grandchildren. The vibrant pioneer, nevertheless, had no regrets.

In other sessions, Walt heard tales of nearly impassable roads that were little more than trails. The reporter got to see the ruins of primitive houses constructed from hand-hewn logs. He learned the meaning of homesteading, Alaska style.

Some of the pioneers were drawn to America's Last Frontier because of the lure of gold. Others came from the southwestern states as part of the fledgling oil industry when black gold was discovered on the peninsula.

A few, stationed on military bases, never left after they were discharged. Several had their own landing strips. One bush pilot took Walt up for a ride he would never forget.

The apprentice reporter did his interviews early in the week, shot drafts off to Hannah, and submitted them by the Friday deadline. He became increasingly more confident compiling on his computer straight from his notes.

Walt's appreciation for his two editors grew steadily. The one in North Carolina cleaned up his structural untidiness, and the other at the newspaper taught him how to write a more expressive narrative. Walt rarely received feedback directly from readers, but the folks at the paper said his features were well read.

"Unintended consequences" was a new expression making its rounds. Walt's avocation was inadvertently forging an on ongoing connection with Hannah through which neither was ever very far from the other's mind.

How did I do?

Walt knew a specific "why" question from Jesse was inevitable. It was not a matter of if, but only when. The widower father rehearsed how he might approach the natural curiosity of his three and a half-year-old, but he knew ultimately that he would have to wait and see what the specific question was. The "when" came one day after he picked up his boy at the babysitter.

"Daddy . . . Why does my mother not live with us like Nate's does?"

"Let's talk about that when we get home."

Walt went to the dresser and retrieved the picture of his son's mother.

> Jesse . . . Long before you were born, I met this wonderful woman named Ginny. We fell in love and got married. She was the most amazing wife, and I loved her with all my heart. We went camping together and took photographs of wildflowers. We went berry picking, too, and cooked our meals and washed our clothes. Ginny and I slept

together in our bedroom. Your mother and I talked about the time when we would have our own little boy named Jesse.

Son . . . Your mom was a nurse, but she did not just work in a hospital. She went all over Alaska taking care of people. To get there, she had to fly in an airplane. On her last trip, the plane flew into a storm, and the pilot was unable to find a place to land. She could not get back to me, so I am raising you without her. Your mother would be so proud of you.

"Is my mother dead?"

Walt was unprepared for that question. He was unaware that his son was familiar with the concept of death.

"Yes, Jesse—your mother's body is dead, but her spirit is here to help guide us."

"Oh . . ."

The time frame and specifics about his surrogate mother would have to wait until the boy was older. The next round would begin, not with "why," but "how." For the time being, this was as far as either was ready to go.

Hello, mother of our amazing child. How did I do?

Tonya!

"Hi, Dad. Got your turkey bought, yet?"

"Well, no. With just Jess and me here, I was not going all out this year."

"What if it were not just the two of you?"

"Are you saying what I think you are?"

"More. Could you handle two guests?"

"Are you bringing a man home to meet your father?"

"You wish. Maybe I do too, but that's not what I had in mind."

"I'm having trouble reading yours—so out with it."

"I think I could persuade Hannah to tag along with me if you were to invite her. I'd hate for her to have to spend Thanksgiving alone."

"Dad . . . Are you still there?"

"I'd love to show Alaska to Hannah, but early winter might not be the best time."

"Oh, Daddy . . . I'm reading your mind right now, and it has nothing to do with what season of the year it is."

"You know this house is small. I only have two bedrooms and . . ."

"No problem. I'll bunk with Jesse, and Hannah can sleep with you."

"Tonya!"

"Seriously, Dad. We can work out sleeping arrangements. Don't forget about the futon. Hannah said just yesterday how much she would love to see Jesse. She never mentioned you, though. Would it make any difference if I told you we had already booked our flights?"

"Tonya!"

"You'll have to meet us in Anchorage. Couldn't find any empty seats to Kenai this late. Anyway—why not let Hannah's first impressions be of that awesome drive? Have you had much snow?"

"The mountains have gotten a good coating but not a lot here. The roads shouldn't be a problem unless we get more. There's not been enough snow to cause any avalanche danger. What am I doing? I'm talking like this is actually going to happen. When are you going to tell me that you were just messing with me?"

"Daddy—go buy a turkey."

With the phone back in its cradle, the other resident had been put on hold long enough. He knew something was up and was waiting.

"Sissy?"

Walt had to make a call. Did he go ahead and tell Jesse, or wait until closer to Thanksgiving to keep his son's exuberance from boiling over?

"Jesse—go look on the desk and bring me the calendar."

He then pointed out what day it was and the day Sissy and Hannah would be arriving.

"Tell you what—let's take a pencil and mark off each day until they get here."

"Okay."

"Othell . . . You sure fell for that. You know—I'm not a slob, but neither am I a Martha Stewart clone. Just look at this house. It has not had a good cleaning in months, and company is coming in a week. What would Ginny think if another woman came in here with it looking like this?"

As Walt walked away from the conversation with Tonya, something about it did not ring true. He could not see Hannah agreeing to something like that without first discussing it with him. Even then, it would take some serious arm-twisting. Exactly when were those airline tickets purchased? Was he the only one in the dark?

Doing his chime thing again, Gus II interrupted the bewilderment. Not even a hint of doubt was in Walt's mind about who was on the other end.

"Walt . . . Thank you so much for inviting me to come to Alaska for Thanksgiving. I was hoping to spend it with Tonya, but when I found out she was going to see you guys, I started preparing myself. It was so thoughtful of you to anticipate that being alone would be a struggle. I would have never agreed to this if you had not already bought my ticket. I hope you know what you're doing."

"Hannah . . . As a matter of fact, I have no clue what I'm doing."

When Walt told her his side of the story, a simultaneous reaction zipped past each other at the speed of light somewhere along the transmission lines.

"Tonya!"

"Othell . . . Miss Bizzy Belle is—well—you know what I mean."

When Jane came to keep Jesse while Walt went to conduct an interview, he shared the Thanksgiving news with her. She offered to vacuum and dust while he was gone if he would point her in the right direction. Two cars were in the drive when he returned a couple hours later. The babysitter had called for a backup. Mrs. McCain was just finishing mopping the kitchen.

"Walt . . . You need to do something about those curtains. How long have they been hanging in this house?"

"I don't know. They were here when I first moved in."

"They are so dingy and saturated with candle smoke. Come on. Let's go into town and see what we can find. Jane will keep working in the bathroom. If you don't have a good tablecloth, you can borrow one of mine."

Walt had to admit that the house had a brighter look and a fresher smell. When he offered to pay extra for the babysitting, they blew him off. Mrs. McCain inquired if he needed any help with the cooking, but he assured her that he was waiting until the guests arrived. He did make an exception and prepared one dish ahead of time.

His concern about Jesse's excitement was misplaced. The boy was handling the daily countdown better than his father was. In the meantime, his admiration for his daughter's savvy only amplified.

Jesse was right in the middle of the grocery shopping. Walt explained how each item would be part of the much-anticipated meal. Tonya almost waited too late to spring her gambit. The Williamsons got the last frozen turkey in the rack.

My darling Ginny . . . Excitement is in the air. Our home is about to become the setting for a big Thanksgiving feast. Ground zero of my gratitude is for the time we had together. Because of you, my life is so much richer and fuller. I did not think I could go on living after you left me. Many sleepless nights, I wished I had been on that plane, too. Somehow, I kept fumbling my way through it.

Wow! How my life has changed since you've been gone! I have an amazing daughter, and we have a terrific son. Gratitude fills my heart.

MPD . . . It was not of my doing. Never-the-less, Hannah will be spending Thanksgiving with us. I'm so glad you got to meet her. Because of her, I was a better person when you came along. When I stand back and look at who she is, what she has accomplished, and especially what she has overcome, my eyes fill with tears. Wishing so much, you could be here to help make everyone feel welcome. I guess little Jess will have to stand in for you.

"Othell . . . My *over* is both *whelming* and *flowing*."

Welcome to Alaska

Light snow was falling when Cornfield headed toward Anchorage. Across the summit, the flakes were the size of quarters. Walt wondered if the road would be passable on the way back. With Radar as his primary wintry vehicle, he was negligent in getting studded tires for Tonya's Legacy. Since the roads were not icy, he could count on the four-wheel drive unless the buildup made it impossible to see the contour of the highway.

Jesse seemed lost in thought during the three-hour drive. Walt wondered what was going through the little boy's mind. Snowing had stopped as they drove down off the peninsula. The entourage would have only an hour or so of daylight once back on the road.

Walt breathed a sigh of relief when no delays had slowed them. He had withheld a surprise from Jesse if time allowed. Downtown, they joined a crowd gathering in anticipation.

"Look. Jesse—here comes Santa Claus with real live reindeer pulling his sled. Ho . . . Ho . . . Ho!"

He took the boy to an observation point near the airport, and they watched planes coming in and taking off. Most were either smaller commuter craft or supersized jets with familiar freight logos. Walt got a glimpse of an airliner as it banked in the distance.

"Jesse—that may be the one."

As the passenger plane was touching down, Cornfield pulled into a parking place near the terminal entrance. Two excited fellows headed toward baggage claim. The wait seemed endless for the boy, but eventually, weary travelers came strolling through the corridor. Walt picked his son up so he had a better vantage point.

Jesse bounded for his sister.

"Sissy! I saw Santa and real reindeer pulling his sled."

Walt reached for Hannah.

"Welcome to Alaska."

Rooms were not cheap in Anchorage any time of the year, so Walt decided to risk making the trek back to Kenai. Tonya crawled in back with her brother and gave Hannah the catbird's seat.

"Before we get home, you'll understand why I say you're not qualified to use the word *awesome* unless you've been to Alaska."

A few miles out of Anchorage, Walt steered the vehicle into a rest area. Doors flung open and snowballs started flying.

Not far down the road, the driver pulled in at Beluga Point. Walt shared with his longtime friend how it was at that very spot where he felt a strong kinship with Alaska on his first journey, and that he had never felt like a stranger or a tourist since. He did not mention that it was also one of the settings for his and Ginny's epic progressive wedding.

The headlights were reflecting on the vast whiteness when they reached the summit. The road had already been plowed, and Cornfield glided safely atop the thin snowpack. Sixteen hours after Eli had deposited the women at the Asheville Airport, the exhausted passengers arrived at their final destination.

"Walt . . . This is so quaint—not at all like I imagined—but I really had little to go on."

"It's nothing elaborate, but it does have all the comforts of home sweet home. According to your body clock, it's well beyond your bedtime. Did I mention cozy? Jesse is excited about sleeping on the futon. You'll have to fight Tonya for the cover in his room."

The host could hear giggling as the women unpacked some essentials and prepared for bed. Tonya came out in her pajamas and Hannah in a robe to say their good nights. Jesse was out like a light. Walt was wired.

"Good morning, sleepy head."

It was after midnight before Walt dozed off. Hannah had never experienced jet lag and was up four hours after he went to sleep. As he joined the others, the aroma of coffee filled the air. Tonya was cooking breakfast still in her PJs.

Jesse had taken possession of Hannah. Wisely, she had waited until morning to give him the Thanksgiving coloring book and a fresh box of crayons. They were sprawled out on the floor face painting the friendly American Indians.

Three gleeful persons were soon around the table. Tonya pulled the fourth off to the side.

"Relax, Dad. You're too uptight. Everything will be fine."

"This all happened so fast that . . ."

"It's not easy for Hannah, either. You have no idea what I went through to get her here."

Walt mimicked a grimace.

"Stop letting Ginny be the elephant in the room."

"But . . ."

"Get off your ifs, ands, and butts. Ginny would want you to be happy. Let her release you so you can move on. I'm not saying you and Hannah have a future together, but you do have a past. Just be yourself. Let's have some fun. See what happens. Did I tell you how much I love you?"

A hug rounded out the conversation. Later that morning when Tonya went to the bathroom, the picture of Ginny on the dresser had gone missing.

Walt and Hannah had agreed to keep Tonya out of the loop regarding their awareness of her ruse. They started making sport of it and then reading her smug satisfaction. This lightened the tension as the two old friends tiptoed around on the unfamiliar turf.

W'us eat

"Chef Williamson? What's on the menu for tomorrow? I see the turkey is about thawed in the fridge. Do we need to make a last-minute grocery store run?"

"Tonya . . . I think I have everything we might need. If there are no objections, I'll smoke the turkey this afternoon and have it ready. If you prefer it baked, then have at it."

"Smoked."

"Is there an echo in here? Sounds seem to be coming from all directions."

"Hannah has agreed to cook the cornbread and dressing. You smoke the turkey. I'll take care of everything else."

Walt had never viewed himself as a paternalistic figure, but when the clan gathered around the Thanksgiving table, all eyes turned to him. Words did not come easy so he suggested a few moments of silence. Jesse pronounced the benediction.

"W'us eat."

As plates were filled and the feast began, one dish, prepared ahead of time, drew attention.

"Walt . . . This is the most unusual and the best cranberry salad I have ever tasted."

"It's actually a cranberry salsa. Jesse . . . Tell Hannah and Sissy about the day we picked those berries."

"Bear—we saw a mama bear and two cubs, but we didn't get between them."

Happy Thanksgiving, Ginny. Our son has taken on a new calling. He has appointed himself the family clown. If the word deadpan had not already been coined, it would be now. The boy can tell a yarn with such a straight face, if you did not know any better, you would swear he was telling the truth. Then again, he gets so tickled at himself that you would think he took lessons from Red Skelton.

Tonya offered to entertain Jesse so Walt could show Hannah around the area. As he pointed out things, he reeled himself in a couple of times when about to make references to his late wife.

"Walt . . . It's okay to talk about Ginny. She was just as much a part of your life as Phillip was mine. Unlike with me, though, she is ever-present because you're raising her child."

"Talk about a baptism in fire. I jumped in from no parenting experience whatsoever to playing the role of both mother and father. I would do it all over again, but sometimes I think it is so unfair to Jesse."

"He will be fine. You know far more than most how people come into our lives and bridge the gaps. Jesse will be no exception. Just keep being who you are and let him be who he is. And by the way, I kind of like who you are. Always have. In case you haven't noticed, that little boy of yours keeps trying to steal my heart, too."

"Oh, look. The sun is breaking through the clouds. Zip up your jacket, and let's go walk on the beach."

P. S.

"Dad . . . We must do something about my car situation. Your old gray mare just ain't what she used to be."

"Tell you what. If you play your cards right, just maybe Jess and I will bring Cornfield and give her to you for your birthday. I do want to make that drive with him, and I think he's about ready."

Tonya winked at Hannah.

"That's something we can all look forward to."

Walt ignored her.

"I'll start looking around here for something I can afford, and we'll fly back. I'm not sure either of us would want to do a round trip."

Walt had to steady himself as he watched his daughter and Hannah navigate the tarmac and climb aboard the twin-engine plane. It was snowing just as it was the last time he laid eyes on his beloved wife. This aircraft was headed in a different direction for a routine winter flight. Emotionally drained, he went to bed at the same time Jesse reclaimed his. Under his pillow, he found a note.

Dearest Walt,

I was so afraid that my presence would be intrusive. Tonya did agree for me to reimburse her for the cost of my ticket. You have no idea how many times I tried to talk myself into just forfeiting that money and staying home. I am now "thankful" that I did not. And thank you for being such a good sport. This Thanksgiving went from one I was so dreading to one I will never forget.

When I'm editing for you, I now have a visual of you sitting at your desk. When you describe places, I will have a better grasp. I'll have to admit that I could never understand your fascination with this place until now.

I know you would have preferred me seeing Alaska first in summer, but let's face it. If I had waited on an invitation from you, or you had held back for me to invite myself, I would have never made the journey. That daughter of yours is something else. So is your son. My heart is overflowing with "gratitude" because you share them with me.

165

I am so proud of you and for the man, you have become. Perhaps, I should say, the man, you are still becoming..........

Hannah

P. S. Next time you clean house, don't forget to vacuum under your bed.

Walt went to sleep with a smile on his face. He forgot all about the postscript until two days later when Jesse was halfway across the kitchen floor before he remembered to take off his muddy boots. That prompt put Walt on his knees but not for bedtime prayers. Two neatly wrapped Christmas packages were tucked away under the bed. The gifts would stay put for about a month.

Nothing about going to Seattle for Christmas excited Walt. With a major car purchase looming, he told his in-laws that he and Jess would go out of their way on the trip to North Carolina in a few months and pay them a visit. This would provide a nice break in the trip.

Jesse received parcels from his grandparents and his sister. On Christmas Day, Walt retrieved the ones hiding since Thanksgiving and told his son they were from Hannah.

"Daddy . . . You first. I've already opened several."

The almost square flat box was heavier than he anticipated. Jesse gave his daddy a hand ripping off the wrapping. A totally unexpected new laptop was inside the box. Walt read the card. Hannah said she wanted to give Jesse some computer games, but the techie indicated that his old computer could not handle them. So—she had no choice but to buy him a new one, just for Jesse's sake—of course.

"Your turn to open a present. Look—computer games—this one's a flight simulator. It will be like you're in the cockpit flying a plane."

"Show me, daddy."

An hour later, the boys with their new toys took a break for breakfast. It was already past Hannah's lunchtime when Walt dialed her number. Jesse took the receiver from him. Five minutes later, he handed it back.

"Hannah . . . You shouldn't have."

"Just why not? Admit it. You don't have an answer for that. Merry Christmas! And I will be anticipating less editing with this much-improved word processor."

"Let me see if I've got this right. You gave me a new computer so Jesse could play games, and you would benefit with less work."

"Walt . . . You're so smart."

What about Hannah?

Walt's Old Sourdough series gained increasing popularity among the readership. The newspaper made plans to publish the expanded profiles in book form after the interviews were concluded. Once housebroken, he found the new computer much easier to work with.

One pioneer widow lamented that she could no longer drive. She supposed that she just needed to sell her vehicle and use the money elsewhere. Walt took a look at the low mileage four-year-old Subaru Outback. He asked what she would take for it and then went home to get his checkbook.

Tonya was delighted with that news and asked if he had named his new ride.

"I think I'll call it my 'Old Sourdough.' I've made almost enough money from my newspaper work to pay for it. I'll concentrate on finishing the interviews so Jess and I can head your way after the thaw."

The robins returned about a week before the departure. Jesse went out every day and chattered with the mother bird. Walt had his own private conversations.

"Ms. Robin . . . What 'must' I do about Hannah?"

Abruptly, the red-breasted bird took flight.

"So . . . You don't know either."

> Jesse . . . The trip we're about to make is nothing like anything you have ever done before. It will take us about five or six days to get to Seattle and that many more to go to Sissy's. That's a long time in the car, but we'll stop whenever we want to. We can take the cooler and have a picnic lunch every day and find somewhere to sleep

each night. Take your books and some toys, but I want you to help me watch for wildlife. Waterfalls will be all along the way. In one park, we can walk right up to a glacier. We'll also stop and play in steaming water from a hot spring. Let's keep the camera handy and show the pictures to your grandparents and then to Sissy.

"Daddy . . . What about Hannah?"
"Of course—we can show them to her, too."

Aunt Polly

Although no day was like any other, the vagabonds, nevertheless, settled into some routines. After an early start each morning, they stopped along the way to get some breakfast. The wanderers picnicked beside streams, some with waterfalls, along glacially formed lakes, and in parks with spectacular views of the mountains. Jesse kept up with the "noculars." Uploading the pictures, was the first thing he wanted to do once they were checked in for the night.

Across the interior of Alaska, within the Yukon, and throughout British Columbia, wildlife sightings mounted. The two enthusiasts spotted several moose, swans swimming in pairs, eagles both perched and soaring overhead, caribous in a pack, at least half a dozen black bears, one old brown bear, a coyote, a big bull elk, a herd of bison, both Dall and bighorn sheep, and a lynx. They got photos of everything except the big cat with pointed ears, which scampered away too fast.

Walt did not bother correcting anyone who commented on a grandfather making a trip with his grandson. He might not be a "grand" father, but he certainly had a "grand" son.

After crossing the border, Walt suggested to Jesse that he find a different way to address his grandparents.

"Do you know why you call them Ice and the Iceman?"
The boy shook his head.
"You could not say, Alice, so you used just the last syllable. Since Dave was her man, you dubbed him the Iceman."

Walt doubted that his proposal garnered any merit, and he was right. Jesse had no trouble saying, "Aunt Polly," and she spent a couple hours with him flying and crashing planes on the flight simulator. Walt was pleased that she mostly ignored him, although more than once, he could feel her eyes.

He wondered if Jesse visiting his Seattle family might prompt more questions about his mother, but it did not. The boy did make one astute observation the morning they were back on the road.

"Aunt Polly hugs me too tight. Those bumps make it hard for me to breathe."

Walt feared he was putting his son into a sensory overload, but he was not sure if they would ever do this again. The duo spent the better part of two days in Yellowstone National Park. Jesse picked up on something he heard his daddy say and started repeating it.

"This is beautiful, but it's not Alaska."

After exiting the park, the driver was like a mule, headed for the barn. Through the valleys and across the plains, Tonya's Cornfield picked up the pace. Three weeks to the day since leaving Kenai, the weary passengers rolled into Ephesus.

Tonya heard the vehicle in the drive and ran out the door. As she lunged for her brother, Walt gave her a heads-up.

"Don't squeeze him too tight."

Jesse refused to go to bed until he showed at least some of the pictures to his big sister. Walt was more interested in a glass of Sin.

The next morning, he was still sleeping it off when Jesse bounced out of bed and went bounding up the stairs to the kitchen. Tonya had been up for some time.

"Where's Hannah?"

"Well, good morning to you, too, little sunshine. Hannah is at her house."

"Can she come over so I can show her the pictures?"

"Let's give her a call."

When Walt finally came crawling out, he climbed the stairs to the sounds of several voices. The jester was holding court.

"Hello . . . Einstein."

"Hannah . . . If I'd known you were here, I would have at least brushed my hair and combed my teeth."

"This little super salesman of yours has certainly convinced me. The next time I go to Alaska, I want to drive, at least one way. Those photos are amazing."

"Who said there will be a next time?"

"Jesse did. He's already invited me."

"Then, I guess the two of you will have to make your own arrangements."

"Daddy . . . You're so funny."

Sounds like a plan

"Did Tonya tell you? The birthday party is Saturday at my house. I don't want to spoil the surprise, but I think we'll have pizza. I'd be willing to wager that Jesse has not had any since you were here last."

"You'd lose that bet. We stopped for one somewhere back up the road."

"Would you prefer Turkey Fried Chicken?"

"Oh . . . Tonya told you what she called the Colonel's chicken when she was a kid."

"Walt . . . That sounds just like you."

"It's not my birthday. You need to ask the honorees what they want."

Hannah got her answer in stereo.

"Pizza!"

The hostess did not give away all her secrets. When Cornfield deposited her passengers, two other cars were hidden out of sight. As the guests of honor came through the door, the occupants were already assembled.

"Surprise!"

"King . . . May Beth."

Jesse remembered the other woman from his last birthday as his sister's grandmother, but he was not sure how that applied to him. He had learned to put his arms in front of his chest if older women were about to give him a hug.

"I thought we might as well make this a family reunion. Shall we go ahead and start making plans for next year?"

"Hannah . . . You did it again."

After Jesse had an ample serving of the birthday cake that Connie Bell had baked, Earl started baiting him.

"Little man . . . Are you going home with me?"

When Walt saw his son look first toward Tonya and then at Hannah, he rescued him.

"We just got here a couple days ago, and our bodies are still getting over butt-lag."

Before he could say anything else, Earl intervened.

"Then, why don't you guys come and stay with us a few days before you fly back? If you can get someone to drive you down, we can take you to the Atlanta airport. It's only an hour from our house."

"Sounds like a plan."

Jesse had been a bystander long enough.

"King . . . I'm four now. Can I drive the tractor all by myself?"

"Only if you have on a new pair of overalls. I see too much leg sticking out of last year's. They look about worn out to me."

"He would've put them on every day if I had let him."

Mary Beth took it from there.

"Jesse . . . You and I are going shopping, again."

Walt and Hannah made eye contact, and they were thinking the same thing—no wrenching airport goodbyes this time. Walt turned away, but after surveying the room, his eyes returned to her. She was still looking at him.

Bloody hell . . . Othell

"Dad . . . Why don't you take Hannah out on a real date—maybe dinner and a movie? She might still be a little hesitant about being in public with another man. You know small town gossip. Take her to Asheville. I'll let you borrow 'my' car. Ha. Ha."

"Let me think about it. What if she turns me down?"

"You're secure enough within yourself to know that would not be anything even resembling rejection. I don't think you have anything to worry about, though. Maybe you shouldn't mention it to Jesse. He would want to tag along and chaperone. Do it properly—with a phone call."

Walt could not believe how angst-ridden he was. He mulled it over for two days before requesting a helping hand from Gus. Hannah downplayed his proposal, and he was about to apologize for being too forward when she had a question of her own.

"Did Tonya put you up to this?"

When he hesitated, she knew the answer. Tonya had given her an out.

"Hannah . . . Don't make this any harder for me than it already is."

"Walt Williamson . . . I would love to go on a date with you, even if you didn't have enough imagination to come up with it all on your own."

The afternoon of the big night, Tonya said she had an errand to run. Hannah welcomed her presence as she was getting ready for her first date in thirty-something years. After trying on several outfits, they settled on just the right one—a blue dress that accented her blond hair. Tonya went for her purse.

"You look dazzling. Now, splash on just a hint of this."

"Tonya . . . I've not had any perfume on in . . ."

"Trust me. Dad will never know what hit him. Let me go home and see if I can smooth out some of his rough edges."

When Walt found out where Tonya had been, he asked why Hannah did not just hitch a ride so they could leave from there.

"Oh, no. You'll pick her up at her house. Here—put on this shirt I picked up for you. I've already washed it. How long has it been since you bought yourself any new clothes?"

"Can't say that I need any."

"Don't you have to look presentable in your work?"

"Just imagine how far I would get if I showed up looking like some slick city reporter."

"Tonight, you're taking a lady out on a date. If you don't make it home, I won't report you as a missing person."

"I'm glad somebody's enjoying this."

"Dad . . . Please tell her how beautiful she is."

"Othell . . . Why do I feel like a senior on the way to a prom? At least I won't have to pin on a corsage."

To make matters worse, he had to ring the bell twice. When the door opened, Tonya's advice was unnecessary.

"You look amazing."

"You don't look half bad yourself, Mr. Williamson. Nice shirt. I don't think I've ever seen it before. Would you like to come in?"

"If I do, we might not make it to Asheville."

"Then, let me grab my purse and wrap. It might get chilly."

On the way through Ferndale, Walt pointed out Tonya's grandparents' now restored old mountain cottage.

"Right there in the drive and on that porch, I saw my daughter when she was a child, and I had no clue who she was."

He steered Cornfield into the "No Bidness Creek" access, and they got out.

"I stood right here on this spot many times in reverential awe of these glorious ferns and never understood why I was so drawn to this place. I suppose—some things will always remain a mystery. We may never know what close brushes we had with angel wings."

"I'm so glad that first, your mother found you, and then Tonya."

"Isn't it strange how some people fuss and fret their lives away, never able to fill the debilitating voids, but in my case, things just fell into my lap?"

Hannah did not respond, but she was not aloof. Rather, she was imagining sitting on Walt's lap. She slowly moved her hand along his back and put her arm around his waist. He spun her around, and they embraced. The odds were stacked in favor of him kissing her, but only a fool would put a wager on Walt Williamson.

On the way back to the Legacy, Hannah started second-guessing herself. Had she been too forward? Was that why he turned away? At the same time, the pressure was off regarding how she would have responded. The chances were good that she would have turned the other cheek.

Back on the highway, Walt took his right hand off the wheel and reached across the seat. Hannah took it and had a question, as though she did not already know the answer.

"Where are we going to eat?"

"I was thinking about the food court at the mall. Years ago, when we ate there, you were a married woman and so worried about being seen in public with another man."

"I hate to disappoint you, sir, but I saw on the news they're tearing down that old mall."

"What a shame. I have such fond memories of the place. It was where we had that deep discussion about identity. So many things clicked and came together for me that day."

"Don't forget, it was also in that same food court where I had the fortitudinous encounter with Tonya, with no inkling that she was your daughter. What is your second choice?"

Walt reached in his shirt pocket and passed across a note.

"Tonya made reservations for us here. I've been gone for some time, and I know Asheville has changed. See if you can follow her directions."

"Oh, goodie. It's Italian. I love Italian."

"You may have to order for me. I might not be able to read the menu."

"You really do need to get out more."

Throughout the meal, Walt looked at Hannah when she was looking away. She glanced at him when his attention was elsewhere. After dessert and coffee, their eyes met.

"Walt . . . This is such a special night. The dinner was divine. Will you be too disappointed if we skip the movie?"

On the way back to the vehicle, he wondered if he had offended her, or if she had something else in mind and wanted to get back home. Once they were buckled up, she reached over and took his hand.

The conversation was light and frivolous until they were well out of town. Both then seemed to retreat somewhere deep into their respective beings. When the headlights were doused in the drive, Hannah sat still until Walt came to open her door. Another pivotal moment was awaiting them on the porch.

"Would you like to come in?"

"If I did, you might have to run me off with a stick."

"Goodnight . . . Walt. I had such a wonderful time."

"Me too. Goodnight . . . Hannah."

"Bloody hell . . . Othell. For heaven's sake, why didn't you kiss her?"

The safe-haven

"Look, Daddy. Sissy and I are painting a picture of a bear eating wildflowers."

Tonya had taken the seldom used dining room and converted it into a studio where she did her own painting and also taught art lessons.

"Why are you back so soon? How did it go?"

"We had a really good time. The food was delicious."

"Hannah said she thought you would like it. No movie?"

"I don't think either of us could have endured anything but a comedy. They just don't make funny movies anymore."

Tonya was certain she would not get much else from her father. She also had a sneaking suspicion not a lot was left to tell.

"I'll make good use of some of the wildlife shots you guys got on the way down. Maybe Jesse and I can get several going while you're here. He's a good dabbler."

"All you have to do is look at his face and see that. I'm off to bed. Jesse . . . Come in quietly."

Ginny . . . I'm a little worried about Hannah. I can't tell where she is in her grieving process, but I don't think she has any reasons for regrets. It is near impossible for her not to wonder if she should have done some things differently. We can talk about you, but I cannot get her to open up about Phillip. Their relationship was always off-limits, and it still is. I'm trying so hard to respect her space, and I wouldn't do anything intentionally to make it more difficult for her. What "must" I do?

Walt thoughts turned to home when he buckled up in the middle seat. He and Jesse were gone the entire month of May and two weeks of June. Forever etched into both father and son's beings were the bonding experiences of the long drive from one corner of the continent to the other.

Waiting for clearance to lift off, he sat ruminating. Tonya was concerned that Jesse was too sheltered, and she might have a point. Yet, the kid had already logged more miles than many folks do in a lifetime. He was safely strapped in the window seat—amused by what was going on outside.

"Daddy . . . There goes our luggage. I just saw them put it on the ramp."

As the boy's mind was developing, it became more and more of an enigma to his dad. When Walt looked back to his own youth, the adults in his life certainly had no indications of what he was up to.

Spending time with Tonya was invigorating, and his daughter's tenacity brought a smile to his face. Miss Bizzy Belle especially enjoyed her little ploys. He could see why Mrs. Thornhill had so dubbed her and could only imagine what she was like as a child.

At the same time, he sensed that she was unsettled. They had discussed how she was open to a relationship, but both were thankful that she had not plunged into something reckless and irresponsible. He knew it would take a special kind of man to rise to her levels, and she would inevitably have to deal with whether she would settle for one who didn't.

Hannah's image then flashed through Walt's cerebral processor. During the last leg of the voyage to her hometown, he had wondered what might or might not develop during this visit. From the complicated circumstances when they first met, this period in their lives was the first when, hypothetically, nothing stood in the way. Did she prefer the safe-haven of the fantasy to the risks of reality?

Abruptly, Walt's thoughts turned to Ms. Robin. Would she have a new brood to show off when they got home? The deliberation was interrupted when the passenger beside him tugged on his sleeve.

"Daddy . . . I wish Hannah was my other mother, and she lived with us."

Jane met the exhausted passengers at the airport in Kenai and piloted them back to their lair. She had looked after things while they were gone and watered the flowers. Nate was with her, and the boys chatted in the back seat. Walt asked how many parties she threw. The teenager made a face and reminded him that she was Plain Jane.

"Hi, Honey . . . We're home."

Once the cases were rolled inside, a candle lit, and the chauffeur and her brother thanked and sent on their way, Walt and Jesse spontaneously went out the back door. Simultaneously, they were greeted with a familiar sound.

Chup . . . Chup . . . Cheer up, Cheerio!

Chee . . . Chee . . . Chee . . . Tut . . . Tut . . . Tut.

Three baby bird heads popped up to see what the excitement was all about.

Vanity

Walt checked in with his editor, and she had three new leads for interviews. When he placed a call to a man who kept the vintage vehicles running when parts were sparse, a woman answered the phone. She identified herself as the early settler's daughter and mentioned that she and her father were reading the articles. After a pause, the second-generation Alaskan indicated that her dad felt honored to be included.

"Can you come for lunch tomorrow? I'm fixing moose chili and Mexican cornbread."

"How could I refuse such an offer? Since I'm violating an unwritten rule about mixing business with pleasure, may I bring my four-year-old? I'd hate for him to miss such a treat."

"By all means. I'll entertain him while you and Dad talk."

A slender woman, with stunning long wavy prematurely grey hair, met the reporter and his sidekick at the door and identified herself as Darleen. Walt introduced himself and then Jesse.

"I'm sure Dad will want to show you around before we eat. His house really is a museum. Mother died two years ago, and he insists on living alone. I come over one afternoon a week and some evenings to clean, cook, and keep him company."

"Jesse . . . Do you smell that aroma coming from the kitchen?"

The boy was not as impressed with relics, old photographs, and the stories that went with them as his daddy was. He took a seat on a stool and started telling his new friend all about his recent adventures. By the time they gathered around the kitchen table, Walt had more material than he could possibly use for a newspaper article. Concurrently, Darleen had gotten an earful.

The cook did not have to wait for reviews to come in regarding the victuals. One guest raved and the other refilled his bowl twice. Walt noticed the woman was not wearing a wedding band.

As the pioneer's daughter saw them out, she took Jesse by the hand.

"You're such a cute little fellow. I'd love to see more of you. Do you think your daddy would let you come over again sometime?"

The boy answered in body language.

With four eyes fastened on his father, Walt shrugged.

"Then, it's a done deal. I'll give your dad a call soon."

Jesse had piqued the woman's curiosity, and she wanted to find out more about the unusualness of the family circumstances. Walt was intrigued by something. He sensed nonverbal communication coming from the woman.

"Othell . . . Is it possible that Darleen really wants to see more of me?"

The day after the feature was published, Gus II got a friendly jolt.

"Daddy and I are so grateful for the great job you did. Can we get extra copies?"

"Sure. I'll pick some up for you. When would be a good time to drop them by?"

"I'll be here again on Monday. Is that a convenient time?"

"I have another interview at two that afternoon, and I could either . . ."

"Come by beforehand, and let Jesse stay with us."

Walt cautioned that he had to drive some distance, and he was not sure when he would be back. She eased his mind that the boy would be no problem.

"Don't let your head swell . . . Othell. Vanity rhymes with both profanity and insanity."

Darleen sported with Jesse, and he revealed in his newfound notoriety. The boy had no secrets. He just did not know everything the grown folks did. When his daddy came to pick him up, she had heard all about Jesse's sister, but otherwise learned little that she did not already know.

"You must stay and have supper with us. Jesse helped me make the spaghetti. We're using up the moose meat before next season. The chili did not seem to kill either of you."

"We would not want to be any trouble . . ."

"Walt . . . This is spaghetti. Nothing could be any easier."

Little pitchers

Jesse finished his meal, and not all of it made it to his mouth. The hostess helped him wash his face and hands, and he scampered off to play a video game. Walt was ready to go and start on the article before his notes got cold, but he did not wish to be rude. Darleen had no such compunction about decorum.

"Jesse told me he has a sister in North Carolina. He did not say anything about his mother, though."

"The boy knows her only from a photo. He's already asking questions, and I'm trying to answer them according to his ability to understand."

"Is this too personal, or is it something you can share?"

"It's been published in the paper, so I guess nothing's confidential."

As Walt began intimating some basic details, the old man got up and left the table. He was not as nosy as his daughter. Unbeknownst to his dad, Jesse had learned a new skill. His son could play a game and listen in on a conversation at the same time.

As they were leaving, Walt mentioned that things might be getting a little out of balance.

"You've fed us twice, and it seems that we're about to become indebted."

"You're still very much in the black for all your efforts and talents with the story you did on Dad, but I do not want you to feel guilty. You guys can have me over or take me out to dinner anytime you wish."

Walt was caught flat-footed—but not Jesse.

"Daddy loves to grill on Saturdays."

"What time, and I'll bring the makings for a salad?"

It was the boy's bedtime when they got home. Walt went to tuck him in, and Jesse had a question.

"Is Aunt Polly my other mother?"

Walt greeted Darleen at the door with an encrypted message.

"Little pitchers have big ears."

"I hear you."

Jesse heard the commotion and ran out of his room.

"Just the person I'm looking for. I brought the salad fixings. While your daddy works his magic on the grill, you can help me put it together."

"Daddy won't let me use a knife, yet."

"Then I guess you'll have to use our hands. You can also drizzle on the dressing and mix it all up."

When they had a moment of privacy, Walt told Darleen about Jesse's question. She immediately began apologizing, but he stopped her.

"He was ready to go to the next level. I took what he picked up on and turned it into a teachable moment. Most of the words he heard the other night went right over his head. Honestly, I look forward to the day when I can tell him everything."

"Jesse's story is so amazing."

"I've always just dealt with whatever life dished out, and this time was no different."

"My dear man. Surely you must know by now that it is not just the cards you hold in your hand, but how you play them."

"Othell . . . Does she think I'm not playing with a full deck? I wonder if she has an ace up her sleeve."

Accolades flowed freely as the three feasted. King salmon were in the river, and Walt snagged a fillet at the market. He bragged on the salad and asked Jesse if he wanted to become a chef. The way the boy wrinkled his nose indicated that he was not familiar with that term.

Who is Darleen?

Playing to his new audience, Jesse took over the jester duties around the table. Soon after he finished eating, he excused himself and began playing within hearing distance. The boy had discovered a new way to gain information.

Walt learned that Darleen owned and operated a greenhouse. She sold herbs and some vegetables to stores year-round and potted plants and hanging baskets to the public all summer.

"I'm not open on Mondays—as you might have noticed. I make just enough to get by. It's somewhat confining during the busy season, but the rest of the time, I can come and go pretty much as I please. Drop by some time, and I'll give you a tour. The salad was made from stuff I plucked just before I came over."

"No wonder it was so good."

Walt wanted to know more about Darleen's story. She disclosed that she lost a son in infancy and was a first-year empty nester. Her daughter withdrew from college and left with her boyfriend when he took a job in Montana. The attractive woman did not mention her children's father or fathers.

After she left, Jesse asked his dad if they could go visit Darleen and see her plants.

"You like her, don't you?"

"Do you like her?"

"She seems like a nice woman."

Walt was hammering out an article the next day when Gus II did his thing. Since the phone was used for business purposes, he had taught Jesse to answer with, "The Williamson residence." The boy began chattering away, and he assumed Tonya was on the other end of the line. After about five minutes, he brought the cordless phone to his daddy. The call was from North Carolina, for sure.

When Walt said, "Yes," Hannah asked, "Who is Darleen?"

"You've already read her name. I mentioned her in the first article I sent to you after we got back."

"Oh . . . I see."

Thirty minutes later, Walt's thought processes were interrupted again. This time it was his daughter calling.

"Hey, Dad. Who's your new girlfriend?"

Jesse's girls

Darleen was more Jesse's girl than she was his dad's. She was kind and thoughtful, and Walt was especially appreciative of the attention she gave his son. The boy badgered him until they took her up on her invitation.

As they strolled through the greenhouse, Darleen held Jesse's hand. As she plucked some things for them to take home, Walt suspected that she was keeping the kid's fingers from doing their own plundering.

"I wish you could have come earlier in the season. Many of the more spectacular arrangements have already found new homes. Alaskans love colorful foliage. After enduring so much whiteness during the winter, they rush to liven up things."

"Darleen . . . You certainly know how to do that."

The woman blushed. Jesse grinned.

By the time the summer solstice rolled around, Walt had almost finished the Sourdough Spice series, but much work still lay ahead. He had gathered far more material than space allowed. The reporter started devoting time to organizing the larger profiles and getting them ready for publication in booklet form. The newspaper wanted them ready to promote as Christmas gifts. Hannah continued her yeoman duty as his finishing editor.

Darleen invited Jesse to come over whenever his daddy would drop him off to help her run the greenhouse. The boy thrived as much as the plants did. Customers fascinated him, and he showed them around when she was busy with others.

Walt was taken back to the time when he helped his Granddaddy Williamson at the roadside stand selling apples, fried pies, vegetables, sorghum syrup, and sweet potatoes. When he came to pick his son up, they often stayed for supper. Tonya put her own spin on what was happening.

"That's one smart woman. She knows the way to a man's heart is through both his stomach and his son."

Walt had no comeback. He was not sure what his feelings were for Darleen but certain of one thing. He was not doing such a good job being both a mother and a father for his son.

Tonya then put him on the defensive.

"Dad . . . You're killing Hannah. Don't you think you should settle things with her—one way or the other—before you get too involved with another woman? She's kicking herself for pushing you away when you were here."

"Push me away? I thought I was the one who held back."

"Oh, dear . . ."

Who is Hannah?

Walt should have anticipated it, but it still took him by surprise. Jesse met him at the door and announced that he was spending the night with Darleen.

"Don't I have any say in this?"

"Please—she already has my room ready. We went to town and bought me some new pajamas."

"You can just move in with her for all I care."

"Daddy . . . You're so funny."

When Darleen brought him home the next afternoon, Walt was in the backyard. They found him chattering with Ms. Robin.

"Jesse . . . You'd better tell them goodbye. The robins are about to leave for the winter."

The mother bird muttered something—as if displeased—and flew into the forest.

When Walt walked Darleen to her car, he searched for the words to thank her for being so good to his son. She did not stumble on her own.

"Who is Hannah?"

Beginning about the time of the fall equinox, Walt and Darleen shared something else in common. They were both caught up with their work. She was a touchy-feely person, and he was not above ruffling his collar so she would straighten it. Neither did he go out of his way to run a comb through his hair when he took off his cap.

What to do with his own hands was another matter. He laughed at himself when he revisited many times in the past when he did not know what to touch, or when it was permissible to touch it. After coming in chilled to the bone one afternoon, all three were warming in front of the wood-burning stove. Playfully, Darleen put her cold hands on Walt's face, and he reciprocated. Jesse jumped between them.

The boy was spending the night again. When Darleen went out on the porch to see Walt off, she squared herself to him. Before he had time to put his gloves on, she reached for his hands and put them back where they were before Jesse intervened.

"Walt . . . Don't be afraid to touch me. I don't bite. That is—unless you want me to."

She then took his hands and put them around her waist, pulling him close in the process. Walt thought she was going for his lips, but instead, her mouth veered and made its way to an ear. After a nibble that sent a shiver through him, she whispered.

"You can spend the night, too—if you want to."

Before he had time to react, the front door squeaked, signaling the private party on the porch was over.

When Walt came out of the shower, Jesse was on the phone. From the conversation, it was hard to tell which of his women he was talking to. After he hung up, his daddy was curious.

"Who was that?"

"Hannah."

"Did she ask about me?"

"No—she just called to talk to me."

That damn shovel

When Darleen was visiting one evening, Jesse surprised them when he announced his bedtime. Walt was suspicious of a ruse, but to his astonishment, the boy was sleeping soundly when he checked on him.

"I guess he's finally beginning to trust us."

"And well, he should. Walt . . . Don't you think you've taken this southern gentlemanly thing far enough?"

"What do you mean by that?"

"We're consenting adults. It's nobody's business what we do behind closed doors. I admire you. I'm attracted to you and yearn for your hands to caress me. I want to run mine all over your body. I'm not asking for any kind of commitment. That might or might not come later. For now, why can't we just have some fun and enjoy ourselves?"

"You mean—like friends with benefits?"

"I need to go home. Sometimes it goes without saying that a spade is just a spade. There's no cause for you to hang a label on it, and call it a damn shovel."

"Othell . . . I think I know that woman's favorite song. 'If you can't be with the one you love, love the one you're with'."

Walt poured himself another glass of Sin. When he felt quite mellow, he went to bed thinking about asking Gus II for some assistance. Up before Jesse the next morning, he reached for the phone. He knew what his first words were going to be, but he was still unsure who would hear them. Eventually, he dialed a number with a one in front of it. On the fourth ring, she answered.

"Can we talk?"

Hannah fell back in the chair, as a wave of lightheadedness washed over her.

Walt had always disliked the phone and found it near the bottom of the barrel as an effective means of communication. That instrument was inept in ciphering subtle nuisances and virtually worthless for reading body language. He made an entry into his electronic journal.

> Words are just words. When emotions are seeking expression, words are vastly inferior to touching and tears, to spontaneous bursts of joy and the oozing of sorrow and sadness. Vocal sounds cannot compete with standing tall or falling prostrate. Words are used to redirect and misdirect, as weapons, as rational attempts to connect and find common ground, and as a mantle behind which to conceal. Perhaps, the poet is more adept than most in using words as a vehicle to convey the longings of the soul, but I'm no bard. The phone is so woefully inadequate, but sometimes it's the only channel available.

Walt walked away frustrated after each conversation with Hannah. When they first connected, he was captivated by her straightforwardness. There were no uncertainties about where she stood. She fully intended to remain faithful to her marriage and was neither hesitant nor bashful in keeping her stance at the forefront.

Now, she sent mixed signals. One week, she seemed buoyant about the possibility of going forward, but the next, her words were vague and ambivalent.

Walt suggested that they rely more on written messages via the medium of email. She reminded him that he was a writer, and she was not. He suspected that it had more to do with her unwillingness to sign off on what was going on in her head and heart.

Tonya suggested that Hannah just needed more time.

"Dad . . . You're the counselor. Try putting yourself in her place. Like so many mountain girls, she married young. He got drafted, and they were separated while still getting settled in. Then, you came along. Hannah could only dream of being with the man who really knew her, who connected with her at a deep level. She could feel it, but it was outside her grasp. Just listen. Don't jump in.

"Simultaneously, you were snatched away from her by Uncle Sam, and her husband came home shot to pieces. Hannah did what she had to do. Over time, she came to accept her lot in life. For three decades, she dutifully went to work in a career that became increasingly less fulfilling. For thirty years, she came home to a marriage that was just as dysfunctional as her husband was disabled.

"Are you getting the picture? In a nutshell, Hannah has not yet given herself permission to be happy. Meanwhile, her professional life is suspended in uncertainty. The only definitive decision she has made thus far was to take a year off and explore the possibilities of doing something else."

"I know all that's true . . ."

"I'm not through, yet. Just suppose that she comes to terms with the past. Give her some space to do so independent of you. You pointed out in your book the fallacy of making two moves in one. Hannah is trying to reinvent herself and figure out who she is at this stage in her life.

"Dad . . . This is her 'identify dilemma.' Brace yourself. Once she emerges from this cocoon, she might have no interest in taking on a crotchety old man who needs help raising his cantankerous kid. She might not fall in love with Alaska as we did. And one more thing. In all this, I have not heard you say one word about how you feel."

"Tonya . . . When are you going to hang out your shingle?"

"Can we talk?"

Walt eventually got around to dialing the local number.

"I think sometimes you talk too much."

"That's one of the things I want to talk to you about."

"Walt Williamson . . . Did anybody ever tell you that you're impossible?"

"If they did, I must not have been listening."

"If you want to come over, I'm about finished giving the plants a good drink of water."

"Son . . . Put your coat on. We're going to Darleen's."

No need to distract the little pitcher with big ears. Walt did not anticipate saying anything too delicate for them.

"Darleen . . . I'm sorry I was so abrupt the other night. I've never liked deception. I put my cards on the table, but I forget that's not the way the game is played. Life is so much simpler when people just say what they mean and mean what they say."

"So—you think I'm playing games with you."

"I didn't say that."

"Why do we have to talk about this? Do you ever just follow your gut?"

"I trust my instincts far more than knee-jerk reactions."

"Okay—what are your instincts telling you?"

"There are saying that we have a beautiful friendship, but if we take it to the next level for our own personal pleasure, we'll spoil it."

Darleen rolled her eyes. Walt continued.

"When you're young and crazy, you are blind to the risks. As we get older, we grow more cautious. Besides—I might be at a different place in my life than you are. If I were to make love to you, two other women would be looking over my shoulder. I just got a stark reminder from my own daughter about how foolish it is to go forward in a relationship with other unresolved issues."

"I suppose that you are talking about your late wife and Hannah. Or, is there somebody else I know nothing about?"

"Your first presumption is correct. Can we just be friends with limited benefits?"

"Only if you promise not to play games with me."

"I don't find it necessary to make any such promise. It never even occurs to someone genuine and forthright of say, 'I don't play games.' On the other hand, when people proffer those words preemptively, I've found that they generally mean, 'Now that I have distracted you, maybe you won't notice when I'm pulling your strings'."

"You just won't put that damn shovel down, will you?"

Ginny . . . Why are women so complicated? I appreciate a little mystery, but I am weary of consistently being caught off guard and thrown off balance. Just about the time, I think I have something figured out, the rules have been changed yet again and the goalpost moved. Damned if I do, and damned if I don't. No matter what, I'm the bad guy. Thank you for making it so easy for me. I never had to guess where you stood, and you took me at my word without twisting things out of context and putting me on the defensive. Baby . . . You spoiled me.

Oh, well . . . Othell

Walt and Jesse were preparing to spend Thanksgiving alone. Distances from loved ones were exacerbated, among other things, by limited funds. Christmas would likely be no different.

Berry picking had gone without incident. As the days grew shorter and the weather colder, father and son got outside two or three times a week. Jesse had settled into a pattern of wanting either his daddy's undivided attention or none at all.

Walt was not sure how much space to give Hannah. A nagging pit in his stomach had taken up residence. His concerted efforts would likely be either too much or not enough, too soon or too late. Fortunately, he had an ally.

"Dad . . . Don't forget to call Hannah and wish her a Happy Thanksgiving. Where did the year go? It seems like just a couple months ago when all of us were in Alaska for Turkey Day."

"What are your plans?"

"They're still open. Nothing special."

"How is Hannah?"

"What do you mean?"

"I think you know what I mean."

"I'm not allowed to give out trade secrets."

"Whose side are you own?"

"Both."

"Can you tell me this? Is she seeing someone else?"

"Oh, Daddy . . . Are you?"

Walt walked away from the conversation scratching his proverbial noggin.

"Oh, well . . . Othell."

After putting a ham in the cart, Jesse helped as they searched for other items on the shopping list. It would not be the feast of yesteryear, but the father and son would celebrate in their own peerless way. The boy was becoming quite useful in the kitchen. His dad was teaching him how to use a knife.

By the time the two had finished pigging out, it was already late afternoon in the Eastern Time Zone.

"Who do you want to call first, Sissy or Hannah?"

Walt was not surprised when Jesse chose his sister. It did catch him off guard, however, when he realized the boy was not conversing with her. Hannah and Tonya were celebrating Thanksgiving together. The talk was fluffy, and the conversations were not nearly as fulfilling to his spirit as the meal was to his belly.

After Jesse was down for the night, Walt's thoughts were redirected.

Our son is helping me in the kitchen. I have given him a few preliminary lessons in using a knife, and so far, he has managed not cut himself. He has also learned that a stove is hot. Jesse has never been a picky eater, but when he is actively involved in putting food on the table, he takes pride in the meal. Our boy certainly has his favorites. He is especially fond of sweet potatoes, anything made from the berries we gather, and what comes from the water.

Cleaning up afterward is not among his passions. I wish you were here to mess around with us in the kitchen.

The elf on the shelf

Walt did not know what to do about Christmas. His in-laws had sent overtures, but nothing about a trip to Seattle excited him. Two of the three people that he cared about most were in North Carolina. Too much was still tentative with Hannah, and he did not give his son a say.

Darleen called and wanted to bring a present to Jesse. Walt braced himself.

"Daddy . . . Look—a puzzle of the state of Alaska."

She showed up dressed like a Christmas elf in a costume about a half-yard short of an outfit. With a twinkle in her eye, she told Walt that she had a gift for him, too.

"Just so you know—I am playing a game with you—and it's an adult game. No kids allowed."

Walt tried to buy some time.

"But I do have a kid, and I can't just lock him up in his room."

"Can't you get that girl to babysit for a few hours?"

Jesse to the rescue.

"Darleen . . . Help me put the puzzle together."

Jesse put the elf back on the shelf.

"Othell . . . If I've said it once, I've said it a thousand times. 'When you compromise who you are—to play somebody else's game—everyone loses'."

Three days running, a card was in the mailbox informing the recipient of parcels too big for delivery. After all the gifts were picked up and unwrapped, Walt asked Jesse which was his favorite.

"It might be the new watch from Ice and Iceman. I really like the painting Sissy sent of me driving King's tractor. But I think my favorite is the computer game Hannah gave me."

Jesse paused with a far-off look on his face.

"Daddy . . . Do you think Hannah will ever want to be my other mother?"

"She would adopt you in a heartbeat, but I come with the package."

"Don't you love Hannah? I know she loves you."

"Just how do you know that?"

"She told me so."

"Oh . . ."

I surely do need somebody to talk to. The calendar just rolled over to 2004, and this is a big year for us. Jesse will start kindergarten next fall. I don't know anything about the local school system here. Do you think I should make Ephesus my residence and just summer in Alaska?

Boy is our little boy shooting up. He outgrows his clothes before he wears them out. I fear that he does not have enough interaction with playmates, but there is nothing shy about him. He never meets a stranger. I am so amazed by the unique little person that he is becoming. You would be so proud of him.

Jane is a senior and not very reliable as a babysitter. I am still writing a few feature articles for the paper and often have to take

Jesse with me. Hannah is still my trusted editor and sometimes calls to discuss her ideas and suggestions. She is thriving as an educational consultant, and I sense a softening. We actually enjoy some playful banter.

Tonya is not teaching at the private school any longer and has added more art students. I fear the house is not big enough for all of us. She is taking more of a hands-off approach in helping me understand what is going on with Hannah, but I am never sure what the women might be plotting behind my back. Did I tell you how much Jesse adores her? He asked the other day if she might be his other mother. What do you think about that?

Kicking the can

When Walt placed WOWs on the dresser and went to the bathroom before putting his head on the pillow for the night, the candle beside Ginny's picture was burning. He did not remember lighting it.

Before restocking the pantry, he stopped by the newspaper office to check in. His editor had nothing new but mentioned something else.

"With your master's degree, have you thought about teaching a course or two at the college? I know the president personally. It's hard to fill the faculty with what they pay. The school is ever on the lookout for adjunct instructors not wholly dependent upon their salaries to make ends meet."

The suggestion started worming its way through Walt's mainframe. Thus far, he had managed to get by without tapping into Jesse's annuity. The cost of raising his son would only escalate with each new rung of the education ladder. This proposal only added to his consternation about where to enroll the boy in kindergarten.

Walt decided it was time to have a talk with Tonya. She assured him that she would be thrilled to share *his* house with him and Jesse and further theorized.

"Perhaps, if you were living here, you might be in a better position to resolve things with Hannah."

"Speaking of Hannah, do you think she would ever consider moving up here with me and Jesse?"

"Why don't you ask her? Better still, why don't you invite her to come back for another visit? I think she has some gaps in her schedule this spring. You two are never going to get anywhere long distance."

"I don't know. Why does the thought of that terrify me?"

"Oh, Daddy."

"Will you test the waters for me?"

"No!"

Walt knew Tonya was right. Should he send her an email or give her a call?

"Othell . . . This rings that familiar bell again. Once more, I feel like a teenager about to ask a girl out on a date. Oh, well."

He called and left a message on her machine. An hour later, Gus II sounded the alarm. Hannah knew he had not placed a call for just small talk.

"Walt . . . Where is your head? Something bothering you? Is Jesse okay?"

"Everything's fine."

He was about to let it go at that when he realized he would just be postponing the inevitable.

"Did I ever tell you I thought I invented kicking the can down the road? When I was a kid and had to walk to my grandparents' houses, selling soft drinks in cans was new. I would find one beside the road and just keep kicking it, until I got to where I was going.

"I kicked one Coke can back and forth so many times that I flattened it. After I was grown and started hearing that expression, I wondered how anybody found out what I had originated."

"Maybe you should apply for a copyright or patent or something. I can just hear it now. 'I give you the famous Walt Williamson—the man who coined the expression kick the can down the road'."

"Hannah . . . That's what you and I have been doing. We've just been kicking the can down the road."

"You scare me. Where is this going?"

Walt was surprised by how easily the words came. He was equally amazed when Hannah accepted his invitation.

"Othell . . . My *up* is *beat*, and my *upper* is *most*."

Dearest Ginny . . . Hannah is on her way. When she gave me her schedule, I did not notice at first that she would be here for Jesse's birthday. He is so excited. I'm a little nervous myself. More than anything, I want our son to have everything he needs. I need a sign from you. Always . . . Walt

When Walt put his pen down and went toward the kitchen, the candle he had lit earlier beside Ginny's picture had burned out.

This is so exciting

"Jesse . . . It's time to go. We don't want to be late meeting Hannah's plane. If we leave now, we'll have time to stop some along the way."

The roads were clear, but an occasional berm created by the snowplows was still a menace. Runoff was already swelling the streams, but avalanche danger had passed.

The three-hour drive seemed to fly by. Belugas were cavorting just off the point named for them. These dwarf whales looked more like giant white dolphins, and this was another first for Jesse. It was also just the distraction Walt needed to keep him from getting all tangled up in what was beneath his surface.

An airliner circled overhead on its way to the airport. Jesse wanted to know if it was Hannah's, but his father told him it was too early.

"Daddy . . . This is so exciting."

Walt checked the board when they entered the terminal, and Hannah's flight was on schedule. He looked at his watch, and her flight was still an hour out.

"Let's go back to that place where we can watch the planes coming in."

Walt did not know what to anticipate. Hannah's visit could have far-reaching implications. Might they just kick the can on down the road?

The incoming flights were about five minutes apart. Some were smaller crafts, and the guys knew they were not the one. Two big ones were teasers, but they were cargo planes.

"Jesse . . . Look. Do you see the airplane way out there? It's banking and turning in this direction. Now you can see it better. It has its landing lights on."

"I see it . . . Hannah's plane."

"Let's go park and head to baggage claim."

Jesse sat on his dad's shoulders as the passengers streamed into the area and found places alongside the carousel. He scrambled down when Hannah waved to him. She let go of her tote, reached out her arms, and gathered him up.

"Don't you suppose I'd better say hello to your father?"

"I guess so."

Jesse yielded his spot in Hannah's arms, and Walt stepped in.

"Welcome to Alaska—again."

Once the luggage was stowed in Walt's Old Sourdough, and the trio was out of the parking lot, Walt turned to Hannah.

"Don't know about you, but Jess and I are starving."

"I did grab a bite on the plane. My innards are not sure what time it is, but I think I can eat again."

"I know just the place to get some great halibut and chips."

Jesse signaled his approval. While they were waiting for the food, he told Hannah about the beluga whales.

"Maybe they will still be there when we go by. I remember seeing the sheep high on the mountainside before."

When they pulled in and parked at the turnout, Walt did a quick perusal.

"No whales—no sheep—I guess we're just stuck with the scenery."

"I'll see if I can suffer through it."

The long flights and the four-hour time differential were working on Hannah by the time they got to Kenai. She noticed that Ginny's picture was not in its usual place when she went to prepare for bed. Jesse had agreed to surrender his room and sleep on the futon, but he changed his mind. Walt had to pry him loose so Hannah could get some rest.

Morning breath

Walt was fatigued after six hours of driving. His emotions had also been on quite a ride, and slumbering did not come forthrightly. It seemed that he had just fallen into a deep sleep when he heard Hannah rustling around in the kitchen. He got up, put on a pair of sweats, and went to join her.

Clad in a bright colored robe, she already had Mr. Coffee doing his thing. The two faced each other squarely, alone for the first time. Hannah broke the spell.

"Yesterday, I did not have a chance to give you a proper greeting."

With arms extended, she moved toward the stoical Walt. Layers of clothing were between them, but he could feel her warmth. His hands? What to do with his hands?

With her head snugly on his shoulder, Hannah ran her fingers through his hair. As his digits made their way around her braless back, they began flexing and kneading. Abruptly, she stiffened, and her moist eyes gazed into his.

Both were transported back to that magical time when their eyes initially locked the night they met. Then it happened. After countless close encounters, spanning more than three decades, their lips touched for the first time.

Sipping coffee at the table afterward, a sly look showed up on Hannah's face. A devious smile transmuted into laughter.

"Of all the fantasies I've ever had about you kissing me, it happening with morning breath was not among them."

Jesse missed the action but not by much. He woke up with an appetite, too, but it was for food. Cooking breakfast with Hannah had a special feel about it. He had the table set when the first sourdough pancakes came off the griddle.

Walt had been expecting other guests to arrive any day. After the dishes were soaking in the sink, he took Hannah by the hand. As they went out the back door, the sun was bright but the air still a bit brisk. His eyes followed a glimpse of movement, and his ears perked up when he heard a familiar sound. Ms. Robin leaped from the ground and landed on the limb cradling her nest. Her exuberance was unmistakable.

Chup . . . Chup . . . Cheer up, Cheerio!
Chee . . . Chee . . . Chee . . . Tut . . . Tut . . . Tut.
Cheer up, Cheerio! Cheer up, Cheerio!

Chee . . . Chee . . . Chee . . . Tut . . . Tut . . . Tut.

Hannah had no awareness of why Walt was emotional. Were they tears of joy? She was not sure. Neither was he.

Ta-licious

"Okay, birthday boy . . . Tomorrow, how do you want to celebrate number five?"

"I want Mexican. Daddy never takes me to get Mexican."

"Mexican it is. Shall we bring him along, or let it be just the two of us?"

"Well . . . I guess he can go, too. I want a taco supreme."

"A taco supreme it is. Let's go for lunch."

Nothing was said about presents or a cake. When Jesse went to bed, Hannah took over the kitchen. Walt's birthdays had never been a big deal, and he had not made much of his son's, either. He had already given him a pocket knife but told him to keep quiet about it. Others might think him too young.

After giving the spicy food a chance to settle, Hannah strolled into the living room singing the legendary song. Five candles were burning atop a black walnut cake.

"Jesse . . . I hope you like this. I know for certain your daddy will. Since I might not be here for his birthday, I made this for both of you. I brought the walnuts with me since I was not sure I could not get them here."

This time, Hannah did have some indication of why Walt's eyesight was a bit blurry.

"Now—close your eyes and make a wish before you blow out the candles."

Why was Jesse taking so long? Did he not know what to wish for, or was he just concentrating intently on his wish? A big smile burst across the boy's face as the five little fires were extinguished.

"This is so ta-licious."

Jesse still held onto a few of his infantile expressions.

"Close your eyes again, and keep them tightly shut."

Hannah slipped out of the room and back in carrying a wrapped present.

"You can open them now—and this."

With a smile taking over his face, Jesse glanced over at his daddy. Walt nodded for him to go ahead. The boy's expression morphed into astonishment as the picture on the box came into view.

"Oh, thank you, Hannah. A Nintendo Game Boy was exactly what I wished for. Thank you! Thank you! Thank you! How did you know?"

The words were then translated into more tangible expressions. Meanwhile, Walt's tear ducts were crying for some relief.

Over the next several minutes, Hannah pored over instructions, and Jesse acted them out. Walt hovered over them like a proud mother hen. Once the game action began, he slipped unnoticed out of the room.

Hello, Ginny. Thank you for not just one sign but two. I hope I got them right, but I'm never sure. You do understand how hard my head is sometimes. I know you want what's best for me. You always have. I also know you wish only the finest for our son. You will forever be Jesse's mother. I will never let him forget that. But it is so hard for me to raise him alone. I cannot be sure what Hannah is thinking. She has certainly charmed Jess. She might be willing to step in and give me some help. Step in—is that why it's called a stepmother?

Tonya got up thinking about Alaska and had difficulty concentrating on anything else the rest of the day. She thought about taking herself out to eat but settled in for a pity party. Not even Gus was her friend. Then, he surprised her when a chorus of three wished to sing her a birthday song.

"Sissy . . . Hannah gave me a Game Boy."

After Walt conveyed birthday wishes, Hannah reached for the phone.

"Before you go to bed, you might want to look under it."

Gus was not through for the night.

"Hannah . . . You shouldn't have."

"And just why not?"

"I love my new threads. Thank you so much. Don't guess I'll be wearing them on a date anytime soon."

"We'll do something when I get back."

"Oh goody. You can tell me how everything went."

What to do with his eyes?

When bedtime rolled around, Jesse planted himself firmly in the bed on loan to Hannah. He was soon joined by the others, one on each side, and all dressed for the night.

Hannah put one arm under Jesse, and her hand playfully found Walt on the other side. Using her free hand to stroke and distract the birthday boy, the other made its way upward, and she started tickling his daddy under his arm. Walt struggled to remain impassive, and the lad was oblivious to the flirting going on behind his back.

Two can play that game. With his father's arm also cradling him, the five-year-old thought for sure he was the center of the universe. When Walt went exploring under the covers, Hannah's other hand guided his to where she wanted it and did not want it to go.

Walt was unsure which conked out first. With the other two resting peacefully, he slipped away to his own bed. First, he leaned in and kissed each sleeping angel on the cheek. Hannah roused and puckered.

He was up early the next morning, but not before the sun. The summer solstice, little more than a month away, had been on the job for several hours. He had left Jesse's bedroom door open, but it was closed. After coffee and reading yesterday's paper, he approached it quietly. Faint sounds were coming from the other side. When he tried the knob, it was locked.

"Okay, you two. What's going on in there?"

The voices hushed.

"I guess I'll just have breakfast by myself."

"Oh, Daddy."

Walt heard the click, but the door did not open. He waited a moment and burst into the room.

"Wake up sleepy head. Wake up sleeping beauty."

Giggling and frolicking soon reached a fever pitch.

Walt made note that Hannah did not put on her robe when she made her way to the kitchen. Whether intentional or not, the top button of her pajamas was not pulling its weight.

After pouring herself another round, Hannah leaned in and drained the coffee pot into Walt's mug. His eyes—what to do with his eyes? As she settled back into her chair, she put her feet in his lap.

"Giving the Game Boy to Jesse, was brilliant. Look at him now. We can talk without him being right in the middle of things. Whose idea was it to lock the bedroom door?"

"His."

"So—he wanted you all to himself. Do you know how much that thrills me?"

Teamwork

When Walt booted up his computer, an email was waiting. His editor wanted him to write a feature story about a true survivor—a woman who lost her husband in the Vietnam war, then her home and a child in a fire, had overcome cancer, and walked away from a single-engine plane crash a few months earlier. Hannah was intrigued.

"Would I be a distraction? I think it would be fun to see how you go about conducting these interviews. If I'm a fly on the wall, I could then edit from a whole new perspective."

"The only disruption would be Jesse. Let me see if I can schedule so Jane or her mother can look after him."

Walt did not record the sessions, even though his newspaper editor had suggested it. The columnist could have done so surreptitiously but considered that an invasion of privacy. Furthermore, he feared a tape recorder in plain sight might be intimidating and cause someone already in the spotlight to clam up. He supplied Hannah with a pad and pen and suggested that she take her own notes.

The toughened middle-aged Alaska woman seemed pleased when Walt introduced, both himself and his companion. When they got to the cancer part, Hannah stepped in and took over the delicate elements of the story.

As was his inclination, Walt went right to work when they got home while his memory was fresh. He did not have to explain to Hannah that after his notes got cold, he could not always decipher his handwriting. Neither did he find a need to put any binders on his copy editor. She saw things he missed, and he welcomed her input.

He did mention that he did not forward articles immediately. Rather, after a day or so, he went back over them with fresh eyes. It went without saying that both thrived in this auspicious stint of teamwork.

Game on

Jesse became less possessive of Hannah. He even relinquished his side of the bed and went back to sleeping on the futon. The five-year-old was not above being the intruder, but the others found more time to talk. Walt kept reminding himself that talk was all words, but for the time being, words would have to suffice.

"Hannah . . . To use the juvenile analogy, we finally got to first base."

She smiled.

"I know where you're going—so get on with it."

"Miss Smarty Pants . . . You take it from here."

"You were about to circle the wagons a few times talking about the turf between first and second base, and then how to get from second to third. You're not ready, yet, to discuss hitting one out of the park."

"Why would I ever try to keep anything from you? Game on."

"Don't you even think about trying to steal second. That's a privilege you'll have to earn one pitch at the time. And I mean no foul balls or wild pitches."

"I'm more uptight about getting picked off first."

"Then, don't take a big lead."

"Are you also the umpire?"

"But of course—I'm a woman."

Hannah celebrated her gamesmanship skills but was concerned that she had bruised Walt's ego. She got up and went behind his chair. After massaging his temples, she continued.

"What you really want to know is whether I would ever consider living here in Alaska."

Jesse came running in the room to report the winning results in the game he was playing. Game over.

"Jesse . . . Do you think Hannah would like to build a bonfire? We could run to the store and get some wieners and marshmallows. Why don't you go ask her?"

"No—let's surprise her."

"Okay—you keep her entertained until I get back."

Hannah knew they were up to something, but she let them have their fun. While in town, Walt also picked up the ingredients for chili. Jesse blocked her path to the kitchen while his daddy got things ready and started the fire. Walt burst into the room brandishing a cast iron skillet.

"Who's been bad? Who do I need to use this on?"

He got the same "Not me" response from both parties.

"Then, I guess I'll just toss it in the fire. Come on."

Jesse was tickled that they pulled it off. Hannah let him stir the pot, cooking over the open coals, while Walt went to cut forked alder twigs. The lad sharpened the points with his pocket knife.

They did their own hot dog roasting, but the kid took charge of the marshmallows. He deliberately let them catch on fire and then quickly blew it out.

"I cannot imagine a better evening. Those dogs will have me barking for days. The dessert was a little burnt, but it was so sweet and gooey. You guys are the best."

With the flames smoldering, Hannah snuggled with Walt on the quilt. Jesse was playing in the fire and did not notice or seem to care. The star-crossed lovers lay back and did some gazing. Walt reclaimed first base, and the umpire called him safe.

The earth moved

After a laid-back day of beach walking and hiking a steep trail down to the Kenai River, Jesse put himself to bed earlier than usual. Walt got up from his chair and joined Hannah on the sofa. The conversation was going nowhere in particular, but his hands were venturing.

A sound resembling a noisy rushing wind interrupted the mood.

"Earthquake!"

The frame house vibrated from the sonic waves. A split-second later, a ripple went through the floor, ramped up to a rumble that shook the structure for several seconds, and ended with a big thud.

Hannah impulsively wrapped herself around Walt and closed her eyes. He could feel her body trembling.

"Is it over?"

"There might be some aftershocks."

Sure enough, another lesser wave washed under the house. Hannah held on tight. She eventually released her grip but was unable to relax.

"I've heard of earthquakes all my life, but that was nothing like anything I had ever imagined. You feel so helpless."

"Something like this reminds us of just how insignificant we are when compared to the forces of nature. Things got rattled around in here. Let's see if anything is broken."

Walt turned on the radio and tuned it to the Emergency Broadcasting System. The quake was a moderate one, measuring 6.8, but there were no tsunami warnings. The epicenter was not far across the Cook Inlet and nine miles deep.

"How could anything that far underground shake things like this at the surface?"

"Think about a skyscraper. If the bottom floor collapsed, everything above it would get tossed around."

"Walt . . . Next time the earth moves—I hope you have something to do with it. I will also be anticipating some aftershocks."

Jesse slept right through all the excitement.

A good plucking

On the last morning of Hannah's visit, the adults sat at the table sipping coffee. She was about to go home with much still unresolved. The timetable was more urgent for Walt because of Jesse's kindergarten predicament. As she put her feet in his lap, he tried one more time to move the conversation off center.

"We still have so much to talk about, and I'm not sure where to begin."

"Me neither."

Attention shifted to the caffeinated diversion as both caressed the mugs and sipped in silence until Hannah broke it.

"Please tell me what you're thinking. Why did you invite me here?"

"Isn't that rather obvious?"

"No—Walt—I want to hear it. Talk to me."

She put her feet back on the floor.

"Jesse just turned five. He will start kindergarten next fall, and . . ."

"I don't want to talk about Jesse. Tell me about Walt."

"Only if you will then talk to me about Hannah."

"That all depends on what you say first."

Walt grimaced, relaxed just a tad, and put a foot in her lap. She started rubbing it and just couldn't help herself.

"I never knew you were so ticklish."

"Now you know everything about me. Your turn."

"Walt Williamson . . . You're impossible. Come on counselor. You're such a genius at getting others to open up. Please tell me what's going on in your head. Then, I want to know what's going on in that heart of yours."

"Hannah . . . Do people have only one soul mate? Can there be more than one love of your life? Or is that a contradiction?"

"You tell me."

"You were my first love, but because of *your* circumstances, I had to restrain myself endlessly. I'm having trouble breaking that pattern. I think you are, too."

"Do you think Ginny was the only love of your life, and that she can never be replaced?"

"I don't like the word replaced. I didn't think you could be replaced, but I found a different place in my heart for Ginny. What I'm wondering is whether you can reclaim what has *always been yours*."

"Walt . . . A part of me has loved you from the moment we met. I will *always* love you no matter what. I'm so thrilled that we reconnected after all these years."

She paused, squeezed his hands, and looked into his eyes.

"I love you, but I want to be madly *in love* with you. I want you to court me, to woo me, to take my breath away, to sweep me off my feet. I've never had that."

Walt's heartstrings had just gotten a good plucking.

"I would love nothing more."

> Othell . . . What the hell did I just agree to? How can I romance that woman when we live thousands of miles apart? If she moved here, could that happen if we lived in the same house? How does this square with Jesse's schooling? Maybe kicking the can down the road was not so bad after all. I might get canned, but this Casanova is about to give it the good old college try.

On the road again

"Jesse . . . Let's go check one more time before we get on down the road."

Ms. Robin was all excited. Walt retrieved the step stool and peered into the nest. Two of the eggs had hatched. He hoisted Jesse so he could see the tiny featherless birds.

"You take good care of your babies. We should be back from our summer vacation before you all leave for your winter break."

Old Sourdough, the Subaru, was loaded for the long haul. Walt always carried along emergency supplies, and he left room for the seats to recline—in the event, they had to sleep in the SUV. Jesse had packed his entertainment stash and books to read if he got bored. Before they were hardly settled in their seats, he had something on his mind.

"Daddy . . . What did I look like, when I was born?"

"I think there's a picture or two somewhere. Did you never see them?"

"I don't remember it if I did. Did I look anything like those baby birds?"

"You were much bigger, and you had hands and feet. Your eyes were open, but you couldn't see, yet. You even had some hair on your head."

"Did I hatch from an egg?"

"Yes, you did."

"Was my mother there, then?"

"Son . . . Your birth was different from most boys' and girls'. Your mother left the egg behind before she went away. It was kept in a safe place until it was time for you to be born."

"Was I hatched in a nest?"

"Yes, you were, in sort of a nest. Aunt Polly took your mother's place keeping your egg warm."

"Oh . . ."

Jesse crawled in the back and reached for his tablet and crayons. He would not let his daddy see what he was working on. When they pulled in at Tern Junction to stretch their legs and take in the glorious scenery, he held up a colorful but rough sketch of Ms. Robin sitting on the side of her nest with three blue eggs in it.

"Son . . . That is so beautiful. I can't wait for you to show it to Sissy. Maybe, she can help you touch it up, and we'll get it framed."

Before they crossed from the Yukon into northern British Columbia, Walt could see the smoke from a massive wildfire. When he stopped to top off the tank, he learned that the Alaska Highway was closed. He also found out that the limited number of rooms at the outpost was all filled, and the lone eating joint had run out of food.

"Jesse . . . Looks like it will be sardines and crackers for supper. I think we can make room for you to sleep in the back, but I'm sitting in my bed for the night."

By the next morning, pilot trucks were leading vehicles through. Even with the windows rolled up and the flow through ventilation shut off, the smell of smoke got inside. Radio stations were scant but when the scan settled on one, Willie Nelson was belting out, "On the road again. Just can't wait to get on the road again . . ."

A woman's touch

The father and son were ready for a break when they crossed the U. S. Border. Seattle was only a couple hours on down the road. Walt wondered if Jesse would address his grandparents differently, but there was not a chance. They were still Ice and the Ice Man.

After dinner, Dave invited Walt to join him for another evening walk. His son-in-law had no objections because his legs needed a good workout.

"Alice and I were hoping Jesse could spend some time with us this summer. He is such an experienced flier. If you thought the boy was ready to travel alone, we were going to offer to purchase his ticket.

"When we found out that you were coming by for a couple of days, we came up with a Plan B. Would you consider letting him stay with us for a while? It would be fine if he was here until you came back through—or if you wished—we could put him on a plane at any point. Think about it if you need to. I wanted to have this talk with you alone and leave Jesse out of it until you decided."

"I'm open to the possibility. The boy is a trooper, but he gets so tired being confined on these long trips, especially after we get out of Canada. Let me discuss it with him and see what he thinks."

When they got back to the house, another car was in the drive. Jesse was showing off his Game Boy to his Aunt Polly. She glanced up at Walt, and the five-year-old had to pull on her arm to regain her attention.

Jesse's surrogate mom did not stay much longer, and Walt walked her to the car.

"Polly . . . You look nice. Have you lost weight?"

"Yes—I would have lost even more if I had known earlier that you were coming through."

He could feel himself blushing and was appreciative of the subdued light.

"Mother told me what Daddy planned to discuss with you. I do hope you let Jesse stay here. Please understand why I want to spend some time with him, too. I'm out for the summer and would love to do things with him. He might need a woman's touch now and then. And you, too, for that matter. Who is Hannah?"

"She's just an old friend from graduate school."

The conversation with Jesse would have to wait until morning. Another communication was more pressing.

> My precious Ginny . . . Your parents want Jesse to stay with them while I drive onto North Carolina. I have no problem with him being around them more, but I'm torn about Polly. Jesse is asking questions about his birth, and I'm answering them as best I know how. I do not want your sister to divulge anything causing our son to think I have not been honest with him.

> Perhaps, I have not been fair with Polly. I was so caught up in my own universe that I was unable to put myself in her position. She is truly a remarkable woman. I would not have the boy without her. How can I make amends without her reading more into it than what I mean? And by the way, Polly is taking good care of herself. She looks amazing.

Jesse did not jump at the notion of sending his dad on without him. He was really looking forward to seeing his Sissy and playing with Hannah. Walt asked if he would be okay flying alone. The boy shot him a look right out of his mother's playbook.

"Daddy . . . Did you forget? I'm five."

The opportunity to prove his point was the tipping point. Saying goodbye was harder for Walt than it was for Jesse. The sky was overcast, and the driver was in his own fog. He almost did not see an oncoming motorist waving at him as he turned the corner, and he barely got a glimpse of Polly on the way to her parents' house.

Always on my mind

"Othell . . . This might work out quite well. On the plus side, I'll be more relaxed not worrying about Jesse's well-being during this long stretch. Anyway—why should I have to carry the burden of Jesse's beginnings alone? He might learn things that will make it easier for both of us. Besides— I have some serious courting to do, and the little intruder won't be sticking his nose into everything. Come on, you Old Sourdough. Let's get on down the road."

About that time, Willie chimed in again. This time, he was strumming and singing, "Always on my mind . . . You were always on my mind."

Finding motels with Wi-Fi was not always easy except in cities where the nightly rates were steeper. Walt saw a sign advertising the service in a small town, and he pulled in for the night. He needed to get a message to Tonya informing her of what to expect and considered surprising Hannah. The chances of the boy's whereabouts remaining a secret were somewhere between nil and nada.

"Othell . . . Sometimes surprises rise up and bite you in the butt."

He hammered out an email to his daughter and copied it to Hannah. Answers to both messages were awaiting him before he checked out the next morning. Tonya seemed more disappointed than Hannah did. Both encouraged him to be safe.

Walt found the solitude satisfying. He loved his son, but this aloneness reminded him of just how much their lives were intertwined. Once the kid started to school, both could claim a new measure of independence.

He turned the radio off for hours, and the silence gave him time to think. Walt had always been an incurable romantic. The happiest days of his life were while he was with Ginny, and his amorous impulses were unfettered. The possibility of a second chance excited him. His creative juices flowed as he started plotting things in his mind. The woman said she wished to be courted and romanced. Did she have any idea who she was dealing with?

"Othell . . . My *over* is *due*. I just hope my *other* is *wise*."

Plans change, again

The fourth day was a killer. Since leaving Kenai, this was Walt's eleventh under the wheel, with three off in Seattle. He was averaging more than six-hundred miles per day, and his back and neck were not happy campers.

"Othell . . . You know full well you're not as young as you used to be."

The weary motorist imagined soaking in a hot tub. His thoughts drifted to Hannah's hands soothing his throbbing muscles. While his mind was taking a little mental vacation, so also did the Outback. The driver coxed the vehicle back on the road, careful not to over-steer. It was time to take one last break.

Only fifty miles from Ephesus, he had not planned on making another stop. Plans change.

When Walt finally got to his other home, perplexing news awaited him. Hannah had left the day before for a seminar in Durham. Tonya was unaware that she had not mentioned it.

"Othell . . . My *flabber* is *gasted*—my *thunder* is *struck*—my *dumb* is *founded*. So much for getting run over by the welcome wagon."

"Oh, Dad—She's just playing a bit hard to get."

"Hard to get? We're not in junior high. Is she acting like the age group she worked with? When will she be back?"

"I believe she said in four days."

"Hmm. Just about the time I was planning to go see Earl and Mary Beth."

"Ho-hum, you two."

Hannah had blindsided him. Walt's mind circled back to when his vehicle drifted, and he had to regain control to avert a disaster. Another correction was necessary, and he was trying not to overreact. He had planned to visit his uncle and aunt during the summer, but with his entire focus on Hannah, nothing was prearranged. Rather than sit around and wait for her, he decided to make use of the time.

When Hannah got back into town, she was not thrilled when she learned of his whereabouts. He had given no indication of how long he would be gone. Tonya was thrust in the middle.

"Hannah . . . I'm not going to tell you what to do, but I think you made a serious mistake. You have known about that conference for weeks and could have at least given him a heads-up. Dad could have timed his arrival to correspond with your return. You had a golden opportunity to alert him when he sent the joint email to us after he left Seattle."

Tonya waited for her to take ownership of what she had done. When Hannah remained impassive, she went on.

"Try to put yourself in his place. I could see the hurt in his eyes when you were not here to greet him after such a strenuous journey. That's a long, long haul, and you have to believe his thoughts were more and more on you the closer he got. Remember—it was your idea for him to come all the way here and court you."

"Do you think I'm subconsciously sabotaging this thing?"

"You're the counselor, but it seems to me that you might delete subconsciously. Hannah . . . I love both of you, but make no mistake about it. I do not want to see my daddy get hurt."

"What do you think I should do?"

"I'm not going there. You messed in your nest, and you'll have to figure out how to clean it out. If you want to, that is. I will say this, though. A gesture of goodwill might well be in order. If you'll give him a chance, I think you'll find my father understanding and forgiving."

The Kings were not online, so an email was out of the question. Hannah knew she could call but also realized how much Walt detested resolving things over the phone. If she got in her car and made the three-hour drive, she might look like a blithering idiot crawling back to him. Discussing it with him when he got back, seemed the best plan.

Get a grip, girlfriend

The more Hannah contemplated what happened, the more she convinced herself that what she did was not that different from what Walt had done. She tried to justify herself to Tonya.

"I think the playing field is just about level. No really, it isn't. My seminar was already scheduled, but he deliberately changed his plans to make me look bad and to show me up. How dare that man not be here waiting for me when I got back? He made me feel like I'm not important."

"Get a grip, girlfriend. You made yourself look bad. When you ducked out on him, you sent a strong signal that he was not a priority. He was not showing you up but just giving you a dose of your own medicine."

"It's his own fault that he doesn't like to talk on the phone. If he were not so eccentric, he could have called me in my room, and we would've worked things out before he got all riled up."

As she fumed, her disdain kept ramping up for how *she* was mistreated. If he did not see things *her* way, then he would just get what he deserved.

Tonya countered but got nowhere. She suggested again that the next move was Hannah's.

"I did what was right for me. What do I have to apologize for?"

"Hannah . . . Do you ever listen to yourself?"

Striking out

Walt was devastated when he heard nothing from Hannah for a full week after he returned to Ephesus. With every passing day, it appeared more unlikely that Jesse would be making his first solo flight that summer. He did not even bother looking into the possibility of enrolling the boy in the local school.

"Dad . . . Don't be so stubborn. Go talk to her."

"I'm being stubborn? She created this confusion, and it's up to her to make things right with me."

"I know you're right, but women don't think the way you do."

"Huh—If there's something wrong with my thinking, then the last thing I need is a woman in my life."

Each time he talked to Jesse, the more unsettled Walt was. He set a deadline in his mind of sufficient time to hear from Hannah. It passed, and he placed a call to let the Sullivans know approximately when to expect him. His son was at Polly's, and Alice told him that Jesse's visit had meant the world to their daughter.

"Thank you so much for sharing him with his other family. He's such a good kid."

Walt's body was about recuperated when he buckled up in Old Sourdough's driver's seat for the about-face. Conversely, his spirits were nowhere near mended from the ordeal he had just been through.

"Othell . . . In some ways, this was a wasted trip, but in others, I found the answers I was looking for."

The day before he departed, he went to a greeting card store, purchased a generic note, and addressed it to Hannah. He inscribed only three words.

These were not the three she thought she might be hearing by the end of the summer. Simply put, Walt penned.

"I struck out."

The balls

Walt limped out of town, while Hannah was celebrating her Pyrrhic victory. It was her way or the highway, and even though she did not know it yet, the other party was trucking on down the road. He drove aimlessly but attentively.

"Othell . . . My *down* is *trodden*. My *brow* is *beaten*."

Walt tried to assess what had just happened, but none of it made sense. The Old Sourdough kicked into overdrive.

Hannah could bear the silence no longer, and she called Tonya to get a reading.

"He's gone. Left early this morning."

"What? And he didn't even tell me goodbye?"

"Hannah . . . You were not here to say hello to him! What makes you think he owed you a goodbye?"

"Ahhhhh . . . Men! Do you think it's over?"

"I feel like the proverbial broken record. That's up to you. You've known the man far longer than I have. What do you think his reaction would be if you were to get down off your high horse and assume your *own* accountability for what *you* did to run it off the rails? The ball is in your court. Or, I should say, the *balls* are in your court."

"Tonya . . . I thought you were my friend."

"If I were not your friend, we wouldn't be having this conversation. Let me see if I've got this straight. Not only do you think you did nothing wrong, but you were also the one wronged?"

"Why would I see it any other way? He came all the way from Alaska to see me. Then, he turned around and went back without even laying eyes on me."

"You think you had nothing to do with that?"

"I didn't hold a gun to his head."

"Oh, Hannah . . ."

"I guess it's all just as well. Walt already had his mind made up before he even got here. Besides—I could never live up to his precious Ginny's standard. He didn't come right out and said so, but I knew he was trying to lure me into leaving everything behind and moving up there with him in that God forsaken place. I could never be happy in another woman's home, especially one where Walt shared such a passionate relationship. I felt creepy both times I was there."

"That's not what you said at the time. Dad came here this summer— open to the possibility of putting Jesse in school here. If things had worked out for you two, would you have wanted him to move in with you?"

"Sure. Why not?"

"Why is that different?"

"I don't know why it's different. It just is."

"You mean—the same home that you and your husband lived in for decades—and the same house where he took his own life?"

"If I'm okay with it, why should that be any kind of problem for Walt?"

The conversation ended awkwardly, and Hannah went to check the mail. A big smile came over her face.

"He just admitted it. HE struck out. This is ALL his fault, and HE knows it."

Unintended consequences

Previous cross-country voyages were adventures, but this time, Walt just wanted to get to the Pacific Northwest. Attractions along the way would wait until he could share then with Jesse.

"Othell . . . Tell me something. Why is it that a woman says she yearns for romance and then cuts her man off at the knees? What is he supposed to do when she then turns the tables on him for not being able to stand on his own two feet?"

When the anguishing motorist checked in the first night, he did not even look for Internet service. Walt did, however, take his laptop into the room. He opened his electronic journal and scribed some things running through his head.

> Everything within my being hurts right now, but my real pain is for Hannah. I kept superimposing on her the woman I first met. Back then, she was vibrant and so full of life. I had never known anyone that honest, thoughtful, and caring. Nonetheless, I made a serious miscalculation

> when I did not factor into the equation what life threw at her after we went our separate ways.
>
> Hannah's wounds seem not to have healed. They may never. Some individuals get into a self-preservation groove. After years of developing strategies to safeguard themselves, they are terrified of pealing off the layers for fear of being vulnerable and getting hurt all over again. The warning signs were there all along. I just refused to see them.
>
> It also appears that Hannah is following a familiar pattern. Professionals often busy themselves trying to fix others so they do not have to deal with their own broken parts.

When he finished, he copied and pasted what he had written into an email to send Tonya the next time he was online. He added a personal note at the bottom.

> Tonya . . . I have been processing what happened. I'm working hard to see beyond my own disillusionment, and to get some kind of handle on what is going on with Hannah. See what you think. Sorry I did not have more time to spend with you. How is your love life?

After another grueling day, Walt pulled in a little early. Crossing the plains, the Old Sourdough had a tailwind, and Walt loosened the reins. He stopped twice before finding a motel with Wi-Fi and got the message off to Tonya before jumping in the shower.

He was up early the next day, disappointed that she had not responded by the time he checked out. About mid-morning, he went into a library and used one of their computers. A message was waiting.

> Dad . . . Three things leaped from the computer screen when I read your email. First, I was so needlessly worried about you. I do not know another person who would not have taken what

Hannah did to you and perceived it as rejection. Yet, you tried to see it from her perspective. Much of what you derived about her is spot on. It was almost like you eavesdropped on our conversations. Never doubt for a moment my love and admiration for you.

Unlike that old Timex commercial, you not only take a licking and keep on ticking, but you also take licking after licking and keep on ticking. Just don't get the impression that I feel sorry for you, though. You are also fully capable of getting in your own licks.

The second is this. For the life of me, I cannot see why anyone would want to be a counselor.

The other thing that rattled me prompts a confession. In something you wrote, you were describing me, also, in so many ways. Dad . . . I'm thirty-five-years-old, and I've been devising strategies all my life to keep people, especially men, from getting too close. I have been so obsessed with not becoming my mother that I've neglected, as you say it, my "I am."

"Wow . . . Othell. Talk about unintended consequences."

Part IV: Jesse's two Mothers

Tea leaves

On the fourth day of ten or more hours behind the wheel, Walt got into Seattle ahead of his projected schedule. The reunion with his son would have to wait a few more minutes.

"Jesse is with Polly. She was going to bring him back in a little while, but you got here first. She wanted to spend as much time with him as possible. Why don't you go on over to her house and save her the trip? I know she'll be happy to see you, too."

"Othell . . . Did you hear that? Save her the trip. Huh—I'm the one who's been glued to this seat all summer, but I've got to save Polly a fifteen-minute drive. Mothers always protecting their children. Huh—then again, maybe she was doing me a favor. If Polly brought him home, she might stick around. I can go gather up my son and leave."

"Daddy! Daddy!"

"Son . . . Did you miss me?"

Walt was a tad miffed when the boy hesitated.

"I sure missed you."

"Hello . . . Walt. Did you miss me, too?"

"Of course, I did. I missed Jesse. I missed Aunt Polly. I missed Ice. I missed the Iceman."

Polly was chagrined with his response. She had already read the tea leaves regarding his cross-country turnaround. All decked out in a bright summer dress that accented her assets, she was hoping for a better reaction when he gave her the once-over.

For the first time ever, Walt did not disappoint her. Feigning a southern drawl that had long since faded, he poured it on thick as molasses.

"Good golly, Miss Polly. If you ain't-a sight for sore eyes."

"Have mercy—Mr. Williamson. I shore do hope yore old sore eyes keep gittin' better and better."

Polly's elation was short-lived.

"Jesse . . . Get your things so we can go."

It was worth a try, but she braced herself for yet another big letdown.

"Why don't you stay here? It won't be the first time you slept in this house."

"Daddy . . . Have you lived here before?"

"I stayed with your Aunt Polly a few days when you were a baby."

"I didn't know that."

"Walt . . . I do hope you won't just rush off back to Alaska. You must surely be exhausted."

"My body hurts in places that I did not know I had places."

"You pore man. Come on—let me run you a tub of hot water."

Nothing to fear

"Jesse tells me that he will begin kindergarten this fall."

"Yes . . . Dave. It's hard to believe, but it's true. Our lives are about to take a decided turn."

"I'm sure you have good schools in Alaska, but the ones around here are acclaimed for their excellence. The offer I made to you before is still on the table. I know you want to hold onto Ginny's house, but if you would consider moving here, I remain in a position to help you relocate. We have enjoyed Jesse so much while he's been here."

"Thanks again for your generosity. This is just not my home. Anytime I leave Alaska—I cannot wait to get back."

"Well, then. Jesse did not make a flight this summer, but we both agree that he can do it alone. The attendants gush all over kids like him. Anytime you can spare the boy for a few days, let us know. The least we could do is pay for his ticket."

"From what he's told me about this visit, I think he'll be all for it. He really enjoyed going golfing with you."

"Such a good caddie he was, and my buddies are now calling me the Ice Man. I hear it every time I line up a putt. Walt . . . Don't deprive us of enjoying our grandchild. I know this is a little delicate, but don't keep him away from Polly, either. You have nothing to fear from her—and perhaps much to gain."

"Othell . . . What the hell did he mean by that?"

"Jesse has told me all about Ms. Robin. He said his sister was going to help him with his drawing, but since he never made it that far, we worked on it some together. I hope you don't mind. Did he show it to you?"

"No—he didn't. Jesse might have told you what he knows about Ms. Robin, but he certainly did not tell you everything."

"What do you mean?"

Walt looked for a way to backtrack, but he could not find reverse.

"Starting the spring after Ginny's death, I felt like some kind of channeling was going on, and I seemed to get messages from her through the robin."

"Walt . . . That is amazing and so exciting."

"Then—you do not think me a kook?"

"Heavens no. Tell me more."

"Soon after I found out about Ginny's three frozen eggs, I told Ms. Robin about them. I was so undecided about what to do. The bird got all excited, and I could tell she wanted me to look in her nest. I went for the step stool and looked down at three blue eggs. Three eggs—can you believe that? I didn't get it at first, but then I figured out Ginny was telling me to go forward."

"Wow!"

"Remember the 'Little Boy's Second Christmas' ornament you gave Jesse? Do you have any recollection of the way I looked at you when I saw etched on the back a robin on her nest looking down at the three eggs?"

"Wow! Times two."

"Can you see now why Jesse's colored sketch is so important?"

Polly sat in stone silence looking straight ahead before she could respond. Her eyes then turned to him.

"Walt . . . Do you realize what just happened? We had a moment. You did not have to share this. It thrills me that you care enough to take me into your confidence with something so special as this. I have chills. I'm shaking. Will you hold me?"

Bedtime stories

The Sullivans seemed fine with Walt spending time with Polly. She and her mother insisted on taking Jesse shopping for school clothes. They were not sure what the Alaska kids wore, but his daddy assured them their duds were not that different.

"You take care of everything else, and I'll get his overalls after we get back."

Jesse especially liked it when Aunt Polly read him bedtime stories in her lap. After one session that lasted longer than usual, he fell asleep in her arms. The boy hardly roused when his dad picked him up. Walt sat several moments on the bedside looking down at his precious son.

When he returned to the den, Polly had dressed for bed.

"Come over here, big boy, and I'll now read you a bedtime story."

"Will you rock me to sleep?"

"I'd rather keep you awake."

"Then, it'd better be an interesting story. It's getting late."

Walt was in reach, and Polly pulled him down beside her. She took his hand and put it on her flat tummy.

"Not the first time your hand has been there, but it feels much different now doesn't it?"

"You must be talking about when you swallowed that pumpkin seed."

She started moving his hand upward, and he offered no resistance.

"Not the first time it's been there, either. What do you feel now?"

"What kind of bedtime story is this?"

"It could be one that ends, 'And everybody lived happily ever after'."

Alaska is calling

Walt was concerned about Tonya, and he used Polly's computer to send her an email. He was spelling out what a nice time he was having in Seattle when Polly not so subtly glanced over his shoulder to see for sure whose name was in the address box.

He did not want his daughter to think that he had an ulterior motive and was checking on Hannah. Walt was uncomfortable with how much Tonya was caught in the middle. If Hannah had anything to say, she knew how to reach him. He got a reply through Polly's mail, with an attachment that she asked her father to delete after reading.

Tonya supposed that she must be having her own "identity dilemma." She had earned two college degrees but had found no fulfilling way to use them. Never before, had loneliness become an issue. Something kept worming its way into her mindfulness. It certainly felt like Alaska was calling her again.

A wave of regret washed over Walt. Single-mindedly tussling with the Hannah mess, he had missed a prime opportunity to be there for his daughter when she needed him. He scheduled a phone date from the Sullivans where he had more privacy.

When they talked, he reassured Tonya that if she wanted to return to Alaska, she could crash with them for as long as she wished. That settled it, but one thing in particular concerned her. She was a little edgy about driving through the vast wilderness areas alone. Walt suggested that she angle across the country to Seattle, and then they would go the rest of the way in tandem.

"Are you in a hurry? It will take several days for me to pull things together."

"Remember—I had planned to be gone all summer. I just need to get Jesse home in time to start kindergarten, and that's still a few weeks away."

After he ended the conversation, Walt turned to Alice.

"Looks like you're stuck with us a while longer."

"Walt . . . You, your son, and your daughter are always welcome here."

Polly made no attempt to contain herself when she heard the news. The hug he got was not only tight but also animated. Unlike his son, Walt did not put his arms in the way.

Jesse's eyes sparkled when he learned Sissy was going back home with them. He would get to see her after all. And so much more.

A chain and a splintered board

Bidding farewell to her art students was spirited, but saying goodbye to Hannah was awkward. The mutual friend did not come right out and say so, but Tonya knew what she was thinking. First, Walt turned his back on her, and now his daughter was abandoning her.

Deciding what to take and what to leave behind was a work in progress. Almost every available inch in Cornfield's cargo area was utilized. It was a bit out of the way, but she went by to see her Grandmother Connie.

Tonya was drawn to the city cemetery the morning she left Sand Mountain. Tears flowed unabated standing at the foot of her Pa Bell's tomb. Numbness consumed her when situated between the graves of her mother and grandfather. Tonya then did something long overdue.

Not far up the road, her thoughts circled back to the first time she drove across the continent. She had just met Hannah but had no clue regarding who the woman was. Tonya recalled another cemetery she took a walk in the first morning on the road. The odds of finding it again were not good, but she stopped at a rest area and reached for her ragged atlas. Three town names sounded familiar.

Hours later, she was hopeful that she had gotten off the expressway at the right exit. The little burgs had a sameness about them, but one was different. She spotted the motel she had stayed in, but it had long since closed. The cemetery was still open for business.

Tonya revisited her yearnings of yore when she contemplated the veiled messages on the markers. She was struggling once more with her own sense of significance and what might one day be her epitaph. As if guided by an unseen hand, she had found the hallowed burial place again.

What about the little country church? Would Mrs. Hattie's house be razed and another in its place?

After rambling for about an hour, she had just about given up when she saw a sign at an intersection pointing to the church. The members had modernized it. Tonya had trouble breathing. Mrs. Hattie's house was just down the road. Cornfield went on autopilot.

The caved in roof was the first thing Tonya noticed when she turned into the drive. She then looked for the swing. Decaying remnants cluttered the ground, but the chains were still dangling.

Breathing deeply, she opened the car door, got out, and went to where the back door once stood. The old kitchen table had surrendered to the collapsed timbers. Tonya squeezed in and salvaged a splintered board. She then went and yanked on one of the rusty chains until a section broke free.

The sketch of Mrs. Hattie was one of the last things Tonya had packed. She retrieved it and held it out in awe. The ethereal woman whispered in her ear. "Follow your inner voice."

Ties that bind

Tonya was physically and emotionally exhausted when she got to Seattle. She was relieved that Walt and Jesse were in no hurry to get on up the road. Dave and Alice put her up. Jesse went back and forth.

"She's in love with you, you know."

"Who?"

"Polly."

"I thought you might be talking about Hannah."

"She is, too, but—sometimes, I think Phillip is still controlling her from the grave. Why do people allow that?"

"Tonya . . . Is your mother still pulling your strings?"

She glared at her father with, "How do you do that?" written all over her face.

"No—I cut her loose five days ago, standing by her grave."

She paused to let that sink in.

"Is Ginny still controlling you?"

Abruptly, Walt got up and went out the door. The saturated firmament was leaking, but he did not notice. Pure mist commingled with salty drips.

An hour later, Alice was putting dinner on the table, and Tonya was getting worried. Walt ambled in drenched to the bone, but at one with the elements. A peaceful appearance was about him that had been missing in action for months. He excused himself and said he would rejoin them around the table after a good drying out.

Before he and Jesse left to go back to Polly's for the night, Tonya pulled him off to the side.

"I don't want to intrude, but we didn't finish our conversation earlier. Now—back to Polly. Dad . . . Is some rebounding going on here?"

"Tonya . . . I've about decided that this old coon dog has been barking up the wrong tree the whole time."

Once upon a time

Walt was never sure what Jesse was taking in. Much involving his providence was swirling all around him. He did not want to overload the kid, but he longed for the day when everything was out in the open. At the moment, some serious antecedent business needed tending with the woman who carried the boy and birthed him.

Polly sensed nothing urgent that evening and insisted on reading Jesse stories until sleepiness prevailed. Walt paced in the background until finally taking possession of his son's limp body. He caught Polly by surprise when he came back in and spoke rather curtly.

"We need to talk."

"Why? What have I done this time?"

"It's not you. It's about me and what I've done and not done."

"Walt . . . You frighten me."

"Nothing to be afraid of, my dear. Then again, maybe this is a little terrifying."

"My dear? Did you just call me my dear?"

"Would you hush? I feel like a big ticking time clock is hanging over my head. We have to get on up the road soon, and so much needs to be said."

"Take a deep breath, *my dear*. We've got the night."

During the next wee slice of eternity, Walt tried fervently to clear both the air and his conscience.

"First of all, I was so caught up in my own world that I rendered myself impervious to any understanding of what was going on in yours."

"Don't be so hard on yourself. The baby was never meant to be mine. It was yours and Ginny's. I went into it rationally, and I honestly thought I could go through it without getting emotionally involved. It's not your fault. The one thing I had not counted on was falling in love with you. That put an impossible strain on us and screwed up everything. For that, I am genuinely sorry."

Sparkle shined through the tear trying to form.

"Not sorry for falling in love with you, but for the screwing it up part."

"I was flattered that you had feelings for me. Honest, I was, but I just could not let myself go there. I felt it would be a betrayal of Ginny."

"You were so right. Thank you for being strong. I'm not sure how you did it. Then again, when I remember how I looked, I can't imagine why any man would have found me attractive."

"Not the case now, is it? Polly . . . You are a beautiful woman."

"That's terrifying, but don't distract me. Walt . . . You don't know what it's like having a little person growing inside you. Jesse will always be a part of me no matter what, and there's nothing you can do about it."

"I'm so sorry for what I put you through. Right now—I'm struggling with what I *can do* about it."

"Oh, really?"

"Do you know what one of my biggest obstacles has been? Think about it. Before a woman's death, she leaves behind frozen eggs. One is eventually implanted into her own sister's womb, and fertilized, no less, by the late wife's husband. The surrogate sister and the widower unintentionally fall in love and raise the kid as their own. That sounds far too much like something in a romance novel than anything that could possibly happen in real life."

"Walt . . . I believe in fairy tales. Don't you?"

Walkie-talkies

Walt Williamson had departed Alaska with a twofold dilemma. Top billing went to what was best for his son. Secondarily, he went seeking a way to bridge the spatial gap between himself and someone firmly rooted and grounded elsewhere. He returned with the same quandaries, only with a different woman.

The first box might be a bit easier to check. Polly's devotion to Jesse would never be in doubt. Other unknowns were all over the map. Both he and Polly had been single the majority of their adult lives. Compatibility issues and potential differences in child-rearing policies must be addressed— if they explored the possibility of going forward raising Jesse together. Walt suspected the boy's other mother might be lenient and have a propensity to pamper him.

"Othell . . . Might that be offset with a tendency for her to spoil me as well? Hmm."

Polly had a gift for the caravan before it pulled out—walkie-talkies. Jesse took on the role of the switchboard operator. It was a good thing she sent along extra batteries.

The five-year-old had a reserved seat in each vehicle, but he favored the one bringing up the rear. That was fine with Walt. This gave him space to bounce things back and forth in his brain. Communication between him and Polly was unbelievably uncomplicated once he broke through his obtuseness. Her sly sense of humor put him on the other side of comic relief, and he found that incredibly satisfying.

Walt revisited the discussion he had with Tonya about the three words all starting with the same letter—*whatever, whenever,* and *wherever.* If the chance of a committed relationship were to unfold, they looked at their various options.

Both were in agreement not to move too hastily. Polly assured Walt that he could move in with her almost seamlessly. Jesse would have to change schools since it would be impossible for things to come together before the upcoming academic year.

Another alternative was for her to join him in Alaska. The teacher would likely have no difficulty finding a job, and she assured Walt that living in her sister's house would be no problem. That took a big weight off his shoulders. Polly surprised him when she suggested that making a fresh start somewhere else actually appealed to her.

That led to a third possibility. Nothing prevented them from settling anywhere they wished. His house in North Carolina was a neutral site and not off the table.

In the wilderness of northern British Columbia, something about the situation amused Walt. No one could see the devious look that appeared on his face.

"Othell . . . I don't believe I'd get all tripped up courting that woman."

He had just put his finger on the crux of the matter. Unlike the agreement they had forged before Jesse was born, this was no mere business arrangement. While Jesse's welfare was uppermost, this had to be right for both parents as well.

"Othell . . . Only time will tell."

The hots

As the lead dog, Walt was the sentinel on the lookout for spectacular scenic views and wildlife within range. The airwaves were also open when someone needed a break. Jesse often chimed in for no apparent reason.

Walt tried not to read too much into it, but Polly's contribution was highly symbolic of how barriers can be bridged with open channels for communication. Was she that much like her sister?

Jesse told Tonya all about the Liard Hot Springs, and how on the way down, his daddy had just about scalded him. On this visit, the boy entered the water one toe at the time in his underpants. Walt donned a pair of cutoffs.

Tonya was hesitant to step in with shorts and a top, but her father had advised her wisely that no one was out to make a fashion statement. She relaxed when she saw others dressed in all kinds of garb to cover their bodies, some barely at all.

While his daughter and son cavorted in the less temperate shallows, Walt took a seat on a bench where the hot sulfur water washed over his tired neck and shoulders. He closed his eyes and imagined Polly adding her magic touch.

The place they stayed that night had slow and unreliable Internet service, but Walt got off an email.

"Today, I had the hots for you."

Walt was in his own world and Jesse just along for the ride, but this was yet another trip of a lifetime for Tonya. Standing beside her mother's grave was many miles back down the road, but its significance was still evolving. The evocative words of Mrs. Hattie were fresher than ever.

The brakes were applied to Cornfield at will. She told her dad that if he was in a big hurry, just to take Jesse and go on ahead, but there was no chance of that. The father and his two offspring might never again have such an opportunity to do this together.

The staleness that had taken over Tonya's existence was being routed by one visual feast after another. The terrain kept reinventing itself as though each portal was endeavoring to outdo the rest. Her camera card was drained into her laptop each evening just to keep pace.

Tonya was still unsure what her inner voice might be telling her. Not in doubt was that her "I am" was all in.

New leaves

The Alaska residents and former resident were waved on through at the Alaska Border after a brief inspection. The agent reminded them that soon, passports would be required. An eagle came up from behind and gave them an escort. Wows were audible in both vehicles—echoing over the airwaves.

When the entourage finally pulled in, Walt when on ahead and opened up the house. While Tonya was fidgeting with what to take in first, he went out the back door. No one was there to greet him. He gasped when he saw that a storm had broken up the bird's nest, and the pieces lay on the ground. The widower went inside, bypassed the candle, and put his Ginny WOWs journal away for good.

Two days later, Tonya went with Walt to the Peninsula College campus to check on job possibilities. He learned that the last position had just been filled. Neither were there any openings in her fields, but the dean said he thought the Homer campus was still searching for an art teacher.

"You have your master's degree, but your teaching experience is limited with none at the college level. Let me give them a call and not waste a trip."

While he was on the phone, Tonya mused to her dad.

"How could a drive from here to Homer ever be thought of like a wasted trip?"

"Great news. They would like for you to come for an interview."

The tall peaks across the inlet were shrouded in clouds, and Cornfield had to negotiate patches of dense fog. None of this dimmed Tonya's spirits. Alaska had called, and she had answered.

Arriving about an hour before her appointment, she made her way to the Homer Spit. Bekka had been gone for as long as she had, and the art gallery was open under different management. The former employee and exhibitor sauntered about looking at the works on display without mentioning her prior affiliation.

Tonya had just enough time for a walk along the rocky beach. The pondering of the day was synchronicity. Stepping gently on the uneven terrain, her eyes were drawn to a flat rock with intersecting white streaks forming a T. Since that was the initial of her first name, she picked it up.

After meandering for about a half hour, she turned back. Another smooth gray stone sporting a distinct Z caught her attention. Something about being at the end of the road and finding a rock with the last letter of the alphabet engraved on it enticed her to take it along, too.

Tonya went back up the road with a job, a place to live, and two rocks. A local contractor had just completed a four-unit furnished apartment complex, and she had her picking choice. The street it was on was aptly named, Fairview, so she chose one on the ground floor.

Tonya reflected on the first time she came to Homer. She anticipated a quick turnaround to get back to a job and a boyfriend. When she packed up and left ten years later, the notion that she would return for an encore was just as far-flung.

Walt . . . Are you still there?

When Walt called Polly on Sunday afternoon, she burst into laughter.
"This is like old times. Are we going to have phone dates again?"
"Why not? But I don't want another kid."
"Me neither. Are you sitting down or pacing?"
"Why do you ask?"
"Before Jesse was born and you called to check on me, I could just imagine you on your cordless phone, walking the floor. You were so formal and business-like. You tried your best not to trip all over yourself and give me any reason to think you actually had feelings for me."
"That would be a fair assessment."
"In your mind's eye, what were you seeing?"
"I don't know. I guess I was just envisioning what you looked like as your body was trying to accommodate the little intruder. What was I missing?"
"Walt Williamson . . . You don't know how many times I sat here talking to you while fantasizing about you making your donation up close

and personal. And how hard you kept trying and trying before you finally got it right."

"Walt . . . Are you still there?"

Mrs. Claw Hammer

Jesse insisted on wearing his new overalls on his first day of kindergarten. Polly called the night before to remind his daddy to take pictures. Walt drove him to school and went back to pick him up but said he would ride the bus from then on. Jesse liked that schedule.

"What's your teacher's name?"

"Mrs. Claw Hammer—or something like that."

"Did you mean Mrs. Krauthammer?"

"That might be it. She talks funny."

"She's German. Did you know that kindergarten is a German word? Let's get the globe and find where that country is. Kinder is the word for children, and I think you know what a garden is. You are enrolled in a place where children can blossom and grow."

"When will I learn how to read?"

"Do what your teacher tells you. You already know the alphabet, and you'll be reading simple words soon. But school is not just about reading. You'll also learn how to write and a lot of other stuff."

"Mrs. Claw Hammer said the first thing we had to learn was to sit down and shut up. What does 'schnell' mean?"

Walt was hoping Jesse would someday learn a foreign language. He just had no idea that lessons would begin so soon.

When Tonya called to see how his day went, she cackled.

"Did I ever tell you about my first grade teacher? Her name was Mrs. Berger and I called her Mrs. Bugger. Don't laugh. It gets worse. The assistant was Mrs. Harbaugh, but I dubbed her Mrs. Hair Ball."

Va-BROOM

Halloween was on a Saturday, so the students dressed up on Friday. Walt thought Jess only needed a straw hat and a red bandana to go with his overalls, but then a package came in the mail. Aunt Polly sent him a Spiderman suit. His son was being corrupted with societal crazes that this father would just as soon the boy knew nothing about.

Sissy came to the rescue and took her little brother trick or treating. That was by no means the only reason for her visit. It also just happened to be their dad's sixtieth birthday.

While the goblins were out hobnobbing, Walt enjoyed a little treat of his own. From the freezer, he retrieved a slice of the black walnut cake Hannah had baked. He thought about calling her or sending her an email. Then, he stopped himself.

"Othell . . . You can do your part, but you cannot do someone else's. You heard nothing from Hannah on your birthday. Oh, well."

Gus II broke the spell.

"This is your favorite witch—twitch—twitch. Happy Halloween."

"You know what they always say."

"No—what do they always say?"

"If the broom fits, wear it. Va-BROOM."

"Maybe next year, you can make me twitch."

"You know what they always say."

"No—what do they always say?"

"If you can't stand the kitchen, get out of heat."

"I thought you had the hots for me."

"Thanks for sending Jesse the outfit. Tonya came up, and they are out on the town."

Nothing was said about Walt's birthday. He had not mentioned it and presumed she had no way of knowing. When Tonya and Jesse got back, he was carrying a sack full of loot, and she came in with a black box. Walt noticed that it was sent to a Homer address.

"Looks like somebody left some treats for you on the porch. You might not want to open this before Jesse goes to bed. Me, too, for that matter."

It was getting late and an hour later in Seattle, but when Walt dialed Polly's number, he knew she would not be asleep.

"Let me guess. You're in bed—wearing nothing but a smile."

"You know what they always say."

"No—what do they always say?"

"A smile is the prettiest thing a woman can wear."

"Thank you for my birthday goodies. You sure put a smile on my face."

"You know what they always say."

"No—what do they always say?"

"Abstinence makes the hard grow fonder."

"Walt . . . Are you still there?"

The summons

Jesse came home from school with a note from the teacher. All kinds of things started worming their way through Walt's mind when it said that he was scheduled for a parent-teacher conference. The boy denied being in any trouble. As his father went into the classroom, Jesse waited outside.

"Mr. Williamson . . . Please do not be alarmed. We routinely invite parents in after a few weeks to go over their child's progress. Jesse is a bright kid. That is both good news and bad. The good is obvious. The bad is that he gets bored, and there's no end to his mischievousness."

Walt tried to contain the smile taking over his face.

"He still has trouble pronouncing my name, and it annoys me when he just refers to me as 'teacher.' Will you help him with this?"

"I'll be as supportive, as I can."

"I noticed you said, 'I.' Most of our students come from regular homes, but we have our share from non-traditional families. I've asked Jesse about his mother, but I've been unable to understand what he is saying."

Walt then laid out the basics and asked for no special considerations. The conference ended with him thanking Mrs. Krauthammer for introducing German words to her pupils.

Hungry as a bear

After the Thanksgiving table was cleared, Tonya decided to give Hannah a call.

"Dad . . . We had such a good time last year, and I hope she's okay."

The phone rang and rang. Neither did the answering machine kick in. Walt mused.

"She likely saw my name on Caller ID."

"Oh, come on. Give her the benefit of the doubt."

"How many times am I required to do that? I doubt that she will ever make things right with me. I doubt that she ever wants to see me again."

"Okay—let's talk about the Christmas holidays."

"Everything is up in the air. Or, I should say, who will be up in the air. The Sullivans have invited all three of us. They, for sure, want to see their grandson, and they're willing to tolerate us."

"I guessing that this has nothing to do with Polly."

"She's already mentioned hanging some mistletoe. I invited her to come here, but she didn't want to cut her parents out."

"Why don't you and Jesse go on? I promise I won't have a blue Christmas without you."

"Let me guess. This has nothing to do with your new neighbor across the hall."

"Schnell . . . Jesse. We don't want to miss our flight."

"Ich kommen, Daddy. Vergessen my pocket knife."

"You can't take that on the plane. Here—let me stick it in the suitcase."

When they were buckled in the hop, skip, and jump commuter to Anchorage, Jesse tugged on Walt's sleeve.

"Do you think Aunt Polly will like the bear I carved for her?"

"If not, I'm sure that she will let you know. When she sees the blood stains on it, she might give you a scolding. Let me see your finger. Has it about healed?"

"Oh, Daddy—it was nothing."

"Jesse Sullivan Williamson—you're a tough Kenai kid."

"Danke Vader."

The big bird to Seattle/Tacoma was packed. Jesse made friends with a girl in a seat behind them, and Walt had to rein them in a couple of times when they got a little rowdy.

Aunt Polly saw them before they saw her. She slipped up behind Jesse, and much to his delight, lifted him in the air. When she put him down, much to her liking, her feet came off the ground.

"Mother has been cooking all day. Let's not disappoint her."

Jesse winked at Walt.

"I'm hungry as a bear."

"Leave your things in the car. You're going home with me after dinner."

As they were unpacking, Jesse could wait no longer.

"Aunt Polly . . . I made this for you."

She handled the crude carving for the priceless treasure it was. Tears were added to the existing blood and sweat.

"This deserves a big bear hug."

"Danke . . . Aunt Polly."

Jesse was wired, and then he unwound all at once. The mistletoe soon worked its magic on his dad.

Here comes Santa Claus

"Jesse . . . Come and sit on my lap and tell me about this German thing."

He wiggled out of the lap part and sat beside her. The kindergartener told his Aunt Polly all about Mrs. Claw Hammer, and how she was teaching her students words from her native tongue.

"I can sing *Silent Night* in German. Do you want to hear me?"

His rendition ended with two exclamation points.

"Wunderbar! Sehr gut!"

"Danke . . . Aunt Polly."

Jesse did not realize it, but he had just auditioned for a Christmas Day performance.

After the boy went to bed, in contrast to his son, Walt's lap offered no resistance.

"Walt . . . I don't know how you feel about this, but I want Santa Claus to come for Jesse."

"We've never made much ado about Christmas, but he's been hearing all about it at school."

"Let him be a kid. It will mean so much to me."

"What about your other son? Is Frank coming home for Christmas?"

Polly was wobbly. Walt had said her "other son."

"He was here Thanksgiving and has little time off from his new job. You know he's also taking graduate courses and eventually wants to get his doctorate. He said he needed the time to finish a research project."

"Please say Merry Christmas to him from me and Jesse."

"I'll let you tell him yourself. We'll give him a call before we go to Mother's."

Jesse had trouble going to sleep and got back up twice rubbing his eyes. Walt was not sure what Polly did or how she did it, but when she emerged from his room, she said it was safe for Santa to come.

"Polly . . . You overdid it. You've created a standard that I will have a hard time living up to."

She did her best to ignore the "I" in what he just said.

"How about a Christmas Eve toast?"

When Walt popped the cork, he had trouble containing the fizz.

"Careful there, big boy. Don't get too carried away with the symbolism."

After the bottle of bubbly was slowly drained, they went to bed. Santa came again.

Zane

"Tell me, my sweet daughter. How was your Christmas?"

"Very nice. We finally got some good snow. I was beginning to think we weren't going to have a White Christmas."

"Is that the royal we, or the plural of I?"

"You're the writer. You tell me."

"I don't think you're into royalty. Well?"

"Zane and I had a candlelight Christmas Eve dinner and then went cross-country skiing the next day. I'm so sore I'm still having trouble walking."

"From the skiing?"

"Yes—Smarty Britches—from the skiing. I guess I don't have to ask about your Christmas?"

"Now that you mention it, Jesse and Polly have this most remarkable connection. I know they share the same genes, but it goes well beyond that. If something were to happen to me, she would fight you for custody."

"Who says I would want custody of the little brat? What about you and Polly? Is she having trouble walking?"

"When we left, she was dancing on air."

"You wish. Did you guys start making any plans?"

"She wants to come here next. We talked about when school is out. She couldn't get here in time for Jess's birthday, though."

"Whose birthday?"

"Yours and Jesse's birthday. If I were a betting man, I'd wager that she adds some personal leave to her spring holidays."

"That desperate, huh?"

"It's so comforting to know that I can always count on you. Now—let Jesse tell you about his Christmas."

When Tonya ended the phone conversation, she looked down at the two rocks on her kitchen counter. Why had she not noticed it before? T for Tonya—Z for Zane.

Bosom buddies

Walt went online, found a florist, and had flowers delivered to Polly at school. Two Valentines' Day cards were in the mailbox from her. Jesse came home from school with a sack full. He claimed he got more than anyone in his room, but his eyes lit up when he saw the big one from Aunt Polly.

"Can we call her? Bitte! Bitte! Bitte!"

"Yes—but we'll have to wait. She's still not home from her school."

Waiting was not one of the boy's most noble virtues.

"Is it time, yet? Is it time, yet?"

"We'll try at three. That will be four where she lives. You can tell time. Let me know when the clock says three."

Walt called out the numbers and let Jesse dial them. He remembered his camera and took a picture of his son talking to his other mother. When the boy showed no interest in relinquishing the receiver, Walt attached the digital photo to an email that would go out when the phone line was available. He got back just in time to hear Jesse say, "Auf wiedersehen."

"What? She did not want to talk to me?"

"She didn't mention it."

Moments later, Polly's phone rang again.

"This is Walt. Remember me?"

"Are you by any chance the fellow who sent me flowers? The card said it was from my sweetheart. Been trying all afternoon to figure out which of my suitors that might be."

"If no one else came to mind immediately, then I'm not all that worried. What are you wearing?"

"I dressed up just for you, set the timer on the camera, and got most of me in the picture. I was about to email it to you. I'll call you right back."

Walt's impatience was now put to the test. Five minutes turned into ten. No email and no phone call. Gus II startled him even though he was expecting the intrusion.

"Walt . . . The flowers were so special. But the picture of Jesse talking to me, well—I was so touched that I forgot how to attach the one I was sending you. You'll just have to use your imagination."

"He really loves you. Are you okay? Do I need to call back in a few?"

"I'll try again to send the picture. Let me know if it comes through."

Walt sat at the computer checking for incoming mail. Eventually, a message started uploading. The attachment slowed it, but finally, the photo opened.

"Good golly, Miss Polly. Red is my favorite color."

"Where is Jesse? Can he hear you?"

"He's in his room sorting through his valentines."

"Good—you know what they always say."

"No—what do they always say?"

"A boobs man has an overabundance of titstosterone."

"What makes you think I'm a boobs man?"

"Your eyes. Your hands."

"Does that make me your bosom buddy?"

"Times two."

"Sounds like a booby trap to me."

"You are so Scorpio. Now, delete the picture and go back to your imagination."

"Othell . . . My *over* is certainly in *abundance*."

Hungry as a wolf

Schoolteachers taking days off around holidays were frowned upon. Students were not focused on academics, and their teachers were better equipped to maintain discipline than substitutes. Polly's principal remembered well the extra consideration necessary when Jesse was born, and she worked with her to extend the spring holidays for another full week.

Polly left school early on Friday to hop a flight getting into Anchorage barely in time to catch the last shuttle to Kenai. Jesse got off the bus in high gear, but he had to pull back on the throttle. Aunt Polly was still four hours out.

Walt kept the boy busy in the kitchen. The two cooked up a storm so they could have more time to do other things. Topside, a pot of clam chowder simmered while green beans cooked down with a slice of bacon. Walt still preferred them southern style.

Meanwhile, a pot roast was baking in the oven. Jesse helped peel the potatoes and scrape the carrots, showing off his dexterity with a knife.

With only one more scheduled incoming flight for the night, no guesswork was involved when the aircraft came into sight. Aunt Polly had grabbed a front seat and was the first passenger to come down the steps. When she came through the glass door, four arms were awaiting her. Walt yielded.

Jesse winked at his father and had a question for Aunt Polly.

"Are you hungry as a wolf?"

"Absolutely."

"Then, let's go home. We made chowder from claims we dug on the beach."

The newly arrived guest, had to clear her bowl, before she could dip from the pot.

"Jesse . . . Did you carve this wolf for me?"

He winked again.

Part V: First Responder

Hold that thought

Reconnecting with Polly was like starting all over again for Walt. What to do with his hands? Not so with her. It was more like picking up where she left off. The houseguest made no attempt to keep hers off him as he gave her a little tour of the place. He was pleased that she seemed in no ways ill at ease in her late sister's house.

Jesse had no difficulties with the lapsed gap, either. He demanded a bedtime story and thought Aunt Polly was planning to stay by his side. After he drifted off, she slipped off the bed and into something more comfortable. Walt then got his own bedtime story.

Most of Saturday and Sunday was spent showing their visitor around the area. Polly lamented that she never got to Alaska while Ginny was alive.

Parents were invited to join their children at school for First Responder Day on Monday. Jesse's teacher got to meet his other mother. The boy came home all abuzz about the neat gear and uniforms of the firemen and paramedics.

Polly took it upon herself to get Jess off to school each morning, and she was the first to greet him when he got off the bus. While he was snacking on cookies hot from the oven, she put an arm around Walt.

"You have no idea what this means to me. I don't want to disappoint you, sir, but all my dreams were not about you. Want a cookie?"

As the time for Polly's departure grew nearer, an unavoidable gloom overshadowed them.

"You know what? I might just call in sick for the rest of the year."

Polly's flight to Seattle was on Saturday. The Alaskans wanted to spend every possible minute with her. They also wished that she might experience the incredible slice of Alaska stretching between Kenai and Anchorage. Walt was hoping for some sign, some signal of her intentions. He got it at Beluga Point.

"I think I could live in Alaska. I could not understand why my sister never left until now."

"Does that mean you're coming back when school's out?"

"Hold that thought."

After Aunt Polly checked her bag and was about to go through security, she picked Jesse up.

"You're getting to be such a big boy. This might be the last time you'll let me do this."

"I love you, Aunt Polly."

"I love you, too, baby."

235

When she put him down, she reached for Walt and whispered in his ear. "I know—you don't have to say it, yet—but you will."

"Dad . . . Are you sure you know what you're doing?"

"If you could see Jesse and Polly together, you wouldn't have to ask."

"He's always been a little lady's man."

"This time is different. It would be criminal for them not to be together."

"What about you? How do you feel about Polly? I have a good indication of how she feels about you."

"Tonya . . . Your capacity for love changes as you get older. It's somewhat like with children. I love you different from the way I love Jesse. Neither is lesser. Do you know what I mean?"

"I think I do. What about the age difference? You're almost a decade older than she is."

"She doesn't seem to mind. Anyway—don't worry about me. I'm still in my prime."

"What are you going to do when she gets in her prime?"

"Dad . . . Are you still there?"

First class

The day before Jesse's sixth birthday, he took his first flight without his father. The school year was still not over, but Mrs. Claw Hammer went ahead and promoted him to first grade. Walt was not so sure about the boy making a connecting flight alone, so he drove him to Anchorage.

When they checked his lone bag, the airline representative took his time printing the boarding pass. Walt did not know what was taking so long and hoped there was not a problem.

"The flight is almost full, but I see one empty seat in first class. If I hear no objection, I will upgrade Mr. Williamson—at no additional cost."

None was raised, and Walt walked him to security.

"Auf wiedersehen . . . Herr Williamson. Have a good flight."

"Auf wiedersehen . . . Mein Vater. Have a good drive home."

Under any other circumstances, Walt would have been beside himself. His beloved son was in good hands, and the boy's father would also be making a solo flight in about three weeks. Polly had sold her house and bought a burgundy GMC Denali AWD. Jesse was going on ahead to spend some time with his grandparents.

Polly had already reserved a rental tag along to bring along the treasures she could not part with. The two most valuable would be riding up front with her. Walt dubbed the vehicle, the "Alcan" since its maiden voyage would be up the Alaska Highway.

The young couple that bought the house was soon to be married. They told the previous owner to leave what things she did not want, and they would either use them or dispose of them. She did store a few things in her parents' basement.

With everything loaded, Polly, Walt, and Jesse went to the Sullivans for the night. After dinner, the men took another one of their walks.

"Walt . . . That's a noble thing you're doing letting Polly help you with Jesse. She has always loved the boy like her own—because in so many ways, he is. Now mind you, we would have preferred that you moved here with her. Our daughter has assured us, though, that you put no pressure on her to go with you."

"Sir . . . That is correct. I let her make the decision. For one thing, she did not want to disrupt Jesse. It also appears that she's excited about living in Alaska."

"It makes it easier for us knowing that she is fond of you, too."

"Dave . . . Rest assured that I also care about Polly very deeply."

"You know we're always here for you if you need us."

"I've never questioned that for one moment."

"Be careful . . . Son. And keep on taking good care of your family."

"Thank you . . . Sir."

We're a family

Walt started out under the wheel, but Polly wanted to get the feel of the rig once they were out of the city. She turned it back over to him before they went through customs. The agent asked the usual question regarding their destination and then inquired about alcohol, firearms, and tobacco. He stamped their passports and waved them through after only a cursory look at the cargo.

"Walt . . . We're a family. We just crossed into Canada on our way to Alaska, and that border guard assumed as much. He treated us like we've always been one. Isn't that a wonderful feeling?"

Jesse unbuckled, hopped up on the hump, and stuck his head in.

"Aunt Polly . . . Do you think Ginny would mind if I called you Mother?"

She yanked him between the bucket seats into her lap and answered with hugs and kisses.

"Okay, you two. Canada has a seatbelt law. Don't get us deported on our first day in the country."

"Then, pull over and stop. Let this mother get in the back with her son."

Walt was in the front seat with no one beside him, but he did not feel alone. The word family was swirling in his head as well, and it made him giddy.

Since they had gotten over the hump, he and Polly had not had a misunderstanding. Even the best of families had disagreements. His new partner was spirited, but she was not self-absorbed. He could not foresee anything that they could not work through together. His notion of commitment had been consistent since the first time it made sense to him.

"I'm on your side, and you're on my side."

Walt understood the prerequisite of trust. Polly earned his in record time because of her devotion to Jesse. Apparently, that road went both ways. Once she made her resolve, she never wavered in moving on with her newly minted family.

The trip was so much more enjoyable having someone to assist with both the driving and the basic decision-making. He did not have to carry the burden alone of finding places to eat and sleep. Most important, he had someone to talk to, an individual who cared about his feelings and his inner-workings.

While the two other family members were reveling in their back seat world, Walt pledged to himself to ever uphold Polly in the place of honor she deserved. At that moment, he knew he was in love with her.

Boiling over

"You still got the hots for me?"

"Boiling over."

Polly had packed what they would need for the hot springs in a separate tote bag. Jesse's other mother held his hand as they walked down the boardwalk. Once out of the changing rooms, the guys watched as she tested the waters. She reached for the boy's hand again and helped him down the steps.

Walt played with them for a few minutes and then found a spot on the bench with the overflow spilling across him. He did a little mental inventory of how much had changed since the first time and the last time he sat in that spot.

When he looked up, company was coming. Jesse watched from the decking as his parents took turns rubbing each other's shoulders amidst the torrents. The boy could not see what was going on beneath the steaming waters.

"Walt . . . How is it that you never got into a rut and settled there? I've tried to imagine when you first came up the Alcan in your camper and the freedom you must have experienced. You did not let a career own you or debts swamp you. You never became a slave to anyone nor addicted to anything. Do you know how rare that is?"

"I just had to be who I am and true to myself."

"I repeat myself. Do you know how rare that is?"

"This is not just about me. Has it hit you, yet, what you're doing? You left a comfortable life behind to take off into the wilderness with a man you hardly know with a kid to raise. Do you know how exceptional that makes you?"

"That man you say I hardly know knocked me off my feet. And that kid is not just any kid. He's mine, too, Walt. The only two worthwhile things I've ever accomplished in my life are named Frank and Jesse."

"What about all the hundreds of students you taught?"

"I'm not sure I ever *taught* them much of anything. The good ones got it on their own. The lazy ones just kept switching classes until they found a way out. Did your teachers make much difference in your life?"

"Not really. I thought it was just me."

"I don't want you to think for one minute that I needed rescuing. At the same time, Walt Williamson . . . You've afforded me an opportunity to take possession of my life as I have never done so before. The best part is that I just get to be who I am, too."

"Moose!"

"Where, Jesse?"

"Just over the hill. He's a big bull."

239

Bullwinkle initially paid them no attention as the load lumbering toward him slowed. Polly and Jesse both snapped pictures. Then, he scampered into the forest.

Since they were already stopped, it was a good time for a leg stretch and to change drivers. A mile or so down the road, Walt picked back up the previous conversation.

"When you get a chance, I want you to read my book. As I was compiling it, your sister was such an inspiration. So much of life is about people just being who they are."

"Why don't you write another book, something like a memoir? Don't you think others might gain inspiration from you? I certainly have."

"You're not the first person to suggest this. It would have to be fiction, though. The ups and downs, the ins and outs, and the twists and turns in my life have been so off the wall that no one would believe the truth."

"If I can get a teaching job, will you get to work on it?"

"We'll see. Right now—slow down. A herd of bison is in the road up ahead."

Oops!

"I don't know about you boys, but I'll be glad to get home."

"Me, too."

"Me, three."

"Jesse . . . You're so cute. One of the first things we'll do is get you set up. You're going to have a boy's room."

Polly had brought along Frank's old bed and a number of kid things to get started. Also packed, was her newly purchased mattress set. The master bedroom was about to get a makeover as well.

The restyling would not begin the day they arrived except for two things. The wood-carved bear and wolf pieces found homes in the kitchen window. Over coffee the next morning with Jess still sacked out, Walt went out of his way to encourage Polly to make herself right at home. She responded with a bit of attitude.

"It's so nice to know that I have your permission."

Oops!

By lunchtime, the cargo was all unloaded, much of it still on the front porch. Walt went into town to turn in the rental trailer. If there was one, he would have won the popularity contest when he brought home a pizza. As the assimilation of two households continued, Jesse was the front door patrol.

"Polly . . . You'll have to get used to mosquitoes. A breeze is blowing today, and they're not too bad. Even so, we'll have to get in and out as quickly as possible. They do love to hitch a ride inside."

The summer sun was nowhere near the horizon when the resident family members settled into their beds, both replete with new foundations.

"Walt . . . Will you just hold me for a few? It feels so good to be home and in bed with you."

"I won't start anything if you don't."

She didn't. The next morning, she could not remember falling asleep in his arms.

The masterpiece

The most pressing matter for Polly was finding a teaching job. Having frozen her retirement plan back in Washington, with twenty-five-years to her credit, she could always start drawing from it if necessary. She also had some savings and had pocketed a tidy sum from the sale of her house.

With four high schools within commuting distance, the odds were good that at least one was looking for an English teacher. Sometimes, there is no winning ticket. With her credentials, Polly was assured that she would get a call if a position came available. She was also reminded that people come and go in Alaska, often on short notice.

Walt told her to chill and assured her they would not go hungry. She put her sentiments into words.

"I've been employed since I graduated from college. It's hard to imagine getting up and not having a job to go to. Even most summers were busy with recertification stuff and such."

"Get used to it. You might like it."

"Being a bum has certainly worked well for you."

Walt watched as Polly slowly unwound. Days were filled with spiffing. When the weather permitted, the three were off to explore favorite trails, and Polly was enamored with the wildflowers. A camera, field guides, and the binoculars went with them on every outing in a backpack.

Jesse's eyes were now about as good as his dad's for spotting wildlife. The three huddled when in their regal presence. As it got closer to the time for school to start, Polly suggested that they not answer the phone.

"How could I go off and leave this—to teach uninspired young people, with little interest in their native tongue—nor much curiosity about those who have woven words into masterpieces?"

"Polly . . . You're my masterpiece."

"Do you mean that in a literary sort of way or literally?"

Tonya was teaching remedial English classes during the summer, and her new love interest occupied her spare time. Zane Patterson was a nurse practitioner, a paramedic, and was in training to become both a medical transport and a search and rescue helicopter pilot. After grades were turned in, Tonya invited him to go with her to Kenai to meet her family.

"Don't worry about Dad. He'll be on his best behavior. He's so caught up in his new family life that he'll forget all about being his daughter's guardian and protector."

"You mean that you've not already warned him about how I'm taking advantage of you?"

"You are? I thought it was the other way around."

Tonya did not think to prepare Zane for Jesse. The boy was fascinated with emergency operations. He told his new friend about his first computer game—a flight simulator—and he wanted to know all about flying a helicopter.

Tonya was mostly right about her father. She did catch him sizing up her main squeeze, but they did not go for a walk and talk. His daughter did find a few moments of alone time with him.

"It seems that Polly is making herself right at home. This place looks so fresh and livable. Jesse is happy. It shows. I know how important that is to you. Occasionally, you might wipe that silly grin off your face, though."

"Why?"

The Kenai Kid

Jesse had long since traded in his OshKosh B'gosh overalls for Carhartts. On the first day of first grade, he picked out his light brown ones. The six-year-old did not understand why he could not take his pocket knife to school. He was not properly dressed without it. His parents had already met his teacher at the open house, but Polly insisted on taking him—after a round of pictures before they left.

Walt never imagined relinquishing that honor, but he felt really good about stepping aside and letting Polly become the chief school parent. The pupil had no objection, either.

When she returned, she went straight to the computer and sent digital photographs to the boy's grandparents. Then, she found Walt.

"This is different. We have a few hours of time on our hands without a kid keeping tabs on us."

"What do you suppose we should do about it?"

"Let me count the ways . . ."

Jesse fared better in the teacher name department. Mrs. Walker had been teaching for so long that some of her new students were grandchildren of earlier ones. Since his last name was near the bottom of the alphabet, sitting on the last row at the back of the room suited him just fine.

When the first grader came home each day, he found that some rules had changed. His father had left the teacher alone to do her job with little interference on his part. His longtime teacher mother saw things differently. She was waiting for a daily report and then went over his lessons with him.

"Walt . . . Did you realize how sloppy this child's handwriting is?"

"I never thought much about it. He knows what he means, and that's the important thing."

"What if his teacher can't make heads or tails of it?"

"I guess she'll need to have a better understanding with him of what she expects."

"Go wash the dirty dishes in the sink."

Jesse enjoyed tinkering with wood. When they walked on the beach, he always came home with pieces of driftwood. He had an eye for seeing anomalies in the grain and carving around them.

By professional standards, his work was crude. He was, after all, just in the first grade. The kitchen window sill was becoming a zoo. The boy was not haphazard and only occasionally came in with a small cut or scrape.

Jesse also continued to draw. What many of his sketches represented was known only to him. If Polly asked him to tell the story of what was going on, his imagination knew no bounds. One particular cartoonish figure kept reappearing. When his dad asked him who it was, he said, "The Kenai Kid."

Contrarily, Walt's creative juices were not flowing so freely. Polly nudged him now and then to get on with writing his story. For the time being, he was too caught up in the present to go trampling around in the past.

Resourceful resolutions

Walt made good on his promise from the year before. On Halloween, his favorite witch twitched. He got to open a life-size birthday present wrapped in black. That all took place before Jesse came home from school.

Polly took their son into town to go trick or treat with Nate. The boy would have it no other way than to go as a first responder. His mother could not find a ready-made outfit so she put together a makeshift fireman suit with a plastic helmet she did find in a store. The new Alaska resident was finding out about limited resources in her new environs.

Walt wondered if Polly would suggest going back to Seattle for Christmas. She balked at the thought and wanted to spend their first Christmas together, as a family, at home. He had never done much decorating, but he had to admit that Jesse and his mother had made the place festive.

The woman of the house was not sure about a makeshift tree, but she acquiesced. Walt said the forests were full of spruce, and he was not about to pay a ridiculous price for something shipped in. He and Jesse brought one home that was only a grade level above a Charlie Brown.

Mistletoe was another matter. Since the woodsy parasite associated with romance was not common to Alaska, they had to settle for a plastic replica. Nothing was spurious about the results it got.

The couple had agreed to go easy on gift-giving. Walt violated the rule, and after a Christmas toast, Polly opened a package that nobody but the two of them would ever know anything about. Resources might be limited, but Walt was resourceful.

Both the post office and Ma Bell did a booming business during the season. Tonya and Zane came up from Homer on the 26th. Jesse added a passel of drawing supplies to his bounty.

Walt could not remember the last time he was not in bed by the time they sang "Auld Lang Syne" on the East Coast. Polly made good on her pledge to keep him up for the fireworks.

On New Year's Day, all three residents gathered in the kitchen to help prepare dinner. Walt introduced the others to some southern traditions. Jesse stirred the black-eyed peas representing coins. Polly cooked the turnip greens symbolic of green folding money. The pork seasoning signified the hope for prosperity. Walt made cornbread to sop the potlikker.

Jesse escaped just ahead of time to clear the table. Walt washed the dishes and Polly dried them. He then led her to the sofa.

"My dear . . . I like the traditions we're establishing. You've brought so much excitement and energy into my life. Jesse is thriving."

Polly had learned enough about Walt to know when he had something on his mind, so she turned, faced him, and took his hands.

"You know—two other things are associated with this holiday. You don't hear much about them anymore, but they are opposite sides of the same coin. One is taking inventory, and the other is making resolutions. Polly . . . How are we doing?"

She released her grip, slumped back, and closed her eyes. Walt knew her well enough to know when she was digging deep. Abruptly, she sat up with raised eyebrows.

"Did I frighten you?"

"No."

"Thank God. I'm still getting used to a man who doesn't decide for me what I'm thinking or feeling or doing."

"That's why I asked."

"How are we doing? Let me begin with the easy part of we. Do you agree with me that Jesse is doing well? The boy is a wonder. He switched gears from one parent to two without missing a cog."

"Agreed."

"My biggest concern was that you and Jesse would carry on as usual, and I would be an outsider. He had always looked to you for everything. I feared you might not grant me much say so, and he would not recognize my role and authority. Thank you so much for letting me be his mother."

"Trust me. That required little effort on my part. You made it so easy for all of us."

"I could throw it back to you now and ask how you're doing, but I doubt you'd let me get away with it."

"I called this meeting to order, and the speaker controls the gavel."

"You're so cute. Let's go to bed."

"Oh, no, you don't."

"How am I doing? Be careful what you ask for. My entire life, I've yearned for a man who listened, who took me seriously, who valued my opinion, and was concerned about my feelings. When it happens, it's a little unnerving. There's no end to what you can get away with when you keep telling yourself that he does not understand you—that he thinks more about himself."

Walt took her in his arms. Nonverbal confirmation was more important than anything he could say.

"How am I doing? You asked for it. Drop the hammer—anytime you wish."

"I love you . . . Polly."

"I know, but my darling, but I would be less than honest if I did not acknowledge that this has been a big adjustment for me. I uprooted myself from everything familiar and distanced myself from my parents and my other son. I found myself among the ranks of the unemployed but then took on, not one but two new roles both simultaneously and in a whole new world. I fretted that you might want your space back and send me packing."

"Oh, Polly."

"How am I doing? These are the happiest days of my life."

Walt dropped the gavel.

"You're so adorable. Let's go to bed."

"Okay."

"We never got to the New Year's resolutions part."

"I was not the one who adjourned the meeting."

"Polly . . . Where do we go from here? What can we do better?"

"My life is so rich and full with you and Jesse now in it. Yet, I have always had girlfriends. Some were at work. I know I used them, as they did me, to help fill empty spaces. I need to get out and become more involved in the community. I want to be known as more than just Walt Williamson's kept woman, or whatever they call me around here."

"Go for it. Now, I have a question for you. What is your biggest unfulfilled passion? If no obstructions were standing in the way—if nothing was holding you back—if money was no object—what is the one thing you'd like to do?"

"You're so charming. Let's go to bed."

"Been there and done that."

"Darling . . . For years, I taught both American and European literature. I know I could never compete with the great masters, but I already have quite a collection of poems that I have written through the years. Some are about you, by the way. Do you think I could get a book of poems published? Perhaps, Tonya could illustrate it."

"You won't know until you try."

Poetry

Walt's New Year resolution was to get started on his own book. He had never given it much thought until his mother convinced him that he was a good storyteller. The novice writer contemplated weaving embellished tales from his youthful experiences into a saga that illustrated some of the life lessons he had learned along the way. When he asked Polly her opinion, she said that he wouldn't know until he tried.

She spent hours poring over poems of yesteryear. It was one thing to amateurishly string words together, but quite another to make them worthy of publication. She delighted in sharing little jewels and nuggets with him as she rediscovered them.

Walt just sat down one day and started writing. He had no notion of where he was going, much less how he would get there. With his mother as his inspiration, he envisioned enunciating the yarns to her and watching for her reaction. The aspiring novelist was surprised by how fast the pages added up.

Polly picked up her pen now and then when new inspirations seeped into her soul. Walt was the recipient of an original on Valentine's Day. He was so awed that he did not know how to respond. She said he could count on its inclusion in the book.

Walt had seen nothing more of the red negligee Polly was wearing in the photo she emailed him the previous year. After Jesse was asleep, he got to see it with his own eyes. When she waltzed out of the bedroom into the candlelight, he was transfixed. He knew he was not being original when he said it, but it was the best he had to offer.

"Polly—that's poetry in motion."

The Memory Lane exit

Polly asked Jesse if he wanted a birthday party, but he did not seem too excited. Mrs. Walker said he played well with his classmates but did not have a particular close buddy. He did agree to invite his friend, Nate, to go with them for burgers. Nate was a year ahead of him in school.

His teacher said Jesse was reading above his grade level, and she credited his mother for much of it. If Mrs. Walker had any inkling of the boy's biological beginnings, she never let on. Their son had made no further inquiries, but Walt did not want Ginny to fade from Jesse's mind. Polly suggested that as he got older and learned about reproduction, he would get a good refresher course.

As the school year was nearing its end, Jesse had big plans. His grandparents had sent him a plane ticket, and the Ice Man had purchased a set of juvenile golf clubs. The up and coming second grader assured his parents that he had been through the routine enough times to make the connecting flight, but Walt overruled him. His dad saw no need to mention that he had booked a room for two nights so he could show Polly around Anchorage.

Jesse did not want anybody fusing over him after he was checked in. After watching him head to security, his parents walked solemnly back to the Alcan.

"Our little boy is growing up."

"Tell me about it."

Walt was fearful this might put a damper on Polly's evening, but she rallied. Without mentioning he had been there before, he took her to the same salmon bake eatery that he and Ginny had frequented years earlier. It had hardly changed, and the food was just as good as he remembered.

Concerned about Polly's mood, he was now the one stumbling about in nostalgia. She suggested a movie—something they had never done before— and Walt took the first exit off Memory Lane. The couple sat on the back row with her jacket draped across their laps.

On the way back to Kenai, Polly reached over and took Walt's hand.

"I'm sure going to miss that little fellow, but one thing I'm really looking forward to."

"And that would be?"

"I can parade around the house dressed any way I please."

"Othell . . . In some ways, those sisters are as different as cotton candy and peach brandy. But in others, they are the handy-dandy twins."

Walt had picked himself up another editor. Each time he revisited an episode from his childhood, and changed the names to protect the guilty, he showed it to Polly. As he framed anecdotes in his patented humor, they shared many laughs.

Polly continued sorting through her handwritten collection of poems but had not come up with any recognizable theme. The task was daunting and beginning to seem overwhelming.

Come summer, they were both ready for a break. While Jesse was with his grandparents, the couple tackled some strenuous mountain trails that he was not ready for. Soon after they set out on one, slow drizzle set in. Instead of turning back, they trudged on. By the time they got back to the Old Sourdough, not a dry thread was touching skin.

As they soaked in the tub together, determining places for elbows, knees, arms, and legs was ongoing. Walt had no problem finding what to do with his hands.

> Othell . . . My concern for keeping Ginny alive in Jesse's mind has brought me face to face with my own memories. When the things that Polly and I do overlap what Ginny and I did, Gin's image is fading. I often have to stop myself. If I make a reference to some previous experience, I forget it was not Polly with me back then.

As Jesse started second grade, his mother made good on her resolve to become more involved. Locals were ever on the lookout for fresh talent. She accepted the position as president of the parent-teacher organization. When added to the library board, she soon leapfrogged to head the Friends auxiliary.

Jesse had done a complete turnaround with his penmanship. Some of that had to do with his drawing ability. He did sketches of Sesame Street characters, but his favorite pastime was drafting emergency rescue workers and their vehicles.

Each new work of art took its place in the family gallery—the refrigerator. As older pieces were taken down to make space, Polly carefully filed them away.

Starting with a pencil, he often added color with his crayons. Sissy had given him a watercolor set, but it was too messy.

The boy's favorite Christmas gift was a pair of ice skates. Walt had not laced his up in years, and Polly strapped on her sister's. The three held hands going around the rink a couple of times until Jess broke free and went off and left them.

The Alcan

"Walt . . . Where did this year go? It really is true how time flies when you're having so much fun. School is almost out, and Jesse is two inches taller. I don't know about you, but I'm looking forward to going back down the Alcan in our Alcan. I hope we're teaching by example that it is not just the destination that matters, but also the journey along the way."

"Polly . . . With you, the ride is always exciting."

"The SUV will not be so packed this trip. We'll have more space and can stretch out."

"You're not suggesting that you might take a little power nap now and then, are you?"

"I love it when you read my mind. What am I thinking right now?"

"Hmm."

The Kenai residents were not the only Alaskans with summer plans. Walt was a bit uneasy about the unoccupied bungalow in North Carolina. Tonya was not teaching summer classes and decided to take a vacation. Zane had two weeks off and was flying down with her.

"I hope Brusky has not died and gone to car heaven."

"Eli uses the vehicle like a second car. He said he would meet you at the airport."

"He's never been to that part of the world, and I'm looking forward to showing him around The Great Smoky Mountains."

"Say hello to Eli for me. And Hannah, too. Or not."

The earth belched

Jesse breezed right through third grade. He started bugging Walt for a four-wheeler, but his mother said that was not going to happen, at least anytime soon. As the days grew longer and got warmer, he spent more time in the storage building that he and his dad had converted into a shop.

On birthdays and Christmases, the boy put in his order for hammers, screwdrivers, sanders, drills, saws, and wrenches. When in town, he wanted his daddy to take him to the builder supply store to shop for tools and add more to his chest.

Carving wood pieces and giving them away, thrilled him the most. On the last day of school, he presented an oddly shaped root to his teacher, and she said she would treasure it. He was working on Christmas presents for Ice and the Ice Man. His second most special recipient was Sissy, but his all-time favorite was his adopted mother. The kitchen zoo kept adding more animals.

Mt. Redoubt, the ten-thousand-foot mountain across the Cook Inlet, had been rumbling for several days. Seismologists warned of the possibility of an eruption, and one morning in mid-March, 2009, the cone turned red, the top blew, and magma spewed. Kids were sent home from school, and the area braced itself for volcanic ash. The air might be dangerous to breathe, and the intake of vehicles could quickly choke.

The mountain's peak was visible from a spot just down the road. Walt, Polly, and Jesse walked to view the spectacle. The fourth grader came home, sketched the scene, and then colored it in with his crayons.

The ash became more of a menace to aircraft than for the people on the ground immediately below. The currents carried it for hundreds of miles. Some flights were canceled and many others diverted.

As they were discussing it afterward, Walt reflected.

"Living in Alaska is never without excitement. Fires, earthquakes, volcanoes, avalanches, plane crashes, tussles with wild animals—but I would not live anywhere else."

Jesse was thinking something different. His reflections were on the brave people keeping everyone safe.

Just be yourself

While Jesse was spending time with his grandparents, Gus II intruded. A sobbing Mary Beth was the bearer of bad news. Earl had succumbed to a massive heart attack.

"We'll get there as soon as we can."

"Walt . . . I was so hoping you would say that. Your uncle would be honored if you might say a few words at his memorial service. Let me know your schedule, and somebody will meet you at the airport."

While Polly was packing, Walt talked with a booking agent. Because of the extenuating circumstances, the airline representative used due diligence in finding the best possible itinerary. Most flights going toward the East Coast were red-eyes, and this one was no exception. She scheduled a layover in Seattle on the way back, with an open ticket to Anchorage.

As the couple buckled up on the first short leg, Polly reached for Walt's hand.

"This is another first for us. We've never taken a flight together. I'm so sorry it is under these circumstances."

"Polly . . . You just don't know how much it means to me to have you by my side."

She curled up and got some sleep on the nonstop to Atlanta. Walt kept turning things over in his mind of what he could possibly say even approaching anything appropriate. Other than his two grandfathers, Earl and Mary Beth were the most important persons in his youthful life.

One of the King's longtime friends was waiting for them at baggage claim. He said there was no need in them renting a car, and he had a spare one they could use while they were in Adamsonville. Walt turned to Polly.

"Welcome to the South. Welcome to good old southern hospitality."

Walt made no attempt to hold back the tears when he stood by Earl's casket.

"I didn't realize how much he had grown to look like his father. And like my Grandpa, I'm glad Earl went the way he did without lingering."

Once back at the house, Walt took their things to the basement and his old room. Mary Beth embraced Polly in more ways than one.

"It's so nice to meet you. We were hoping this was the year we were coming to see you, but something kept holding Earl back. Now, we know what it was. The man lived his life is such a way that he left this world with few regrets. His biggest was never seeing Alaska and not getting to meet you."

"Polly . . . When I was a little boy, I never had any new clothes except for my uncle and aunt. Mary Beth always took me shopping. She probably knows what I'm about to say now. I don't own a suit of clothes that I can still get into. Looks like you might have to take me shopping again."

"That won't be necessary. It matters not that it is the First United Methodist Church. Earl would want you just to be yourself. Wear what you feel comfortable in. That will be fine."

Adamsonville turned out to honor one of its most successful business and civic leaders, and the church was filled. Walt sat between Mary Beth and Polly until called to the stand. The minister introduced him as the boy who was like a son to this childless couple.

"I guess you can say I'm Earl and Mary Beth's prodigal son. Only, I went off into the far country and never came back."

Getting those first words out broke the logjam.

After Earl's body was laid to rest, an impromptu receiving line formed. Polly had Walt by his left arm as others reached for his right hand. Person after person told her man that he had given the most impressive and meaningful eulogy they could ever remember.

The family friend meant what he said about the loner car. When he found out that Walt and Polly were going on to Ephesus, he insisted that they use one of his. He also pledged to escort them back to Atlanta when they were ready.

The three-hour drive turned into four when Walt took a detour through his boyhood hometown of Mason, Georgia. He showed Polly the house he lived in, now renovated. Dogwoods he set out were old and decaying.

His Grandpa and Grandma King's old home place was abandoned and in a state of disrepair. He took her to the mule barn where the faint smell of dung still hung in the air. Around back, he showed her the ancient GMC where his Grandpa died. Walt reached in the cab, removed the gear shift knob, and put it in his pocket.

The area around where his Williamson grandparents lived was hardly recognizable. All the original structures were gone, and the land was in pasture.

"My granddaddy breathed his last breath reading his Bible in wood shop that stood right over there. I wonder what happened to his tools. I wish Jesse had them."

Nothing was left of the school he went to except the gymnasium, now converted into a senior center. Walt told Polly about going to his biological father's memorial service in that building without knowing who he was. He added that his natural mother was sitting with the woman feigning to be his mom, and how he had no clue about the big family secret.

"My real father was a test pilot for the Air Force, and he died in the crash of an experimental plane. When various decorated veterans spoke of him, it was the first time I had given any thought to the concept of a hero.

"Since then, usage of the word has become so widespread that it's lost much of its significance. These days, if a Boy Scout helps an old lady across the street, he's hailed a hero. I think the term is used far too loosely and should be reserved for the truly heroic."

"Walt . . . I could not agree with you more. Whatever happened to unsung heroes?"

The cemetery was on the other side of town. They came first to Maude's grave, the woman who raised Walt. His Grandpa and Grandma King were buried in the adjoining lot. Arm in arm, they paused when he took Polly to the final resting place of the mother who gave him up at birth and then reclaimed him before she died. His genetic father's grave was a few lots over. As they headed on up the road, Polly turned to him.

"I just keep finding out so much more about you. I can see better now how you did what none of us thought possible when my sister gave you her heart. Who would have ever believed that I would be here with you now, and not her?"

"How could one man be so fortunate? For reasons far beyond me, both Sullivan girls found me worthy of their love and devotion. I am the luckiest man on the face of this earth."

"It didn't turn out too badly for the baby of the family, either. Walt . . . I need a hug."

Mrs. Williamson

The bungalow was stale and needed a good airing. As Polly walked through the house, she could better envision the woman who also viewed Walt as the son she never had. It was a special treat to sit with her man in the fabled swing where so many dramatic episodes had played out.

"I'm convinced more than ever that you must finish your book."

"That reminds me—while we're in town, let's go by the university press and see if they would be interested in publishing it—and perhaps your poems, too."

Walt was not surprised when no one at the press knew who he was. One of the flunkies was sent scrambling. He found a copy of his book in the archives, along with numerous clippings.

"So—I'm standing here looking at a living legend. It says here that your book was the first ever published by this press. You must have made a mint for the university when it hit the big time."

"That was a long time ago."

"Send us a manuscript when it's ready. We'll be happy to take a look at it. You, too, Mrs. Williamson. We might be able to kill two birds with one stone scheduling book signings."

When they got back to the house, Walt made his way to the swing. Polly soon joined him on the cool summer evening in the mountains of North Carolina.

"Walt . . . He called me Mrs. Williamson. Can we get married?"

> Othell . . . History sure has a weird way of repeating itself. It was just before my first book was released that Ginny asked me to marry her.

Seated in a cramped airplane was an atypical place to plan a wedding.

"I cannot compete with you and Ginny. That progressive ceremony is one for the ages. You must include it in your book. I want something quiet and simple. What do you think about getting married while we're in Seattle—just us, and Jesse, and my parents?"

"Sounds fine. Who do you want to officiate?"

"One of Dad's golfing partners is a Presbyterian minister. Jesse already knows him. Is that okay with you?"

"You're the bride. Just make sure somebody cues me when to say, 'I will,' 'I do,' 'I already did,' or whatever it is that I'm supposed to vow."

"I'll make sure Jesse jerks your chain when it's time to kiss the bride."

"What about a honeymoon?"

"My darling . . . It began the first time you made love to me."

The Sullivans had not told Jesse where his parents had been. Walt took him into the bedroom and closed the door.

"Son . . . I have some news I want to share with you. King died a few days ago. Your mother and I have been to his funeral. He was an old man, and it was his time to go."

"Why did my mother, Ginny, have to die?"

"Jesse . . . Your mother was a nurse."

"I didn't know that."

"I told you before, but I guess you were too young to remember. She was not just an ordinary nurse who worked in a hospital, but a very special nurse. Your mother went on plane rides to remote places all across Alaska to help care for sick people. On her last flight, they flew into a storm, and the pilot was unable to bring it through. It fell into the Bering Sea. Nobody on board survived."

"I didn't know that."

"Now—I have some good news. Do you know what a wedding is? Polly and I are going to get married."

"Oh . . ."

Strapped in plane seats was not the most ideal place to deal with postnuptial jitters. As Mr. and Mrs. Williamson winged their way high above the Inside Passage, with a piece of paper certifying that they were husband and wife, the Mrs. had a question.

"Are you going to start taking me for granted—now that you have a noose around my neck?"

"But of course, I am. Granted to you, is my body to ravage anytime you so wish. Granted to you, are my worldly possessions, meager as they are. I grant to you my promise that I will always be by your side and on your side."

"Even when I'm wrong?"

"Mrs. Williamson . . . You surely do drive a hard bargain."

"See—you're having regrets already."

"The only thing I regret is not hogtying you earlier."

No Mark Twain

After trampling among the roots from which he sprang, Walt renewed his writing with a new resolve. His editor in residence also now had a better perspective from which to nudge him. By the 2010 fall equinox, his manuscript was almost ready to submit.

Polly was not yet ready to let go of her poems. She had become Walt's biggest fan, but he was of little help in assessing the quality of her work. He tried to convince her that if rejected, they had not lost anything.

"If neither gets published, we've done it. Just to have these to hand down to our sons was worth all the effort. And for our grandchildren, too, if we're ever so blessed."

"Walt . . . No way will they will reject your book. Remember—I taught literature. It's southern fiction at its best with a big family secret and real down-home characters that everyone can identify with and relate to. It has suspense, mystery, and intrigue.

"You're no Mark Twain, but your humor is the kind that sneaks up on people. They often have to back up and come again before they laugh out loud."

"I feel more like Ichabod Crane."

"Thanks for making my point. Seriously, you have taken the theoretical framework of your book about identity and woven it into your narrative through your characters."

"You're biased, but I love you for it. What will it take to get you over the hump?"

"I need an objective opinion."

"That might not be possible because your sentiments are subjective. One so-called expert might love it and another not think much of it. Let's send them in at the same time. If need be, the press has all kinds of literary resources they can appeal to right there at the university."

Following the submission guidelines, both Walt and Polly hit the Send icon, and the manuscripts winged their way through cyberspace. The waiting game began. He kept assuring her that no news was good news. At least, the book proposals were not immediately rejected outright.

After almost two months of anticipation, a parcel came in the mail with two contracts. In the cover letter, the managing editor stated that the board immediately and enthusiastically embraced *Jesse's Two Mothers, A Fairy Tale Comes True, and Other Poems of Promise.*

The press was much more hesitant about *The War Baby*, though, with the disclaimer that the woods were full of southern family sagas, and that they were a dime a dozen. The reviewers did note that Walt's book had a compelling storyline, and was well-written. Because of his prior notoriety and previous connection with the university, they had decided to publish both books and promote them as a husband-wife tandem.

"See there, Mrs. Williamson . . . The only reason my book is being published is because of you and yours."

"Walt . . . Please hold me. I'm shaking."

"My darling husband . . . Now that we're legal, I want another piece of paper."

"And what would that be? Do you want me to sign everything over to you?"

"No silly. I want to officially adopt Jesse. Now that I'm about to become a famous poet, married to a renowned novelist, I want him to have the same legal protections as Frank."

"So—If you ever leave me—you want an equal shot at custody?"

"I'm as stuck on you as the glue is to a postage stamp."

"I'm surprised we've not thought about this earlier."

"Then, you're okay with it?"

"I think it's a great idea."

"Let's go to bed."

"Okay."

Pure bliss

Walt had been through the routine before, but it was new for Polly. The gears of the printing press grind slowly. Writers are not always apprised of the steps being taken behind the scenes. Copy editors were going over everything with a fine-toothed comb. The type had to be set and cover designs developed.

Tonya painted a pair of swans, and it was accepted for the jacket of Walt's book. Jesse's childhood sketch of Ms. Robin and the three eggs was used as the cover art for the book of poetry. Now a sixth grader, he was hardly impressed and perhaps even a bit embarrassed.

After submitting the manuscripts to the Library of Congress for copyrighting, the authors had to sit back and wait. Polly knew it would not put a rush on anything, but right after Labor Day, she insisted on placing a call for an update. The receptionist had no definitive information, and the key staff people were all unavailable.

"Walt . . . as you put it so succinctly. Oh well . . . Othell."

The writers got their first glimpses of what the final products might look like when galley proofs were sent digitally. After suggesting a few tweaks, hard copies showed up about a month later.

Polly held up and out the facsimile of her book of poems reverently and in slow motion. Walt stood by as tears welled up in her eyes. It already specified so in the dedication, but she said it aloud.

"This is for Jesse and for you."

"I know, baby. And we both love you so very much."

He took her in his arms in what could only be described as moments of pure bliss.

"Now—let me wrap my hands around your novel."

"Walt . . . Can you believe this?"

News finally arrived of the official publication date. Walt got a birthday present when two boxes of books were on the porch when he and Polly got home from a Halloween event at school. He took out his pocket knife and ripped each open.

Thousands of words that had flowed through their fingertips were encapsulated in the volumes they held in their hands. Momentarily, their voices were unable to manufacture any more.

Readers of *The War Baby* would discover a reciprocal dedication. The book also had a tribute page. Walt's grandfathers, his Uncle Earl, and his mother were memorialized. A special accolade was reserved for Ginny.

Lacking this time around, was a hack to propel the books into national prominence. The authors understood that sales might be limited to a few hundred copies. Walt also explained royalties to Polly. With the books purchased and given away, they would be fortunate to break even.

"This is not about money."

"I know."

Déjà vu

The published books were on the market in time for Christmas presents. A press release was sent to local newspapers where the authors had connections. The one in Kenai where Walt was a feature writer joined hands with the library and threw a big bash. Polly got her first taste of book signing.

Tonya started planning an autograph party in Homer for right after Thanksgiving. Walt was not surprised that Polly's poems were outselling his novel.

The Sullivans had good reason to lure the Williamsons to Seattle for the holidays. They planned a big reception for their daughter and son-in-law. Polly's friends also sponsored a gala event.

Jesse was not sure what to make of the festivities. Soon after returning to school in January, he took a copy of each book for show and tell. His sixth grade teacher invited his parents to visit his classroom. The girls gathered around his mom and wanted to know more about writing poetry.

The university press agreed to wait until school was out for the authors to come to Ephesus. Tonya went on ahead and helped set up a book signing at the campus bookstore where she had worked. Jesse stayed behind with his grandparents who met him at the airport between connecting flights.

The event was well publicized, and a steady stream kept them busy. As the crowd began to dwindle, Walt's eyes were drawn to a woman coming through the door.

"Othell . . . It's déjà vu all over again."

"Polly . . . I'm Hannah. I met your sister right here at Walt's first book signing."

"Hi, Hannah. Please accept this copy of my book as a gift. Walt told me you were the one who suggested the title for his. Maybe the cheapskate will pay you back in kind. And by the way, your name is mentioned in *The War Baby* credits. I insisted."

Jesse continued to establish his growing independence. Like both his mothers, he made good grades. As his father, that mattered little to him. He did not talk much about school, insisting that he needed no help with homework.

One of Walt's biggest concerns was that Polly might be a permissive parent. Rather, she leaned more toward being overprotective. She had raised Frank in a very different environment. In Alaska, the risks were much greater and the consequences more extreme. As with any kid, they felt certain theirs did not tell them everything.

Jesse's parents were not sure what he was studying in seventh grade science. Eventually, students would be introduced to reproduction. Would that be the catalyst? Both wondered if the title of Polly's book might generate a reaction, but apparently, it raised no red flags.

No how-to manuals or child-rearing guidelines were on the market to shepherd these parents through this anomalous set of circumstances. Should they be proactive, or wait and let him come to them? For all intents and purposes, Polly was his mother. Ginny's picture was on the dresser in his bedroom, but he had not mentioned her in some time.

The book release hoopla, what little there was of it, died down. Meanwhile, Polly never laid her pen down for long. That was her way of journaling. Walt was not sure if ever again he wanted to sit in front of a computer for long spells.

When he got a call about a job opening at the college, he went for an interview. Teaching introductory psychology was not on his bucket list, but he decided to give it a try. He had never told Polly about the counseling session when he wrote bucket as in list and let the tail of the b fall below the line. Understandably, she thought the contrived F word was hysterical.

One winter Saturday afternoon when Jesse had gone off with some of his friends, Walt came out of his office after grading papers. Polly was stretched out on the sofa.

"Walt . . . Come over here and lay beside me. Did you realize we're acting like an old married couple?"

"Do you want to take this discussion to the bedroom?"

"What's wrong with right here? You know what else is on my bucket list?"

"Don't tell me all at once. I might kick the bucket."

They went scrambling when Jesse came home unexpectedly. After reappearing a few minutes later, his mother had a question.

"What did you guys do today? You were gone for hours."

"Oh, nothing special. We just did a little ice fishing."

"You what???"

Tonya and Zane were now sharing an apartment. He was working four ten-hour shifts each week at the hospital and commuting to Anchorage to continue his training. Her job was shaky. The department was having difficulty enrolling enough students to justify the position. Saving some money seemed the sensible thing to do.

Walt teased her about that being the same rationale he and her mother used.

"I can promise you one thing. This outcome will be much different."

"You didn't turn out so bad."

Tonya was a tad miffed when Jesse always seemed more thrilled to see Zane than her. That was offset with admiration for how much time he took up with her not so little brother. The paramedic answered questions about rescue missions without going into gory details. If he could arrange it, he promised to give Jesse a tour of the helicopter the next time it touched down in the area.

A month later, he made good on that promise. After replicating rescues from the oil platforms in the Cook Inlet, the squadron set down at the airport for the night. Zane was impressed by how much Jesse already understood the operation of an aircraft. He reminded Tonya's boyfriend that he had upgraded his flight simulator software three times.

"Jesse . . . What conditions do you practice the most?"

"Bringing a plane through a storm."

A cool kid

In ninth grade, the proverbial you know what finally hit the fan. Jesse came home from school with an unsettled look well beyond typical adolescent volatility. He went looking for his dad, but he had not gotten home. When Polly found out what was on his mind, she called Walt and told him to come as soon as possible.

"Do you want us to answer your questions, or start from the beginning and fill you in?"

"I don't know what to ask. Just give it to me straight. I can handle it."

Walt went back farther than might have been necessary. He told Jesse about how he and Ginny had met, and he described in elementary terms the nature of their loving relationship. He asked his son if he remembered the discussion about his mother being a nurse and how she died. He did.

Walt looked to Polly for some reassurance that he was doing okay so far. She stepped in.

"Jesse . . . It's the time frame that makes no sense. Is that right?"

He nodded.

"Your father found out that Ginny had donated some of her eggs before she died. They were kept frozen and were still alive. I volunteered for one of them to be implanted into my womb, and it was fertilized by one of your daddy's sperms. Genetically, you were my sister's child, but you grew inside of me like you were my own. That's how you have two mothers."

Walt and Polly looked to each other yearningly for mutual moral support. It was out there. It was finally out there. After years of agonizing about this moment, they had faltered their way through it.

The intensity of their locked eyes began to dissolve. Each head swiveled slowly toward the audience of one, the only one in the room that mattered at that moment.

Jesse's countenance had likewise undergone a transformation. He tilted his head back and had a one-word response to this potentially life-altering information.

"*Cool.*"

He bounded from the room and went to the wood shop. Both Walt and Polly had trouble going to sleep that night. He tried to put it in perspective.

"After fourteen years of dreading this day, of trying to figure out what to say, of wondering how he would react, all he had to say was 'cool'."

"Thanksgiving is next week. We have so much to be thankful for because we have such a cool kid."

Radar

One rite of passage Walt had been concerned about was now defused. On Jesse's birth certificate, his mother was listed as Virginia Sullivan (deceased). When he took their son to get his learner's permit, no questions would be prompted. As they were waiting for him to be called, something about his birth mother was, nonetheless, on his mind.

"Dad . . . Can I have Radar?"

"That old truck is worn out. I'm not sure it's even safe to drive."

"I want to restore it. I'll get a job if I have to—to buy the parts."

"Sure. Why not? But I don't want you falling behind in your grades."

Jesse knew nothing about the annuity that his grandfather had assigned to him, and it had grown exponentially. Facing his future, Polly thought it was time to discuss the funds with their son.

As with any teenager, he had given little thought to the expenses involved in getting to where he wanted to go. His parents told him that he was all set for college, but depending on where he went, he might not have enough to pay for everything and would have to budget carefully.

They impressed upon Jesse the importance of keeping up his grades. His dad reminded him that he was at the age when distractions were appealing, and how easy it was not to take school seriously. His mother was concerned about him both getting a part-time job and also spending other free time working on the truck.

Polly eventually came up with a plan. She proposed making small withdrawals to cover the cost of truck parts so long as Jesse maintained his good grades. Both parents were pleased that their son's chief extracurricular activity would bring him home from school each day.

The boy had always been good with his hands, but Walt stood back in amazement as Jesse put Radar on blocks and went to work. The truck restoration became a group project. The Williamson backyard soon became the gathering place for their son's friends. Comrades brought their specific expertise with them, along with their fathers' tools and some much-needed muscle. Nate served as the unofficial crew chief.

Jesse had picked up a repair manual and they referred to it often. The first stage involved replacing the worn-out suspension with a jacked up version, which included a complete brake job and oversized tires. Rewiring the vehicle, followed next.

When school was out, the boys started rebuilding the engine. Walt came in one afternoon and heard the motor idling. He got home just in time to go along for the first road test. Jesse got out and adjusted the carburetor.

The body still needed work. When the weather permitted, the truck owner and his buddies grinded and sanded. The paint job would have to wait until the next summer.

A mentor

On his sixteenth birthday, Jesse was sitting behind the wheel of Radar when he went to get his driver's license. Tonya and Zane were at the house when the father and son got back from the Public Safety licensing center. Jesse was glad Sissy was there to help share one of the proudest days of his life. Zane got to kick the truck tires and do his own personal inspection.

It was Tonya's birthday, too, but her boyfriend captured her brother's attention. They had a long talk while the others were gabbing around the kitchen table.

"Jesse . . . You need a plan. Search and rescue is not a full-time profession. It's something you prepare for and go when called."

"What was your plan?"

"I joined the Coast Guard. The military taught me all kinds of survival skills. I also got my first experience in a helicopter and knew then I wanted to become a pilot. When I was discharged, I used my veteran's benefits to go to nursing school."

Tonya was intrigued by what was going on and came and sat on the arm of Zane's chair.

"The highlight of being in the Coast Guard was my assignment to the cutter stationed in Homer. I knew right away that I wanted to live in that seaside town. The best part of all—I got to meet your sister."

Tonya gave Zane an affirming hug and sat in on the rest of the conversation.

"Perhaps, the most direct route is to become a fireman. You can likely get a job right out of high school and undergo training in fire rescues. During your days off, you can enroll in other programs."

"How does that work?"

"Public Safety is responsible for all emergency operations. Becoming a state trooper is another option you might want to consider."

"I don't think I'm interested in law enforcement."

"Alaska has several volunteer organizations that work hand in hand with the troopers. Its members are highly skilled in water rescues, in snow emergencies such as avalanches and snowmobile accidents, and even in plane crashes. I belong to one where I have been trained in all these areas, and now, I'm nearing getting my license as a rescue helicopter pilot."

The teenager was taking it all in.

"Jesse . . . We need to talk about something else. Search and rescue is no place for adrenalin junkies. Skilled leaders spot them quickly and get them out of the program. Those out for thrills put themselves in unnecessary danger. They also put the lives of the ones they are trying to rescue in an even greater peril. If you're interested in this for any reason other than the love of humanity, then do us all a favor and find something else."

Think snow

The next day, Jesse drove the truck to school. That night, Walt opened his digital journal for the first time in a while.

> Grandfathers are on my mind for some reason. I never knew my biological granddads, but I cannot imagine a boy being any closer than I was to the two who raised me. I wonder if Jesse's mechanical skills were handed down to him by ancestors he never met. I'm so happy for him that he has one grandfather in his life. I suspect the bond between them is beyond anything that anyone else is privy to. That is certainly true of me and my son. And with my daughter, too. The one thing yet unfilled in my life is being a grandpa. I can only imagine what a thrill that must be.

"Dad . . . One of my friends is moving, and his snow machine is for sale. Let's buy it. We can get it for a song. I think you'd enjoy it almost as much as I would. Maybe even Mom could go riding with us."

"I'm in. Do you think you can sell her on it?"

Jesse was more confident than Walt was, and in the end, she relented.

Think snow.

Some Alaskans were not yet convinced of climate change, but one thing was undeniable. A White Christmas was no longer a given in any given year.

The Kenai Peninsula got a good dusting of powder around Thanksgiving, but nowhere near enough to support a snow machine. Mushers were hitching their huskies to four-wheelers while training them. It finally came the second week in January. After about six inches were on the ground, Jesse motored up the road. Walt turned to the boy's mother.

"He took to that thing like he'd been riding it his entire life."

It was not the first time Jesse was on that same recreational vehicle, but his parents did not know that. With some coaxing, Walt tried it out. When he limped back from a short excursion, Jesse gave him an instruction.

"It's like skating. You have to get up some speed, some momentum. Here, Mother . . . You try it."

"Oh, no."

"Then hop on behind, and let me take you for a ride."

Jesse was in his element.

Two weeks later, Tonya took her first ride with her own personal guide. Afterward, Jesse made a suggestion.

"My friends have told me about a place up near Sterling where you can ride for miles on land cleared along a gas pipeline. I think I can find it."

"You boys go on. I'm staying here with Polly."

The men loaded the winter ATV on Radar and headed up the road. Jesse had been there before, too, but he played it coy finding just the right turnoff. Over the next two hours, the three took turns putting on the helmet, riding off into the wilderness, and returning to the starting point. The terrain had its ups and downs providing thrills proportional to the speed.

Zane taught Jesse some new maneuvers. Walt was a slow learner, and the dead man switch did its job when he did a rollover leaning the wrong way. He was delighted to see his son having so much fun, even if that included making sport of his clumsy dad.

"Othell . . . My *over* is *joyed*."

He's the one

The Tonya-Zane visit was not just a social call. They had twofold news to share, and Zane set it up.

"Do you want the good news first, or the other good news?"

"Your call."

"First, we're moving to Anchorage. I have a job at one of the hospitals. Also, I'm now certified in all rescue areas. Anchorage is the main base, and I need to be nearer."

"Nice—I hope you both will be happy living in the metropolis of Los Anchorage. You know what the locals say. It's only about fifteen minutes from Alaska."

"I'll let Tonya tell you the rest of the story."

She paused to make sure everyone was paying attention.

"Well?"

"Zane and I are getting married."

"Congratulations on all counts. When is the big day?"

"Next Saturday. The wedding will be on the deck of the Coast Guard Cutter docked in Homer, and the captain will perform the ceremony. If he can still get into it, Zane will wear his old uniform."

"Does this mean Polly and I can finally expect to have some grandchildren? Frank is all caught up in his teaching career and on the fast track to becoming a full professor, so we can't count on him."

"Then, it might all rest on Jesse's shoulders. We've been trying for about a year and nothing has happened so far."

"You could always . . ."

"We thought about it but decided that one test tube baby in the family might be enough."

It was time for a father-daughter talk.

"Are you sure he's the one?"

"Dad . . . I could give you a laundry list extolling Zane's virtues, but you already know what they are. I could tell you how much he cares for me, but you can see that in his eyes."

Walt nodded in agreement.

"Do you recall when I said Alaska was calling me? Remember me revisiting Mrs. Hattie's rundown house again and hearing her whisper once more, 'Follow your inner voice'? I listened.

"I took the plank from the shattered table and etched those words on it so I could see them each and every day. I framed it with the links of the rusty chain. Isn't it amazing how a chain can support you when relaxing in a swing, or bind you should you get all tangled up in it?"

"Tonya . . . That gives me chills. It's true in so many areas of our lives."

"I had wondered why I was going through the motions of getting a master's degree, thinking I would never use it. And then the improbable job opened up for me in Homer. When I moved away, it was unthinkable that I would ever reside there again. Less than a week after I was in my apartment, Zane moved in next door."

"Amazing."

"How he got to Homer is its own fascinating story. Do you have any idea how many things had to fall into place for us to move in at the same time? I guess you would."

She then told her dad about finding the T and Z initialed rocks on the beach of the Spit.

"Dad . . . All the things you said about synchronicity are true. He's the one."

Jesse and his dad decided together that the last stage of the Radar restoration should be left to professionals. Walt took him to the body shop to get it when it was ready. The gleaming black finish was stunning.

"Ginny would be so proud. That's what she was driving the day we met. And by the way, I'm kind of proud of you, too."

Radar became one of the most recognizable vehicles in the area. The high school student loved his wheels. Accolades were sure to include the word classic. Jesse's buddies fought for the right to ride in it and on it in parades. A homecoming queen waved from the tailgate, but his other mother was the only female who had earned the right to ride shotgun beside him on the bench seat.

Auf wiedersehen

Jesse's grandparents encouraged him to apply to one of the universities in Washington, but he could not imagine living anywhere other than in Alaska. His immediate goal was to get through his senior year without causing a mutiny. In the meantime, he wished to climb as many of the EMT rungs as he could by the time he graduated.

On Jesse's eighteenth birthday, he did three age-related things. He registered to vote and went to the hospital to sign up for an EMT class. The third was something very personal.

Zane's mentoring was invaluable. While Jesse had enormous respect for firemen, he wished for a career with ongoing involvement, not just in the event of a fire or medical emergency. He was still not drawn to law enforcement, and nothing about the military appealed to him.

Something in healthcare seemed Jesse's best option. He was not cut out to become a physician, but radiology was a possibility. When he applied for nursing school in Anchorage, it mattered not if it was in his genes, or he got it by osmosis from Zane. The high school senior was ready to get started.

Jesse wanted to skip out on his graduation, but his mother threatened him to within an inch of his life if he tried it. He was recognized as an honor student, but he yielded the top prizes to those who coveted them. Mr. Williamson was not the only member of the Class of 2017 with overalls underneath his robe.

It was not easy for Walt and Polly as they steadied themselves for an empty nest. She had been through it before, but this time was different. If ever there was anything, bitter and sweet at the same time, it was the day Jesse loaded his gear in Radar. He gave his mother a big hug. Walt extended his hand.

"Auf wiedersehen . . . Herr Williamson."

"Auf wiedersehen . . . Mein Vater und mein Mutter."

"Did I ever tell you what Jesse told me when he was a kid about you hugging him so tightly? He said that you just about smothering him with those bumps, and they made it hard for him to breathe."

"He didn't."

"Oh, yes he did."

"His daddy never complained, though, did he?"

"About you taking my breath away? Not once."

Tonya offered her brother a place to stay for a week or so while he looked for his own housing. On the first day of classes, he took a seat on the front row.

When their work schedules permitted, Jesse and Zane hooked up for a coffee break and talked shop. About a month into the semester, his mentor took him to the headquarters of the volunteer search and rescue agency of which he was a member. This gave Jesse an inside track to begin his own training.

The nursing student strived to keep up with his school work so he could use free time to learn the ropes, literally. His first assignment was rappelling.

Next, he went out on the water and took lessons in how to navigate an inflatable raft. Each session became more intense as his group put in where the currents were swifter. Jesse tried on a wetsuit, learned how frigid Alaska water temperatures are, and was taught how rapidly the window of opportunity closes for a successful rescue.

Once again, he found himself thinking snow. The one area of his preparation that he already had a modest amount of experience in was handling a snow machine. He finally got his first lesson in January under the tutelage of an expert. The apprentice found out quickly how little he knew.

A proud day

It was a proud day for Jesse Sullivan Williamson when he was handed a cell phone with GPS and other advanced technology. It was an even grander day when he went out on his first emergency rescue.

The poise and expertise of the veterans made their marks on him as they motored to an island in Skilak Lake where three fishermen were stranded. As the men were treated for hypothermia, he knew his role and stayed within his bounds. When he got back to his room, he used his phone to call his folks.

As Jesse's snow machine skills ratcheted up, so did the challenges. This ramped up piece of machinery was often the first means of reaching someone in trouble. He became familiar with the emergency equipment efficiently designed into it.

On a bright sunny mid-March afternoon, Jesse was taken to a training site in a remote area with still a good snowpack. His assignment was to use the GPS and locate a dummy about ten miles into the wilderness. The supervisor noted the time when he sped away.

Closing in on his target, the trainee saw a snow machine on the side of a mountain. Tracks indicated the driver was high-marking. In this increasingly popular but very dangerous sport, operators climb progressively higher on the side of a mountain to reach the steepest point possible without stalling out or rolling over. Jesse hit the brakes and took out his binoculars.

"The fool—he has a passenger—likely showing out for his girlfriend."

This was not part of the drill, and Jesse used the phone to report what was happening. His trainer told him to temporarily suspend his mission and to keep an eye on the grandstander.

"WIPEOUT! WIPEOUT!"

As Jesse raced toward the base of the mountain, he lost visible contact. Back and forth he went until he finally spotted the wreckage of the mostly buried snow machine.

He cut the engine of his and listened. Faintly, he could hear a cry for help. The first responder slogged in the direction of the sounds and located a young male. He assessed that the teenager had a broken leg and suspected possible internal injuries.

"Find her. She's out there and she's hurt."

"First—let me get you stabilized."

Jesse put a splint on the leg and wrapped the boy in blankets. He had remembered to leave the phone mike open, and the instructor in charge of the aborted mission called for backup.

"What's her name?"

"Macy . . ."

Jesse started making wider and wider circles calling out for her. He was fearful that she was either unconscious or buried in the snow. His supervisor told him to keep doing what he was doing, but if he did not find her soon, he would have to go back and try to save the young man.

"Help!"

He could barely hear it.

"Where are you?"

"Over here."

When Jesse located the passenger, she had lost her helmet and likely had a concussion. Chances of them surviving, were much greater if they could share bodily warmth. He brushed away the snow she was mostly buried in, gently gathered her in his arms, and trudged painstakingly to where her boyfriend was some fifty yards away.

After both were wrapped around each other and under all the blankets he had, Jesse got the good news. Captain Zane Patterson had the GPS coordinates and was on his way. He was at least half an hour out—probably more.

Jesse was instructed to keep the accident victims talking until help arrived. His unmentioned concern was high above. Spring-like temperatures, combined with all the snow machine hot dogging, had made the snow unstable. He resisted rebuking the boy, knowing that was not his place. Muted voices were suddenly interrupted with an ominous cracking sound— and then a rumble.

AVALANCHE!!!!!

"Walt . . . Polly . . . Your son died a true hero. When I dug them out, Jesse had positioned himself atop the other two and arched his body. He spent his last minutes using superhuman strength to protect them from being crushed and to form an air pocket so they could breathe."

"Did they survive?"

"Yes—they had some frostbite in their extremities and the injuries from their accident, but in a few weeks, they can get on with their lives."

"Thank you . . . Zane."

"Here's something else you should know. Jesse was an avid believer in organ donation. He was such a strong young man, and because his body was suspended in the frozen snow, parts of him will live on in people all across this state."

"That's what Jesse would have wanted."

"If you wish, I'll pack up his things and drive his truck home."

"Thank you . . . Zane."

"Auf wiedersehen . . . Herr Williamson."

Baby Robin

After walking through the next few weeks, zombie-like, Walt and Polly decided a change of scenery might help. They booked passage through to Asheville, with a two-day layover in Seattle. Just as they were about out the door, Gus II shattered the silence. Walt bellowed in disgust.

"What now, Gus? How much more bad news can I stand from you?"

He let it ring, but Polly picked up the receiver, realizing that it could be about a flight delay.

When she hung up, she told Walt that she just had the strangest request.

"The young woman said she had copies of our books and wondered if she might get them autographed. I told her about our plans, and she agreed to meet us inside the terminal at the airport."

"I hope she's not late. We don't have a lot of wiggle room."

"You did leave a key with Nate to take the Alcan back to the house?"

"Of course—and a house key so he can look after things while we're gone."

When they rolled their luggage in, a woman in her early thirties approached with an infant under one arm and two books in the hand of the other.

"You must be Joy. I'm Polly the poet and this is my husband, Walt."

He took the books and then a seat. Polly reached in her purse for a pen.

Not wanting to be rude, but also in somewhat of a hurry to get the baggage checked in time, Walt was all business. It had been some time since either had signed a book. He asked the usual question.

"Is there a particular way you want this autographed?"

"You could say, 'For my granddaughter, Robin'."

Polly gasped. The author dropped his pen and looked up.

Walt and Polly missed their flight.

"Would you like to come with me to my house? We don't live far from here."

Walt had driven to the airport, but Polly took the keys from him. The mystified couple sat in stone silence as they followed the vehicle ahead until she broke it.

"Walt . . . Is there something you haven't told me that would explain this?"

"I swear—there was no one else. I have no idea what this is about."

"Please come in. Jason is at work. You can meet him later. Would you like some coffee or tea?"

Both declined but thanked her for the offer.

"Jason and I had been trying for several years to have a baby. We finally went to the new fertility clinic and soon found out that he has a very low sperm count. At first, we were reluctant to try in vitro fertilization, but we wanted so much to have children that we finally consented."

Walt's hand went searching for Polly's. She pushed it away, but then reached back for it.

"When I got pregnant, the doctor asked if we wished to know the name of the donor. He had not signed a confidential agreement. We declined, but then the physician called later and suggested that we reconsider in light of what was on the news. Yesterday, we learned who he was.

"Mr. and Mrs. Williamson . . . Your son, Jesse, became a sperm donor on his eighteenth birthday. Robin is his biological daughter—and your granddaughter, too. She was born the day he died."

Polly's arms stretched out for Baby Robin, and the infant's mom joyfully handed her over. The new grandmother drew the infant's face to hers, kissed her on the cheek, and smiled for the first time in weeks.

Polly sprang back from the brink of the black hole. Joy and Jason gained an instant babysitter. After checking with her father, who approved without reservation, Jesse's annuity was reassigned to the new member of the family.

Walt did not rebound so quickly. He was still trapped in a pit of despondency, unable to escape. Polly suggested that they go ahead and use the trip tickets, good for a year.

As she was putting the last few things in the suitcase, he called Tonya to wish her a happy birthday. Everyone was tiptoeing around that it would have been Jesse's nineteenth.

Walt went out the back door to start Radar. The truck had not been run since Zane brought it home. Abruptly, he stopped in his tracks. He heard a familiar sound—missing from the yard for some time.

"Hello . . . Sister Robin. Why don't you build your nest right over there in that tree where your grandmother always did?"

Chup . . . Chup . . . Tut . . . Tut . . . Tut.

Chee . . . Chee . . . Chee . . .

Cheer up Cheerio . . . Cheer up!

The bird flew to the branch and turned facing Walt. It grew very still, and he looked into her eyes.

"What's that you say . . .?"

In appreciation

A special thanks to Eugenia Hambrick for providing both the incubator and the nursery for Walt's baby. Much of the book was written at Genie's dwelling in Homer, Alaska.

This setting was not always conducive. The author was amid endless distractions created by snow-covered mountains and glaciers ever in view, glorious sunrises and magnificent sunsets, beckoning hiking trails with breathtaking vistas, a White Christmas, and food to die for with an ample supply of "cooking wine." He was also amongst moose, eagles, cats, and friendly people. The writer was furthermore rattled by a series of earthquakes. Nonetheless, he was able to hammer out the narrative.

Kudos to fellow lodger, Zane Peterson. Zane shared his Alaska expertise and was rewarded by having a character named for him.

Also, accolades to Wanda L. Eidson who read and reacted to the manuscript as it was evolving. Her critiques and encouragement were most welcomed.

About the author

The writer has his pivotal character, Walt Williamson say:

"What a relief it is not to have to know everything all at once. Think of three words starting with the same letter. Being open to *whatever*, to *whenever*, and to *wherever* is the first step in embracing the possibilities—as their moments in time announce themselves."

Those were not just random terms strewn together in a work of fiction. Rather the assertions are personal reflections of the author's own sentiments.

Becoming a writer was not even a *whatever* possibility until it declared itself. *God's Frozen Chosen* is his third novel in the trilogy that includes *The War Baby* and *Miss Bizzy Belle*.

Neither was being an accomplished photographer something he set out to do. His book *Frozen in Time* is a photo journal of some exceptional snapshots with poignant stories to go with them.

One reader remarked that the author/photographer must have spent hours waiting to get some of the pictures. Johnson responded. "No—I just snapped what was right in front of me at the time."

The author also had Walt say:

"People have to be who they are. And some folks just do an outstanding job of being who they are." Then, he chuckled to himself, "Thank God, I am one of them."

While most folks speculate about their significance and contemplate the nature of their being, Larry G. Johnson does not just stop there. He welcomes and grasps—whatever, whenever, and wherever—one moment at the time.

thewarbaby@mindspring.com

Also, by the author

The War Baby
Miss Bizzy Belle
Frozen in Time